personally, makes her journey one you'll want to follow. The story's blend of witty dialogue, unexpected twists, and heartfelt moments keeps you hooked from start to finish. If you love stories with strong, resilient women and a dash of Southern charm, this debut novel is a must-read!"

—Jennifer Moorman, bestselling author of *The Vanishing of Josephine Reynolds*

"This charming debut has it all—second-chance romance, a balmy Southern setting, and plenty of long-held secrets that kept me turning the pages. As easy to imbibe as a glass of cold sweet tea on a hot summer day, *Southern by Design* is perfect for fans of Kristy Woodson Harvey, Karen White, and Mary Kay Andrews."

—Colleen Oakley, *USA TODAY* bestselling author of *The Mostly True Story of Tanner & Louise*

PRAISE FOR GRACE HELENA WALZ

"*Pretty as a Peach* is a heartfelt story that will have you cheering for each of five lifelong friends as they navigate love and loss, honesty and betrayal, and what it means to choose yourself while navigating the complicated bonds of friendship. Walz expertly weaves a story of loyalty and ambition into an unforgettable tale that is both tender and sharp."

—Elizabeth Bass Parman, author of *The Empress of Cooke County* and *Bees in June*

"Southern fiction full of heart and hope, *Good Hair Days* combines small-town charm, second chances, and fierce family love. It's one of those rare books that leaves the reader smiling through tears and longing for a trip to June's."

—Audrey Ingram, *USA TODAY* bestselling author of *The Summer We Ran*

"*Good Hair Days* is a story as heartwarming as it is heartbreaking and is told with a heavy Southern accent and an even heavier dose of charm. The love between sisters is 'brighter and sparklier' according to Walz, and the connection between Junie and Georgia is a palpable one that encompasses forgiveness and hope and everything in between. Throw in a hair salon, a large family of women, a long-lost love, and a devastating legacy and you've got the kind of book you won't want to put down."

—Karen White, *New York Times* bestselling author

"With plenty of Southern charm and juicy family drama, a second-chance romance with her lost teenage love, and a mystery surrounding the identity of Mack's father, this appealing novel sits nicely alongside other Southern fiction focused on women's lives, like the novels of Kristy Woodson Harvey and Mary Alice Monroe."

—*Booklist* for *Southern by Design*

"With this Charleston-set debut novel *Southern by Design,* Grace Helena Walz has taken her place among such treasured Southern novelists as Dorothea Benton Frank and Anne Rivers Siddons. Her stories and her voice is one readers are bound to adore."

—Mary Kay Andrews, *New York Times* bestselling author of *Summers at the Saint*

"Fans of interior design, Southern secrets, and good, old-fashioned family drama will flock to Grace Helena Walz's page-turning tale. A story of second chances and long-lost love as atmospheric as the Lowcountry itself, this is a positively charming debut from a standout new voice. Add it to your TBR list immediately!"

—Kristy Woodson Harvey, *New York Times* bestselling author of *A Happier Life,* for *Southern by Design*

"With bright, snappy dialogue, characters so real they jump off the page, and a Charleston setting to swoon over, *Southern by Design* is a sparkling debut! Walz is going to win fans with this sweet story of big dreams, to-die-for design, and real love."

—Lauren K. Denton, *USA TODAY* bestselling author of *The Hideaway*

"What's not to love about a humid Southern setting, a second-chance romance, and a family full of secrets? This debut novel sets Grace Helena Walz up to become an instant favorite for fans of Karen White, Kristy Woodson Harvey, and Patti Callahan Henry. *Southern by Design* is pitch perfect for book clubs and just the right amount of sweet."

—Kimberly Brock, award-winning author of *The Fabled Earth*

"*Southern by Design* is a refreshing and lighthearted read that beautifully captures the charm of Southern living while delving into the complexities of single motherhood, family dynamics, and second chances. Magnolia 'Mack' Bishop is a relatable and humorous protagonist whose determination to succeed, both professionally and

PRETTY AS A PEACH

ALSO BY GRACE HELENA WALZ

Southern by Design

Good Hair Days

PRETTY AS A PEACH

a novel

Grace Helena Walz

THOMAS NELSON
Since 1798

Pretty as a Peach

Published by Thomas Nelson, 501 Nelson Place, Nashville, TN 37214, USA. Thomas Nelson is a registered trademark of HarperCollins Christian Publishing, Inc.

Thomas Nelson titles may be purchased in bulk for educational, business, fundraising, or sales promotional use. For information, please email SpecialMarkets@ThomasNelson.com.

HarperCollins Publishers, Macken House, 39/40 Mayor Street Upper, Dublin 1, D01 C9W8, Ireland (https://www.harpercollins.com)

Library of Congress Cataloging-in-Publication Data

ISBN: 978-1-4003-5285-2 (softcover)
ISBN: 978-1-4003-5286-9 (epub)
ISBN: 978-1-4003-5287-6 (audio download)

Printed in the United States of America

26 27 28 29 30 LBC 5 4 3 2 1

For my dear friend, Sarah Berke.
Forgive me, I killed the peach tree.

PROLOGUE

Delilah

1998

ONE CALL FROM VIRGINIA Kate, and the phone tree stirred the four of us sixth graders from the covers of our warm beds. In less than an hour we were loaded in the back of Eliza's mother's hunter-green Chrysler Town and Country minivan and on the way to our friend in need. The headlights cast a dancing spotlight along the quiet small-town road, the familiar path to Virginia Kate's house tucked among pine trees, freshly mowed lawns, and brick-front homes. As soon as the vehicle shifted into Park beside the newly painted mailbox, we threw back the sliding door and poured out across the lawn. Down the street, a neighbor's sprinkler kicked into gear, then hissed as water escaped across the grass. All locals knew that at the height of summer, after sunset was the best time for watering.

"An hour. Two tops, girls!" Eliza's mother called after us from her lowered window. "I'll be right here!"

Betsy, in the lead, broke into a jog and yelled, "Ginny Kay! We're here!"

"Shh! People are sleeping," I said, slinging a bag across my body before following.

"She's not lost in the wilderness. She put out an SOS," Sloane muttered, adjusting her beret, the centerpiece of the French phase she was currently living out.

I reached back and linked arms with shy, strawberry-blonde Eliza, and tugged her along lovingly. As she neared the house, Betsy slowed to a stop, allowing the rest of us to catch up. Together we formed a circle on the lawn.

"I feel horrible for her. What if we say the wrong thing? Are her parents going to be mad we're here?" Eliza had a habit of spilling her worries like marbles from an overturned jar, and the rest of us had gotten into the habit of collecting them for her.

I patted her arm. "It's alright. The adults know we're here, and Virginia Kate needs us."

Betsy's eyebrows danced, a devious look spreading across her face, and I knew just what that meant. "Your au pair *knows*, right?"

Betsy shrugged. "She was asleep. She hates being woken up."

Eliza gasped and covered her mouth with both hands.

Sloane cleared her throat and said cooly, "Come on, y'all. Let's find Ginny Kay."

Though the street was dark, the upstairs window to Virginia Kate's parents' bedroom was lit, showcasing her mother and father in heated conversation. Sloane led the way toward the house—until the quiet sound of sniffles reached us.

"Tire swing," I said, pointing to the sweeping oak tree at the far side of the house.

We redirected like a flock of birds flying expertly in a V toward our downed member. Last summer I broke my arm when I fell off this swing. The girls—our group dubbed The Five—had responded like a trained platoon of EMTs, checking on me, calling for help, distracting me to get my mind off the pain. I thought then it would be the toughest thing we'd face together. But it took only a single glance at Virginia Kate, perched on the swing with her head hung and shoulders curled in as she shuddered and cried, to know I was wrong. So very wrong.

Sloane got to her first and hugged her. "I'm so sorry, Ginny Kay." When she stepped back, she took her Eiffel Tower charm necklace from her neck and looped it around Virginia Kate's.

Betsy followed and pulled something from the front pocket of her jeans. "They're probably melted by now, but I brought M&M's. When my parents are gone, a sweet treat makes me feel better for a minute."

Virginia Kate took the candy, and Eliza scooted in for a hug. She whispered something into Virginia Kate's ear that made her smile—but only briefly.

When it was my turn, I unloaded my bag and set my offerings at the feet of the tire swing. *Tiger Beat* magazine. Cokes. Friendship-bracelet-making supplies. The latest Spice Girls CD. Maybe none of it would help, but I'd thrown in everything I thought might make a dent in our friend's hurt.

There wasn't anything I wouldn't give away if it meant putting things right.

"Y'all are the best friends I could ever have," Virginia Kate said. "You got a flashlight in that bag, Delilah? 'Cause I could sure use a look at the Leo DiCaprio *Tiger Beat*."

I grinned in pure delight and nodded furiously. "I have a CD player too, but we'll have to take turns with the headphones."

Betsy took the chocolate candy and shared it among us. The pieces were warm, and with the slightest crack of the candy shell, the liquid chocolate flooded my tongue.

We didn't talk about the divorce. We gossiped about celebrity news. We made bracelets. None of us knew what to say, but we did know how to be friends.

When Eliza's mother flashed the headlights, we said goodbye.

As the others took off jogging across the lush front lawn, I stood and waited—watched. Virginia Kate's world was still on its way to falling apart, but before she walked into her house, she pulled her shoulders back and lifted her chin. I knew then that our showing up mattered.

"Delilah!" Eliza called, waving wildly. "Mama says it's time to go!"

I took off toward the van after one final look back.

The Five might've just been a gaggle of sixth-grade girls, but what happened when we came together was something special, something powerful. Something people spend a lifetime searching for.

Something that was surely built to last.

CHAPTER 1

Delilah

Twenty-three years later

I ALWAYS LOOK FORWARD to Saturday mornings at the Pearl farmers market, my table a rainbow of handmade soaps laid out in front of me. I'm bright and early this morning, one of the first to arrive, and when the breeze picks up, it delivers the fruity scent—peach, my favorite—from the soap to my nose like a gift wrapped in a bow. I hand-painted "Bubbles & Suds" on a burlap tablecloth I rescued from a thrift store bin, and atop the cloth my homemade soaps are set out in a colorful array like French macarons.

Before long the crowd mills happily along the quaint Main Street of Pearl, Georgia, a crispness on the breeze that pairs well with the leaves that've turned to fiery oranges and reds. Panting dogs on leashes tug by, small children tote too-big snacks, and frazzled parents chase behind. The scent of fried food carries from the food trucks, along with the chatter and laughter of the crowd.

I double-check that my tablet is connected to the card reader, then pull out the roll of branded stickers I special ordered. I had to bend the numbers to make the purchase fit in my budget, but for my beloved operation it was worth pinching pennies.

My niece, wearing sweatpants and a super-oversized tee that hangs low, slides in beside me. Her long brown hair, streaked with blonde highlights, hangs loose, tousled and damp.

"Sorry I'm late, Aunt Lilah. Mama needed me to help her with some cute, new party project," Roxie says. She's the sixteen-year-old daughter of my older sister, Darcy.

Roxie may adore her mother, but the feelings between Darcy and me are far chillier. In fact, strain runs through all of my family relationships. Mostly I try to keep my head down and keep the peace, and so far it's worked out pretty well.

I pull Roxie into my side. "Not to worry, honey. I'm glad to see you."

From inside the crowd, my four best friends—*still* known as The Five—approach in a huddle that moves as one. Sloane wears a pressed button-up and those oversized slacks I once tried on that made me look like I'd borrowed Steve Harvey's suit pants from the '90s. Probably she picked up the items on one of her fancy business trips. Though she long ago ditched the beret, she's still into travel and culture.

Betsy pushes baby Huddie in a stroller, four-year-old Rex following alongside, and her auburn hair is up in a messy bun that glints in the sun like a halo. Eliza, forever strawberry blonde, is wearing a cotton midi dress and a denim jacket. She's notably hands-free, so baby Jack must be at home with her husband, Ted. Virginia Kate catches up from the back wearing jeans and sneakers, chasing behind her twin eighteen-month-old boys, Dawson and Banks.

"I've already sent two women your way, ladies," Betsy calls from behind the stroller and winks at Roxie. "I could tell they were from out of town, so I had to spread the word."

Betsy—all of them, really—have been wildly supportive of my soapy endeavor ever since we made the first shoddy batch in Betsy's family kitchen while her au pair was out grocery shopping. Eliza wore protective goggles the entire time, fearful that she would somehow be blinded. Virginia Kate, grateful for any distraction from her parents' contentious divorce, was the scent master, and Sloane hung around "supervising," or something of the like. By high school the others had grown busy with extracurricular activities of their own, and I was happy to take the reins.

Sloane pulls her sunglasses down the bridge of her nose as she turns over a soap in her hands. "You really should ask around to get placement in boutiques. This stuff would sell."

"The margins must be incredible," Virginia Kate mutters, a reminder that as well as being a top-notch mama, she is also a financial pro, if temporarily sidelined by motherhood.

Eliza beams. "I just love them. I'm going to need some for my baby sister's wedding favors this summer! You know she . . ."

And with that The Five is officially in session. Despite the fact that it's only been three days since we spent an evening playing Mahjong and sipping wine, the chatter takes off like a match dropped on a dry haystack. We bat around job wins and job woes, recount whose spouse said what about the preschool Spring Fling, share perils in parenting—well, the moms do while Sloane and I listen—and the occasional piece of neighborhood drama.

Eventually people begin circling the booth, and Betsy speaks up. "Come on, y'all! We can't be blocking customers. Let's go to the coffee shack. Ginny Kay, we'll bribe those two to sit still for a minute with a cake pop."

"If the toddlers wear us out, we might be calling you in for backup, Miss Delilah," Sloane says before following the others.

Virginia Kate wrangles the last loose twin, and the lot of them disappear into the crowd.

I smile as I return to my soaps. I may not have my own children yet, but I have earned quite the reputation as the "toddler whisperer." I never imagined working in the Blissful Bunnies two-year-old class at Pearl Prep Preschool would be anything more than a stopgap on my way to transforming Bubbles & Suds into a thriving corporation, but I have been wholly surprised. Spending my days covered in finger paint, applying Band-Aids, and wiping tears just feels . . . *right.* So much so that I take the time to memorize each of my pint-sized students, learn their sensitivities and strengths, and bond with them over their favorite things so I can be their best possible ally in the classroom.

Then again, I'm not sure it's enough to suffice as a lifetime calling, not in a shiny town like Pearl where the young—including my younger self—are trained up to be top achievers, bound for excellence and nothing less. The salary also doesn't exactly leave room for much beyond necessities. This place is nothing if not worthy of its gemstone namesake, as it sits sparkling at the top of the highway ring that encircles Atlanta.

A fit middle-aged woman walks up to our table, a canvas tote stuffed with vegetables tucked under her arm, and she gently lifts a soap to her nose and sniffs.

"These are just beautiful." She taps her pointer nail on the allergen information sheet that sits propped in the center of the display. "And I'm terribly sensitive to chemical perfumes, so this might just be perfect for me."

The customer gathers a small selection of soaps into a stack and reaches into her bag for her wallet.

"Same here—reaction wise," I say.

Twelve-year-old me had been elated when a popular line of super-scented lotions was dropped into the party bags at Betsy's birthday bash. For once, her parents had actually shown up for her and not until the bounce house was packed up, the mobile petting zoo hauled off, and the popcorn machine scorched from overuse did they disappear as they typically would. Mere minutes after applying the sweet-scented lotion, I broke out in a nasty red rash, and to my young heart, not fitting in felt akin to dying a slow death, one foregone lotion scent at a time. The Five made it our mission to find a fix.

"Which is your favorite?" the customer asks.

"That's sort of like asking me to pick a favorite child," I say and lean in, "but between us girls, it's the peach one."

She picks up the milky peach soap, adds it to her stack, and slides them in front of Roxie, who holds the tablet. Roxie bags the soaps, then holds out the card reader.

The woman pulls in a deep breath. "Just being around these fresh scents feels like walking into a spa."

"Thank you." I tuck my business card into the bag before handing it over. "Feel free to reach out with any questions, and we take orders online in case you're interested in the future."

Across from us, through the gaps in the moving crowd, a pastel-peach banner is hoisted to the top of a freshly erected tent. In curling script it reads, "Peach Pit." Below, a subtitle in uniform text reads, "All-natural, organic products for your best self." A striped white-and-peach tablecloth billows at the hint of a breeze, and a woman in a flowing patterned silk dress, one far too dressy for the farmers market, carries a brown box over and begins unloading items. Lotions, small cosmetic items, and to my horror, *soaps*. Her partner, a glossy blonde wearing a burgundy maxi dress, cinched with a trendy rattan belt at the waist, clicks a speaker to start their music. From a bag they pull a bottle of champagne, then playfully cower as they wiggle the cork off, shrieking as it pops and disappears into the crowd.

They're late to set up—late for the market season—but neither fact appears to be standing in their way.

Already a few people have gathered around them, drawn in by the tray of champagne they pour into plastic flutes, a party come to life. Within moments one woman is gathering a lotion bottle from the table and squirting it onto a forearm held out, massaging it with a manicured hand, wearing a delighted expression as she speaks. She passes a clipboard to the customer, who takes a pen and writes.

I look down to the table before me, the thrifted burlap tablecloth, the wax-paper-wrapped soaps with simple twine, the basic signage. Homemade and crafty. It's taken longer than I'd hoped to build Bubbles & Suds into a legitimate company, but I've always kept the faith. Setting big goals and believing they will come are simply part of being raised in this town. Staying the course.

I might not have been able to be the daughter my family truly wanted—one exactly like my older sister—but *this,* I thought, was something I could do. Transforming a beloved hobby into a thriving company.

Now the glossier, more grown-up version of my own soap table has moved in across from me. I look again at their banner—*all natural, organic, clean.* Sitting here across from them, I'm forced to stare down the very dream I had for my own Bubbles & Suds, and it only brings to light the shortcomings.

Unpolished, unconventional, unfinished: the same arguments for why I don't entirely measure up. The very reasons I don't fit in in this town.

Roxie grabs my upper arm firmly. "What the heck? Why are they letting these peachy people set up right across from us? Natural, organic cosmetics? No way this is acceptable."

She doesn't keep her voice down, confident in her disapproval.

"It's alright. It'll be okay." I wrap a hand around her wrist and pull her in to calm her, as I whisper, "Let's lower our voices, yeah?"

"Why on earth would we? We were here first and have been for a long time. Not to mention it looks like a big business, not homemade. This is supposed to be small businesses only."

Roxie points at them with her free hand, and I rush to take it in mine. My stomach drops at the thought of them seeing us pointing the literal finger at them. I don't want to start trouble with the newcomers; it's simply not in my nature.

"If that's the case, I'm sure they're just passing through. Here for the weekend, I bet."

Roxie's eyes bore into me. "You sure? 'Cause I'm not convinced."

I flash her my best smile, and the tightness in her arms releases enough that I'm comfortable letting go of her hands.

"Yes, I'm sure," I lie. "This is nothing to worry about."

"It's okay to say something, Auntie Lilah. Stand up for yourself. You wouldn't be starting a world war."

I shake my head. "It's not worth it. I don't want to upset anyone. I just want things to be calm and peaceful."

Roxie looks back at me doubtfully.

"I'm sure it's nothing worth making a fuss over," I say, staring down the peachy display. "I'm sure it'll all be fine."

Despite my words, a creeping sensation runs down my spine. I know for a fact the farmers market doesn't allow drop-ins, and this company will be across from us for the rest of the season, a season they considered worth joining in its last weeks. I repeat my mantra—*keep the peace*—to reassure myself, but my mind wanders. I can't help but wonder, in the face of this new peach company before me: What if I'm wrong? What if this doesn't turn out fine?

I dismiss the thought as quickly as it comes.

There's simply no way.

CHAPTER 2

Delilah

Eighteen months later

A CONFETTI POPPER ERUPTS, casting peach paper sprinkles across the women perched on the living room furniture, and Betsy squeals in delight watching it fall across the dozen or so guests gathered in her home. She lowers her manicured hands to the sides of her block-print dress, a warm smile pulled across her face as she takes us in.

"It's official, ladies, this Peach Pit party has commenced! Raise your hand if you've tried the products."

I'm squished in beside Sloane on a love seat, chowing down on my second peach cupcake frosted with a delicate floral design. There is never any question about my attendance at these Peach Pit parties: I come for the food, not the cosmetics. Well, and to support my friends, of course.

Betsy's gaze floats over the group. "Virginia Kate, I see you with a hand up."

Ginny Kay pops up onto her feet and runs her palms down the front of her pink linen shift to flatten it. "Yes, ma'am," she sings. "I, too, am a Peach Pit Darling—thanks to Betsy—and I cannot say enough about these products."

"Darling" is the name given to a sales consultant who buys into the Peach Pit multilevel marketing business, a company built out of tiers of saleswomen tasked with hosting parties to sell Peach Pit products to their friends and family.

Betsy catches the invisible ball Ginny Kay lobs to her and takes off running. "The age-defying night cream was the reason I fell in love with Peach Pit and took the leap." She giggles like the whole thing is a secret club we're lucky to be privy to. "With the revolutionary power derived from the depths of a Georgia peach pit, this cream is better than any time machine at turning back the effects of aging."

Sloane leans in and whispers to me, "Have to say I think I'd prefer to take a DeLorean."

I rush to slap a palm over my mouth as a laugh erupts.

When I glance up from my crumb-laden plate, Betsy shoots me a look that says, *"Hush it, girlie."*

I pull an apologetic grimace, and the presentation carries on.

In the year and a half that's passed since Peach Pit landed in Pearl, it's taken our town by charge. At first it was a novelty, a few parties springing up here and there, but within months the parties were everywhere. Women of any and all ages couldn't take ten steps outside their door without a Peach Pit Darling inviting her to a sales party or inquiring about her skin-care routine.

The Darlings tout the "life-changing" qualities of their products, promising to help Pearl women "bounce back" after childbirth, to find energy and avoid the ghastly traps of aging. I can't say I get it. When I look around Pearl, I see women who don't need to be revolutionized. Not one bit. I see tired eyes that are a predictable by-product of motherhood, a fluffy waistline that *shouldn't* be a priority for a woman caring for an ailing relative, wrinkles that are the result of fun in the sun, laughter among friends.

Beyond their sky-high promises, it's obvious how Peach Pit truly took hold: Invitations for women to join the business scheme are delivered like bids to a desirable sorority. Women want to belong. It is a club as much as it is a business, and for those Pearlites who most desire the "it girl" status, buying in and being crowned a Darling is a ticket directly there.

"You're getting me in trouble," I whisper to Sloane.

She shrugs almost imperceptibly.

"My other favorite is the peach lip gloss." Betsy unscrews a tube, grabs a hand mirror from the table supporting her elaborate display castle of product, and applies it to her already glammed-out face. "It has a slight taste, and it's *enhancing*, so if it burns a little you know it's working. Like a Red Hot, but on your skin."

I blink once. Then again. And again, trying to make sense of setting one's skin ablaze. I glance around the group, and not a one of them seems to falter at the suggestion of self-inflicted discomfort in the name of a little beauty. Maybe it's me. I've never been a hair-and-makeup-obsessed Pearl girl. I fought my mama tooth and nail on the pageants she tried to push me into as a child, alongside my sister—and Betsy. I still have the same hair dryer I got in high school and none of the other hot styling torture tools. In fact, it was the support of The Five from a young age that gave me the confidence to be me.

"Now"—Betsy grabs a large canister from the table of products—"this is the tummy-trimming Peach Tea. Many of us have had babies, and there's nothing better for bouncing back to your pre-baby self. Ditch the love handles, get your glow back, and even regrow all that hair you're finding in clumps in the shower. Yup, I was there too. I had my third baby, Hattie, six months ago, and I was left feeling exhausted and just not myself—"

I lean over to Sloane. "Isn't exhaustion an occupational hazard of having children?"

Childfree Sloane shrugs, bewildered.

"I started drinking this tea three times a day, and I dropped ten pounds in the first two months, noticed a tightening of my skin, and even saw baby hairs of regrowth on my scalp."

"I bet it just gives you diarrhea," Sloane whispers to me.

My only response is a grim look. I can't imagine opting for self-inflicted diarrhea on top of juggling a new baby. Bless the moms. They deserve better than this.

"Who wants a sample of the Day Glow body shimmer lotion? It's unconfirmed but highly suspected that Kesha uses it preshow." Betsy makes her way around the room peddling samples.

I risk a glance at Sloane, who is grinning like a Cheshire cat.

"Stop," I say, fighting a laugh. "Betsy's going to think we're laughing at *her*."

To be entirely honest, I haven't trusted the mathematics of the scheme—the promise that every Darling will make oodles of cash—but I keep it zipped and mind my own soaps. Especially since Betsy and Virginia Kate signed on.

I support them how I can, but it does hurt a little knowing I'm also supporting this mega-company that's sprawled all over Georgia and into the surrounding states like kudzu. My Bubbles & Suds sales at the farmers market have dipped, some customers who routinely ordered on my site dropping off and later announcing their new job as a Peach Pit Darling. I know it's not personal, that these women are still lovely and kind, but when I look at my sweet little soaps unsold, my chest cramps.

Betsy arrives in front of us, props a hand on her hip, and blows a stray lock of auburn hair out of her eye with a pronounced puff.

"I'm not even gonna ask if y'all want a sample." She rolls her eyes lovingly.

I don't use Peach Pit products because I've learned my lesson too many times to trust a corporate "all-natural" claim, breaking out in a signature ugly rash. I could only imagine the chorus from my tiny bunnies tomorrow morning: *"Miss Delilah, boo-boo!"* on repeat. They really don't miss a thing, and when those tiny brows knit in worry, it breaks my heart right open.

Sloane throws out a reluctant forearm. "Work your magic, but if I don't leave here feeling far more like Kesha, your boss might be getting a strongly worded email."

"I'll take a hug from Pearl's greatest hostess instead," I say.

Betsy's face breaks into a grin, and she tucks the bottle under her arm and takes me into her arms. "I love you, Delilah Thomas, even if I'll never make you a Darling."

"Well, we can't all be Darlings," Sloane chimes in, a reminder of the points she's made repeatedly regarding the math of a network sales model and market saturation.

"I'm not sure they'd have me even if I wanted in." I laugh, but anyone could take one look at me and see the evidence laid out before them.

I wear leggings, T-shirts, and sweatshirts 90 percent of my life, and otherwise I'm in something fun I found at the thrift store. Overalls are a top favorite. I'm happy with my homemade soaps and I auto-buy cheap shampoo that has yet to cause any skin issues, not a complicated ten-step skin-care routine in sight. My shoulder-length mousy-brown hair resembles a chinchilla most days, and I can't say it bothers me. I could blame my aversion to glamour on the messiness of my day job, but it's always been my way. Visually floating under the radar.

I couldn't manage Darling glossy if my life depended on it.

"Well, I appreciate y'all being here for these parties. I know it's not your thing, but you come anyway," Betsy says before swanning off to help a woman at the product table flagging her over.

I wander over to a side table set up with a smaller display of products. The lotions are in modern cylinders, matte peach, like something a Kardashian would design, and the makeup items are in sleek, translucent peach shapes. Everything is branded in peach and gold, heavy card stock, quality linen ribbon closures. It feels expensive, luxurious. It's a perfect sell here in Pearl.

I feel a hollowness in my chest when I move down the table to the basket of soaps. They're a milky peach, not entirely unlike the ones I make myself, wrapped in a chic white card stock sleeve with the peach-and-gold branding.

Eliza lifts herself from the deep-set armchair and dusts cupcake crumbs from the top of her large baby bump. She waddles over, glowing despite the bags under her eyes, and Sloane joins us from where she'd been standing examining her phone.

"Here, take the love seat," I say.

Eliza glances at it and sighs. "Not sure it's worth it, knowing how hard it'll be to get back up."

"Fair. How much longer now?" Sloane asks.

"Less than six weeks apparently, but Jack was early. I have to work right up until I go into labor because I have basically zero time off." She looks up to the ceiling. "I just want more time with baby girl when she gets here. Is that too much to ask?"

I reach out and wrap an arm around her, the beginnings of tears welling in her eyes. The HVAC company where she works as an administrative assistant isn't a bad gig, but at the end of the day, they're a small business that needs customers scheduled, materials ordered, and bills paid, and they can't accommodate a long leave.

"I'm sorry," Sloane says.

In private I've wondered if Eliza and her husband, Ted, could swing her staying home for a while, but I don't want to ask. Probably if they could afford it, she would be planning to take the time she wants.

Eliza sighs. "I've actually been wondering about giving this a whirl."

Collectively we look around the picture-perfect party dressed in peach, and something deep inside me hitches.

"*This?* Like being a Peach Pit consultant?"

"You mean a *Darling*." Eliza smiles serenely. "Both Betsy and Virginia Kate are making it work, so why couldn't I? Plus, it's *fun*. And all the girls are a club. It could be nice to be part of it."

"You know there's a base investment, right? And then a per month requirement of product ordered." Sloane looks at her with great focus.

Eliza bristles slightly. "Are you suggesting I couldn't keep up?"

"No. Of course not. I'm sorry, I didn't mean it like that." Sloane takes a sip of her drink. "It's just . . . a lot. Competitive."

"We just want the best for you." I rush to smooth out the brewing disagreement. "With the baby coming and all, you have so much on your plate."

I smile as I relay these comforting words, but the same concerns Sloane raised buzz in my head.

"I know," Eliza says, her voice catching a little. "I'm overwhelmed and worried about delivering the baby. Sloane, I'm sorry. I didn't mean to snap."

In the pause between us, Betsy looks over and catches Eliza's eye. Her blue-and-white floral dress flows out behind her as she approaches, hair tucked neatly behind her ears, and stops in front of Eliza. She takes her hands and squeezes them.

"So what do you say? Are you ready to say yes to Peach Pit sisterhood and become a Darling?" Betsy gushes.

Despite the fact that I know Betsy would never—*never*—knowingly lead one of us astray, a discomfort I just can't place wells inside me as I watch Eliza field the question. If Betsy recruits Eliza, she would be making a commission off all her sales, just like she already is off Virginia Kate's sales. It's the way the recruitment model works, but I can't mentally reconcile taking a cut of your *actual* friend's income.

"I'm sure she'll want to talk it over with Ted," I say in the sweetest tone I can muster.

"Aren't you always the one saying women are capable of making their own decisions?" Betsy says to me, a playful brow cocked. "You can't have it both ways, girlie! You can't say it only works when she's making the same choice as you." She sings the words to soften the impact of the statement.

In this moment Betsy looks so much like the pageant-winning young woman of our youth, the one who followed in my older sister's footsteps so closely that she might as well have been the second daughter of my parents' dreams. Certainly my mama would've been happy with that.

"I'm coming from a place of love. And you're right." A tightness mounts in my throat.

"I do appreciate it," Eliza says.

"Maybe just think on it. You just said how overwhelmed you are, and it's a sizable financial commitment to make when you're already stressed." Sloane sounds reasonable and unemotional like the lawyer she is, and I'm grateful for the grounding effect of her voice.

Eliza nods rapidly, her head bobbing around the circle of her friends. "Probably a good idea."

Finally, Virginia Kate swans in behind Betsy, filling the gap beside her head. "You're in, Eliza, right?" She squeaks, clapping. "I can't wait for you to be *one of us*."

"'One of us'? What the heck?" My hands lift to sit atop my hips. "The 'us' is The Five."

It's about as sassy as I allow myself to get, but for that sort of comment it's beyond warranted.

"Yeah, what the hell?" Sloane says, as if the comment takes a moment to sink in.

Virginia Kate has the decency to blush. "You're right. Peach Pit comes second."

Betsy's smiling veneer remains intact, and Eliza's eyes dart from friend to friend, as if she's scrambling for purchase on a crumbling road. As if they're too afraid that perhaps, maybe a little, Peach Pit has become something to them that contends with our decades-old group.

"Maybe even third. Or fourth." A familiar shame burns at my cheeks as I hear the boldness in my voice.

I just can't help myself. The Five has been the heart of my life for as long as I can remember. Especially when I, the caboose baby late to a party I wasn't invited to, never fully imprinted on the family to which I was born.

The Five was once sleepovers, trick-or-treating with group costumes, and talent show performances. Next it was homecoming dances, sports cheering sections, and collective tears over broken hearts. We endured braces, bad haircuts, and bad decisions. It became big life choices, losing people we loved, first love. Eventually, engagements, weddings, and babies. Their children in my class every weekday morning.

Virginia Kate pulls in a breath and speaks with complete nonchalance. "I just misspoke. Can we not make it such a big deal, Delilah?"

"Yeah," I say. "Of course."

The memory of racing to Ginny Kay's house the moment the news of her parents' divorce broke back in middle school returns to me. How she camped out in my room for a week starting the next morning. "Such a big deal" might as well be the story of our lives.

At least that's how I've always felt.

I look to Sloane, who rode with me. "You about ready to go?"

"Sounds good. Thanks for having us, ladies. My house Tuesday night? Anton's traveling for work. As always." She pouts slightly.

Sloane and her husband are a tried-and-true power couple with high-flying jobs and a polished loft in a trendy local building.

Betsy presses a hand on Sloane's back. "Thanks, girl. I'm excited for it."

We say our goodbyes, and before we're even out the door, Betsy and Virginia Kate take off to chat with their down-line ladies, the ones they've recruited to flow business into their group.

I turn back to Eliza. "I'm here if you need me. Anything, okay?"

She smiles and nods, her hand running over her bump, her tiny daughter inside. *Another one of us,* I think.

Sloane calls to me over her shoulder. "You coming or what?"

I pull Eliza into a quick hug and then go, and as I walk out behind Sloane, I try to ignore the feeling that nips at my heels—the feeling that things are about to change.

CHAPTER 3

Betsy

BETSY MCCLEARY CLOSES THE door behind the last guest and turns back to the party wreckage. Her heart flutters, despite the fact that the special-order paper cups in peach seersucker are now scattered across her living room, despite the matching napkin stack being knocked to the floor. A serene smile opens across her face as she pulls in a deep breath, savoring the sugary peach scent the festivities have cast into the air.

If there's anything in the world she can count on being good at, it's being a Peach Pit Darling, and all she wants is to hold tight to this feeling.

Betsy was once a floundering mom with nothing but a résumé full of retail jobs to show for herself. Landing an incredible husband was her greatest accomplishment. She closes her eyes, and—now planted firmly past that low—she allows herself to remember it.

College graduation was a day of excitement for the rest of The Five, all of them certain of where they were headed next. Virginia Kate to earn her accountant's license, Sloane to law school, Eliza into a permanent, full-time administrative job, and Delilah to get her early education teaching certificate while she continued to build her soap company.

Betsy had no plans.

She'd spent so much of her childhood swimming in the quiet

freedom of her jet-setting parents' absence that she never truly anchored to much. Besides The Five. Probably she had too much freedom too soon, too little guidance, and part of her felt like she'd missed the boat on finding a calling. In her sorority she was the best social chair they'd seen in a decade, effortlessly throwing together lavish parties, and it was there she thrived.

When that was stripped away, Betsy became unmoored.

The years that followed dragged as she worked retail jobs and continued to date Jared. Their engagement—the first of The Five—quickly erased Betsy's woes as she was thrown into a series of parties, showers, planning, and a shopping list a mile long. Soon after the big day, she became pregnant and jumped into another season of showers, shopping, prepping, and planning. But once the wrapping paper had been balled up, the thank-you notes written and delivered, and the quiet fell, a familiar emptiness crept in.

Virginia Kate emerges from the kitchen, flapping a garbage bag that billows open, and it stirs Betsy back to the present. Her eyes pop open and at the sight of the party remnants around her, the tightness in her chest releases: All of that is firmly in the past, thanks to Peach Pit.

"How were sales tonight?" Virginia Kate circles the room, sliding discarded plates piled with cupcake wrappers and icing blobs into the bag. Unlike Betsy, Virginia Kate's party-ready bubbliness has vanished, and she yawns through cracked lipstick.

Betsy marches over to her laptop that's set up beside the products and clicks around. "Eh, not bad. A hundred sixty bucks."

Virginia Kate doesn't look up from her cleaning. "And what did you spend on all of this stuff?" She gestures to the food, beverages, and paper goods.

Betsy pops upright. "Oh. Well. I'm not sure, but I just don't really count it."

"You don't?" The surprise in Virginia Kate's voice takes Betsy aback. "It's a cost of operating."

"Well, it's an *investment*."

Virginia Kate looks entirely unconvinced. "I guess Peach Pit doesn't follow basic accounting rules, huh?"

Betsy isn't sure if there's a true annoyance behind her friend's words, but it's not a surprise, seeing as Virginia Kate was once a serious finance professional used to the stuffiness of boardrooms and spreadsheets. Betsy believes what she said—it's an investment, one that will pay off in the long run. It's such a big part of being a Darling, believing enough in yourself and your business to invest now so that in the future the fruits can be reaped.

Virginia Kate slumps onto the sofa, letting her head drop back. "I guess you're right. Got to keep the faith."

Betsy props a perky hand on her hip. "You know you're killing it right, Darling Virginia Kate? Don't get the blues on me now, sister!" She crosses the room in spirited bounds and drops onto the sofa beside her friend, then pulls her into her arms.

Betsy just knew Peach Pit was the solution when Virginia Kate mentioned she needed to go back to work. Betsy wanted to share the wealth—literally and metaphorically—of Peach Pit. Once upon a time, Virginia Kate was a finance pro living in Charlotte, North Carolina, but she left it all behind when she married Hunter. When Virginia Kate had issues reestablishing her professional license, it might as well have been the universe herself pointing Virginia Kate to Peach Pit. All her friend needed was to be a tad more aggressive with recruitment, and she'd be on her way to explosive growth.

Betsy rolls out of the full body hug.

Virginia Kate sighs. "You don't think Sloane has a point? That maybe the structure is . . ."

Betsy startles at the blasphemy. "No! Not one bit. To start, Sloane hasn't experienced it firsthand like us, so how could she truly get it? I was *meant* to be a Darling. Just like Delilah is in her element at school. I mean, she doesn't even have her own kids, but she was the only one who could get Rex to use the potty at school. Every single mama relies on her to be the toddler whisperer."

"I'm not sure Delilah would agree," Virginia Kate says, glancing away.

"What do you mean?"

"Sure, she likes the preschool—and there's no denying she has a knack for it—but what she really wants is for Bubbles & Suds to make it big."

Betsy wrinkles her nose, then swats the air. "That's just a hangover from her parents trying to make her someone she's not. She's the star teacher at the preschool now and total Pearl royalty. What more could she need?"

"Either way, there's a limiting factor on how the down-line can grow, especially if you're getting in late."

Betsy purses her lips jokingly. "You're not in the financial district anymore, Ginny Kay! This is the South. We have business among friends, and we have faith our hard work will pay off. Just look around Pearl: Everyone's doing well. There are always new people moving here—did you see the new development over off Highway 3? How can we lose? Only by negative self-talk. That and lack of effort."

Virginia Kate is quiet, and Betsy hopes she's chased off her misgivings. She hates seeing Virginia Kate worn out, but it's normal for things to feel difficult at the beginning. Betsy truly wants the best for her dear friend, the same success she's had. Virginia Kate is a hard worker, and she's charming; she's going to kill it.

Honestly, *any* of The Five could be a winning Darling.

"So." Betsy hops up and heads back toward her computer. "It sure seems like Eliza's ready to join. I mean, it's obvious she wants to stay home with her kids. That job at the HVAC place is way too blah for our gal. This is literally a match made in heaven."

Virginia Kate nods. "You really think she could make enough?"

Betsy's insides bubble, knowing the numbers on her account.

She makes more from this than she did in any prior job, and she gets to throw parties and sign other women up for the same life. *Of course* she believes. Peach Pit turned her life around, so why wouldn't she recruit her friends?

Sure, she doesn't actually see the sales the girls on her team are making. They buy product from Peach Pit, and Betsy receives a cut. From there the Darlings work their magic and sell it out into the world, but there hasn't been even the slightest hint of turbulence among her team in selling through.

"Ginny Kay, *yes*. I've been here awhile, *trust me*."

Virginia Kate's face softens. "Trust is hard for me, you know that. I'm glad I've got you here to encourage me."

The scandalous divorce poor Virginia Kate endured after her mother's affair shook her to her core. The Five were there for her; they did their best with sleepovers and implementing a buddy system in the school hallways, but Virginia Kate didn't really recover from the aftershocks of her mother being socially cast out. Sure, Ginny Kay still came to the country club with her father, but the adults should've shielded her better from their gossiping. Not to mention the teasing that came at school—mostly from the cruelest boys. Despite it all, Virginia Kate studied hard, passed her accountant exams, and turned it all around.

Then before long, Hunter swept her off her feet and ferried her back home to them, a freshly minted Mrs. Virginia Kate Rhodes.

The welcome home party The Five threw was one for the books. Betsy picked a "Travel Home to Me" theme, and it was as if Delilah had moved into her head with how fabulously she pulled off the handcrafted decorations. A dotted path covered the wall, and along it, milestones in their lives as The Five were marked. Everything looked sleek and professional as Delilah delivered it hot off her Cricut.

"Is this too much?" Delilah had asked, physically shrinking like she always did in her most shining moments.

"Oh, cut the bull, Lilah. You and I both know these are killer," Betsy had said with a wink.

Delilah's blush had been about as deep as the hug Betsy pulled her into.

Betsy smiles to herself at the memory.

"Follow up with Eliza in the morning? I can just feel it—she's ready to leap! It'll be fabulous. I mean, imagine if we could get all five of us in Peach Pit!"

Virginia Kate laughs. "We both know the chances of that. And I should probably get going. Hunter's got a client meeting early, so I'm solo getting the kids up and to school in the morning."

"Sure thing, honey. I've got the rest of this mess."

Virginia Kate stands and grabs her purse from the kitchen, and Betsy walks behind her to the door. As her hand falls on the handle, Virginia Kate turns to face Betsy.

"I want to make sure this Peach Pit stuff doesn't mess up things between The Five. I could tell it upset Delilah when I accidentally suggested this was—"

"We're good, girl. We're *The Five*—nothing can touch us, especially not a few sweet cosmetics."

"Right." Virginia Kate casts her eyes downward.

Betsy hugs her friend again, then Virginia Kate slips out into the evening. Betsy watches her climb into her weathered minivan and wonders if Virginia Kate will be able to replace it soon with her Peach Pit earnings.

Surely it's only a matter of time.

CHAPTER 4

Delilah

AFTER I DROP OFF Sloane, I head to SweetGum Lane and pull into the narrow driveway that runs alongside my Craftsman-style bungalow. The street is lined in mismatched landscaping, wildflowers when the season allows, patches of dirt where some folks would demand mulch be laid down, streetlights that flicker on reliably after sunset. People who run small businesses or work trades and creatives of many sorts live on this street, the most affordable as well as the most vibrant vein in Pearl. Homes are painted in a rainbow of colors—not an HOA color guide in sight—and we lovingly refer to ourselves as the backwoods Rainbow Row.

When I step out of the car, the street is quiet in the dark of the evening, the chirping of nighttime bugs slowly returning with spring, and the cool breeze rustles in the Georgia pine trees. My azaleas have bloomed, and I stand and enjoy them, knowing I won't get to keep them hardly long enough. Down the street music is playing, and it reminds me that Teo is celebrating his retirement this week with a series of gatherings, family coming and going as their lives allow.

Before heading inside, I walk to the mailbox I haven't checked in a couple of days and pull out a short stack that I tuck under my arm. Intentionally I wait to look through it. If there's something from *him* today—a postcard, or even a full-length letter—I want to savor it. My heart flutters. At minimum I saw one of my favorite coupon books poking out, so I won't be entirely disappointed. Not that any coupon holds a candle to one of Jasper's messages.

Through the picture window of my lavender house, Scooby the tabby cat sits illuminated by the glowing table lamp, seemingly awaiting my return. Her brother, Doo, a larger, surly tabby, is probably curled up somewhere far more comfortable, happily hidden away from prying eyes.

I climb the deck, it creaks lovingly, and my keys jingle melodiously as I sort through the ring for my house key that's stacked amid the school-related ones. This house is my own pocket of the world, a place I can be entirely me without worrying about keeping anyone else happy. Here, I'm entirely free.

I glance next door to the tangerine house, and the only light on is in Mrs. Chopra's bedroom. Curled up with a book and a cup of tea is my guess.

The door hinges squeak as I push in, and Scooby drops to the weathered wood floor and tangles herself around my ankles, purring a beautiful "welcome home." I crouch and gather her into my arms, and she burrows into me in response. I pass into the kitchen and drop my keys and the mail on the tiny butcher block island. In the would-be dining area attached, my soap-making supplies sit stacked on a metal prep table. Bowls, measuring beakers, tiny pots of essential oils stacked precariously in the small space. An oversized box of sleeves sits at the end, dwarfing the rest, but the wholesaler was having a sale, so I took advantage.

As I head for the fridge, Virginia Kate's question echoes through my mind: *"Can we not make this such a big deal?"*

Such a big deal.

Honestly it hurts to hear one of The Five say that. It makes me feel like I should—by this age and maturity—be cynical enough to act cool about the comment. To not care so much.

What if the others simply don't see our friendships as they once did? Could I be the only one of us living in the past? Certainly the lot of them have added significant others, children, careers, but I never imagined that would mean recategorizing The Five. Maybe I *am* being too much about it. But one thing remains constant: I care. Deeply so. Perhaps embarrassingly so, but no degree of mortification would change the fact.

What I worry about most is that this company, Peach Pit, will be the thing, despite all life's challenges we've endured side by side, to come between us. Betsy was one of the first few in the Peach Pit door, so considering the way the women join in layers below the most senior Darlings, it would be understandable for her to be flush with cash. But for a new recruit like Eliza? I couldn't throw a stone in a room in Pearl without hitting a Darling. Who would she recruit to build a team? Where are the customers for her to sell to? From where I stand, I can't make sense of it.

But maybe I'm the one overthinking it. Not to mention, it would be nearly impossible to say anything without insinuating wrongdoing by Betsy and Virginia Kate. And the last thing I want to do is upset everyone by stirring things up. In The Five—much as in the rest of my life—I'm terrified of rocking the boat. Since I was a child, no good ever came from me speaking up.

Scooby wiggles in my arms, and I realize I'm holding her too tight, my grip intensifying as my mind whirls. I set her down.

"Sorry, Scoobs."

She looks over her shoulder, as if to accept my apology.

I reach for the bundle of mail I set on the counter, and my heart picks up again as I page through the stack and my gaze lands on a plain envelope. I slide it out, and at the sight of Jasper's handwriting, my heart does a somersault. The sound of the envelope ripping open under my nail sends a shiver through me, and I pull the letter hungrily from the paper casing.

Delilah,

This assignment is a doozy. Started off great, but then some of the team got sick, and now we're living with only the basics. Fortunately, we got the story we came for, and we're heading back stateside for a break in ten days or so. This one will be welcome.

I did get to see a lion pride up close—a first for me. One of the locals offered to take me out in his Jeep for a tour, so naturally I took him up on the offer.

Did you end up doing a new soap for the spring? I hope all is well at the lavender house with your two feline friends. I have a month off until my next assignment, ~~and I was thinking maybe I'd~~

~~Could I~~

What if I came to Pearl? It'll be the last break I get for a while.

Talk soon,

J

It's as if a surge of energy rushes into me, and I suck in a gasp. My palms are at once covered in sweat.

Jasper has been my pen pal since we were matched in a school-to-school program in fifth grade, and despite our keeping in touch all these years, we've never been in the same room. Initially I was disappointed that I'd been paired with a boy rather than a girl as requested, but Mrs. Rogers was fresh out of girls, so it was Jasper from the Pacific Northwest or nothing. It started with gel pens and me spraying my Hello Kitty stationery with perfume because I saw it in a movie. Eventually I saved all the best stickers for him. Little did I know we'd never go long without communicating, that he'd become someone I confided in, someone I looked forward to hearing from.

Nowadays Jasper is a travel journalist, so he's taken to sending me postcards from all over the world as he lives his life on the road. I still get full-length letters when he can swing it. We've had a few spotty video chats—thanks to his tenuous connections to Wi-Fi—and each time I'm left grinning ear to ear and giggling like one of my students. I hate to admit it, but he reduces me to a blubber.

At the rumble of my stomach, I yank open the fridge door. In the glowing interior are only a few dinner options, so I grab a container of Chinese food leftovers and toss it in the microwave. It's enough along with the cupcakes I ate earlier to call dinner. The microwave beeps, and when I slide out the food, the container nearly burns my hands.

It reminds me of the burning peach lip gloss, and I giggle to myself at the idea of slathering Tsu's sauce on my lips.

I make my way back over to the living room, the quietness of my solo life wrapping me in its familiar embrace. I tug the curtains shut and drop into the dip of my well-worn spot in the corner of the sofa. Scooby curls up in my lap, and her warm weight presses against me and slows my nervous system.

I hold the container elevated above her feline perch and eat.

The truth is that I'd like to have others in my life to share this cozy home. A partner, children one day. It's a reason I love my job as a preschool teacher, a reason I hungrily grab at time with my beloved niece, Roxie. I just haven't gotten around to figuring out the *how* of it yet, considering there are zero suitors on the horizon. The Five have given me pep talk after pep talk after a bad date as I lament about my forever-single status.

That, and steered me toward Jasper.

I have to admit: Jasper is absolutely a person of interest, but the problem is that he won't stay in one place long enough to be a real option. He loves being a travel journalist, and even if his postcards from exotic locations make my heart skip a beat every time I pull them from the mailbox, I don't want to float around the world. Pearl isn't perfect, but I love so much of my life here: the bunnies, Bubbles & Suds, The Five.

When I finish eating, I pick up Scooby and head upstairs. My bedroom and the attached bathroom, nestled into the crooks of the dormers, is the entire floor. Trees line SweetGum Lane, and up here I let myself imagine I have a treehouse. I change into pajamas, brush my teeth, and wash my face. I flip on my table lamp, casting the room into a warm yellow, and then climb into my spindle bed. I adjust the mountain of pillows and hand-me-down quilts until I'm comfortable, then dig around for my TV remote.

I turn on a competition baking show, and I'm almost to sleep when my phone chirps. I don't rush to answer it. Eventually I lift the phone, and a groan erupts when I see my class assistant's name, Amber, pop up. A text from her at this time on a Sunday evening is always a call out.

I click to the text, and my suspicions are confirmed. Her daughter has a fever and will need to stay home tomorrow. I text back something understanding. Really, it's not like it's within her control, and to be fair, Amber was talked into taking the assistant position when the school couldn't find anyone else to do it. They put on their own version of the Peach Pit hard sell.

I hop up out of bed and pull back the blinds. Mrs. Chopra's light is still on, so I text her.

> Any chance you'd be up for hanging with me and the bunnies tomorrow? Amber has a sick kiddo.

Mrs. Chopra is a well-established sub at the school who jumped through the required administrative hoops a couple years ago, and she's always my first choice when Amber is out.

All I had planned was a long walk and working in my garden, so why not?

Mrs. Chopra is in her mid-sixties, a widow and retired chemist who spends her days exploring nature, volunteering as a reading tutor at the local elementary school, and enjoying a robust calendar of senior social activities. She spreads delight wherever she goes, and I eagerly befriended her as soon as I moved in six years ago.

I reply: You're an angel. Pick you up at 8:15?

I'll have my lunch packed.

I settle back into my pillow and am seriously considering turning off the television to sleep when my phone jumps to life, shaking as it rings again.

I click to answer, and Mama's voice flows out sounding like a heavy musk perfume.

CHAPTER 5

Delilah

"WELL, HEY THERE, HONEY child, you sound like you're about halfway to sleep." The clink of ice in a glass follows, and I can see my mama, Trudie Thomas, sipping her nightly whiskey on the rocks. She sits in her rocking chair on the wide wraparound porch overlooking their sprawling property. Well out of the way of my mercurial father.

"Everything okay? You don't usually call this late," I say.

"Well, I'm calling with a surprise!"

My insides shuffle as I internally brace myself. How she and I categorize good versus bad surprises is polar opposite.

"I'm chairing the Pearl Easter Egg Hunt!" Mama cries.

"Congrats, Mama. I know you've been wanting to chair for years now." I sigh, relieved her surprise doesn't pertain to me. "You'll do a fabulous job."

"But that's not it! I've also gotten special permission to choose my co-chair."

I close my eyes, knowing what's coming next: another stint of being caught in the painful middle.

Now don't get me wrong. I would love to be included in the inside track of my family, but when it comes to Mama and me, it's as if her every attempt to include me is one exercise after another in highlighting my shortcomings. Of course, I dare not utter a word about this lest I make it worse. Best to grip tight the fragile peace we have.

When I was a child, it was the pageants. Glitzy Darcy took to them so naturally she was curling her own hair in grade school, but when Mama entered me, it should've come with a storm warning. I pulled ladders in the pantyhose, smudged my makeup, and sobbed the moment I was supposed to go onstage. My fussing over not wanting to participate threw the whole family into a tailspin for so long, I lived to regret saying anything at all. It would've been far less painful just to suck up my unwillingness and do the pageants.

Later she'd include me in her weekly nail appointments. I went along with it as long as I could—for the sake of wanting to be close to her—but the way the nail salon smelled made me sick to my stomach until I left with a throbbing headache. There was also one foray into keeping horses on the property like many of their neighbors do in that area. But I was hopeless with the horses, and though I kept my struggles quiet, before long the horses were surreptitiously rehomed to a neighbor with state-of-the-art stables.

I made my efforts too, inviting her as I could into things I liked, but she called bingo at the community center a bore and declined an offer to hike based on the off chance of sighting of a snake. When she brushed off my invitation to the most precious olive branch I could ever imagine—soap making—I stopped asking.

It's sad that out of the entire family, it's still Mama I'm closest to.

I pull in a breath. "Nice. I'm sure—"

"It's you! You're going to be my co-chair, sweetie. You'll have firsthand access to all the who's who of Pearl as we plan the best egg hunt of the century. You'll be so well connected by the end of it, you won't know what to do with yourself." Mama's cheery, high-pitched gushing sends a quiver through my middle.

I might've lived most of my life in Pearl, but when attending these upper-crust events, I always feel like an intruder. I won't ever belong there.

"Oh, Mama, are you sure—"

"It's going to be fabulous, honey. I've already been chatting with

Betsy's and Sloane's mamas at the club about how nice it's going to be to have one of y'all on the organizing side. Though all of us are still alive and kicking just fine, it won't be long until we need you young folks to step in on this sacred tradition."

"*Sacred* might be a bridge too far."

Mama laughs. "Well, to some of us it is! I know it's a little outside your usual wheelhouse, but I think you'll simply adore it once you get into the fun of organizing."

Mama and Daddy have taken Darcy and me to Easter brunch at the country club since before we could walk—just as Pearl tradition dictates. Darcy always wore her frilly Sunday best, patent leather shoes slapping and clacking as she strutted through the grand building as if everyone had gathered on her account. Later, fashionable dresses with strappy heels. She drank in the attention that inevitably came her way.

I much preferred to play outside in the dirt, but they tugged me behind them fielding looks of chagrin over the smudges of mud on my white shoes.

"I think I might fare better than the pageants," I said.

"Oh, hush." Trudie's words are playful. "You would've been just fine, honey, if you had just stuck the course. You were so darling with your hair all curled and sprayed—"

"I tore holes in my tights before I even left the dressing room."

"The red cupcake dress was perfect on you—might've given your big sister a run for the crown had you made it onto the stage!"

Mama and I both know that last part isn't true, but I appreciate her attempts to soften Darcy's constant dominance. Darcy's showboating at the club was exactly as it was at home, the favored child who checked all the boxes. Nothing I did garnered a similar response, and I learned quickly that being helpful and quiet were the best ways for me to get along. I helped my mother in the kitchen while Darcy was off practicing her singing for her pageant talent. I set Daddy's slippers out in hopes of mitigating the bad moods he always brought home from work. I ate less of everyone's favorite potato salad when we were running low. I always cleaned up behind myself—and others if they forgot. I kept myself out of trouble at school and otherwise and relied heavily on the kindness of Eliza's mom to get me to any special events.

My parents praised me for my maturity, and I clung to the bare-bones recognition.

"I must already be asleep and dreaming, Mama, because Darcy Rawlins, née Thomas, would come after you with a hot curling iron if she heard you say that."

"Well, let's keep it between us. Heaven knows your sister could use a bit of a reality check with how she's running around drinking mimosas all day like she's on *The Real Housewives of Pearl*. She needs to get involved with a philanthropy to busy herself. Or start pageant coaching."

"You could always ask her to co-chair," I say, imagining the reprieve of the responsibility lifting. "Sounds like it could be good timing."

"I want *you*, Delilah."

An extended pause comes across the line, and I know it's time for me to accept this offering. To try as I might, once again, to close the gap between us. After all, there is nothing I'm better at than trying to please others—my mother included.

"I might live to regret this, but . . . count me in."

Mama lets out a cry of joy. "Oh, I'm thrilled, sweetie! I can't wait! We'll get to pick out the details, do it our own way. Well, to an extent—we need to please the crowd!" Mama lets out a throaty laugh.

"Sure thing, Mama. It'll be great." I put effort behind my words.

"It sure will be, honey. I'm so glad to have you at my side. Honestly, it's been a dream of mine for so long."

"I know you've wanted to chair since I was a child, and I'm happy for you."

"Well . . ." Mama pauses for a moment. "Yes, child, I have."

We agree to meet in a couple days to go over the preliminary information, then say our goodbyes. We hang up, and when I'm left in my cozy room nestled in the dormers, I smile.

For Mama I'll try my best.

Even if this Easter egg hunt ends in disaster.

CHAPTER 6

Delilah

WHEN I STEP OUT onto my porch the next morning to sip my coffee, Mrs. Chopra is already on hers next door, dressed for the day and topping off her bird feeder. The sun is up, and the coolness of the morning is beginning to lift with the morning dew, spring birds chirping happy morning songs all around us.

Her dark shoulder-length hair is streaked generously with gray and tucked behind her ears, but the way her eyes sparkle when she greets me betrays youthfulness.

"I'm afraid my favorite cardinal might be getting skinny what with all the spring birds coming back."

"Big Red won't be elbowed out," I say. "I'm 80 percent sure I saw him go toe-to-toe with a squirrel on that feeder a couple weeks ago."

"I don't think birds have toes." Mrs. Chopra grins as she settles the bird feeder.

"Claw-to-claw? You know what I mean."

She heads for the door. "I usually do. Depart in thirty?"

I nod, and she waves as she dips inside. My phone buzzes in my pocket, and I pull it out as I drop into the rattan egg chair on my porch. I smile as I catch sight of the notification on the screen: The Five group chat has woken up for the day.

Sloane: It's before business hours, and I already have three briefs in my inbox, two depositions to take, and a last-minute presentation on the docket. The famous Moretti lasagna I promised for tomorrow might not actually be in the cards. Thoughts on Lunchables?

I smile to myself and take a long gulp of coffee. Sloane's mother, Lucille Moretti, is well known for her lasagna and recently bestowed the recipe on her devoted daughter. Even after marriage, Sloane kept the Moretti name and waited patiently to inherit the family recipes. I set the mug on the floor so I can text.

Delilah: The sun isn't even all the way up!

Sloane: And I barely slept, as per usual. Worrying about work. Knowing my boss was awake sending me emails.

Eliza: Been dying to use my new bread maker.

Betsy: Anything but a Spice Girls' dinner.

The laugh pops out of me so involuntarily that I almost spit out my coffee. I remember the Spice Girls' dinner so vividly, it's as if my mind transports me back in a heartbeat.

Our freshman dorm at the University of Georgia was hosting a talent show as part of homecoming week, and we decided to dress up as the Spice Girls and lip-sync their hit, "Wannabe." We'd been doing it since the song came out back in elementary school, so it didn't require any practice.

Eliza had donned a cute babydoll dress and pulled her hair into two high ponytails to easily pass for Baby Spice. She'd stared at a photo we pulled up on Sloane's laptop and asked, *"Should I cut bangs to make it even more authentic?"*

"No. Absolutely not." Virginia Kate slammed the computer shut, already decked out in a dazzling cheetah-print jumpsuit and elaborate eye makeup as Scary Spice.

Betsy huffed in front of the mirror. *"So much for glitter. All it does is make me look like I have crazy dandruff."* She stood waving a spray can of temporary hair glitter, teetering in high heels and a Union Jack–flag dress she'd dragged us all through the mall to find.

I swanned over to rescue her in the Sporty Spice tracksuit I'd found in a thrift store bin. Despite my lack of athletic ability, my aversion to high heels made me a shoo-in for the position, with The Five in full support of me being me.

I dusted the excess glitter from her hair. *"I think it's good as is. Don't forget the choker."*

Betsy frowned at her reflection. *"But Jared's going to be there. You know, my future husband. It's got to be just right."*

At the time the two weren't even dating, let alone engaged, but Betsy had called her man. I was about to assure her that she would have his full attention, but Sloane, our sleek Posh Spice for the evening, pulled open a deep drawer on the side of her desk and grinned as she pulled out a liquor bottle.

Eliza gasped. *"Sloane! You're not supposed to have that in here!"*

Betsy lit up. *"Gimme, gimme! Exactly what I need to take the edge off."*

"You haven't eaten dinner. Get a snack first or something," Sloane said.

"Fine." Betsy slipped out of the room to return to hers next door.

The rest of us, also on empty stomachs, forgot the bottle and got back to our primping, slathering on body glitter, and practicing parts of the routine. About thirty minutes later, Sloane slid open her desk drawer and eyed the interior.

"Where's the tequila, y'all?" she asked.

Each of our heads swiveled to scan the room for the contraband when, as if on cue, Betsy reappeared in the doorway. Tequila bottle in hand.

"How much of that did you drink?" I asked. She looked wobblier than usual.

Betsy swatted at the air. *"Only like . . . three sips."*

Sloane marched over, swiped the bottle, and lifted it to check the level. *"Too much is what she's had."*

"We have to go on!" Eliza began to pace. *"And we cannot get caught with booze in the dorm."* She shot daggers at Sloane.

Sloane held up her hands. *"I'll take the fall if we get caught. Betsy, we need to get a little pep in your step."*

Betsy stood up straight, saluted Sloane, and said, *"Aye, aye, Captain!"*

We changed her into flats, and by the grace of God we made it through the show in one piece—even earning a second-place prize. Before we went back to the dorm to put Betsy to bed early, a jittery Jared had stopped her and said, *"Nice job up there, Betsy. We should hang out sometime."*

Betsy had nodded and winked. *"You know where to find me."*

The smile lingers on my face as my buzzing phone pulls me back to the present. Betsy and Jared are such a perfect match. I couldn't be more grateful we prevented the tequila from sending it off the rails before it had a chance to get started.

Virginia Kate: I'll stop by Publix and grab chicken and salad.

Delilah: I'll bring dessert.

Sloane: Guess that leaves wine to me! Oh, and sparkling water for Ms. Eliza.

Eliza: 😊

I get to my feet, noting the time.

Delilah: I've got to get ready for school. Love y'all and have a good day! See some of your squishy ones soon! xoxo

I drop the phone into my sweatpants pocket and head back inside for a quick shower, smiling to myself. The phone continues to buzz as I climb the stairs toward my bathroom. I turn on the shower, and while I wait for the water to warm, I pick out jeans and a lightweight flannel shirt from my closet. I pull the phone from the pajama pants I'm about to shed and set it on my nightstand. I can catch up later. The Five will always be there, my place in the circle waiting for me.

CHAPTER 7

Delilah

MRS. CHOPRA AND I meet at my Toyota, which I love because the engine runs and the AC is still kicking well enough to blast cold air my way during the warm months. I drop my student Neil's nap mat in the back before I slide into the driver's seat. He got sick at school Friday, and in the rush to get him home, his mom forgot the mat. I brought it home and washed it to have it ready for his return.

We drive to school in comfortable quiet, and when we arrive Mrs. Chopra heads straight to the main preschool entrance to help unload car-pool vehicles, and I wait by the classroom door to welcome the students. Each picks their greeting: Asha and Fox take high fives; Morris waves; and Braylen, Tia, Madeline, and Collin take hugs. Jack, Eliza's son, gives me a hug and a kiss on the cheek. Cici's mom emails me that she's sick. I'm to the point of wondering if Huddie, Betsy's son, might have gotten sick too when I hear his sweet humming nearing the door. Warmth floods me as I catch sight of the chunky boy toddling down the hallway independently, dragging his bag behind him.

He never waits for staff.

He knows he's coming to Miss Lilah's room.

I kneel and open my arms, and it's the best start of every morning when Huddie barrels into me and sets his fluffy head on my shoulder. Every morning his greeting is a bear hug.

Mrs. Chopra appears at the end of the hallway and moves in a slow but effortful jog toward us. She stops before us, breathing heavily. "I'm not convinced there's anything to stop that sweet child from booking it to you on his own accord."

At the sound of Mrs. Chopra's voice, Huddie breaks from my arms, takes Mrs. Chopra by the hand, and shows her inside the classroom. I follow and shut the lower section of the Dutch door behind me.

While the bunnies dig in the canvas totes of toys designated for early morning play with Mrs. Chopra looking on, I head for the craft cupboard just above our sink. I bundle into my arms dot markers, a rainbow of paper options, and thick foam stickers perfect for those chubby two-year-old fingers. Cici has a tendency to put the stickers in her mouth—on one occasion consuming it whole, whereafter she visited the ER—so those strike me as a good fit in her absence.

I start singing the song we all know signals cleanup time, and the toddlers faithfully pile their toys away into the totes, head for the tables, and drop into their chairs.

"Would you mind?" I ask Mrs. Chopra and hold out the dot markers.

She nods, and without further instruction hands them out.

"Make sure to give a blue to Braylen. She's obsessed and will eye anyone else with the blue until they hand it over. This way keeps the peace."

"If this isn't a well-run ship, Miss Delilah."

I smile, accepting the compliment. I take pride in my work of creating a warm and welcoming classroom. It's one of the most unexpected positive side effects of growing up with the Thomases: my ability to anticipate the needs of others.

Back then, if I anticipated that my father would want to watch the Falcons on *Monday Night Football* and I had it playing when he got home, he might give the yelling and complaining a rest for the evening. If I went ahead and got dressed appropriately for lunch at the club, Mama wouldn't huff over having to redress me. If I steered clear of Darcy when she had her friends over, I wouldn't get told off.

A while later, I pull out the maracas and tambourines, and my students toddle over and drop down, crisscross applesauce, into a lopsided circle. Poor Fox wriggles and writhes impatiently, his eyes trained on the big drum that is his absolute favorite. When it's time, I slide the instrument to him, and he hammers it with his palms in delight. His classmates grab from the basket of shakers and tambourines, bells and whistles, and join the fun. Admittedly the sound does hurt my ears a little, but I'm happy to endure it for the joy it brings.

When the children gather back at the table, Mrs. Chopra shakes Goldfish crackers into small bowls for snack, and I slide in quickly and replace Collin's with the gluten-free option his mom brings from home. The children eat hungrily, the classroom near silent for the first time since their arrival, and in the lull, I prep bags for the children who will leave after our playground time.

They're all loud and fast—if a bit wobbly—on the playground, running and climbing until their cheeks turn pink and sweat beads on their foreheads. When it's time to head inside, I start the cleanup song.

Slowly the children join in, and with the familiarity of a deeply embedded routine, they begin returning toys to the bin. We line up quietly, and the group, now tired and sagging slightly, follows me single file back into the building. They are the most precious bunnies I have ever seen.

"Remind me, who is a lunch kiddo?" Mrs. Chopra asks back in the classroom.

"Everyone except for Huddie and Asha."

"I'll start prepping lunch boxes."

Asha's mom, Devi, appears first at the door, hanging back and waving hesitantly. Her toddler runs right to her mother, and I follow, snagging her tote bag and zip-up hoodie on my way.

I hold out her belongings. "Asha had a fabulous day—*as usual*." I smile at Devi, and when I make eye contact, it strikes me that something is different about her appearance. My face must pucker inquisitively, because she jumps in.

"The lips." She covers her mouth bashfully as she laughs. "Didn't realize when Betsy said the gloss might burn, she meant actual skin damage." Devi laughs it off, but there's no missing the hurt underlying her no-big-deal attitude.

"Oh. The party." I'd forgotten I spotted her there last night among the attendees.

Devi nods. "Guess I must be allergic."

As she reaches out to take her daughter's items, I get a closer look, and now that she's pointed it out, the redness and swelling around her mouth is obvious.

"Does it hurt?"

Devi shrugs. "You know, nothing much compares to childbirth, which is still fresh in my mind. But yes, it's sore. I took Benadryl when it started to swell, then ibuprofen this morning for the pain."

"I'm so sorry." I want to tell her that she's beautiful without any lip plumping anyway, that Asha adores her regardless of the way she looks, that her being the incredible mom she is, is enough, but that isn't my place.

Just then Betsy comes down the craft-project-lined hallway and stops behind Devi, baby Hattie propped on her hip. She's dressed in matching athleisure wear.

"Oh hey, Devi!" She reaches out and touches the other woman's arm. "Did you have fun last night? Any products you can't get off your mind? I know you were one of the sad gals who didn't order."

I'm nearly overcome by a sudden urge to press my palm over Betsy's mouth—like, *put the tequila down*—so the words stop.

Devi's face darkens, her brows drawing together. "The only reason I'm sad today is because I have actual damage from the lip gloss on my skin." She points to the irritated area.

"Oh!" It comes out of Betsy in a high-pitched yelp. "You're sure it's from the gloss? You didn't use anything else yesterday? You know, we use all-natural, clean, organic ingredients. None of the nasty stuff, nothing synthetic."

Asha begins to yank on Devi's arm, and she shifts away. "It was all I used. Please let your company know there was an issue." Devi gives in to her yanking toddler and starts down the hallway. "See you tomorrow, Miss Delilah!"

Betsy pops her brow, incredulous. "Can you believe that?" She pauses, her face settling back into herself. "Was Huddie good today?"

"He's always great, a total sweetie." I head for the hooks and grab his bag. "Umm, but Devi?"

"I know, I didn't realize she was so uptight or I wouldn't have invited her to the party. Virginia Kate was trying to recruit her too. Thank *goodness* she declined. I mean, can you imagine?"

I bristle slightly. "The woman has burns on her face, Bets."

"That can't happen from all-natural, organic products."

I dodge the urge to correct her. "It makes the lips burn and plump. There has to be *something* chemical in there."

She pauses as if she's considering that for the first time. Betsy may not have been the honors student Virginia Kate was, but she's also not the dummy she plays herself to be. She gulps.

"Yeah, maybe that—"

Huddie pushes out of the door and wraps his mother's legs in a wide hug. I reach out to her and squeeze her arm.

"It's okay. We're all just doing our best."

I let the rest go unsaid—that she just put on the sell at school pickup and then blew off a woman who was maimed by the products she's selling. That I'm starting not to recognize this side of her.

Betsy might've always had a tendency to get swept up in things, but never before at the expense of being compassionate.

She wobbles slightly, her children on opposite sides, tugging and yanking at her, and her face falters. The hard glossiness drops for a moment, her brow creasing.

"They're not paying bonuses this year at Jared's office, so I have to make as much as I can. Plus, I already gave up everything else to be a mom. I need *something* that's mine."

Hattie starts crying in her mother's arms, pawing at her chest like she's ready to nurse. Huddie barks demands for a snack and his favorite yellow Tonka truck. When Betsy's gaze meets mine, it feels like looking at all the versions of her over decades. The free-range kid who once seemed so lonely. The girl who was all knees and elbows before she blossomed in middle school. The event-designing siren. The jittery bride the night before her wedding. She is all of those to me at the same time.

Before she turns to go, I swear I see a mistiness in her eyes, a tenderness she used to splay before me anytime the need struck. No hesitation. But that tenderness has been under wraps. I can't put my finger on it for certain, but I suspect the change lines up with her Darling initiation.

We exchange a quick goodbye, and as I watch her leave, stacked under the weight of children and their baggage and demands, a heaviness grows in my chest. Perhaps if I were anyone else, I wouldn't have let this go, I would've pushed, but it's simply who I am to let things lie for the sake of keeping the peace. Once she's out of sight, I release a tight breath and head for the lunchroom.

CHAPTER 8

Betsy

BETSY IS KICKING HERSELF all the way down the school hallway, out the door, and still as she struggles to keep a grip on both of her children as she traverses the parking lot laden with bags and her children's increasing demands. She slips her hand into the side pocket on her leggings for the keys, which requires her to momentarily let go of Huddie's hand. The SUV unlocks with a luxury *bleep* just as Huddie darts around the car.

"Huddie!" Betsy dashes after him in the busy lot. She snags his arm and tugs him away from the moving cars. Even before he protests, she knows her nails grazed him too roughly and he won't be having it.

Huddie melts into a red-faced rage and falls limp atop the grimy asphalt. Hattie remains propped on Betsy's hip, so she has no option but to scrape her toddler from the parking lot with a single arm. Huddie thrashes, writhes, and cries out in tearful yelps. Betsy grits her teeth and tucks him under her arm, her own pulse racing as passing moms stop and stare. Betsy shovels Huddie into the car and sets him in front of his seat while she buckles in Hattie, who has since started to fuss at the commotion.

Betsy swallows hard, hoping it flushes out the rising shame at being seen so publicly imperfect. There isn't much she's done successfully, so continuing to be a good mom is of critical importance.

To Betsy, certainly, but also to the Pearl community, the passing drivers constantly appraising.

"Bless her," they'll say.

Once Hattie is fully buckled, Betsy walks around to the other side of the car to settle Huddie. By the time she opens the door, his face is wet and snot runs all the way down his neck. His breath hitches in shudders from the exertion of being so physically angry. Looking at him, Betsy wonders if she'd ever get to do the same: let all of her feelings rip, scream, and cry and be downright honest about all the hard things. She wraps her boy in her arms, and his breath slows, his face burrowing into the space between her chin and her shoulder, a space she hopes he'll always find.

She runs her nails up and down Huddie's back in a gentle massage, and he sighs.

"Snack?" she asks quietly.

Huddie pulls himself immediately upright, nodding hard enough to make his light brown hair shake along with him.

"Let Mama buckle you in, honey. Then snack."

Huddie rears back and screams. "Snack! Snack!"

At the explosion of sound and the child gone tight and wound up in her arms, Betsy's eyes burn with the threat of tears. *Stop. Don't,* she wills herself. Across the back seat Hattie starts to fuss louder. Betsy wrangles Huddie into his car seat as he pushes and fights her. Betsy's throat burns.

"It's okay, buddy. Take a breath. Calm down. *Calm down.*"

Once Huddie's buckled, Betsy grabs his snack cup from her passenger seat, and as soon as it lands in his hands, Huddie goes silent.

Betsy's shoulders drop as she looks skyward, her racing heart finally relenting. She slides into the driver's seat and cranks the car so the air flows. She should probably just give in and sign Huddie up for lunch and nap time because picking him up tired and hungry just isn't panning out well. That way she could get Rex at the same time, one less pickup to make her feel marginally less like a shuttle bus driver. And to think—today Hattie was mostly happy and unbothered. What if Huddie had actually made it away from her when he darted? What if a car hit him? Betsy shakes her head, willing the thought away.

It's a perfect follow-up to the scene with Devi at Delilah's door. Betsy pulls in a deep breath and lets it fizz out slowly, the crunching of crackers floating up from the back seat. She reaches for her phone and clicks her most recent text conversation, the name saved as "Top Peach" with a peach emoji, all so cloak-and-dagger, then clicks to call.

"Hey, Darl." The woman on the other end of the line drags the *a*, so it sounds more like *doll*.

"Hey, quick question. What do we do if people have allergic reactions? A woman came to my party last night and her lips are pretty messed up from the gloss."

The woman laughs. "Beauty is pain."

Betsy's insides pinch at the meanness. For a long time she thought Peach Pit was only the best parts of a sorority, but as she's spent more time in the organization she's run into far more of the cattiness she thought she'd left behind on her college campus. Still, by the time those parts truly came to light as a pattern, she was already far too enmeshed to change course.

"Seriously, do I report it?"

"Ha. Um, I mean, no. That's just, like, sort of their personal problem."

"So I don't need to log it or anything? I figured they'd want to know in case there's a bad batch or something."

"I'm going to forget you ever said that. Peach Pit is made with all organic ingredients, all-natural components found in a Georgia peach. There's no such thing as 'a bad batch.'"

Betsy closes her eyes, a stab at finding patience. "Corporate doesn't have a phone line or anything? Look, the woman is pretty upset—and rightfully so—and I don't want her coming to me directly."

"You're not legally liable."

Betsy's mind spins. She's not worried about getting into a lawsuit with Devi. She wants to respond professionally and appropriately, to make it right. It shouldn't be too much to ask, but alas, the company is so tiered and access to information so restricted that she doesn't have any direct recourse. Even on the website, there's only a general company email that she's heard through the grapevine goes unmonitored.

"Will you make a note of it to corporate, please?" Betsy asks.

"*Fine.* But don't expect me to send her a medical care package. People these days are so whiny."

"Thanks. Just let me know what you need me to do for the report."

"*Sell*, girl. That's what you need to be doing. Plus recruiting."

"Got it. Talk to you later."

Betsy hangs up.

These Darlings, especially the girls at the very top, are not the sort to be messed with.

Betsy simmers with frustration as she shifts the car into gear and heads for home. Peach Pit really should have a better professional plan in place for dealing with these issues. How else is she supposed to show everyone that Peach Pit is genuinely good? What if the rumor mill takes this one-off bad impression and runs with it? What if she's lumped in with a bad batch too?

Betsy just needs to show people like Devi that Peach Pit also makes so much positive impact. That though it may not be perfect, the company completely changed her life—and others'—for the better. She feels the Peach Pit effect so strongly inside, it's a wonder it's not completely obvious to everyone else. Her confidence, her new sense of purpose, all of it is thanks to Peach Pit.

As the tree-lined streets blur outside her window on the drive home, her mind goes back to the time she got her invite to Peach Pit.

Betsy had been sitting on her lumpy living room couch with the broken spring, and no matter how carefully she picked her seat, she inevitably sank into the dip. At the time Rex was only a toddler, and she cradled baby Huddie in her arms and struggled to get him to latch on and nurse. He screamed and cried, and before long Betsy's shirt was stained with breast milk as she darted around the kitchen trying to throw together a bottle of formula. The moment she got the bottle in his mouth, the quiet was almost spiritual, and with Rex glued to a children's show on TV, she took out her phone.

A message waited for her on Facebook from an old friend, one she looked up to and admired from the pageant circuit.

> Hey girl! How are you? It's been so long!

Betsy's spirits lifted almost instantly.

> I know you're a mama these days (Yay! Isn't it so fun?) and I wanted to share the most amazing opportunity with you. Me and a ton of other girls have recently joined Peach Pit. I think you would be a perfect fit!

Betsy pulled in a deep breath that filled her up all the way. The lightness that spread over her felt like she was coming back to life, the old version of herself being called up from dormancy. She was always better in a group.

> The products are super cute, and I just know you'd love them. You'd have your own small business—after a very reasonable start-up cost—and then you basically get to throw parties, make new friends, and make money at the same time. Party planning is basically your superhero power already, so I bet it'd be super easy for you.
>
> I'm having a party of my own on Friday night, and I'd love to see you there! We can chat afterward about signing you up for the sisterhood.
>
> XO

Hattie makes a happy coo in the back seat, and it pulls Betsy back to the here and now. The electricity that had run through her in that moment when she'd received the Peach Pit invite lingers as the memory fades. Betsy will have to figure out on her own how to make it right with Devi. She's a nice lady, and they'll share kids in the same class forevermore. Betsy doesn't want tension with a fellow mom—or worse, for her reputation or that of Peach Pit to be sullied.

When she makes it home, she's relieved that Jared is at the office today. She's not in the mood to explain why she's frenzied and out of sorts, especially when Jared's had his own questions about the lack of information published about Peach Pit—though he's gone quiet since the larger checks began arriving.

In the driveway she puts the car in Park, and when she glances in the rearview, Huddie is asleep. She groans. He won't sleep in his own bed after this, so she'll have to sit in the driveway and let him nap here with the air running.

Betsy grabs her phone and sees a text from Delilah.

> I'm sorry if the moment at the door felt like an ambush. It was just a chance run-in. Luv ya, Bets.

Betsy sucks in a rapid breath and bursts into tears.

CHAPTER 9

Delilah

THE NEXT EVENING I park on a quiet side street off the historic downtown area of Pearl and then cross to Sloane's loft inside an old mill building. The surrounding area is littered with buzzing restaurants and boutiques alongside the lot where the farmers market is held. She lives here with her husband, Anton. He barely seems to inhabit the space with the intensity of his work travel, but the pair makes up for the time apart with lavish vacations when they can fit them in. The floor is thick wooden planks, worn deliciously with age, and although the ceilings are high, the warm textures of the furnishings make the space feel cozy.

Betsy has already dropped her Mahjong set on the cowhide ottoman in the middle of the room, a selection of chairs and love seats scattered around it. The collection is eclectic and chic and the very best work of Sloane's interior designer.

Eliza, wearing a onesie pajama outfit, drops into the oversized armchair. "This is one of the few comfortable things that still fits without my belly sticking out. Ugh, I feel so gross."

"You're *supposed* to be getting bigger," I say. "It doesn't matter how it looks, the cooking inside is what matters."

My heart pinches at the suggestion that busy Eliza, working full-time while also preparing for a new life, is at all concerned over her appearance.

"I panic-ordered three pizzas," Sloane announces as she walks into her living room with gusto, her long almost-black hair flapping like a shiny curtain behind her.

"I'm sorry, what?" Virginia Kate stands at the twelve-foot island unloading the grocery bags of chicken and salad she promised.

Sloane whirls around. "I just get like this when I'm stressed."

Betsy marches up to Sloane, and with a warm smile, she plucks the cell phone from Sloane's grip and circles around the sofa.

"This is an intervention."

Sloane scrambles behind her. "Betsy! No! My boss is going to *kill* me if I'm out of touch."

Betsy raises a brow as she levels a look at Sloane. "Is that really true or are you just overdoing it? Doesn't your company have a policy about after-hours work?"

"That's only for people who aren't on the partner track."

Betsy plops down beside Eliza and hands off the phone with a conspiratorial look.

"Oh no!" Sloane says. "Don't you dare, Eliza Woolridge."

Eliza grins and tucks the phone snuggly inside her onesie. "A couple hours of girl time aren't going to tank your career, Sloane. You need to rest."

Sloane drops into an armchair and releases a defeated breath.

"You don't look like you've been sleeping," I say from across the ottoman.

Betsy slips down onto the rug and begins setting up the game.

"I've sort of quit that whole thing." Sloane nods at the pearl tiles poured out. "I'll sit out the first round."

Virginia Kate joins us with a plate of chicken, salad, and some of Eliza's homemade bread. She pushes it into Sloane's hands.

"And I can tell you haven't been eating either, so get to it, girlie."

Sloane's eyes water for a moment, and her voice turns quiet. "Thank you. You're probably right."

I head to the kitchen to load up plates, Betsy and Virginia Kate not far behind. Eliza struggles to pull herself upright.

"I'll get you a plate, Miss Preggo," Betsy calls to her. "Put your feet up and get ready to Mahjong!"

"Thanks, and no salad, please. The dressing gives me the worst heartburn."

Plates are made, bodies settled on the furniture, and we start the shuffling of tiles. Our rounds always take forever because we start talking, get off on tangents, and then can't remember whose turn we left off on. After two successful rounds—Betsy winning both—I know it's time to share the information I've been sitting on.

"Okay, ladies," I say.

"Oooooo," Betsy squeaks. "An announcement?"

The rest of them perk up, hands stilling, chewing slowing.

"I got a new letter from Jasper—"

"Oh-em-gee, if y'all won't just kiss and call it boyfriend-girlfriend already," Eliza grumbles.

I double-blink. "If you'd let me finish?"

Sloane waves me on. "So we're safe to assume he didn't get eaten by a great white yet?"

"At least not before he sent this letter," I say.

Jasper's phone number changes constantly because he uses cheap phones that won't be missed if they get lost on a forest floor, stolen on a train—or snapped up by a shark, in Sloane's scenario.

"I still heavily suspect he's a spy," Virginia Kate says.

"Well, we'll just have to wait and see"—I drop the letter into the middle of the ottoman atop the Mahjong discards—"because it looks like he's coming to Pearl."

Shrieks erupt and plates are cast aside as they clamber to be the first to read it.

Betsy wins.

She stands and reads out loud to the group. "Oh my goodness, *look*! He crossed out twice. He must've been nervous!"

Virginia Kate slides in beside her to see. "Gah! So sweet. He's coming to see you, Delilah. He didn't know how to say it."

Betsy hands the postcard to Sloane, who says, "That really *is* cute."

Eliza waves at her for the letter. "If *Sloane* says so, it must even be triple-dipple-super-duper cute."

"Sometimes I forget what sort of family you come from, but then you say something like 'triple-dipple-super-duper,'" Virginia Kate says lovingly.

Eliza got the minivan driving, Sunday-school teaching, homemade snack sort of mom who would've been a Pinterest queen had it been around back in the day.

Eliza sighs at the letter. "This is it. It's finally happening. I call matron of honor!"

I walk over and pluck it from her fingers. "I appreciate all of that, y'all, but let's not jump the gun. He basically said he *might* come here, but who knows what that means. Knowing Jasper, it might mean he's here for three hours before he needs to grab a flight out of Atlanta."

"In the past he's always had his breaks planned out, though," Virginia Kate says.

"So would that be in support of or against him being a spy?" I ask.

Virginia Kate grins. "Jury's still out, but it's 100 percent in support of him wanting you."

All my insides feel light and giddy, but I don't let myself feel it too deeply. I don't want to get my hopes up. Jasper is my ideal partner. He's smart, funny, thoughtful, and interesting. But he has that travel bug that means he won't stay anywhere for long, and even if he does stay for a couple days or even a week, it won't last.

"I am excited to see him," I say.

"Alright, I'm on wardrobe," Betsy announces. "We just need to know what the first date will be." She taps her temple like her mind is already brainstorming. "Do we want to hire a hidden photographer? Like in case the wedding does end up happening? It would be a good photo to have. See? Already a top matron of honor over here."

"Hey! I called that," Eliza says.

"Y'all!" I don't yell it—I'm not a yeller—but I say it forcefully enough that they all stop still. "Can we not make this too big of a deal?"

I'm sure my face says the rest: The bigger deal we make of it, the greater the disappointment when it doesn't become the dream moment. They all know I want the happily ever after, but I also genuinely love myself and my life alone. I love my Blissful Bunnies at school, and I love The Five. I love making soap with Roxie. If this is what I'll have from here on out, I'll be happy with it.

"Sorry," Sloane says. "We'll be more quietly supportive—"

"As long as you don't skimp on the updates," Betsy says, then turns to reset the game.

"We're just excited for you. You deserve the best," Virginia Kate says.

"And honestly, I'm grateful for anything positive to distract me from the birthing I'm going to have to do here in a few weeks." Eliza shudders, then pops a nugget of chicken into her mouth.

Her delivery with Jack was complicated, and she ended up with injuries afterward that took a while to heal. Her doctors have assured her they will be watching and monitoring to prevent the same—and even offered to schedule a C-section instead—but it hasn't erased Eliza's worries.

She rubs her belly. "I just wish they could transport the baby out without disrupting my body. Shouldn't we have that technology by now?"

"I think that comes *after* the alien invasion, honey," Sloane says.

The doorbell rings, and Betsy gets up to retrieve the panic pizzas. She carries them to the kitchen and calls, "You'll have lunch for the week, so no excuses to be withering away the next time we see you."

"Yes, ma'am," Sloane answers.

"Do y'all need any help with the shower?" I look between Betsy and Virginia Kate, who are leading the charge on Eliza's baby shower.

"I think we're pretty much set," Virginia Kate says. "Right?"

"Yup!" Betsy replies. "You know there's nothing I love more than planning a party. And especially so for our Eliza."

We're lucky to have a Betsy in The Five. Even with the Peach Pit weirdness, she is our social go-to, knowing the ins and outs of hosting and entertaining. She simply shines in those moments.

Eliza is teary again. "*I'm* the grateful one. I don't know what I'd do without y'all."

The lot of us pile onto her chair and its arms and curl up around the baby bump.

Nights like this are the moments that I feel most like I belong to a family. It's so easy to be together when you don't have to re-explain stuff, the hows and whys of everything.

It's a special sort of love being each other's backstory.

CHAPTER 10

Delilah

THE FOLLOWING DAY, THE Pearl Prep Bunnies are so decidedly *un*blissful that after I sit in a pool of glue one boy-who-shall-not-be-named set out as a "bug trap," I make the call for double playtime. It's not often I'm counting down the minutes until pickup, but today is one of those times. By evening I'm exhausted, sticky, and not feeling particularly festive. Nevertheless, Darcy has a birthday on March 29 every year, and she's absolutely not the rescheduling type, so to my parents' house I go.

Ten minutes across town, the house sits at the end of a long driveway nestled discreetly among ancient oak trees. It doesn't have a gate like the new builds in the area, the vast rolling property of grass and trees that surrounds it the only buffer from the road. The home sits low and wide, a ranch with an attic-style upstairs. A deep porch wraps the entire house, surrounded by lush, leafy hydrangeas waiting to bloom in fantastic blue mops. The green roof glints in the descending sun, complementing the cream siding with black trim.

My parents' chocolate lab, Arnold, stands on the porch looking austere, presumably guarding the entrance. Our childhood dog died years ago, and only recently was Mama able to talk Daddy into getting another one. I suspect she may have traded naming rights, which is how she ended up with a pet named Arnold Palmer.

I grab the gift bag topped with delicate puffs of tissue paper from my passenger seat and beg the universe that Darcy will like the contents. I'd approached the Ulta sales associate with my desperate eyes and repeated the script Betsy gave me: *"Air wrap hair dryer with a full set of adapters."* Before long, I left half a paycheck lighter and toting what looked like a vacuum cleaner nozzle with an array of oddly shaped tips.

I climb the porch, gift bag in hand, and glide inside the double-door front entry without fanfare.

Roxie must've been waiting because she jogs into the foyer at the sound of the storm door banging shut.

"Auntie Lilah's here!"

No one else stirs at the announcement, but Roxie commands my full attention. I pull my niece into my arms for a hug.

"How was school today?"

"Good! I got an A on my bio test, and Mom said I can have cake tonight." Her blue eyes are wide and optimistic.

I balk at that last bit. "What's this about cake?"

Roxie's cheeks flush, and she lowers her voice. "I agreed to do the pageant, and she doesn't want me to not fit into the dress."

I suppress a growl. "Anytime you want cake, come to my house, Rox. No if, ands, or buts."

Her face brightens into a smile. "Are you making soap soon?"

I link arms with her, and together we walk into the living area. I wasn't planning to until I sell down some more inventory.

"You're my first call when it's time."

Darcy sits on the cream sofa, texting feverishly on her phone that buzzes incessantly in her hands.

I plop down gently beside her. "Happy birthday!"

She doesn't look over; she doesn't even look up from the phone.

"Thanks." Her long acrylic nails continue clicking on her phone screen.

"I got you something." I smile and hold out the gift. "From me."

Darcy glances at it like it's something she'd rather not touch, then tucks it beside her and goes back to her phone.

"Thanks. Work is crazy right now."

I gloss right over the comment about work. Darcy isn't traditionally employed. Her husband is a business guy who is gone more than he is home, and his income plus her trust fund keeps them more than comfortable. It isn't a life I'd want for myself, but I must admit I've daydreamed about the ease that accepting my trust fund could grant.

Still, I've never come close to asking for it because I meant it when I made the decision to forgo it. My father has always been moody and cruel, and the last thing I want is for my life to be built on a fund he can manipulate based on his appraisal of me.

"Don't you want to open it?" I ask. "I really hope you—"

"Not right now, Delilah." Darcy pulls her mouth into a puckered smile, like she's trying but doesn't mean it.

I feel my optimism evaporate. "Oh. Sure. Yes, okay."

Only when Darcy continues to smile pointedly at me sitting there do I receive the rest of the message and clamber to my feet. Roxie stands waiting, and I follow her into the kitchen.

"I'm sorry. I'm mortified," Roxie whispers under her breath.

I squeeze her arm. "It's nothing for you to worry about. It's her birthday, and she'll groan if she wants to. Or whatever the song says."

As I'd hoped, Roxie's straight face cracks into giggles.

"That's definitely not how it goes."

In the kitchen an aromatic roasting smell hangs in the air.

"Mama, hey!"

The French country–inspired kitchen boasts an island that could seat my entire class, a designer copper pot rack hanging above, and ornate, hand-carved moldings around the ecru cabinetry with hardware special ordered from France. I know this because I was accidentally held hostage during my mama's design meeting.

Mama looks up over her reading glasses and sets down the hardcover cookbook wrapped in a tatty paper sleeve. She holds out an arm in reply, welcoming me for a hug.

I close the gap and slide under her extended arm.

"Lil' Roxie can settle now that her auntie is here. She has a new idea for a soap." Mama winks over her reading glasses, and her sweet perfume envelops me.

I pull out of her arms and turn to Roxie. "New scent, huh? You're holding out on me."

She nods quickly, lips pressed into a nervous smile. "I was thinking about blending the vanilla bar with the orange and making a Creamsicle flavor. For summer. One of my friends at school has a body lotion that smells like both combined, and now everyone else is buying it."

My insides light up. "Definitely! Since you've got this hot idea, why don't you come over this weekend? Sunday since we'll have the market on Saturday?"

"I have pageant practice," Roxie says, barely containing an eye roll. "But I can text you dates for next week."

Mama calls over, "Hey, dolls, could one of you grab the potatoes out of the oven and give them a good toss? You know I can't rely on anyone else for help."

I grab the oven mitts from the counter. "Yes, ma'am."

I pull open the oven and a wave of herby savoriness rolls out.

"I'm already drooling," I say.

"Thanks, honey. We're close to ready. The chicken is about to come out, and I'll have your father carve it"—Mama glances side to side as if in search of him—"if he isn't already three sheets to the wind."

I shrug. "There's no guarantee."

"Don't I know it," she mutters, barely disguising her exasperation.

When I was a child, my father was aloof, preoccupied with his work as a finance manager for the Pearl elites—or at least that's what Mama told us—but over the years he turned surlier. Probably—*hopefully*—he was different back when he and Mama were Pearl high school sweethearts, or maybe it was a symptom of the times for her to put up with it from the start.

Before they were married, my father knew he had the job waiting for him—his own father established the firm. Still, I can't help but suspect that the true depths of Mama's potential might've been clipped before she grew up and out. She's like a plant I'd love to repot somewhere else. I would bet my whole—*minuscule*—life savings on her spreading out in thick vines, climbing toward the sun.

After tossing the potatoes, I slide the dish back into the oven. "I'll go check on him."

Past the living room, both sets of French doors hang open onto the patio, and the sun twinkles behind the tree line as it submerges for the night. Mama has already pulled out the pots she'll plant once the weatherman is sure the last frost has passed. When my foot hits the brick patio, my father turns, his eyes scanning for the intruder. I stop, and for a moment there's only silence between us.

"Hey." I pop up a hand in greeting. "Mama wanted to see if you would carve the chicken, please."

His eyes are cold on me, and inside it makes me shrink.

"I guess." His eyes linger on me as if he's waiting for proof that I'll turn and leave him be. After a moment he looks back to the glass in his hand, his true priority.

If I were still a child, I'd probably bow my head and leave him to his whiskey. Go do something sweet for him like set the sports section of the newspaper on the arm of his favorite chair to assuage the storm he always seemed to carry around with him. The part of me that's grown up since then wants to spit sharp words at him to stand up for Mama, but I'm not foolish enough to think I've got the guts to follow through on those wishes. I could only imagine the mess that would spawn.

I settle for something in the middle. "She's working her tail off in there, Daddy. A helping hand would go a long way."

He walks toward me, but before he passes by, he pauses at my side and squeezes me into a brief side hug. "Thanks for coming."

I smile and nod like I always do, but I can't get away from how odd the words sound as they land on my ears. Of course I came. It's Darcy's birthday, and I'm a member of the family. Not some stranger doing him a favor. I go back inside, and the air feels thicker, the living room walls pressing in. Darcy remains alone on the sofa, more reclined now than before but still glued to her phone.

In the kitchen I help Mama pull together the last bits and pieces for dinner. By the time my father appears, my mother has already carved the chicken, so he slips out without a word of apology. Mama and I carry the platters and serving utensils to the formal dining room, the table already preset with linen napkins and silverware.

"Dinner's ready!" Mama sings out with an enthusiasm I have to imagine comes only from her years of pretending, of playing happy family.

We eat dinner in tense silence, an effect my father has on every gathering, and only when Darcy puts on her shiny smile does it break.

"Thank you, Mama and Daddy, for such a lovely dinner." It sounds like a canned pageant response, and both parents light up.

"Well, it's just a shame Andy couldn't be here," Mama says.

Darcy nods at the mention of her husband. "He's in high demand these days. They're running trainings out in Sedona, and they couldn't make do without him. He did leave a gorgeous pair of diamond earrings with Rox to give me on his behalf." She winks.

Mama reaches over and squeezes Roxie's hand. "Good job, honey."

Roxie blushes, then drops her eyes to her plate.

Darcy's birthday has always been a big deal, but at least as a child and teenager it made more sense. Once she made it to adulthood and the endless events continued, the demands for all eyes to remain upon her for a "birthday month" became over the top.

"Should I get the cake ready?" I ask, hoping to move things along.

"That would be great. Thank you," Mama says.

I'm already on my feet. "Are we doing candles, Darce?"

She throws me a look. "I'm not a child."

I duck my head and make for the kitchen. What a dumb thing for me to say; of course, Darcy's too fancy for candles. I thought she did them last year, but I must be wrong. One time and one time only have I gotten it right with her—when she briefly hopped on the soap-making train years ago when we were kids, adding glitter as her personal touch. I open the fridge, and there sits a round cake with pale peach frosting ensconced in a white bakery box. I slip it from the box and carry it into the dining room.

As I lean to place the cake in front of Darcy, Mama pipes up, "Don't set it down yet! Let us sing!"

I reverse, bite my lip, and remind myself this is almost over. Darcy beams as the group of us sing—well, what Daddy does is mostly grunting. The song ends, but when I reach to set the cake down, Mama stops me again.

"I'll take it over here, Delilah. I'll slice it."

"Birthday girl gets the first piece!" Darcy sings.

Roxie smiles, but nothing can conceal the look of discomfort that shines in her eyes. My heart breaks for her. I understand.

I don't wait to be asked and instead stand at my mother's side and take the slices of cake she cuts and disperse them among the group.

"Got you one with lots of icing just how you like it," she says as I deliver Darcy her birthday girl—woman?—slice.

The next one she hands me I deliver to Roxie.

I set the next one at Mama's place and leave my father until last.

I might not yet be brave enough to take him on, but small cuts count.

After I deliver his slice, I turn back, and Mama has already sat back down and dug into her piece. My gaze roves the tabletop to double-check, but there is no slice for me.

When she glances up at me, Mama's first look is confusion before she realizes.

"Oh! Sorry, honey! I miscounted."

"No worries." I cut myself a piece and dump it onto a paper plate.

I eat as quickly as I can and make my excuse to head home. When I step outside, the warm night air is utter relief, and I relish the fact that this performance is over. My body unwinds one muscle at a time.

As I climb into my driver's seat, my phone begins to vibrate with a call. I paw through my bag to retrieve it, and the number is one I don't have saved. My thumb hovers on the button to send it to voicemail, but then a little voice in my head reminds me that it could be him.

I click to answer. "Hello?"

"Delilah. Just who I was looking for."

My heart flutters. Jasper.

"We're heading out early." In the background is the sound of shuffling people and voices. "We ran into some issues. This is sort of insane, but we have to leave the country now, and I wanted to see if I should come to Atlanta."

I suck in a breath.

"*Yes!*" My cheeks heat. Surely that was too much.

"Well, great." I can hear the smile in his voice.

It is like lightning running through me when the realization strikes: After all these years, these words written, stamped, and sent, lousy connection after lousy connection, Jasper Rowley will finally be close enough to touch.

CHAPTER 11

Delilah

THE PHONE IS STILL glued to my ear, a giddy smile plastered on my face, as Jasper's voice spirals over the line to where I sit in my car outside my childhood home.

"And as luck would have it, my buddy's uncle has a cabin up in the Pearl area, so I've already got somewhere to stay."

I soak in the words.

I would be lying if I said I hadn't wished to hear this from Jasper on more than one occasion over the years. I'd even casually mentioned that we should meet up in person, but that typically resulted in Jasper inviting me to meet him in Peru or at the beach in Moldova as he jaunted around the world. I was never brave enough to say yes because, quite frankly, the idea of traveling internationally on my own to meet up with someone who made my insides into a whirlwind sounded overwhelming.

Maybe choosing not to accept his invites was also partially an excuse to play it safe.

"No worries if not. I can always hop a flight elsewhere," he says, and it strikes me that I've left a lengthy gap of silence in conversation. A gap long enough to leave him wondering if his proposition landed poorly.

"No, don't change the plans. *Come*." My face turns beet red as I hear the enthusiasm reverberating in that single word. I clear my throat. "When will you be here?"

Too many additional questions flood my mind: How soon can I see him? How long will he stay? How much time can I get? Will it be different in person? Would he even like me off paper? And most pressingly: Why, finally, after all these years, *now*? Surely he knew all along that if he wanted to stop in Pearl, I would warmly welcome him.

I press the questions down, knowing I don't want the conversation to feel like an interrogation—and before he's even gotten here.

"The next flight gets me to Pearl tomorrow evening." Jasper's voice rattles at the end, and I wonder if he has a pinch of the same nerves I have. "It's super-short notice, so I don't expect you to drop everything to see me right away."

Little does Jasper know that of course I would drop everything to see him as soon as possible. It's been *years*. Since elementary school. In fact, tomorrow can't come soon enough.

"Tomorrow is great!" I'm impressed by the collectedness in my tone that is in no way mirrored on my insides. "You can come over to my place and finally meet Scooby—we can see about Doo, but thus far he hasn't shown himself for a single newcomer."

A deep laugh escapes him. "Well, it sounds like the gauntlet's been thrown: Win over Doo has been elevated to the top of the task list."

"Setting your sights high, I see."

"Eh. I like to live on the edge."

My heart swells at the idea of adventurous Jasper slowing down enough to set foot in my humble abode, of him caring enough to attempt to woo my testy cat. Even if he and I are mismatched for long-term romance, there is no doubt in my mind that he will always be one of the most prized people in my life.

"Bring Kevlar if you're going to push it."

"Probably, to little surprise, I have it in all forms."

I always worry about him venturing into territories where war or terrorism is in the cards, but he doesn't share much about those assignments until they're over. Once I wondered if he did it to protect me from worry, but by now I've come to the conclusion that their movements are likely kept secret to avoid detection. Not that I would have much of anyone to leak it to aside from The Five.

Or Mrs. Chopra.

Or my cats.

"How long is your break?"

"Four weeks." He lets out a breath I can hear across the phone line. "And honestly? I need it. This last assignment . . . Let's just say it was a bear. I don't know if I'm aging or what, but I'm beat."

I want to ask if he'll stay in Pearl for the full four weeks, but even with our rapport it feels like too much. The last thing I want is to scare him off—or worse, ruin our friendship by being needy or demanding. What if he sees me in person and is happy to leave it at a one-time meeting? It doesn't seem likely, given our history, but it's also not impossible. For now I'll just take what he's offering—a visit to Pearl.

"Good for you for taking it. I couldn't run at the rate you do for long."

"And I wouldn't last a day with the toddlers."

"They're far less scary than a lot of the people you interview."

A loud commotion rings out on Jasper's end.

"Hey, I've got to go. But there will be plenty of time for debating job woes once I'm there."

"Travel safe."

"I plan to be asleep for most of it. And Delilah?"

"Mm-hmm," I say through a smile.

"I can't wait to see you."

My entire person floods with butterflies and warmth. "Me too."

As I end the call, I feel like I'm floating on air. It's going to be so full circle to finally see Jasper, to hug him, and to cover so much more in less time. To learn his physical quirks, the way he moves and speaks.

I just hope he stays for a little while.

CHAPTER 12

Betsy

THE MOMENT THE TEXT from Delilah comes in, the one far too casually stating that Jasper Rowley himself will be arriving in Pearl tomorrow, Betsy springs into action, her thumbs like wildfire across her phone screen to activate The Five.

Betsy: DROP EVERYTHING. MEET @ WINED DOWN ASAP.

Delilah: Already in the car, so I'll be there in 10.

Sloane: Will they let me in if I'm not wearing a bra? It's already off.

Betsy: Assuming you're not flashing anyone, I'm sure it'll be fine. Whoever's first get the bottle of sauv blanc.

Eliza: Jack is coming down with something. FaceTime me in?

Betsy: Of course.

Virginia Kate: En route.

When Betsy walks into the cozy storefront of the local coffee-wine bar on Pearl's Main Street, Sloane, whose loft is mere steps away, is already there. The walls are exposed brick, and local artists' work is hung and displayed for sale. Smooth jazz music flows from hidden speakers.

Despite the late hour after a long day, Betsy is positively buzzing. She adores an emergency Five meeting when it's about something good. Though to be entirely honest, she's also never thrown off by a bad emergency meeting. Not considering her upbringing. When she was a child, her mother and father were ready to drop her for an interesting adventure in a blink—tickets to a show in New York, joining in on a friend's Bali vacation when a spot opened up, taking the foreign work assignment for visibility.

Betsy remembers one Christmas when the three of them—she, her mother, and her father—had a storybook morning. There were chocolate chip pancakes, presents to open, and plans to see lights after dark. The au pair who had been with them for six months had flown back to Germany a few days earlier, and there would be a gap before a new one arrived in January. Betsy had felt so special, so included, that her parents had made holiday plans that she was a part of—until one phone call on Christmas afternoon shattered it.

A cousin had an extra room at their Vail ski lodge rental. Were Betsy's parents interested? They'd barely hung up the phone before they started packing their suitcases.

"You're okay to stay alone for a few days, right?"

Betsy was fourteen. Sure, she would probably be safe, but it sounded scary to stay alone. She'd pulled her shoulders back. *"I'll be fine. Just leave me with plenty of cash."* It was what her parents wanted her to say, how she impressed them—by swallowing down her fears.

Her mother laughed as she pulled out a healthy stack of bills and set them on the kitchen counter.

"That's my independent girl. You're really going to make a name for yourself one day."

Betsy made it to 10:00 p.m. before she called Delilah and rode her bike over. Delilah had made some remedial attempts at fluffing the daybed for Betsy, and it practically broke Betsy's heart in the best of ways. She'd swallowed the tears that threatened. She had to be the child her parents wanted: one who could be alone without issue, without neediness. Crying over her parents leaving—after a wonderful morning, mind you—was childish.

The sight of Sloane carrying a wine bucket breaks Betsy from the memory. Sloane nods to the apron-clad man at the counter. "He said he'll bring over glasses."

"I thought you might not make it. Isn't Anton home?" Betsy says.

Sloane smiles. "Thanks to jet lag, he passed out two hours ago. Plus, I couldn't miss *this*. We're all invested."

Betsy grins in agreement, pauses at the water station to snag a carafe, then follows Sloane outside to the patio. They've been warned once before that if they're conducting "Zoom meetings" with the volume up, it needs to happen on the patio in order to maintain the relaxed feel of the interior for other patrons.

As Betsy and Sloane settle at the wrought iron table, the others arrive, and a few minutes later the conversation is at full steam.

"Of course I'm excited, but I can't put too much pressure on it," Delilah says.

Too much pressure? Betsy herself is practically about to spill over with enthusiasm because she's certain this is Delilah's shot at love.

"I mean, I get it. The travel bug seems to be a permanent part of him," Sloane says.

"But you said he was tired," Eliza's disembodied voice says from Sloane's iPhone that sits propped against a sweating water glass. "Maybe he's ready to hang up his saddle."

"Is that the saying?" Virginia Kate asks, twisting up her brown hair into a claw clip. "Hang up his boots?"

"His hat?" Sloane says.

"*Y'all.* We're missing the point—he's not hanging up anything," Delilah says. Her cheeks are rosy, and Betsy can tell she's flustered by the way she keeps crossing and uncrossing her legs.

"Fair," Virginia Kate says from inside her glass. "So let's get to the point: What are we doing for the date?"

"Can we not call it a date when it hasn't been declared one?" Delilah says, a hand creeping up to cover her face.

"*I* declared it a date," Betsy says.

"It could be fun if we 'spontaneously' show up with no clue y'all were getting together," Sloane says from a smirk.

"Oh-em-gee, yes!" Betsy says. She's only sad she didn't mastermind the idea herself. Masterminding happy outcomes for her Five girls is her favorite behind-the-scenes activity.

"Absolutely not," Delilah says. "But please help me. What do we do? What do I wear? What should I definitely not say? How do I act? This is happening *tomorrow*."

Sloane puts a firm hand on Delilah's arm. "First things first. Let's take a breath."

Everyone else assembled nods in agreement.

"I have wardrobe ideas," Betsy says. She's been thinking about this for a while, obviously—the perfect meeting outfit. "That chambray top you have that ties in front with the cropped olive pants. You can do tennis shoes or sandals—both cute."

Delilah's brow perks up. "You think? I really like that outfit."

"Well, of course," Betsy says. "That's part of why it's a solid choice. Plus, it looks great on you. It's casual but put together and not over the top like you're trying too much."

Delilah looks away like she's thinking. "Yeah. About the 'too much' bit. I'm worried about getting out of control."

Virginia Kate laughs. "*Controlled* doesn't exactly sound like fertile ground for a budding romance. It's okay to admit what you want, what you like—your feelings."

"It's way too early," Delilah says.

"It's been *years*, and you're finally seeing him. What do you have to lose?" Eliza asks on speakerphone.

"Um, our *entire friendship*." Delilah throws back a healthy gulp of wine.

"Doesn't he venture into war zones for a living? I highly doubt he's the type to be easily scared off," Virginia Kate says.

Betsy agrees wholeheartedly. Delilah just needs to push through, see the guy, and eventually—when the moment is right—seal the deal.

"What about a game night? A simple dinner plus games?" Betsy takes her phone from her purse and types. "Here. I'm sending you a list. You have most of them already."

"I like that," Delilah says.

Betsy smiles and shimmies in place in celebration. Of course, it sounds like it's off the cuff, but only Betsy knows how much thought she put into it. All of them have places to be in the morning, littles to get ready for the day, and after they split the bottle between the four of them, they start packing up. When they stand to give hugs all around, Betsy pulls Delilah close.

"Did Darcy like her gift?"

A disappointed breath leaves Delilah. "She didn't even open it. Cast it aside basically."

Betsy's heart sinks. She knows Darcy will love that gift—even if she's too proud to admit it in front of her sister. Ever since she followed in Darcy's pageant footsteps, Betsy has admired her glossy confidence.

"Being a birthday diva, huh?"

"You can say that again," Delilah says.

When they finish saying their goodbyes and go their separate ways, Delilah has a plan for her date and strict orders to call once the timing is finalized. They all splinter off into the night toward home, excitement hanging in the air for their friend.

Betsy hums to herself as she drives home, feeling cheery about it all. Mentally, she's already planning Delilah's wedding.

CHAPTER 13

Delilah

THE NEXT MORNING I might as well be whistling as I pass through the school doors, my jean jacket pulled over a concert tee I picked up at the thrift store, a tote bag of bulletin board decorating supplies tucked under my arm. It's a Thursday teacher workday before a three-day weekend, so I will spend the entire day redecorating my bulletin board. I have the whole design mapped out: cutesy springtime animals, a pastel rainbow color palette, even little tufts of grass hand-snipped from construction paper. I can already hear the squeals of delight that will come from the bunnies.

At the top of the hallway, Donna, our school administrator, stands twirling a set of keys on her fingers, smiling far too specifically in my direction.

"Delilah! Good morning!"

My feet grind to a stop. "I have the whole day planned." It comes out sounding like the refusal it is.

"I only need you a couple hours."

My shoulders drop along with my face. "What's the assignment?"

"Poor Miss Patti's husband had to be rushed into surgery—gallstones—so I need someone at the desk. Maybe you could do your planning there?"

I stifle a sigh. "Only because it's you, Donna."

I drop my bag of supplies in my classroom and carry myself

and my coffee mug to the office. It's quiet in there, only the occasional hum of the jumbo printer-copier, no chirping phones. I'm no longer a novice teacher, so I have my lesson plans mapped out. I make occasional adjustments, adding new supplies and updating the class library, but the Blissful Bunnies don't require the same razor-fine planning that the elementary classes do as they work on reading and math.

The preschool is part of Pearl Preparatory School, the area's most sought-after educational institution, but in reality it functions quite separately. The preschool has a laid-back, loving feel. Arts and crafts rule, story time might be punctuated by impromptu yoga moves, and playground hour rarely wraps up on time. Sure, we work on letter recognition and basic writing once the students get older, but both Donna and I share the same philosophy: Let them be little. Because once they're ferried on to the next levels of Pearl Prep, they begin their training to become the next glossy generation of Pearlites, steered toward collecting accomplishments, prizes, and luxuries to validate their existence here. The lawyers, the bankers, the tech geniuses. The entrepreneurs. The people throwing lush dinner parties around town.

I picture my current students funneled into career paths, molded, buffed, and polished, and I catalog all the things about them I hope remain untouched: belly laughs, delight in a flower sprung up after a cold winter, untamed paintbrushes splattered on paper, bird-watching, kisses to heal all wounds. A sigh escapes me.

The phone beside me rings, and it pulls me back to my surroundings. I lift it and answer, "Pearl Prep Preschool. This is Delilah. How may I help you?" Out of reflex, I paw around the desk, looking for sticky notes in Patti's handwriting that might guide me. This isn't my first time covering, and she leaves *quite* the paper trail regarding outstanding matters.

"Hey, Delilah! What a nice surprise to hear your voice. It's Madeline from last year. Coco's mom."

I smile at the memory of Coco and her daily pigtails. "Oh hey! How are y'all?"

Background noise floats across the line, kitchen sounds, kids' voices. "We're fine, but look, I was thinking about dropping off some food for y'all today. The girls want to bake, but I can't have it all sitting around my house."

I smile. "If you put something home baked in the staff lounge, it'll be gone in hours. Sometimes the football coaches even come over from the upper school to poach."

"Wonderful. We'll get on it and drop it by."

"We appreciate it!"

"Sure, and actually—now that I have you—I wanted to ask: Did you hear about Devi?" Madeline's lightness fades.

"Oh. Um. I'm not sure." I struggle for an answer that protects her privacy.

Madeline sighs. "I decided to go to Betsy's party, hoping it could be a pick-me-up since I sort of let myself go since my mom got sick last summer, and I invited her to come. Just some fun products to shine me up. Anyway, Devi got a really bad reaction to the lip gloss, and she actually ended up at urgent care the other night."

"Wow, that's awful. I'm sorry to hear it." My mind returns to the moment at my classroom door.

"Well, apparently Betsy and the rest of them—the peaches or whatever they call themselves—are radio silent. I think the right thing would at least be to cover her medical bills."

"Oh no." My guts sink hearing this through the grapevine about my dear friend. I'd assumed Betsy had already done whatever was required to make it right—as she always does.

Madeline pauses and pulls in a breath. "I'm not trying to be ugly about it, but it's a little upsetting, you know?"

"I understand. Is there anything I can do to help?"

"Thank you, but no. Devi's feeling a lot better after they gave her some prescription stuff. You know she and I are close, and we've sworn off all that Peach Pit garbage and are hoping this fad burns out soon."

"I'm glad she's feeling better, and it's totally reasonable that you both would feel that way given her experience."

"Thanks, Delilah," Madeline says. "And I don't mean anything by it mentioning Betsy. I know y'all are friends, and she's always been good to me."

"No worries. Talk to you soon."

I hang up the phone, and I know exactly what Madeline meant. She doesn't have an issue with Betsy, but she's not convinced on Peach Pit. Same here. Sometimes I wish I was more outspoken like her—brave, unafraid.

I sit back in the chair and take a deep breath. Patti has made the station so comfortable, and my muscles relax and my head drops. My eyes catch sight of a list on the desktop that includes Virginia Kate's name. I reach out a hand and slide it closer.

Overdue Accounts is typed at the top with a short list below.

I flush at having accidentally stumbled upon something so private. Certainly it's a mistake—some sort of mix-up. A clerical error on the bill-pay end. Nevertheless, my mind spins. Hunter works in insurance, so I know some of his pay is commission. It's possible he could've had a slow month. But so slow they can't make tuition? Their twins, Dawson and Banks, are in the threes class. I'm probably overthinking it. They forgot to go online and pay, each of them thought the other one did it, or the first of the month got away from them. It could be anything.

I know I shouldn't, it's not good manners and my mother would be clutching her pearls knowing I was about to do this, but I sneak a second look. This time at the second column. *Three months* delinquent. A gasp escapes me, and I bury the paper.

Just then Donna breezes in. "You look like you saw a ghost, Delilah. You okay?" She glances around the office casually.

"Just feeling a little faint. Probably need a snack."

"Well, perfect timing. I'm here to relieve you."

I hop up, grateful to escape this desk and the scene of my overstep. "Thanks!" I call, already halfway out the door. I shouldn't have looked. I wish I *didn't* know, because now I'm thinking about it, mulling it over without the ability to ask more.

My breathing slows as I walk through the halls to my class, and once I'm there I check my phone before launching into the bulletin board makeover. A text waits.

> **Jasper:** Just got into my rental, and all they had left was an F-150. What should I bring tonight? I'm still a terrible cook. Always and forever.

My face breaks into a deep smile, and my fingers run without thinking.

> **Delilah:** Just yourself, kid. No one needs food poisoning going into the weekend.

I tuck the phone away and pluck my AirPods from my tote, and as I begin pulling down the old bulletin board covering, I think about the evening that awaits me.

Even if it's not something that will last forever, I'm determined to enjoy every minute of Jasper while he's here with me.

CHAPTER 14

Delilah

THE GROUP TEXT DINGS nonstop in the hours leading up to Jasper's arrival, but I set the phone aside to focus on the task at hand: getting myself clean and presentable.

I also don't want to hear them call it a "date." I might have had sweaty palms for the last two hours and a whole horde of butterflies in residence, but Jasper hasn't called it a date so neither will I. It's not something to infer between the lines. Not that I'm an expert in dating. In fact, I'm quite the opposite.

Before long, I'm showered and dressed in the outfit Betsy preselected for the evening and drying my hair. I inspect my face closely in the mirror and for the first time I notice the fine lines that have appeared across it after these thirty-seven years of life. Surely Peach Pit has a remedy, but as quickly as I consider it the memory of my sage neighbor, Mrs. Chopra, springs to mind. She laughs in full sun, her face deeply wrinkled like a raisin, and she says, *"Aging? It's a beautiful thing, honey. What a gift to have another day."* I smile to myself as I abandon my primping and head downstairs.

I flit about the house with a new jitteriness. I pull the premade charcuterie board from my fridge and light a candle. My eyes flicker to the wall clock again and again as I track single minutes edging by, and I do laps of the first floor, adjusting pillows and picking lint off the rug. Details I have never before considered. As the time draws closer, my heart beats quicker than usual.

Suddenly I second-guess everything: the outfit, the snacks, the plan to play board games, *this entire endeavor.*

What if Jasper doesn't even like me in person? What if I say the wrong thing? What if I ruin this somehow? What if I'm different than he imagined from the postcards and the handful of spotty FaceTime calls? What if I'm not enough?

A knock at the door transports me out of my panic.

A sudden calm covers me, and I stride to the door. *We're friends,* I remind myself. *Pen pals since childhood.* My hand hesitates on the door handle, but only for a moment, and when I pull it open, my heart nearly stops.

Before me, Jasper is fully human. He's taller than I expected from pictures, with broad shoulders and a medium build. His tattoos show beneath the sleeves of his T-shirt. His dark hair shines in the sun like onyx, and his beard is thick around his jaw. Dark glasses frames complete the tall-dark-and-handsome that currently threatens to lift me off the ground. His warm brown eyes meet mine, and I almost miss the item in his hands.

He pushes out the pot. "I got you a succulent."

I suck in a surprised breath. "I love it."

Jasper pushes his hands into his pockets and glances down. "I had flowers, but then, you know, it seemed like maybe the plant felt right."

"You didn't have to bring anything." The depth of truth in this statement is almost unmooring. Simply having him here, flesh and blood before me, feels like a miracle after all this time. For years he was continents away or mail service away or hurrying off the line because of a bad internet connection, and now he's *here.* On my doorstep.

"Oh, come in! Look at me leaving you standing out here."

I blush as I turn to head inside. The newness of being in person with him pulses between us, and it's hard to find a place in my mind to make sense of it. Objectively I've known Jasper since fifth grade, but everything about this moment feels uncharted.

Jasper ducks slightly as he steps over the threshold. He stops in the living room and turns to me. "Isn't this crazy? You're smaller than I imagined. I don't know why. Maybe because your personality is so strong. Sorry—is that a weird thing to say?"

I laugh. "I'll take it as a compliment. I didn't realize you had all those tattoos."

He pushes up his sleeve to reveal the designs that run up and over his shoulders. "I've collected them from my travels. The best keepsakes for a nomad like me." He leans closer, and my breath hitches. "Just don't tell my mom."

"Pinky promise." It's all in fun because I haven't met Jasper's family, who are scattered across the Pacific Northwest, but from the stories he's told, I imagine they'd appreciate his tattoos.

I wave him into the kitchen behind me. "Let me get you a drink."

I pull open the fridge and list off my beverage options, and Jasper floats toward the formal dining room turned soap-making room.

"Water would be great," he says. "With all the time zone changes, my body is one beer away from a twelve-hour sleep coma."

I pluck two sparkling waters from the fridge and pour them into a set of cut-glass tumblers I found at the vintage store in town. I join him at the metal prep table and hand off the drink. He runs his free hand over the supplies with a surprising reverence.

"Finally, the great Bubbles & Suds magic is before me." Jasper's eyes sparkle in the fading sunlight that streams through the window.

"Humble setup, but it works for me."

His brows raise slowly, and he says, "Don't play like that with me, Lilah. You know this stuff is the bomb, and you should own it."

A rush of butterflies goes through my middle. He sounds just like his written words. I could've read that sentence right off a postcard in his chicken-scratch handwriting. It's thrilling to hear them come straight from him, a real person. It's like finding your favorite book in an alternate universe and getting to read it again for the first time. Somehow, it's exactly the same and completely brand-new at once.

I let my shoulders drop. "Fine. Alright. Yes, it's not so bad."

Just then Scooby appears, and Jasper crouches to meet her. "I'm going to assume you're Miss Scooby." He picks her up. "Yup. Definitely Scooby. Now I just need some tips on wooing your brother."

I reach over and pet the spot between her eyes. "She's my best girl. The pair of them are pretty good company around here."

"I have mentally cataloged all the stories—the diarrhea incident of 2017, the live bird carried inside, the winter we thought we might lose Doo," Jasper says.

I still shudder as I remember finding him limping home from the road out front after what I could only presume was a close call with a car. "You remember all that?"

It was about ten years ago that I got the pair as kittens, and though I do mention them, I talk a lot about work, family, and The Five in my postcards and letters too. It wouldn't be at all unreasonable for them to be an afterthought.

"Are you kidding? We're on season 8 of Scooby Doo, and I am a superfan. I've got the boxed DVD set and everything."

"I have a whole host of Doo photos that would make killer T-shirts."

"Sounds like I've got my weekend plans sorted then."

I cross my arms, and only once I've done it do I realize that it looks sort of strange. The perils of nerves meeting my personality. Still, I barrel on.

"Yeah, so. Uh, like, what *are* your plans? You know, just in general for being here in Pearl?" I do an odd head-cocking motion that probably makes me look like a mosquito just flew into my ear.

He looks over, shrugs, and throws me a devious smile. "You know how I am. Plans are always flexible."

My heart sinks a little at the comment, despite it being firmly on-brand for Jasper. I want to know precisely how much time I have with him so I can make the most of it.

"Yeah, yeah. Of course. How long do you have the rental?"

"Well, my buddy's uncle wasn't using the cabin—a tiny house sort of place—and he said I could stay for the whole month if I wanted. We didn't make anything official, though."

A thrill runs through me at the thought of him staying for a full month, but I remind myself to tamp down my enthusiasm. A month is still only a month. This is not a date. And knowing the circle of friends Jasper keeps, an invitation on his next adventure is never far around the corner.

"Cool," I say.

Inside, I don't feel cool at all. I'm a jumble of flutters and nerves and second-guesses, so I suggest we get some food and play a game. As we settle in on the barstools at my butcher block island, I wonder if it's all too produced. Sure, I want to make an effort and show Jasper he's welcome, but is it all too formal? Shouldn't we—as old, old friends—be posted up on the sofa with a movie and pizza? Does it look like I'm trying to make it a date when it's not? Why don't they make playbooks to help people like me seem less like an idiot in romance?

"Thank you." Jasper motions to the spread. "For thinking of all this."

The tension in my shoulders releases at once. He grabs the deck of cards and begins to shuffle, and we agree on a game of gin rummy.

"Sure thing. Yeah, it's weird to know what's right when we've known each other for years but are only now meeting in person."

Jasper executes a perfect arch as he combines two smaller stacks, then looks up. "You really are my favorite friend in the whole world, Delilah. Have I ever told you that?"

I nod repeatedly like a bobblehead.

Once in eleventh grade. Once again in our late twenties. Yes, I memorized them because they practically made my heart stop. Never before in my life had I felt so special.

I should feel just as good at these words today, but as I smile back, I wonder if he can see the disappointment that thrums inside me as well. It's so nice of him to say, a genuinely lovely compliment. But it's even clearer now with him sitting across my island, dealing cards with a worn-in comfort, that I want something else: to be more than just a friend.

I remind myself that the clock is already running for when he leaves again.

We settle in to the game, and soon the banter we exchange on paper wakes up in real time. It feels so indulgent to have all of him present, to see his eyes squint when he thinks, his brows leap when he's surprised, lines crease around his face when he smiles. I discover that he uses his hands when he talks. His whole body moves and shifts the more animated he becomes.

I notice every detail.

Eventually we begin to yawn.

"I'm afraid I'll wreck on the way back if I push it much later." He rubs at his eyes as he gets to his feet. "My body thinks it's 3:00 a.m."

I stand and walk him to the door. "Please be safe."

He turns to face me, and he takes my upper arm in his wide hand and squeezes. "Thanks again."

I hold my breath and wish for him to pull me into a hug, and there's a moment where he seems to be considering it too. Maybe I should go for it? But what if he's not a hugger? These aren't the things you cover in postcards or letters, even if we've waded into everything else. The last thing I want is to tack a weird goodbye onto tonight.

He turns to go. "See you soon?"

I pull open the door. "Sure thing. *Soon.*"

He pauses and pulls something from his back pocket. "Here. I had it written to drop off at the next mail station, but we didn't make it. I didn't know if I should or not, but—I kept questioning if I should tell you. But then I realized you're my Delilah." He presses the battered, folded-up postcard into my palm. "I can trust you with anything."

He turns and jogs down my front steps, and before I can manage a response he's gone into the night. A vehicle I can only imagine is his rental truck comes to life in a rumble, and headlights track down the street. Even once he's completely gone, I'm still holding my breath.

"My Delilah."

CHAPTER 15

Delilah

IT'S THE DAY AFTER my meetup with Jasper, and it feels like clouds pad my every step. I filled in The Five on the group chat after Jasper left last night, and as promised I didn't spare a single detail. Well, aside from the aggressively blossoming romantic feelings inside me, the ones I'm actively trying to talk myself out of. Which makes me even more grateful for the timing of the activities I have planned for today.

My mother is perched at my kitchen island with a stack of papers and her reading glasses low on her nose. I'm "helping" her with the Easter egg hunt planning, and though it wouldn't typically be my first choice for my day off school, it's a great distraction from the pitter-pattering of my heart.

"I'm not sure why there needs to be three adults in bunny costumes. It looks weird when they cluster, don't you think? Like something from an alternate universe," Mama says.

"Haven't really given it that much thought." I drop a heavy box of shea butter on the metal-top table in the adjoining dining area in preparation for my soap-making date with Roxie later. "But now that you say it that way, three adult bunnies seems entirely too much."

"I guess we can't quite have child bunnies either. I think it's just the proportion—tall bunnies, there's something ungainly about them."

"So it's decided: one adult bunny of reasonable height." I bump into the table and send a box flying.

Trudie removes her glasses entirely and examines the mess. "Honey, don't you have a better space for this stuff without having it half set up in your kitchen?" She tuts and looks around as if her eyes might magically conjure some extra space into my tiny home.

"Mama, it's just me. And I'm not formal, so I don't need a dining room. When the girls come over, we're on the couch anyway."

She raises her hands. "I know better than to push it. Anyway, let's get down to brass tacks."

Mama puts the glasses back on her face and reads the organizer welcome letter out loud. She oozes delight over every word as if each had been crafted for her and her only.

"Did you hear the standards? No misbehaving or we'll get the boot!" She laughs to herself.

"Worst-case scenario, you have a backup daughter," I say playfully. "The favorite, if we're being honest."

A silence passes between us while I wait for Mama to say something witty back—a joke about how Darcy can be difficult without lying about her favored status—but when I look over, she isn't smiling.

"I'm sorry that it hasn't always been easy. With the family."

I turn my back, pretending to root through the soap supplies for a hidden ingredient, glass beakers clinking against the electric burner. It's a balm to hear her say it. But it's also not the first time, so I know her words won't change anything about how the Thomas crew works.

I look at the supplies in front of me like they're my only hope. I pull in a steadying breath and whirl around.

"I love you, Mama, and we'll figure it out. Now let's review the tasks, because Roxie will be here in thirty minutes to mix up a Creamsicle soap blend, and we don't want to take you out with our fumes."

Mama's face lights up. "You're such a good auntie."

I nod and smile, thinking to myself how much I'd also like to be a mother one day too. I realize that might not be in the cards, and frankly, as long as Roxie sticks around in my life, that'd be enough.

Mama reads off the sheet. "We need to plan the physical setup, temporary fencing, decorations for the area and signage, but all of that is closer to kickoff. We do need to get the eggs and prizes ordered so we're not caught out last minute. The Presbyterians are always on top of their game, and we don't want them buying up all the good stuff."

"I can make a list of options," I say, happily accepting an administrative task.

"Great, there's a list of the last few years' prizes in the welcome email we got, so let's cross-reference that to keep things fresh."

"Got it."

"What colors are we thinking?" Mama slides the glasses back down as she looks to me.

"Aren't they always the same regular Easter colors?"

"No, there are two central colors—like a wedding. It's typically a pastel, but it rotates some every year."

"Can't say I've noticed." I shrug. "Whatever you please, Mama."

"Oh good, because—"

"Anything but peach."

"Sure thing, honey. How about cream and robin's-egg blue? A light shade of it?"

"Sounds perfect."

We roll through the last preliminary items, and as the soapmaking supplies mount across the metal prep table, Mama eventually shuffles her papers into a stack and stands.

"Well, let me let you go. I know you girls will have quite the fun."

I walk Mama to the door, keeping an eye out for Roxie to pull up in her old Jeep, and I think about the fact that Mama could've done this all by herself and probably in half the time. She need not explain to me all the details and procedures. Those are things on which she has more than a solid grasp from her experience as a volunteer. She wouldn't have had to drag herself over here.

But she did.

She folds her hands in front and nods once. "Thank you for all your help, sweetie. I was happy to see you today."

I didn't help, not really. But I'd much rather this than attempting an adult pageant or horse riding again. Maybe, just maybe, this could be the start of us finding that missing common ground.

"No problem, Mama. Thank you for coming."

She turns to go, but her phone rings in the pocketbook tucked under her arm, and she reaches for it.

The greeting must be skipped, because the first thing she says to the caller is, "Well, I'm at Delilah's. You're never usually home before seven anyway."

Her face drops, and suddenly it's a sad and tired woman far older than her years standing before me.

"I'm leaving now, so I'll see you in a little."

Mama sighs as she punches the screen to hang up, shaking her head as she tucks the phone away.

"I'm not sure what's going on with your father; he's all ornery these days."

"These days?"

Her eyes go wide as she leans closer. "I swear he's getting worse."

"I'm sorry, Mama." I bite back the comment I'd rather make: *"Why don't you leave him?"* It's not my place.

She reaches out and squeezes my arm. "Thank you again, honey." She turns and hurries out of the house, freshly jumpy and alert.

* * *

The electric burner hums, the ingredients melting down into a liquid, as Roxie stands beside me sniffing the essential oils, her hair pulled back into a messy bun.

She unscrews the cap of the orange and sniffs. "We definitely can't overdo it on this one or it'll be too sour. You know what I mean?"

I lean over and sniff. "For sure. We want it sweet. So maybe we can start with four parts vanilla to one orange?"

"Yeah, or even five to one."

"I like that. Let's start there."

It's quite the shift from the Easter planning of earlier when Mama might as well have been speaking a foreign language. It makes me think of Betsy and how—once again—she'd be better suited to my position as my mother's sidekick. Once they hit it off on the pageant circuit, the two never looked back.

Roxie puts on her safety goggles and a mask, jerks the window open, and mixes the lye on the ledge.

"How was the meeting with Grandmama?" She grins over at me as she stirs.

I shrug. "She's being so nice about it, but it's obvious I'm the world's worst candidate for this job."

"I think she wants to include you." Roxie keeps her eyes trained outside.

Roxie is a bright girl, and she sees how her mother dominates during family gatherings. She often slinks off when Darcy starts showboating, but she would never dare to speak a word against her. Darcy's still her mother, and she *does* dote on her. Case in point is the cute Jeep parked outside that sat waiting for Roxie on her sixteenth birthday several months back. It could be fodder for a documentary series, because despite my efforts, I'm yet to make sense of the fact that Darcy, despite her Darciness, does seem to be a good mother.

"Your mama does so well with the spotlight, it'd be a shame to drag it off her," I say.

In reality she could probably use a break from it.

"For what it's worth, I think you're pretty spotlight worthy." Roxie grins in a cheesy way that allows her teenage side to keep things from getting too sincere.

"Thanks, kiddo." I reach out and measure the essential oils for the batch as Roxie blends the larger mix with an immersion blender. "I wish I had something pretty to put in them."

"Since when was 'pretty' your thing?" Roxie asks, briefly pausing the blender.

I let out a small laugh. For the longest time I was adamantly against anything pretty in the soaps. I was worried it would sully the "irritant-free" quality of the product, but now that Peach Pit has taken off, I've started wondering if perhaps I need to branch out in order to succeed.

"I'm up for trying it with natural things. I'd need to look into it."

"Oooh! For the Easter brunch. What if you're a sponsor? We can make some pastel-colored blends and put dried flowers in them, and the soaps will go out in the goody bags for ticket holders. It would be incredible publicity."

My chest opens wide as a thrill runs through me. "Roxie! Yes!"

She shakes her hips in a happy dance. "I've told you I'm Team Delilah, even if most of the town is Team Peach Pit."

I look away. "Well, it's not exactly me versus them."

"But it is a way to show that Bubbles & Suds is a premium product. Peach Pit is cute, but it's super cosmetic, and although they claim the whole 'natural, organic, clean ingredients' deal, there's no way it's the case," Roxie says. "If we get clear with branding, we can set ourselves apart."

I slide the soap molds in front of her. "*Right?* I haven't been able to stop thinking about how impossible it is that their peach soap is natural. It's obviously highly perfumed and dyed. No one seems to care."

"People are so used to companies lying to them."

Roxie finishes pouring the test batch into the mold, and I hug her from behind. "And you know I'm not trying to bad-mouth Peach Pit, right? I just wish they'd be honest about their products. I have several friends involved, and though I have my concerns about the company, I know for a fact they've got some of the best people in their ranks."

She waves me off. "Of course! Some of their stuff is cool, but they should be honest."

I try to ignore the sting of Roxie calling them cool, even if only in a small dose. "Thank you so much for being part of this thing with me." I gesture to the soaps.

"I love it. Oh, and did I tell you Mama let me sign up for graphic design class at the community college? I have to do a branding project, and I thought maybe I'd use Bubbles & Suds. You wouldn't *have* to use it or anything, I—"

"Yes! Canva is killing me slowly. It takes me an hour or two every time I make a graphic to post about a sale."

She grins. "I already have ideas."

"I'm paying you for it."

"You don't need to."

"I want to."

Roxie stills, picking at the hem on her oversized T-shirt. "I know you're not selling that much soap, and I know Peach Pit is one part of that. I want to help—not be a burden."

I wrap my niece in my arms. "You will never resemble anything close to a burden, peanut. You're total sunshine."

CHAPTER 16

Betsy

THE PARTY GAMES ARE done, the onesies decorated and hung along the clothesline running across Betsy's fireplace, the presents opened and a list of names made for the thank-you cards, wrapping paper gathered and disposed. Everyone, even funky fashion–inclined Delilah, arrived wearing an appropriate dress in rainbow pastels as Betsy requested. The shower has been everything Eliza deserves, and she even cried when she walked into the house, a moment Betsy basked in, knowing much, almost *all,* of it was at her hand. It is a Saturday afternoon for the books.

Only now, tucked away in Betsy's kitchen, Virginia Kate and Eliza alongside, does she hold out the box of specialty cupcakes she had made for the occasion. French vanilla cake with peach buttercream frosting topped with a hunk of candied peach. The wrappers are the signature peach-and-cream seersucker pattern in thick card stock—just like something Joanna Gaines might lay out at her Texas bakery. Only the Pearl version.

Betsy cradles the box in her arms and grins as she pops the lid. "So? What'd ya think?"

Eliza smiles and nods. "Yeah. Sure thing. They're . . . cute."

"I knew you'd love them! I figured why not since you wanted to make your announcement today and everything."

Virginia Kate floats around behind Betsy to look at Eliza. "Everyone's going to be so happy for you."

Eliza's eyes go blank, and Betsy isn't sure what's misfiring. Eliza was all in when they spoke last night. She already paid her start-up fees, and Peach Pit training 101 says that reluctance to pay is reluctance to commit. Not for their Eliza. She swiped the card, sealed the deal, and Betsy didn't even have to put on the hard sell.

Peach Pit has worked miracles in Betsy's life, and it's impossible to consider Eliza would be anything less than gung ho for the same. She belongs somewhere far better than that boring HVAC company, somewhere that can offer her far more than just a paycheck, somewhere with built-in sisterhood and belonging.

"Yeah. It's just—don't you think Delilah and Sloane would rather I mention it to them first? Since we all talked about it. I don't want them to think I'm going behind their backs."

Betsy swats at the air, playfully rolling her eyes. "Delilah's a big girl, and if you've made your mind up, she really needs to respect it. Plus, she'd still give you a kidney if you needed it, so you're golden."

They're The Five—which Delilah is always so ready to remind them. Even with Peach Pit in the mix, it's the solid ground upon which they all walk. Isn't that how friendships work? They can endure a little banging up, a bit of a rough ride, and they'll still be standing.

The memory of the email that popped into Betsy's inbox this morning returns to her. Madison Kingston reported two different issues her customers have had with the glittery body lotion, two cases of widespread rashes and hives. Betsy forwarded it to her up-line, telling herself it would be addressed even if she wasn't fully convinced.

Eliza looks back at the cupcakes and grins. "Why not! It'll make a splash." Her hand flies to the underside of her baby bump. "Oh! And baby girl is kicking like she agrees. Maybe she's a Darling too."

The squeal of joy pours from Betsy as she slides the box onto the countertop so she can pull her friend into a hug. Eliza's belly pushes against hers, and she asks the universe for all things good for this baby.

Virginia Kate stands by, her mouth pulled like she's trying to smile, but it melts into a pseudo grimace.

Betsy laughs. "Did you have a rough night's sleep last night or what, Ginny Kay? You look like you need a nap."

She shakes her head and dabs briefly under her eyes before she joins them and wraps her arms around the pair to create a group.

"Welcome to Peach Pit, Eliza."

Betsy arranges the cupcakes on a tiered platter in seconds, and Eliza carries it out to the living area where her guests sit chatting, milling, and catching up. She stops and gulps visibly.

Betsy pats her encouragingly on the back. "The first few times are the hardest. Promise."

A thrill courses through Betsy as she watches Eliza call the room to attention, as she gushes about joining Peach Pit, how *excited* she is to bring her friends and family products that will fight the forces of aging. Products that will replenish their biological defects, soothe the soul. Products that might even bring them back to life in ways they never imagined.

Really, that's what Peach Pit has done for her.

Here, among the Darlings, Betsy is so much more.

Here, she's important.

Betsy rushes up to Eliza's side. "I know we're on the tail end of the shower, now that all the planned festivities have ended, but if y'all would care to stay, we'd love to share cupcakes and a brief presentation on the Peach Pit products. Since Eliza is new, Virginia Kate and myself will tag in and support her in presenting. Plus, Eliza will be sharing one of our brand-new products we simply *cannot* wait to try."

Right on time, Virginia Kate pushes a rolling cart of Peach Pit products into the center of the room.

"I know a lot of you have seen these products before, and I hope I'm not boring you," Eliza starts.

Betsy catches a glance of Delilah, whose face is so pale she looks like she might be sick. Sloane, beside her, is grumbling something under her breath, a single brow arched. Betsy shoots the pair a look, commanding them to zip it and support their friend in a moment that is decidedly not theirs.

"Oh, you could never, Eliza!" Betsy pipes up. "Every Peach Party is a brand-new experience, and we're thrilled you're launching your own small business."

"Well, now that you say it," Eliza's voice resounds with confidence this time, "I have to say these products have impacted—changed, really—my own life already. Not only has the overnight Peach De-Puff Cream completely removed the bags under my eyes, but thanks to this business, I'm now able to stay home with my baby girl for as long as I want when she's born." Eliza cradles the bump, staring at it adoringly. "If any of you ladies would like to sign up today, I have room on my own Darling team for entrepreneurial women seeking a new business opportunity."

Betsy steps back and crosses her arms over her chest. See? Eliza is already a pro. It'll be a matter of weeks before she has a whole team below her, and she's set. There's no better feeling than sharing the magic of this company with the friends she loves most. Betsy glances over to Virginia Kate, who pauses briefly, then holds up a thumbs-up, her eyes jittery above. Betsy reminds herself to pull Ginny Kay aside later, after the whole party is wrapped up, because there's something off about her. Could there be something in her personal life she's out of the loop on?

Impossible. The Five has no secrets—well, aside from surprises for one another.

Eliza keeps running on her presentation, handing out samples and telling the story of how the power of a Georgia peach pit was harnessed and channeled into these life-giving products.

"And now, without further ado, our latest offering is the Peach Pit Peach Tea!" Eliza holds up the adorable box covered in Peach Pit stripes, the peach brand on a hand-cut paper medallion right on top. "This all-natural, clean tea has restorative powers, enhances the age-fighting forces inside your own body, and even detoxes chemicals found in processed foods."

Betsy lingers on the outside of the party, ready to snag any wily souls trying to escape before placing an order with the mom-to-be, and she overhears Sloane mutter, "I think as long as you have a fully functioning liver, it does the detoxing for you."

Most of Eliza's family members purchase a single item, then slide quickly out the door.

Delilah and Sloane stand and head for the exit, and Betsy is suddenly plagued by a sinking feeling that maybe Eliza was right, maybe Sloane and Delilah should've been told in advance. She crosses the room, feet shuffling quickly to catch them.

Her hand grazes Delilah's upper arm as she crosses the threshold, and Delilah turns.

When Delilah's eyes meet hers, hurt covers them. Delilah is too nice to say anything, but Betsy can tell she's upset.

"Um—" Betsy suddenly realizes she has not a clue what she should say. "Thanks for coming." She snaps back into her smiley hostess mode.

Delilah nods once, says, "Thanks for having us," and continues out the door.

As she watches her friends go, Betsy wonders how much she's messed up. Sure, she realizes now that she got excited and rushed in, giddy over the idea of joining Peach Pit with a classic Pearl baby shower. But surely Delilah and Sloane will be quick to brush it off?

Betsy's mind goes back in time to her early pageant days.

She had been dying to try out a pageant ever since she first saw Delilah's older sister, Darcy, get dolled up and strut around the stage. Mrs. Thomas had required Delilah to attend in support, and various members of The Five often tagged along. The adoration the pageant queen got from the crowd, all the girly stuff involved, the choreographed poses. Betsy wanted it, and she just knew she'd kill it if given the opportunity.

Her own mother wasn't about to commit to the hours of driving and prepping and preening required, but Betsy got her to agree to pay. Mrs. Thomas took pity on her and agreed to bring Betsy along for all the same shopping excursions, training sessions, and beauty appointments she was already attending with Darcy.

Initially Delilah had been excited for Betsy and glad her own mother could help her friend. At some point it became more than just logistics, and Mrs. Thomas took a genuine interest in encouraging and coaching Betsy. At that point Delilah grew quiet about it. Her enthusiasm faded.

Betsy realized that she felt pushed out.

The way Delilah walked out of her house tonight reminds Betsy of exactly the way she looked when the pageant stuff became too much. Betsy eventually took a break from pageants because of it, not reentering until she could drive herself, book her own appointments.

When Betsy considers the same in this situation, a sharp pain runs through her middle.

She would be lost without Peach Pit.

CHAPTER 17

Delilah

THE MORNING AIR IS fresh, the birds chirping and the grass covered in a delicate layer of dew. Pearl Memorial Park has a small network of flat, paved trails that Mrs. Chopra and I like to walk on Sunday mornings, and this morning I have a particularly miffed pep in my step.

"They turned the whole baby shower into a Peach Pit promotional party." I pump my arms at my sides as I recount last night's events.

Mrs. Chopra keeps up with the quicker-than-usual pace beside me. "Well, you said they had most of the party first, right? Just playing devil's advocate."

While I consider, I glance over at the baseball fields where a team is beginning to assemble. "But it was Eliza's baby shower. If Sloane had a baby shower, she wouldn't do a deposition at the end. If I had a baby shower, I wouldn't host a story time at the end."

Despite my assurance behind the words, a tightness consumes me that I'm even thinking these thoughts about The Five. It's as if displeasure with any of them is biologically unwelcome inside my body. I hate it. I just want everything to be good and peaceful and fun, but even though I'm keeping my lips zipped, that seems to be slipping from my fingers.

"Eliza was alright with this plan?"

I toss my hands up, then let them drop. "I can only guess she was a willing participant. She didn't mention it to me or Sloane beforehand, so it felt like an ambush." I let out a long breath. "I feel horrible complaining about the Peach Pit spin, especially when Betsy and Virginia Kate did such a beautiful job with the shower. But why couldn't it just have been a happy day celebrating the baby?"

I've always been able to speak candidly with Mrs. Chopra. She's wise, measured, and steady like an oak that, despite many a storm, is still standing. Like no amount of my turbulence would shake her. We round the bend and a cluster of trees stretches above, casting us into shade. The earthy mustiness rises from the ground as it meets the fragrant pine of the branches above.

"I just wish she would've said something before. The shower was lovely, and then *boom*—out of left field it's a peachy meteor."

"So is this about you having notice or is it about Eliza saying yes?"

Mrs. Chopra's brown eyes shine even in the shade of the trees, and it strikes me how much I envy her inner serenity. As if her own roots are so deeply ensconced that her belonging is merely a simple part of her existence. I'm much more like a sapling—heavens, a weed even—twisting and struggling, despite being physically planted in Pearl my whole life.

I groan, averting my eyes. "I mean, if I'm honest, probably a bit of both."

My chest opens, and it feels freeing to admit it. The ground slopes below us, and in the silence our feet pick up speed with the help of gravity.

Mrs. Chopra shakes her head. "It's never fair and equal like that in a group of girls."

We step out from the tree covering and into the bright light. In the distance a mower rumbles. I consider what Mrs. Chopra says—she's the one who taught me to appreciate a pregnant pause for thought.

And she isn't wrong: Over the years of being The Five, the

leaders and followers have shifted, but if I'm honest, I have never stood out for much aside from potty training their toddlers. I've never once been the prettiest. Or the smartest. Or the most successful. Or the most charming. Yet when I mentally cycle through the others, I realize they've always taken their turn in the spotlight for whatever their talent or accomplishment might be during that moment in time. Betsy has always been socially popular, ever the hostess. Virginia Kate is—and always has been—the smartest among us. Eliza is the kindest, the most thoughtful, the one to text the group to start a meal train for a family in need. Sloane is the cool one. She's successful, independent from her spouse (in a way that evokes chic modernity as opposed to marital strain), and cool under pressure.

Mrs. Chopra reaches out and squeezes my hand, breaking me from my spiraling thoughts. "You've done everything you can, Delilah. And"—she sighs as if she'll regret what she's about to say—"it's okay to let go. These women can figure it out too."

"Let go? But it's changing things between us. I can feel it like a low-grade earthquake."

"Life is constant change."

"One of the moms was actually hurt by a product."

"So you think there's actually something wrong with the products? Or you don't want your friend joining?"

"Devi Patel got a horrible rash—burn, really—on her lips. She ended up having to see a doctor."

"Alright, well, that is horrible. But one bad reaction doesn't make a larger issue."

"I know, but I can just *feel* it, you know? There's more to it. If I could get to the bottom of it, I could stop it from causing problems." Including ones in The Five.

"And what's your plan to do that? Just report it to the FDA online."

She makes a good point. I'm the last person who would make

a big stink about something, upsetting half the town, but I'm just as certain about the fact that I can't do nothing. That would mean standing back while more bad reactions mount. While Peach Pit seeps further into the fabric of The Five.

"At the rate the sluggish cogs of bureaucracy work, the whole town will be broken out before we even get an email back."

"Did I tell you I went to a party last week?"

I stop in my tracks, and Mrs. Chopra turns around from a few steps in front. "No need for the drama, sweetie."

I skip to catch up. "Who? What? Where?"

"Linda from Mahjong. Peach Pit party. Her house."

"But *why*?"

"She's my friend. I'm an old retiree. I'm a widow. And this was a fun party with friends. I didn't realize I needed to run it by you, Delilah."

I flush at the raised brow she throws my way. "No, of course not. Sorry. It's just starting to feel like Peach Pit is ever-present, jumping out when I least expect it."

Mrs. Chopra stretches out an arm and pulls me into her side. "They're not out to get you."

I feel myself relax under the padding of her arm, but despite the comfort she offers, I can't help but disagree. Peach Pit might not be out to get me, specifically, but it is out to get women. They latch on to women's insecurities—about their looks, their social standing—to sell them products. They turn friendships into business deals. And all of Pearl is asleep to it.

"So they didn't try to recruit you, huh?" I laugh.

Mrs. Chopra waggles her brow. "Old Linda put on the sell, but she didn't push hard. She's in it for the parties, and the rest of us aren't buying in. I won't let them talk me into aging being a loss when what I see is fabulous gains: wisdom, experience, joy compounded over a big, beautiful swathe of time. Growing old is such a gift." She runs her hands over her deeply lined face, her warm eyes twinkling in delight. "The rest is just the casing, and you can't take it with you when you go. Not to mention Beverly can't even use the stuff because she broke out in a rash the last time she used the lotion."

"Another reaction. I'm starting a spreadsheet." My brain begins to hum.

I take pride in the fact that not one person has reported a reaction to my soaps—and I even have a tab on my website for customers to report issues.

Mrs. Chopra keeps walking. "Perhaps you're right, love, but you'll have to pry those sweet-scented products from the grips of their dead Darling hands."

It's then the idea strikes, and I close the gap between us, grabbing Mrs. Chopra's hands. "You. It's you—"

"I will not be prying anything peach from those ladies, dead or alive."

"What if you signed up with Linda?"

"One second you're upset I even went, the next you want me joining?" Mrs. Chopra squeezes her brows together.

I shake my head. "You'd be going undercover. Join Linda's down-line, then dig for information, get the inside scoop they don't tell the regular folk. If we get real evidence, no one can get mad at me for sharing it."

"Surely that's a task better suited to a young thing like yourself."

I scoff. "Though I'm sure they'd be proud to coin me as their most difficult convert, the girls are too smart to buy a claim that I've made a complete one-eighty." I gesture to my physical being and Mrs. Chopra nods reluctantly. "Plus, I couldn't do that to them. They're my friends."

"But you *do* want to expose them?" Mrs. Chopra's tone settles into a seriousness she rarely uses on our walks.

"*Expose* sounds so horrible. What I *actually* want is for Peach Pit to simply vanish overnight, and we all go about our lives happily with zero contention."

"I don't think I'm up for it. I don't want to get Linda in trouble."

"I promise it's not about any one person—trust me, The Five are involved. It's about the company, the bigger corporation. I already looked through the website, and there's close to nothing available online except signing up to become a seller. No corporate information, nothing about where the products are made. No complaint line or customer service. It's as if it doesn't exist."

"I see your point."

We walk in silence, and I don't push my request. I can tell from the wrinkle of her brow that Mrs. Chopra is mulling it over. Having once worked as a chemist, she's probably a little more than curious about what the chemical makeup is of these so-called life-changing products that claim to be all natural.

My phone vibrates in the side pocket of my leggings and I slide it out. Eliza's name is on the screen, and I pick up.

"Hey, girl! Is the baby coming? I'm at the park, but my go bag is in my trunk."

I'm signed up to help watch her toddler, Jack, when she goes into the hospital to have the baby.

Eliza sniffles on the other end of the line. "Could you come? I broke out in hives and my lips have swollen up so bad. After last night. I don't know if— Could you come? I need Ted to take me to the hospital. They need to check the baby."

"Of course. I'll be there in ten, fifteen minutes."

I end the call and turn to Mrs. Chopra. "I have to go. Eliza's having an allergic reaction and needs to get to the hospital."

"Oh gosh, the baby."

I nod. "She didn't say, but I have no doubt this was something Peach Pit."

Mrs. Chopra hugs me goodbye. “Just be there for your friend, Delilah. Now’s not the time for the other stuff.”

I release her. “I will. I just hope she and the baby are fine.”

Mrs. Chopra nods, shooing me with her hands. “Go on.”

I turn and take off in a jog toward the parking lot.

CHAPTER 18

Delilah

ELIZA ANSWERS THE DOOR, blubbering through her blowfish lips, tears running down her mottled cheeks. Her hands pat at her lumpy face. She's in her robe, hair thrown up into a seriously messy bun that includes a chunk of hair hanging loose like a rat tail in back. I keep my face neutral, hoping it doesn't betray any sense of how awful she looks, how worried I am about her and the baby, as I cross the threshold and pull her into my arms. Eliza's never been glitzy like Betsy and Virginia Kate, but she's typically put together in a cute tee, jeans, and fun tennis shoes. She has some sort of skin-care routine. It's exactly what I would've pictured for her back when we were kids. Bless her magical mom who ferried the lot of us around in her minivan all those years.

Eliza lets out a sob onto my shoulder. "Thanks for coming. I'm mortified."

I squeeze her and pull back. "All we need to worry about is getting you to a doctor. The ER isn't a beauty contest."

Eliza pulls in a breath. "So you're saying there's no crown?"

A smile cracks my face despite the worry. "I'm sure I might be able to steal one of Darcy's old ones—if you're okay with Jack playing my accomplice."

Eliza steps back, and I pass inside. Ted rounds the corner with little Jack in his arms, looking wrung-out in basketball shorts and a T-shirt with three holes. Jack reaches out with sticky hands, and his father hands him to me.

"After-hours line said you should take a regular dose of Benadryl and go in right away."

I step back to allow him and Eliza some space, pointing to the train on Jack's shirt that falls tight across his round belly. Jack grins and announces, "Choo choo!"

"Thanks for coming." Ted looks at me, running a hand through his already disheveled hair. "We're going to head to the ER up on Highway 7."

I look back to Jack in my arms. "We'll manage just fine here."

Behind Ted's glasses, his eyes dart around, worried most likely, but I can't shake the sense that he's angry as well.

I realize in this moment that at the Peach Pit parties I've attended, I haven't seen or heard any warnings about pregnancy. There hasn't even been a mention of "test a small amount of the product if you have sensitivities." Then again, I was under the impression that most pregnant women simply continued using their regular products.

Ted nods politely before heading toward the back of their ranch house in the direction of the bedrooms.

Eliza sets her heavy eyes on me as she turns to follow. "I'm really sorry, Delilah. And thank you. Again."

"It's nothing. You did nothing wrong."

She takes off behind Ted without another word, and I carry Jack to his play area in the open living room. A cubby hole shelving unit is set up with bins of various toys, a few large, battery-operated options scattered about. I slide out a canvas cube with books and drop onto the carpet.

"Wanna read, buddy?"

Jack picks up his favorite truck, a red-and-blue dump truck with a functional dumper that fits into his palm, but when he glances around the room, it seems to register that his mom and dad have left. He frowns and takes off running toward their bedroom. I get to my feet, but by the time I'm moving he's already down the back hallway.

I call after him, "Jack! Let's play! Want to show me your room?"

Jack veers toward his bedroom door and through it as he yells, "Night night, Miss Delilah! Night night."

I run in after him, grateful to have prevented him from disturbing Eliza and Ted as they scramble to get out of here, but as I slow and turn into his room, their voices follow me. I stand patiently as Jack holds out a hand in a "stop" signal as he begins making me a bed on the floor.

I can't help but overhear.

"I'm not blaming you. I'm just saying that if you hadn't drunk that stupid tea, we probably wouldn't be here," Ted says.

"I told you. I'm *sorry*. I didn't think it'd be an issue. It's all natural and organic."

"And how do you even know that? I told you there was something that didn't seem right about all this."

"It's supposed to be organic and natural."

"Come on." Ted's voice is pleading. "That's marketing, Liza, that's how they sell it. Have you seen the ingredients? Have you been to where these things are manufactured? What does 'clean' even mean? I mean really, what's dirty about a dang cheeseburger? Cut me a break."

"They wouldn't lead me astray."

"Who? Betsy? Honey, she's lovely, and I feel bad saying it, but she's not the brightest bulb."

"That's not fair, Ted."

"It is when she's feeding my pregnant wife a drink that could hurt our unborn child. I mean, she's a *mom*, she's been pregnant. Didn't she stop and think to say, 'Oh, Eliza, maybe hold off on the witches' brew tea until the baby's here'? Or is she just that invested in getting her cut of your sales?"

Eliza sobs, and Ted mutters. A quiet follows, where I hope he's comforting her. I'd bet money on the fact that Eliza blames herself. She's always been that way, the one to take the blame, the one to examine her own actions and conscience before she blames another.

"Shoot, Liza, I'm sorry."

At the sound of Ted's tone shifting to tender, I know I need to remove myself from earshot. I've already heard enough that wasn't meant for me, so I head over to the pallet bed Jack has now piled high with blankets and pillows off his own toddler bed, and on my way I nudge the door so it swings half closed. I grab his music player.

"Ooh, Jack, you have music?"

He stops in his tracks, his entire face creasing in delight, and he rushes to punch the buttons that start the music.

We leave the nursery rhyme songs playing at a decent volume to afford Eliza and Ted some privacy. It's a comfort to know she has Ted in her life, someone who loves her dearly and has her back, someone who cares enough to point out her blind spots. Something prickles in my chest, a sadness I might admit is more like envy, as I sit in the middle of their family. The mess, the fights, the tears, but more so the love, the attention, and the care.

I can't help but think about Jasper, wonder if he and I could ever have something similar. Then an image of him trekking through the Amazon jungle and dodging a low-hanging snake springs to mind, and my daydream deflates.

I turn at a gentle knock on the door.

"Mama is saying goodbye, Jack. Me and Daddy will be back soon."

He runs to his mother, who gives him a quick hug, then returns to play.

Ted dips in for a quick goodbye before they head out, and minutes after they leave, Eliza sends a text to The Five group message.

I send a heart as a reply because Eliza notes in the message that I'm here with Jack. The others chime in with hearty well wishes.

Sloane: OMG, Eliza! Nooooo!

Virginia Kate: That's horrible. Keep us updated! And Delilah, let us know if you need backup.

Delilah: Like I'd share time with little Jack! Nice try, though.

Virginia Kate: No fair, you already get him all day at school.

Betsy: I'm so sorry!

When Betsy's message comes through, it leaves me wondering about her "I'm sorry." Does she assume the Peach Pit products are to blame as I did? Or is she saying it in the amorphous sense we all use to express our condolences?

Her apology reminds me of Eliza's wedding.

She and Ted had an outdoor summer wedding at an event barn ten minutes outside of town, and the four of us were bridesmaids. We were out in an idyllic field across the property, sweating our behinds off for the pre-ceremony photography session when the catering truck arrived and the final touches were put in place. When we got back to the barn from taking pictures, the ceremony soon kicked off in front of a beautiful pond, and we bridesmaids stood lined up beside the floral arch.

It didn't take long to notice the multitiered wedding cake set out in full sun. As they started the vows, the icing began to look thin. Soon it dripped like a gruesome backdrop behind the smiling guests with their eyes glued on the bride and groom. Eventually the tiers shifted on the slippery icing.

"The cake is leaning," Virginia Kate whispered behind me in the line.

When I turned, Sloane was giving wild eyes as she surreptitiously nodded at the cake.

Eliza turned around from where they'd just finished their vows and shot us a look.

"Sorry!" I whispered.

It was a relief when we finally filed down the aisle behind Eliza and Ted, and we went straight for the cake. We dropped our bouquets and spread out around the table, intent on shimmying it into the shade.

"On the count of three, lift," Betsy said.

She counted and we lifted. Immediately the round table undulated in our hands like a wave, and we each almost lost our footing. We righted ourselves.

"Toward me!" Sloane started to inch backward.

We slowly moved her way when the ground beneath me slanted, and I came close to stumbling.

"We've got this!" Betsy announced and pushed the table with force from her side.

In a swift motion it dropped into the shade, and as we let go, the top teetered. Betsy reached up to steady it, accidentally pressing her chest into the frosting.

At the sound of a gasp, we all turned around to see Eliza watching, her hands covering her gaping mouth.

Betsy looked down at her icing-covered breast. "I'm so sorry, Liza."

Eliza shook her head, tears welling. "No. Thank you, Betsy. *I'm* sorry—it's my fault you have an icing boob."

All eyes went to Betsy's chest, and we broke into fits of giggles.

Only time will tell how Eliza takes today's events, whether it's quickness to take blame away from Betsy or if this time she lets it sit. Whether this could ever become something to laugh over, like an icing boob. I set the phone aside and refocus on Jack.

We play with every toy in his room, make a game out of cleaning up, and eat a snack—banana slices and vanilla wafers. Eventually we head outside, and I push him on the swing. I make him boxed mac and cheese, his favorite, for lunch like the fun aunt I am. Eliza calls as I'm wiping orange sauce from Jack's chubby hands.

"They're admitting me, mainly to monitor the baby," Eliza says, her voice far more settled and assured than hours before. "They gave me some fluids and what medications they can with the pregnancy. The swelling is going down . . . It might've been the peach tea. Anyway, my mom's coming over to relieve you. I know there's school in the morning."

Eliza leaves a pause afterward as if she's preparing for me to ask more, but I don't. After this scare I'm far more suspicious of Peach Pit, but my love for Eliza will forever trump any feeling I have for the cosmetics company. Today I want to be here for her like any good friend.

"You poor thing," I say. "Jack's just finishing lunch, and I'll do naptime a little after. I can stay for a while longer if your mama wants to take her time."

Eliza sighs, and it sounds like relief. "You're the best, Delilah. I'll keep you posted."

CHAPTER 19

Betsy

BETSY IS SCROLLING THROUGH Peach Pit social media, scanning for ideas for future parties and marketing, when Eliza's text comes in.

> Hey y'all. I had a bad allergic reaction and am heading to the hospital—prayers that baby girl is all good and it's no biggie! Delilah is home with Jack 💜

Betsy's chest expands like a too-big breath is forced inside at the thought of her friend in trouble. And with baby girl on board, no less. At the mention of an allergic reaction, Betsy's mind goes to Peach Pit, but surely it's unrelated. The same company that transformed Betsy from glum and purposeless to productive girl boss could not be the one to send her dear friend to the hospital. It makes no sense.

Betsy still remembers her first Peach Pit party—the only one she's ever attended as a non-Darling. She'd left the kids with Jared for the first time since Huddie was born, showered, dressed, and did her hair and makeup. Even if the evening had ended there, she would've been a good deal better off than where she'd started—covered in breast milk and diaper cream. But the moment Betsy walked into that party, she knew she belonged.

The women had met her at the door and taken her by the arm—just like they did at sorority rush. The peach decor and the tablescape were an enchantingly far cry from what her living room currently looked like, toys and snack remnants scattered about. It was like being transported to a new world where everything was in order, where a complete conversation might be had. A world where she knew how to succeed.

A senior Darling took her to the refreshments table.

Betsy picked up a small cup of peach lemonade and pointed to the cupcakes. *"I have an app that will create an icing recipe to perfectly match the peach color of the brand."*

The Darling gasped. *"You're kidding! We've been struggling with it since the beginning. Always comes out too orange."*

"Let me help you on the next batch?" Betsy winked. A prickle ran through her like an electric current, a pride she always got from doling out hostessing tips.

"Only if you promise to stick around and join us as a Darling."

Betsy had already been hooked, but that was the moment she promised to come on board, surrounded by the feeling of coming home. It was like waking up from a long slumber, like she'd been revived after going dormant. Of course she loved her home and her boys, but it wasn't easy to feel good at being a mom when the victories were so short-lived, the tantrums ever-present, and the mess regenerating. The Peach Pit world was where Betsy knew how to win.

From there it was history. She'd never been better at anything else in her life—the parties, the relationships, the special touches.

Only over the last few days has Betsy genuinely started to consider how much has happened between then and now. Certainly she and The Five have changed, but has Peach Pit too? Betsy springs to her feet and pads toward the living room where Jared sits watching ESPN.

"Honey, I need to go to the hospital."

Jared whirls around, confusion painted on his face.

"Not me. Eliza's unwell, and she's there. Can you keep the kids?"

Jared grunts, and it's all Betsy needs to take it as a yes.

"Thanks, babe. I won't be long."

Fortunately she's already dressed: white jeans and a floral peplum top she found in a cute boutique downtown. The same place she used to model clothes for before she got pregnant.

Betsy makes a quick stop in the bedroom for some jewelry, a spritz of perfume, and a swipe of lip gloss, and heads for her car keys that hang by the door to the garage. She wants to text Delilah for the lowdown but hesitates, remembering the look on her friend's face after the baby shower. She'll just have to head to the hospital and support Eliza firsthand.

When Betsy arrives at the emergency room registration desk, she's not surprised they won't tell her anything about Eliza, but she spotted Ted's truck in the parking lot, so she's certain they're here. She flashes her ID, gets a visitor sticker, and heads back into the unit.

When she finds the room, Eliza does a double take at the sight of her. Monitors are attached to her round belly, a quiet screen showing a dancing line beside it. An IV is connected to her arm.

"Uh, hey. What are you doing here, Betsy?"

Seeing her friend hooked up to machines of all sorts sends a true pulse of fear through Betsy's middle, and an uncomfortable shiver runs down her spine. She hasn't considered how serious this could get. Eliza looks so different with the swelling and red pock marks.

Ted looks stern and is silent as usual. In Betsy's opinion, he's never been particularly outgoing and has always had a bent toward seriousness. He comes to parties and gatherings, but it always feels like it's only out of obligation.

"Hey, y'all." Her tone lilts up at the end like a question, like a request. "I'm sorry, Liza. I just wanted to lay eyes on you."

Eliza pulls her phone from where it's become tangled in the bedsheets, but once she checks the screen, her countenance falls. "I thought maybe—"

"I should've texted."

Really, Betsy should've called ahead, and it's only now in the middle of her showing up unannounced that she realizes how far she's overstepped. Only real fears, the ones Betsy keeps squirreled deep down inside, would lead her to lose her good sense and her good manners. Fears that this could have something, *anything*, to do with Peach Pit. She needs assurance that it's unrelated. She loves Eliza—truly and sincerely—and she can't let Peach Pit be a bad experience for her. Not when she was shooting for the exact opposite.

"They said one visitor per patient, and I'm that for Eliza. Sorry," Ted says flatly.

A doctor knocks on the doorframe, and everyone turns to look. As he enters the room, Ted and Eliza exchange a few tense, hushed words, and the doctor looks among the adults, as if to figure out who is who.

"Am I good to talk about your health, or do we need to invite people to leave?" The doctor looks over his wire-rimmed glasses at Eliza.

Betsy knows this is the moment she should excuse herself, and she feels crass for imposing, but she can't bear the alternative of being left in the dark.

She leans back against the wall. "Y'all go on. I'm not even listening over here!"

Everyone knows it's physically impossible given the tiny room.

Finally, Eliza nods. "It's okay."

Ted grows red, his jaw pulsing. Betsy will need to do some serious patching up with him, so it's a good thing she's nothing if not charming.

The doctor starts, entirely disinterested in who's who among the group. "First, baby is looking good right now—the news we all wanted. She doesn't seem to be experiencing any distress despite your body going through an allergic reaction. We gave you fluids and a medication safe for pregnancy, and we're happy that we're starting to see the swelling and hives abate. We'll want to admit you upstairs for observation and continued monitoring of your baby until the symptoms subside. Allergic reactions can be tricky, and we won't take any chances with a baby on board."

Betsy's shoulders drop. It seems like mostly good news.

"Is there a way to know what caused it?" Eliza asks. "I don't have any food allergies or sensitivities I know of."

"Funny things happen during pregnancy, and allergies can crop up at any time."

"I'm pretty sure it was that tea," Ted chimes in.

The doctor taps his pen. "It absolutely could've been. And if that's the only new item you've added to your diet, it's likely, but we don't have a test to determine that here and now."

"What about topicals?" Ted asks.

Betsy's skin prickles. Ted might as well pen the paperwork for a Peach Pit Haters Club because it's obvious what he's getting at. Come to think of it, Betsy didn't ask Eliza what Ted thought of her becoming a Darling. It didn't seem relevant until now.

"Topicals are often a cause of allergic responses, but for a systemic response with hives and swelling like this, we expect it to be something ingested. Any other questions?" The doctor looks right at Eliza.

She pauses. "I don't think so. But the tea, it's the only new thing I've tried in the last few days . . ."

"Yes, of course. I would probably skip the tea for now. Folks are getting creative with blends, and it's not always regulated like other foods, so sometimes it's difficult to know what's in it. For the sake of not having to repeat this exercise, I'd stick with your usual beverages."

"Sure thing. Thanks, Doc."

The doctor exits, and Betsy rushes to Eliza's side, hands out to her. "Yay, girly! You're all good! A scare for sure but no lasting results."

Eliza sits there, her eyes vacant and her body still. Like she's sort of existing but not really awake to reality. Between this and the drain of being pregnant while taking care of a toddler, she's likely just in zombie mode.

"I'm not really in the clear until they're sending me home with a healthy baby still inside."

"Well, I personally am relieved it wasn't anything Peach Pit," Betsy announces, tapping her chest with pointed nails as she emphasizes the "personally."

"That's not what he said. Not at all," Ted says. "I'll be reporting the tea to corporate. Or the FDA or whoever is willing to listen."

Eliza reaches out a hand and sets it on her husband's arm to steady him. Finally, she pulls a barely-there smile at Betsy and says, "Thanks for coming. I appreciate you being concerned for us, but I think I'm going to rest for the remainder of my time here."

"Of course." Betsy's voice is bright and high and reeks of "absolutely no worries."

Probably she should put in a call to the higher-ups, just to follow up on the tea. To get evidence that Peach Pit is going to do the right thing, to try to right any wrongs. She believes in Peach Pit so fiercely, she has to believe they'll take this seriously now.

CHAPTER 20

Delilah

WHEN JASPER TEXTS LATER that evening, I'm wrapped in a blanket on my sofa digesting the Eliza situation. Utterly exhausted.

Jasper: Dinner?

I perk up at once, and my stomach lets out a grumble as if to encourage the idea. My thumbs start tapping.

Delilah: Tony's Wood Fire is the best pizza in town.

Jasper: Just tell me when.

I'm already on my feet as we work out the details, and I head upstairs to change out of my sweats. Despite the peachy awkwardness between Betsy and me, I wish she were here to help me. In fact, I would usually text The Five group chat to give a live update, but I don't want to take the attention away from Eliza staying overnight in the hospital.

I drop the phone on my bed and go back to the postcard on my nightstand, the one Jasper slipped me three nights ago on my doorstep. Finally, it makes a bit more sense why he's here in Pearl. Why he's still here. From the date on the postcard, I presume he wrote it before his assignment was called off.

Delilah,

I wish this was my usual letter, but things have taken a turn for the worse. We're out here in Botswana where we traveled to do a story on the native groups working with local government, but we came under fire. I've seen some things during my travels, but this was the first time the crew and I were truly fearful for our lives.

We're hunkered down and waiting on next steps.

I'm not sure of much in this moment, but one thing I was certain of was that I wanted to write to you.

J

It strikes me that if he were still hundreds of miles away, I'd know exactly how to write back, but here in person, I'm not so sure. Does he want to talk about it? Obviously he wanted me to know about the situation, but was his slipping it to me a signal that it's off the table? I always thought having a friendship through the mail was far more challenging than in real time, but perhaps I got it wrong. I pull on a basic T-shirt I got from Goodwill for two dollars and pull on my floral print overalls. Just as I'm about to head downstairs, an idea hits me.

I sit down at my small desk tucked beneath the rafters and pluck a postcard from the stack. I've built up a collection of Pearl postcards from the gift shop on Main. I suspect I'm the primary postcard customer, but Mrs. Finnegan keeps them in stock.

Jasper,

I'm so sorry that happened to you guys. How terribly scary. I'm glad you're safe for now, and hopefully your travels out of there are arranged soon.

> The bunnies are finally back in the swing of things after spring break. No tears at drop-off and everyone is taking turns. I'm already sad about saying goodbye to this group come May.
>
> Your last postcard said you wanted to come to Pearl—is that still in the cards? I would love to host you. :)
>
> Delilah

It's only after I write out the words that a shiver runs through me, as if I'm being bold. Writing from the safety of the preemptive yes of him being here, it feels luxurious to invite him. I fold the postcard, tuck it in my pocket, and then skip downstairs, a new lightness in my steps. Maybe I need to try on some real boldness with Jasper. I want him to stay for the month, and there's nothing stopping me from telling him.

I rehearse it in my head all the way to the pizza place, my nerves mounting as I second-guess. I worry that I'll put too much pressure on him, somehow break our friendship. Make things awkward. By the time I get there, my mind is knotted into a pretzel.

I spot him first, sitting at a table in the sunshine on the restaurant patio. He doesn't see me yet. He wears aviator sunglasses and a plain gray T-shirt with jeans. His leg bobs up and down as he surveys the large plastic-covered menu. When the waiter approaches, Jasper greets him warmly, and before he departs the two are laughing together over something. The look on the waiter's face is how I feel every time I read one of Jasper's postcards: lit up with delight.

I hurry toward him and Jasper stands to greet me. This time things come easier, and when he casually pulls me into a hug, it's as if my heart stops. He smells like laundry detergent and something woody, and I rest my cheek on his chest. The fabric of his shirt is soft, and it feels like madness knowing that it's actually *him* here. The smile that cracks deeply across my face isn't one I can control. Not one bit.

"So I have it on good authority that theirs is the best pizza in town."

I lift my head to look at him. "Only the best for you."

At first I'm taken aback with the flirtiness in my voice, but quite frankly I don't hate it when I consider the company. Jasper pulls off his sunglasses with a single hand, the other still wrapped around me.

"Let me get a better look at you."

I break out of the hug and step back. "Same old me."

He gives me a knowing look. "The sight of you is still brand-new, so let me enjoy it."

I turn to take my seat, an attempt to hide the blush I feel creeping over my cheeks, and the metal of the chair is warm beneath me. I shuffle the menu in front of me while Jasper sits. The waiter walks back to the table with two drinks in hand, and though it takes me a moment, I can tell what they are.

"Shirley Temples?" I'm already half laughing as the words come out.

He shrugs proudly. "You did tell me back in eighth grade that Shirley Temples were the best way to celebrate a special day at a restaurant, and what is today if not a special day?"

I take a sip. "Just as solid as they made them back then. But today? What's the occasion?"

"It's not obvious? We're together. In person." He holds out his glass, and I clink mine against the side.

"You trust me to order?" I flick my eyes to the waiter beside us.

"That, among many other things," Jasper says.

"One spicy diablo, one classic margherita, plus an order of cheesy garlic knots, please."

The waiter scribbles on his notepad, tips his head, and takes off.

In the moment of quiet that follows, I know it's time. I pluck the postcard I wrote moments earlier from my pocket and slide it folded up across the table.

Jasper takes it slowly. "You joining me at my own game?"

"I learned from the best."

He unfolds the paper carefully and reads. His eyes flick up, a fiery eagerness in them. "Thank you for the invite. Even if it's delivered posthumously."

"Hey, hey, now. No one's deceased."

He leans in. "You know what I mean."

"While we're at it—" My voice hitches as the nerves constrict my throat. "I— Well—" I splutter and stumble and reach for my drink to take a sip. "Sorry, this is obviously very difficult for me."

Jasper reaches out and places his hand over mine on the tabletop. "Take your time, Lilah. I've got nowhere to run to."

With his words my breath settles. All of me believes him, and in his calm I find my own. "I wanted to invite you—officially—to stay in Pearl for the whole month." Once the words are out of my mouth, I realize how dumb they sound, and I struggle to explain. "Not that you or anyone needs my permission to stay in town. Obviously you've got your own rental. And if you wanted—"

"Delilah."

I stop my verbal fumbling and lock eyes with him.

"Yes. I would love to stay the whole month, and it means a lot that you asked me to. I understand what you're saying."

It feels like a whole flock of seagulls flapping through my middle, and I am shocked that it worked. I spoke up. And I didn't ruin a thing. Now Jasper will *actually* stay.

"We can make up for lost time," I say brightly.

The waiter returns with our garlic knots and two small ceramic dishes. We thank him before he goes, and I place a knot on my dish.

"I was actually already thinking about staying—you know, before I got your royal decree," Jasper says.

I have to cover my mouth to prevent food from spilling out.

"A buddy of mine—through work—has some freelance connections in the area, so I'm pitching local interest stories. You know, you and The Five might even have some ideas for me as locals."

My mind, which up until now had been consumed by Jasper, comes rushing back down to earth at mention of The Five. My face must show it, because Jasper looks at me curiously.

"Sorry. Did I say the wrong thing?"

"Oh! No! Definitely not." I take a sip of my drink and then begin slowly recounting Peach Pit's arrival in Pearl, the way its tentacles have spread, ensnared far too many women, and how it's beginning to affect The Five. Today's emergency with Eliza.

Jasper listens raptly. Even if he's never met a single other member of The Five, these women have been constant cast members in my life. He knows them too.

"It totally makes sense for Betsy," he says. "She's so good at parties."

"Right? It's just the rest of it. The toxic bits."

He nods. "I worry about Eliza in it. Entrepreneurship requires a certain amount of sharkiness, and she's too sweet to bite."

Usually I would shy away from anyone talking with authority about The Five, but Jasper's practically been there since the beginning. At times I wrote more about The Five than I did about myself—especially during the times I worried I wasn't interesting enough to report on. Possibly to an outsider reader, it even looked like The Five was a cult I'd lost myself to.

I tell him the rest. About Mrs. Chopra and the fact that I've asked her to see if she can join undercover to root out more information.

"If you end up with real evidence that Peach Pit isn't as sweet as it promises, local publications would be all over it." Jasper says it offhand, like a thought his brain is wired to generate rather than as a suggestion. "You could blow the lid off."

I shrug. "Hopefully it doesn't get to that. I don't want to upset anyone. Or break up The Five."

Our pizzas arrive, and the waiter sets up a stand before sliding the trays into place. I assure Jasper he needs to try both, and we fix our plates and dig in.

While we chew quietly, I think about The Five and Peach Pit. My stomach tends to drop now when I think about Betsy and Virginia Kate's dedication to the cause, Eliza now caught in the middle between her friends and her husband—her health and her need to work. Betsy must've known I wasn't happy about the way the baby shower went down, and I can't remember there ever being so many issues at once among us.

Though they do originate from the same place.

For people like me who grow up in families where they don't belong—places they're not necessarily accepted or wanted—it's our friends who fill the void. And The Five is as vibrant of a family as I could ever imagine. I think each of us found something within the group that we needed along the way, things we lacked, missing chapters, people to be by our sides unconditionally. We belonged among one another.

Together, all of us gathered—in spirit or in person—we were home to one another.

I have always been afraid of rocking the boat, and for this very reason I've handled The Five with Bubble Wrap, careful not to ding or dent it lest a small crack beget an irreparable crater. But now, in the face of Peach Pit, part of me feels like finding and telling the truth about the company might be the only path forward. But doing so would send shock waves through The Five. They're two impossibilities I can't fit together.

"You were right about the diablo pizza," Jasper says. "It's incredible."

I look up, and I'm grateful that Jasper pulls me out of my thoughts.

"Well, it's a good thing we've got you in town for a while. Because I have a top restaurants list we can make a tour out of."

Jasper pulls a fist down from the air in celebration, and I wonder if he did the same thing as a boy. I can't help but miss those parts of him I never got to meet in person, and I hope I can hear them replayed in stories.

But for today I'll just have to relish the version of him I have before me, one that is just as good—better—than the one on paper.

CHAPTER 21

Delilah

AT SCHOOL THE NEXT morning Mrs. Chopra brings the last arrivals from car pool into the classroom. Amber returned for a couple of days last week after her daughter kicked her fever, but she's now sitting in the pediatrician's waiting room with a suspected ear infection, secondary to the cold that kicked it all off. I count heads, then glance over my roster.

"Full house," I say, making sure every name is checked.

Mrs. Chopra picks up a coat that has fallen to the floor and rehangs it on a hook. "Not so much for the threes class."

"Oh yeah?"

"Mm-hmm, Mrs. Springfield says they have a bunch out. Illness and vacations."

The comment jogs my memory about the twins, Dawson and Banks, Virginia Kate's boys, who are students in that class. "Well, I know Virginia Kate isn't on vacation."

"I didn't see her at car pool. Usually she makes a special effort to say hi, knowing we're friends," Mrs. Chopra says.

"Hmm." It doesn't necessarily mean the twins aren't at school because the family is past due on three months of tuition. But because my brain is *my brain*, I've already connected the two things even as I try to talk myself out of jumping to conclusions.

I start the cleanup song, and once all the toys are stowed, I call the students to the table. I pull out the flower craft I put together at the tail end of the teacher workday and fan precut flower petals across the toddler-height tables. I set green craft sticks on the table and press a glue stick into each small, chubby hand.

"Does glue go in our mouth?" I ask in a singsong voice.

"No!" the bunnies call back.

"Does glue go on our paper?"

"Yes!" they cry.

Several of them stomp their feet, and when Braylen, our resident rule keeper, nods so fervently that she begins to teeter at the edge of her seat, I rush to her side and catch her before she falls.

"There we go," I say, setting her back upright. "Good as new."

The children get busy gluing paper petals to the craft sticks, and eventually Mrs. Chopra sets out foam stickers to use as centers. I ask her to keep eyes on Cici as I circle the room. Jack and Huddie sit beside each other and work diligently building flowers with rainbow blooms. Neil dots the stickers along the stick, and I rush to his side as his creation takes form.

"Did you make a caterpillar?"

He grins back. I'm not sure if it was planned or serendipitous, but I congratulate him anyway. "How creative!"

The rest of the morning passes with the regular cadence of snacks, the occasional snotty nose, and birdies spotted on the playground. In the background my mind runs like a humming computer, gauging the best way to approach Betsy at pickup today. I've already asked Mrs. Chopra if she could cover me for a few extra minutes, and she was entirely unbothered.

"I'm already sitting down eating with the kiddos, so what good does your presence make?" Her cherry, round cheeks swelled, betraying her humor.

After everything that happened to Eliza and the other issues that have been raised with Peach Pit, I've decided I need to say something to Betsy. She is my friend, and of course I don't want to upset or hurt her. But I also don't want her thinking I'm going behind her back when she finds out I've been looking around for the truth about the company.

I'm still hoping for the best-case scenario wherein Peach Pit has nothing to hide and I come up empty-handed. The version where I don't mess anything up irreparably by sticking my nose into other people's business.

As the clock ticks closer to early pickup, my limbs grow tense, and my shoulders climb. There's no telling how Betsy will take this.

She approaches the classroom door, a Dutch door where the top hangs open and the bottom remains shut to contain the students. I slip out, leaving Huddie behind, which garners a confused look from Betsy.

"Everything okay?" she asks.

"Oh, Huddie's great. I just wanted a word."

Betsy's arms cross over her chest. "Is this about what happened to Eliza? Because I heard it right from the doctor's mouth that they can't determine what caused the allergic reaction."

"It's not, but also kind of." My brain catches up, doubling back to the words it had glossed over. "Hang on—what do you mean right from his mouth?"

"Well, I went to the hospital, of course." Her nose rises ever so slightly.

There was no mention of it in the group chat, and the only messages thus far have been Eliza's basic updates to say all is well.

"Why?" I ask.

"I was worried."

"Me too. Did Eliza invite you?"

A blush creeps up Betsy's throat. "Not exactly, but Eliza was happy to see me."

"And Ted?"

"Ted is Ted. When is he ever happy? Probably only when he's looking at a boring spreadsheet."

"His pregnant wife was in the ER."

Betsy's face drops as if she's realizing her misstep. "I'm sorry. That was unkind. It wasn't supposed to be. You know what I'm getting at: He's not exactly the life of the party."

"I don't really want to talk about Ted. Did you go to the hospital to find out if it was related to Peach Pit?"

Betsy squirms. She's never been a great liar, but she appears to be taking a swing at it. "I mean . . . not entirely. I was worried. Eliza's our friend."

"But not everyone dropped in at the ER. She wasn't admitted until later."

Betsy sighs. "I just wanted to understand the situation."

My chest burns. I believe that she was concerned for Eliza, but between knowing Betsy for longer than most and her dubious body language, it's clear she also wanted to cover her own rear. Or perhaps Peach Pit's; the lines are blurring.

"Look, I don't have a ton of time, so let me say my piece." I pull in a shaky breath as a knot gathers in my throat. "I'm not sure exactly how to say this, and I don't want it to sound threatening because"—my voice catches—"you're my friend, and I never want that to change. But I'm seriously concerned about Peach Pit, what it's doing to the women around here. What it's doing to us, The Five. More and more people are getting harmed by these products, and there's no one to talk to about it. The company is secretive. Why isn't there transparency about the ingredients and the science happening behind the scenes to create these products? Why isn't there a way to log a complaint with a product? I'm going to look into it."

"That's not your place, Delilah. You'd be creating unnecessary problems—Peach Pit is something that's bringing so many people happiness and success. Unlike you, I'm seeing a whole lot more of the happy customers and business owners than unhappy ones."

"Stop calling them business owners."

"It's what they are."

I stop, feeling the adrenaline creeping through my thumping chest as I see where this conversation goes next. I pull in a few breaths. *This is Betsy,* I tell myself.

"Look, I just wanted to let you know that I'm going to be looking into it."

Betsy's chest rises and falls rapidly below her red face. We look at each other long and hard, and I wonder if she's thinking the same things as me. Is this it? The beginning of the end for us? If I think too long about it, the tears will flow hard and fast here in front of my students.

"I'll get Huddie," I say.

I dip back into the classroom and wave Huddie over, taking his tote bag from the hook. I swallow hard as I pop open the door and hand off the bag and child. Betsy won't meet my gaze. I pass back into the classroom after they take off down the hall, and I dip straight into the supply closet and pull the door shut behind me.

It's only then that the tears burst from me in a sob.

CHAPTER 22

Betsy

BETSY MAKES THE DRIVE home glassy-eyed, her mouth hanging slightly ajar, none of the grunted complaints from the back seat making a dent on her emotional permafrost. How could Delilah be so uppity? Really and truly, does she think it's her place to poke her nose in? Then again, Betsy should've just been honest, admitting she wondered about the tea. But once it struck her how Peach Pit's hypothetical missteps might reflect on her, it was as if an invisible needle and thread sewed her lips shut.

She has so much to lose. She bats away the memory of her pre–Peach Pit self.

Betsy dials her up-line's number. It rings and rings before eventually going to an impersonalized voicemail. Betsy curses under her breath as she jabs the button to disconnect.

The woman who recruited Betsy was so charming when she signed up, reminding Betsy of her big, Molly, at the University of Georgia who personalized all her pledge gifts and spent hours hand-painting a cooler for her. Only months later, once Betsy was deeply entrenched and raking in a healthy monthly check, did she first see the veneer crack.

In her mind, the scene plays out like it was just yesterday.

Senior Darling training was reserved for the top tier of Peach Pit sellers, so when Betsy was invited, she felt honored. She counted it as further proof that she'd finally found her place.

As usual, the spread of food set out for the Darlings was picture-perfect and barely grazed over, but it wasn't long after they started the session that Betsy felt things shift. The first clue was when they counted the training manuals and insisted each be checked back in. Why would it matter if a Darling wanted to keep it? Shouldn't additional studying of the material be a positive thing?

The reason became obvious as soon as Betsy flipped open the watercolor cover, scanned the table of contents, and started skimming the materials. A chill ran over her. What on earth? These Darlings—to whom she belonged—were supposed to be good and decent and nothing else. Betsy didn't sleep well that night, tossing and turning as she wrestled with the information in the booklet and how it made so little sense alongside the overwhelmingly glowing experience she'd lived thus far—sisterhood, fun, parties, and profits.

On the second and final day of training, the leader, her up-line, called an early end, popped a bottle of champagne for mimosas, and invited the lot of them outside to her pool. As the music blared on the outdoor speakers, Betsy was afforded a moment alone inside. The stack of manuals sat unguarded. It was the rotten feeling that lingered at the words she'd read and heard confirmed out loud that pushed her to do it. After checking that the coast was clear, Betsy slipped a training manual from the stack and tucked it deep into the depths of her purse.

Betsy sighs and lets the memory fade. She picks up her phone and dials her up-line again. The call goes unanswered.

Betsy pulls a hand to her jaw as it begins to throb; she's been clenching her teeth as she relived the day she discovered Peach Pit had an underbelly. Heat flushes through her as she pulls back her shoulders. If her up-line won't answer her phone, Betsy will simply have to go over there and get her assurance in person.

She calls Jared on the way to the house. "Hey."

"What can I help you with, my love?"

Betsy explains the situation, her worries that the reports of allergic reactions aren't being taken seriously enough, specifically Eliza's case, but she skips over the part about her tense words with Delilah.

Jared pauses, perhaps to check his calendar. "I've got an hour, maybe an hour and a half before my next call. I can keep the kids. Can you be back by then?"

"Yes. Absolutely. Thank you, hon."

* * *

When she reaches her up-line's house, Betsy has to call from the gate. The metal scrolling that runs across the top of the gate is elaborate, a design Betsy once described as "very Versace." Today she can't help but see it as more Olive Garden chic. She used to think the gates were a delicious status symbol, but set beside the memory of a pregnant Eliza heading for the ER, she can't help but wonder if they're simply there to keep the regular folk out.

She presses the call button once, then twice with no answer, but she continues calling.

Eventually an exasperated groan escapes the call box. "Just leave the package in the deliveries box. Can't you read?"

"Hey, it's Betsy."

"Betsy? Uh, what's up? Did I miss something?"

Betsy rubs her sweaty palms on her thighs as she lets out a strained giggle. "Well, all of my calls."

"Ugh. High-maintenance or what, girlie?"

Betsy is relieved of a reply as the gate swings open. She lets out a pressured breath as she drives through and onto the property. The driveway is a straight shot to a house where it dead-ends in a parking pad past the large brick house. Betsy steps out of the vehicle, and female voices float on the breeze from behind the house where an elaborate deck sits outfitted with a grill-bar kitchen. Betsy walks toward it, the very scene of her manual pilfering.

The gate into the backyard is low, and Betsy stops at it before pushing through. Three women are stretched out on a pool lounger, two blonde friends flanking her up-line Darling, the Queen Peach herself, wearing a small swimsuit with tie closures. Behind them sits a heater as well as a beverage cart holding champagne flutes, a carafe of orange juice, and a popped bottle of champagne sitting on ice.

This is what was going on rather than her calls being addressed. *Concerned* calls. About her dear friend and others who are potentially being harmed by the products. If Peach Pit wants to keep its standing in town, they have to take the outlying bad experiences seriously. What's the harm in admitting to a bad batch and moving on with their heads held high? It happens all the time to major companies that've been around for decades. They address the issue, put a PR spin on it, rally, and continue.

The trio barely looks up when the gate bangs closed behind her.

"Hey, ladies!" Betsy musters every ounce of confidence she can scrape from her withering resolve.

"Hey, Darl!" Her up-line squeals with joy, her face squeezed into a deep smile, framed in bouncy golden layers of hair.

Only moments earlier she was annoyed that Betsy was audacious enough to call her. Now this sudden turnaround?

She pulls Betsy into a deep hug, leaving traces of her peach-scented tanning oil on Betsy's clothing. She tucks her arm around Betsy's waist as she pulls back. "Me and a few ladies were just getting a head start on our summer tans, and I was telling them all about Peach Pit. Don't they just *look* like Darlings?"

The other women wave, a mimosa in the opposite hand.

"Uh." Betsy's insides feel like they're passing through a whirling whisk. She's coming—for the second time—with concerns, and the last thing she wants to do right now is play into this fake bestie nonsense to sign up new girls.

"It's nice to meet you gals. Don't forget a round of our Peach SPF." Betsy leans in. "I need a word. Privately."

The Queen Peach's top lip sneers but only momentarily before she snaps back into her sugary-sweet act. "Anyone need a top off? Little Betsy here is one of our most *serious* Darlings, and she's in a moment of need, so I as her big will swoop in to support." She grins in a way that says, *"Isn't this adorable?"*

"Awww," the women sing in unison. "You're so sweet."

Betsy's cheeks burn as she heads inside, and the moment the screen door clicks shut, the woman drops the act.

"I'm about to sign these two on, and you march in here making Peach Pit look all business and no fun."

Betsy takes a step back. "I didn't realize the timing was bad, but this is a serious thing."

Betsy doesn't say the other part: Peach Pit *is* work. It shouldn't be sold as a party only because once a Darling signs on the dotted line, she's obligated to purchase $500 of product a month, then sell most of it before seeing profits. Though she adds a can-do pep talk, Betsy is always honest about this part to the women she recruits.

Her up-line barely contains an eye roll, tipping up her glass. "What is it?"

"What do you know about the Peach Tea? My pregnant friend—a new Darling—drank it and ended up in the hospital."

"Way to go signing up someone new! We need our girl boss fam constantly growing. Look, number one thing: Don't let pregnant women use the products. Tell them they need to consult a doctor or whatever it is all products say."

"But it's sold as regular tea, and tea is okay during pregnancy, so—"

"Betsy, stop being like this. Preggos need to ask a doctor, and that's that."

Betsy's pulse rattles in her throat. "Who can I report it to?"

"We don't report it, okay? The company doesn't care. I'm not a lawyer; I recruit cosmetics sales. Just leave it alone and say it's above your pay grade."

"So who is in charge? Someone has to be."

"Well"—she throws her hands out—"me. I'm the Top Darling, the Queen Peach."

Betsy stops for a moment to make sure she truly wants to ask this question, because uttering it feels akin to hitting a nuclear destruct button. But she's flooded by the picture of Eliza swollen and in crisis, and also of Devi hurt, her own defensiveness a shameful memory tacked on at the end.

"And you don't have a boss?"

The Queen Peach's eyes narrow to slits. "Excuse me?" She marches up to Betsy so they stand toe to toe. Betsy still has a few inches on her, and in this moment she thanks her genetics for giving her this minor upper hand.

"Hmm," she purses her lips in faux consideration, "do I pretend you didn't ask to speak to my manager like some mid-tier Karen or do I just drop you? Because like I said: I'm the boss, and if I wanted you gone, I could make it happen. Haven't had to do it before, but it could be a fun side project for me."

Betsy feels her throat tighten, tears threatening behind her eyes. It's the first time she genuinely imagines life without Peach Pit. Never once has she considered leaving the place that gave her back that feeling of purpose, of doing something that mattered, of helping other women, of building community. There's no way she could've been so wrong about something that made her feel so good.

All the other practical reasons she couldn't leave populate like bees around a honey pot: Her income covers the kids' school tuition, the family vacations, and the MBA they agreed Jared would go after to open up new career options. In a lot of ways, Betsy doesn't have a choice. She doesn't have a way out, not without blowing up so much of her life and setting herself adrift once more.

Betsy nods tightly. "I'm sorry. That was rude of me. I appreciate your leadership, and I'll . . . figure it out."

"Great!" She steps back, breaking the face-off, and yanks the sliding door open. "Now let's go tell my girlfriends how much we love Peach Pit."

The Queen Peach flashes a megawatt smile, linking her arm in Betsy's as they head for the deck. "Sorry to leave you, girlies! Anyone need another mimosa?"

Betsy smiles, greeting the women warmly, but inside she feels like a bag of broken shards of glass. As long as on the outside she looks happy, looks right, she can get through this. She's always been scrappy.

One of the friends lobs a question at Betsy: "What's your favorite part of being a Darling?"

It feels like a robotic part of Betsy deep inside is activated in a snap, like a parasitic piece of computer code she isn't sure she consented to.

"Oh! Peach Pit is *hands down* the best thing that ever happened to me."

Betsy floats through the conversation like she's outside her own body. She excuses herself as quickly as she can, noting that she needs to be back before Jared's meeting. As Betsy scurries to her car, her phone buzzes incessantly in her pocket.

She pauses with her hand on the driver's door to read, but she already knows it's The Five from the pace of the buzzing.

Sloane: Good luck in the viper pit, Delilah. Please don't count any of my mother's words against me.

Virginia Kate: Y'all know my mother hasn't seen the inside of the club in decades, but sending all my love 😘

Eliza: She won't need luck. You've got this!

Delilah: Thank y'all! Packing my holy water and garlic necklace in case they turn on me. LOL.

Betsy's heart sinks. The familiarity of these words, the intonation of the real-life voices in which they'd be spoken ring in her ear. The softness of the space they create among them cuts at her. She feels like a traitor to these women, knowing that Peach Pit—the Queen Peach—has no intention of addressing the issues that just landed one of The Five in the hospital.

She's been hopeful all along that ultimately Peach Pit would right its wrongs. Still, she's not ready to abandon hope. But perhaps that's naive, considering what she learned at Top Darling Training. Trying to make sense of it feels like pawing around in a dark room she doesn't know for a light switch.

She never was the sharpest tack.

Betsy pulls the car door open and drops the phone in the cup holder, texts unanswered.

She doesn't deserve The Five.

And she's likely the last person Delilah wants to hear well wishes from after today.

CHAPTER 23

Delilah

THAT AFTERNOON I PUSH aside my swirling thoughts about my exchange with Betsy as I pull up to the valet at the country club and step out of my beat-up Toyota. It feels like a lifetime since I was last here. A young man greets me and hands off a ticket in exchange for my keys. I fumble with the small cross-body bag I wore for the occasion, taking what feels like hours to extract a tip past the tricky clasp.

Inside the heavy double-wide doors of the entrance I head for the tearoom, sweat prickling under my arms. My borrowed shoes, a half size too big, click and clap on the polished tile floors, and Mary, Betsy's mama, looks up from the table and smiles. Beside her sits Lucille, Sloane's mama, looking very Audrey Hepburn with her curled dark hair, perfect makeup, and pearls.

Mama is the last to look up, and she stands, a wide smile opening across her face as she pulls out a chair for me. "Well, welcome, honey. You're right on time."

I check my watch and confirm I'm still five minutes early. By now, and counting current company, I know better than to arrive late.

Mary smiles. "You must be coming right from school."

I look down at my "Sunday best": some black pants that in the light I realize have faded to dark gray and a button-up shirt that looks decidedly too beachy for the occasion, with its loose, gauzy fit.

"Not quite, but it was a tight squeeze." I shuffle in my seat attempting to find a comfortable position.

"How're things at school?" Lucille asks.

Mama jumps in and answers. "She's doing great. Working with kids is such an altruistic calling, isn't it?" Although she smiles proudly, I can tell her eagerness to gush about school is at least partially motivated by an insecurity that I haven't quite accomplished enough by Pearl standards. Sloane is a fashionable, hot-shot lawyer, after all, and here I am a preschool teacher showing up in the wrong clothes.

Even if I am good with the bunnies, my dream is still to make Bubbles & Suds into a big deal, and I know that when that day comes, my mama will be more than glad to brag about it to all of her friends.

"I'll tell y'all, the children of Pearl *and* their mamas are so grateful for Miss Delilah at Pearl Prep! You whip them into shape," Mary says.

Everyone laughs.

"Remind us, Delilah," Trudie says, "was it the blue box mac-and-cheese fast with Huddie?"

I glance to Mary to give her the chance to tell the story about her grandson, but she only stares back vacantly. Of course she's not so well acquainted with her grandkids; she was barely paying attention when it came to Betsy growing up under her roof.

"*The Hungry Caterpillar* is a magical book, I swear. It broke his food strike and opened his culinary world," I say.

The other women laugh lovingly, fully acquainted with Huddie's personality. I smile at the thought of him too, one of my most adoring students.

Mama nods. "She's known around here for getting them out of the diapers faster than lightning; the class always fills up as soon as registration opens."

Lucille pulls a tight smile. "How lucky y'all are to have grandbabies." She glances off at nothing in particular. "I have to admit I thought Sloane would change her mind once she married Anton. How cute their babies would be."

I look away, knowing I shouldn't be part of this conversation. All of us in The Five know the mamas talk about Sloane's childfree life—bemoan it, in Lucille's case—but it's not something I want to participate in. Sloane tells me she's happy as a clam without children, so who am I to question her?

"I only wish Betsy would use her gifts like your girls are." Mary tuts. "She could be running the event planning scene around here if she pleased, the hostess she is, but instead she's spending her time doing the cosmetics sorority."

Mama reaches out and squeezes Mary's forearm. "Betsy always lands on her feet, and for what it's worth, I think the gals are having fun with the Peach Pit stuff."

Before Mary can reply I pipe up. "So we've got the Easter egg hunt welcome packet information and have already gotten busy on ordering. Mama picked out a beautiful robin's-egg blue for the designs. I've already heard back from the signage folks, and they're sending over some proofs. We'll do some cutesy ones—ducks, lambs, eggs—just for decor's sake, plus ones with the actual details—timing, directions, age groupings, and such. Anyway, that's all to say we're making great progress."

I'm not sure where the words come from, but I sound like someone I don't recognize. I know it's rooted in the desire to cut off the grumblings about my friends without upsetting the mamas. I don't want to hear *anyone* talking about The Five unless it's complimentary.

The three mothers sit smiling approvingly.

Then Mary clears her throat. "Well, very nice, Delilah! I know everyone has things to do and places to go, so let's hand off the last bit. This is all 'day of' info, and I want y'all to have all the behind-the-scenes tips and tricks for timing and rolling everything out. All the churches get out at different times, which helps with the parking at the club, but we still need the attendants. We learned the hard way a few years back." Mary pulls in a breath, but before she can get another word out, a middle-aged woman with bright red hair wearing a club uniform walks up with a cart.

The woman stops beside the table and smiles before she begins to unload a teapot, china teacups with a dainty pink design around the borders, and a tower of finger foods, ranging from cucumber sandwiches to miniature pies to macarons.

The women thank her, and Mama reaches for the teapot and begins to serve the other women as Lucille comments, "Remember the year they had the men's club move the egg hunt to 'the shade' but didn't realize until it was done that they'd put it alongside the dumpsters rather than the other side of the flower arch? Not only did it stink like a fish market, but it was such an eyesore in the family photos! Delilah, surely you remember? Y'all must've been in high school."

I nod rapidly, chewing an entirely too big bite of a pimento cheese sandwich.

Mama jumps in. "I still have a photo of her and Darcy in their matching dresses and that big, ugly green dumpster in back."

"I know y'all will avoid any such pitfalls," Mary says.

"I'm just glad to have one of the younger generations in for the egg hunt. Maybe next year we could get Betsy or Sloane or Eliza," my mother says.

I glance away at the gap in the list that should contain Virginia Kate. Most of the mothers—Eliza's especially, but also Lucille and Trudie to an extent—did their best to make Ginny Kay feel like nothing ever changed. But with the many mother-daughter social events at the club, Ginny Kay naturally soon felt excluded.

"A wonderful idea. But the old guard isn't going anywhere soon." Lucille leans in as she delivers her words lovingly. "We'll help y'all along until it's time to pass the baton."

I lift my teacup, sip without checking it, and suck in piping-hot liquid as if it's a soda. At once I'm sputtering, pawing for a napkin.

"Heavens, child," Mama mutters. "What has gotten into you today?" She adds a laugh on the end to keep things friendly.

Finally, I gather myself. "Sorry, y'all. I forgot how delightful the tea service is here, and I got ahead of myself." I set my hands in my lap delicately, just as I was taught to do in cotillion.

Mary and Lucille smile, nodding enthusiastically. Mama's eyes glint, but wildly, like she's relieved but also prepared to leap into action lest I make another misstep.

Mary hands out copies of her notes, hitting the highlights of each section, as we sip tea—now ever so carefully—and nibble on the treats. "So this year we've got a solid collection of sponsors for the party favors. If you'll take a look." She reads the list.

Only in Pearl would our Easter brunch have corporate sponsors, but for years now businesses have been offering freebies to the country club crowd so that their company can be kept in mind as they mark a special occasion with loved ones.

My eyes land on Peach Pit's place atop the list, and when Mary reads it out loud, Mama rears back in surprise, flicking her eyes toward me.

"Peach Pit is the platinum sponsor, so prepare to see their name and brand on the outside of the swag bags," Mary says without hesitation.

Despite my misgivings heavy and stewing in my middle, I don't utter a word.

"All of these things will run themselves on day of, as long as we're prepared in advance. The men's club will arrange the tents and set out the eggs in advance—y'all just need to keep them on top of it so they have enough volunteers to make light work. We have a list of past volunteers if they need it. It's basically color inside the lines from here." Mary stops and folds the packet shut and removes her reading glasses. "I know you're already well ahead of schedule on the rest, seeing that the eggs and prizes have already come in. We'll be around to support."

"Any questions?" Lucille asks, reaching for her phone as if she has places to go.

"I've been thinking about the gift bags and the sponsors," I say. "Well, Roxie came up with the idea—we'd love to include an Easter Bubbles & Suds soap. We're currently experimenting with having actual flowers inside the soap while keeping everything natural and allergen friendly."

Mama beams. "Oh, I love that! My girls are so entrepreneurial."

Mary nods. "Do we think Peach Pit will be alright with it, considering they're a sponsor?"

Lucille scoffs. "They're not a competitor. Delilah's soaps are far higher end—much more European chic. That Peach Pit stuff is making everyone break out in rashes. At least it's what I'm hearing—never used it myself."

Mama nods as she speaks. "I'm sure it'll be fine. And who doesn't love a freebie?"

"Alrighty, well it's fine by me then too!" Mary announces. "I have to get going though, ladies."

"Same," Lucille says, noting a meeting out at the stables where she boards her horses. "I prepaid and tipped for the tea service on my account, so no one double-pay."

We get to our feet and the others hug, mentioning pickleball and a rescheduled Junior League meeting. I dip in awkwardly to hug each of them, accidentally jostling the table into a clattering more than once.

When they're gone, Mama threads her arm into mine and walks us toward the exit to the deck on the back of the clubhouse building. We step outside and across the deck to the railing. Golden hour sunlight washes over the golf course before us. I let out a long breath that ends in a sigh.

"Was it really that bad?"

"I'm not going to make a fuss about Peach Pit sponsoring," I say. "It's just—I have serious concerns about the company."

Mama sighs. "Oh, it's no big deal, honey."

This is usually the point where I'd nod and agree. Let it go for the sake of keeping the peace among the Thomases. But something new in me, a flicker of bravery, pushes me here in the presence of only my mother to be honest.

"It's a big deal to me. Their stuff put Eliza in the hospital, and it's the reason things are strained between Betsy and me. Not to mention the way they've gobbled up my company."

Mama's brows jump in surprise. "Really?"

"Yes. *Really*. There's something off about the whole thing."

Mama shrugs. "Your soap will be the favorite, I just know it."

I pull in a deep breath and release it. My mother might be missing my full point, but at least she's not exploding like my father has and always will. Among the Thomases she's always been the most sympathetic.

"Rome wasn't built in a day."

I say it for myself—about figuring out Peach Pit, about this family I (technically) belong to, about finding my voice—but Mama pulls me into a quick hug.

"Exactly, *with time*, Bubbles & Suds will be just fine."

"We both know this whole Easter egg planning project is way out of my comfort zone, but I'm doing it for you."

"And I appreciate it." Mama reaches out and sets her hand on my back. "Easter—are you ready for it?"

I pull a face. "Of course. Didn't we just have a conversation about this?"

"I need to know what you're wearing. More people than usual will be looking at you." She touches the sleeve of my shirt. "Let's not do anything like this."

"Oh, I'll probably wear the same dress I wore last year—Darcy's discarded Lilly Pulitzer tea dress."

"You've already worn it two years in a row. You need something new."

"Do I really? The dress only gets used this single day in the year, so I might as well get my money's worth."

"You didn't buy it in the first place. *I* bought it for Darcy, who gave it to you."

"Actually, I pulled it out of a donation bag at your house when you said I needed to buy something new for Easter." Like usual, I was scrambling and found a honey hole of perfect dresses for the occasion.

Mama playfully screams at the sky, exclaiming the words. "Child of mine! Lordy, what girl wouldn't love to be told to go out and get herself a new Easter dress with her mama's credit card around these parts? What have I done to suffer this?"

I laugh. "Set something out for me, and I'll wear it. Something of yours."

"It'll be far too big! I'll ask Darcy for something."

I give her a very specific look.

"What now?" Mama asks.

"Darcy would rather light her old clothes on fire than let me sully their memory by wearing them."

"Oh stop! She'll come around."

"I'll be there, and I'll be dressed. Don't you worry about it," I say.

Mama nods. "I don't know about you, but those pretty little sandwiches didn't make a dent," she says. "Want to order burgers at the bar?"

"You read my mind."

CHAPTER 24

Delilah

THE NEXT EVENING, MRS. Chopra and I are tucked inside my bungalow, and she flitters around trying to help with dinner preparations, despite my insistence she let me handle it. In the big red pot on the stove, water bubbles, and I stir the sauce beside it. When my timer dings, I slide the homemade meatballs from the oven where they've been baking.

Mrs. Chopra's eyes go wide at the sight of them as she inhales deeply. "Delilah Thomas, who knew you could cook, little bird?" She dips down to pick up Scooby. Doo is long gone up the stairs and under the bed.

I spin around, proudly planting my hands on my hips over my apron. "An underutilized skill, I guess."

Although I have zero Italian heritage, I have always been a fan of their cuisine, and in my early adult years I honed a few recipes I can now execute with ease.

"I figured we might want to porch sit. You know we don't do it too fancy around my house."

I glance at the metal soap prep table that resides in the area where I'd otherwise have a dining table. For a brief moment I wonder if my mother is right, that by now I should have a functional dining room. That the soaps should migrate elsewhere. If Peach Pit keeps on doing its peachy thing, there may come a day when my operation shrinks to a size that could be contained in a large box. I shake the thought from my head.

"Perfect. We should enjoy the weather while we have it." Mrs. Chopra sets down the cat in a sunny patch on the sofa and goes to the kitchen sink to wash her hands.

I set the dishes out family style on the counter and direct Mrs. Chopra to fix her plate first. "My mama would probably skewer me for not serving you, but this way you can take what you want."

Mrs. Chopra looks over with warm brown eyes. "The effort of the food is all that matters. And I'd bet she'd be proud of you for preparing this and inviting over your sad widow neighbor."

We laugh together at the absurdity of Mrs. Chopra being called a "sad widow." In fact, I didn't even know she was a widow until the first time I went over to her house and saw photos of her late husband. Between the Silver Sneakers Zumba classes, gardening, and her subbing work at the school, I'd quickly categorized her as independently happy. Someone whose life was so vibrant that she had no need for a romantic partner.

I refocus on Mrs. Chopra. "Can I offer you something to drink? White wine?"

Her cheeks fold into matching dimples. "Twist my arm."

I pull the chilled wine from the fridge and take down two glasses from the open shelving alongside the stove. We settle at my small table set outside, savoring the food and wine in comfortable quiet as the rest of SweetGum Lane comes and goes. I wait until we're mostly finished to broach the conversation.

"I'm going to ask you something, Mrs. C, and I don't want you to get upset."

"Mm-hmm." Mrs. Chopra lets out the sound like a sassy grandmother.

"I want you to reconsider becoming a Darling."

"You have your own down-line now, Delilah?" She eyes me over her wineglass, now cloudy with condensation.

I raise my brows knowingly. "No, but things have changed—escalated, I guess." I fill her in on the details of Eliza's experience after downing the Peach Pit tea. "The company isn't doing anything about the issues. The Darlings are left holding the buck with a flimsy pep talk script."

Mrs. Chopra leans back in her chair, arms folded. "I'm starting to feel like this dinner was a strings-attached situation." She tosses a playful pout my way. "And now I have no qualms asking you to box me up the leftovers."

I lean over the table and squeeze her shoulder. "They're all yours. So what do you say, are you in?"

She looks up like she's thinking. "I want to help you, and I agree that the company is getting out of control. And you know I adore little Jack . . . but before I say yes, we need to be clear about what I'd be doing."

"Just sign up with your friend and let me look at all the insider information. Let me look at what they send you. Let me sit beside you in all of it. We'll treat it like a science experiment."

I know what I'm doing by comparing it to a science experiment. Mrs. Chopra is still as sharp as she was in the days she ran a lab, and I suspect she misses the work.

Her mouth twitches at the corners as she resists, but finally she collapses into a grin. "You had me at 'science experiment.' Plus, I'm more than a little interested to root around inside this company myself."

"And I'll cover the cost of signing up. I don't want you financially wound up in this."

Mrs. Chopra scoffs. "Keep your money, little bird. I could buy the company ten times over and be fine."

I laugh. Sure, Mrs. Chopra isn't struggling financially, and I bet she can afford the buy-in cost easily, but "buy the company" is 100 percent the exaggeration she loves to slop onto her stories. Like when she told me all about her two-week Indian wedding at which ABBA performed, alongside foreign royalty in attendance. The story of her having tea at Buckingham Palace. I listen, actually enjoy the tall tales, but I don't question her.

There's no harm in letting her spin some stories.

"Thank you. And I'm planning for us to do it without ruffling any feathers, so you won't need to worry about upsetting Linda."

She shrugs. "Doing the right thing sometimes requires feather ruffling. I'm not afraid."

I nod politely, but my insides rear back reflexively. She may not be afraid, but I certainly am. Regardless of what dear Mrs. Chopra believes about ruffling feathers, my life has taught me the complete opposite: Only heartache comes from making a fuss over things. *Keep Quiet and Make Nice* would be an appropriate title for my biography. I'm set on bringing out the truth in a palatable way. We'll keep the kerfuffle at a minimum.

I clear the plates and carry them inside to the sink for later on, then pull out dessert. I warm the cobbler and scoop it into bowls, dropping a blob of vanilla ice cream on each, and then walk them out to the porch.

"Honestly, I think this investigation is perfect, the more I think of it. I've been getting a little bored of late, and it'll keep me young. Oh! And I can plan some parties," Mrs. Chopra says with a slap on her knee.

I shrug. "I'm not sure you need to do *all that*."

"If it's a true experiment, the Darling experience should be fully replicated."

I dig into the dessert, and the sweetness of the baked blueberries mixed with the salty kick of the crumble plus the smooth ice cream is enough to pull me out of the mental exercise. We finish dessert, and while I do the dishes, Mrs. Chopra checks my houseplants. She waters a few stragglers, and then we return to the porch with a final nightcap glass of wine.

Eventually I tell her about my worries, about the fact that I'm no longer making enough from Bubbles & Suds to cover the booth cost at the farmers market, about The Five forming peach-colored fault lines.

"I don't know, maybe I shouldn't have said anything to Betsy at all. Just let it lie. I mean, Eliza is really the one with the right to make a stink."

"You're lifelong friends. Why couldn't you express your concerns?"

"Because Betsy's basically let it become her personality lately. She's so far into it."

"What did she think about Eliza's situation?"

"Of course she was concerned, but she wrote it off. Like Peach Pit was invisibly vindicated."

"Hmm."

"School is going great, though. I think I'm going to bring in cookie decorating next week—though I might live to regret it." I imagine frosting smeared across the classroom as sugar-infused bunnies bop about the room.

"They would love it. You have a gift with them, Delilah."

I nod. "I just really want to grow Bubbles & Suds."

It's been the push and pull that's defined the professional scope of my life for as long as I can remember. The pull to scale Bubbles & Suds versus the utter delight I feel after a day well spent with the Blissful Bunnies. It's impossible for both to exist at the same time, and possibly, maybe even probably, Bubbles & Suds is fated to fade into the background thanks to Peach Pit.

Mrs. Chopra cups her chin thoughtfully. "Do you really?"

"Well, of course! It's been my goal since I started it in high school. I love soaps, and leveling it up is my dream."

She smiles. "I see. And don't worry about The Five—you'll get back on track. The lot of you are like a force of nature when you're together. I know I wouldn't want to take you on, peachy disguise or not!"

"I guess you're right. Maybe it's a no-brainer."

But despite Mrs. Chopra's well-intended comments, not all of me believes it.

There's a part of me that doesn't want to admit that perhaps this version of The Five that I've clung to, the one that began when we were kids who didn't have anyone else relying on us, might no longer be viable. It's easy to be a good friend when one's only job is to go to school. Back then if anyone had a broken heart, an overdue school project, or family woes, all it took to make things better was a pizza-and-movie sleepover. The problems were smaller, more easily remedied, but as life has grown, so have the challenges. Perhaps Virginia Kate's parents' divorce was our collective turning point, our first foray into the real hurts of the world. But since then, careers have grown, and marriage has added husbands then children to the mix. Naturally, priorities shift around on the list, but at what position is The Five reprioritized to something dispensable? I wish I knew the answer. I would do all I could to push it into the safe zone.

This time it's Peach Pit—Betsy and Virginia Kate's work—and I can't help but wonder if we're not strong enough together to come through it. Perhaps I simply haven't grown like they have, too stuck on things of the past.

Honestly, I don't know, so the only option is to try.

The way I love those women is too much to let it go, let it all slide, particularly so when things are shaping up in the manner they are.

Eventually we say our goodbyes, exchange long hugs, and Mrs. Chopra takes the mere steps home to her house. In her absence, I think about her diving into Peach Pit, the information she'll find for me. Excitement trills, but only momentarily, and as it recedes, an ache sits in the middle of my chest that surprises me. Why don't I feel like turning cartwheels down SweetGum Lane at the prospect of a good look inside Peach Pit?

When my phone springs to life with a series of buzzes like a drumbeat, it's as good as an answer to my own question.

Sloane: Any news on the Jasper front?

Virgina Kate: Second vote for Jasper update.

Eliza: third

Rarely am I ever reluctant to jump into the group chat. In fact, it's often the silver lining in my days, the good thing that runs through an otherwise mixed life. But today it feels partially insincere to chatter on like nothing is afoot. I pause for a moment and weigh the options. When I decide that a quick, no-further-questions answer is better than leaving them hanging, I type and click Send.

Delilah: It's new. We're figuring it out. We ask for privacy during this exciting time.

The message has barely landed before Betsy "hearts" it. She types another heart emoji and sends it through for good measure. I speak Betsy, so I know what she means: I love you.

Tears well in my eyes.

She's genuinely happy for me. She genuinely loves me back.

Maybe The Five can endure all of this after all.

CHAPTER 25

Delilah

ON WEDNESDAY I STAY behind after car pool to console Neil's mother.

"I just feel like he should know all of the letters by now. Our pediatrician said he might be verbally delayed."

I reach out and take her upper arm. "Let's slow down. Neil is two. He doesn't need to know all of his letters. That's a kindergarten skill—for five-year-olds."

"He's very quiet, though. Surely there's a connection." She picks at her cuticles rapidly.

Neil is over by the Duplo bin building towers higher and higher until they fall.

"I'm no doctor, but with my years of teaching experience, Neil seems very much on track with everything he should be doing for his age. Sure, he's not a chatterbox like some kids, but that's his personality. He knows lots of words, and he always communicates his needs clearly."

Neil's mother's shoulders drop. "You think?"

"If you're really concerned, you can set up a speech therapy screening. Many companies will do it for a reasonable out-of-pocket fee. But for what it's worth, I'm not concerned about him at all."

She pulls me into a hug. "Thank you. Seriously. This really helps."

"Anytime. Neil is a sweetie, and he's lucky to have a diligent mother like you."

A cheery grin pops onto her face almost mechanically. "Have you ever thought about taking on extra work?"

"Like a different job?" I bat away the dreams of Bubbles & Suds that float through my mind like snapshot images. "Really my students aren't old enough for tutoring or—"

"No, like extra? Have you ever imagined throwing a party for your girlfriends and getting *paid* for it?"

I swallow the nausea that swells inside me, my heart flip-flopping in utter defeat. She can't be. She cannot be trying to sell me on this.

"No, I haven't. That's really just not my thing."

She flashes me a smile and calls her son over. "Alrighty, well, if you ever change your mind, I'd love to tell you about Peach Pit and the wonders it's done in my life."

My eyes creep wider at the words, and I hold my breath until the two of them wave goodbye and turn down the hallway. Then the breath spills out of me, and I'm not sure whether to laugh or cry, so instead, I dip into the storage closet to gather my things and get on my way. *Have I thought about throwing a party for money?* I simply cannot with this nonsense. As I lift my purse, my phone inside begins to ring. I pull it out and answer.

"Hey!" The single syllable bursts with enthusiasm.

"Hey there." Jasper's voice is tinged with slight apprehension. From the background noise he sounds like he's in a store.

"Everything okay?"

"On a scale of one to ten, how crafty do we think we are?" Jasper asks.

I'm already smiling ear to ear. "You do realize you're asking Miss Delilah, famed craft leader of the Blissful Bunnies, right?"

"Fair. Well. I don't know. I was thinking— Since, you know—"

My heart pinches at Jasper fumbling over his words. It's nice to know I'm not the only one who gets flustered when we're together—even if it's just on the phone.

"You planned our last da—our last hangout time."

My heart practically jumps out of my throat. He was about to say it. He almost said it. Oh my goodness, *if only* he had said it. Our *date*. He was about to say *date*. I just know it because what else starts with that sound? Unless he was going for *dinner*. We did have dinner last time.

Jasper's voice pulls me out of my mental gymnastics.

"I was looking on a list of, you know, *activities* that people might want to do together, and I found something that might be alright for tomorrow night."

"I'm all in."

I hear a new relaxation in his voice. "Yeah? Sweet. Okay, I'm going to take the swing on this. Promise not to hold it against me if it flops?"

I pull the classroom door shut behind me and begin walking down the hallway. "I would never. And let's be honest, it's fairly difficult to miss the mark with me on crafts."

"Fair point."

"Oh, and I've been meaning to mention—you have to meet The Five soon."

"I'd love to. I feel like I know them already."

"Same goes the other way too, so I imagine it'll feel like a reunion more than anything. I'll ask them tonight and get some dates."

We hang up, and I continue out of the school and across the parking lot with a fresh lightness in my step. I wasn't exaggerating when I told Jasper crafts are a difficult miss with me. In addition to soap, I have also tried hand lettering, needlepoint, screen printing, and candle making. Not to mention the Cricut machine I use near religiously to personalize classroom items.

I slide into the car, excitement bubbling inside me. I cannot wait to see Jasper. To *craft* with Jasper. I mean, never, *ever* in my honest-to-goodness life would I have imagined a dreamy guy like Jasper planning a crafting date with me. He jets around the world for fun, after all, so there's no doubt he's making quite the effort trying crafts.

I can't believe we've only got another couple weeks together before he leaves.

I don't let myself think about it for too long, and instead I crank up the music on my car stereo.

* * *

I can't remember ever feeling nervous for The Five to gather like I am this evening. Not since we went to see *The Ring* in theaters, and I wasn't able to sleep the night before, imagining that creepy crawling girl. I was terrified through and through, not even one little bit interested in seeing the movie, but I went along because it was The Five. I should've just stayed home from that one, but even now I would probably still go along.

In some ways it's the flip side of my dedication to them, my tendency to lose myself in them.

Everyone except Sloane shows up wearing something comfortable. Eliza is back in her onesie, this time the waistline stretched even farther over her growing bump. I imagine the little girl inside, and I wonder if she'll have Eliza's strawberry-blonde hair. Betsy and Virginia Kate come together, both wearing leggings and oversized tops.

Sloane arrives last in her blazer and Ponte pants. "I was this close to canceling." She holds her fingers so close together they might as well be touching. "Whatever is past running on fumes is what I am."

I pull her under my arm. "I'm glad you're here, and you get a pass on egg stuffing. You look like you're about to fall over."

Sloane feigns an offended scowl, then drops the act. "I'm weak enough to accept without contest."

Across my living room sit several Easter egg stuffing stations I designed to make sure we have a variety of eggs for our little hunters to gather. The Five doesn't always stuff eggs, but because of our proximity to the event—through tradition and our families—we've pitched in more than once. Typically we throw on something streaming on the TV, snack and sip, and chat as we stuff.

"I'm also moving at half speed." Eliza is reclined and moving more at a third or quarter speed.

Betsy sits on the far side of the living room, head down, and stuffing rapidly like she's on some Easter version of *Supermarket Sweep*. She passes completed eggs to Virginia Kate, who shuffles them into color-coded bins as the organizational packet dictates.

"We're making good progress over here!" Betsy's words are bright and upbeat, but her lack of eye contact betrays her discomfort.

She and Virginia Kate greeted Eliza and me quickly when they walked in, then got right down to work. They didn't pause to peruse the snacks or drinks I'd set out. They didn't jockey to call the show we'd watch. Instead, it was as if they were arriving for a volunteer shift where they were determined to optimize their every moment of service for results.

Sloane drops down beside the busy pair. "Y'all have somewhere to be after this, or what? Where's the fire?"

Virginia Kate looks up and squeezes an unusual smile. "Just want to do our part for Delilah's Easter egg debut. Plus, I barely slept last night, so I wouldn't mind an earlier night."

I cross my arms as I consider the response. Had I missed something? Because never in my life, never in the lifetime of The Five, has Virginia Kate been a bad sleeper. Not even a bit. She was the one we had to make sure to physically drag out of her cabin at sleepaway camp so she didn't miss breakfast.

Betsy glances up and nods. "I have some Peach Pit paperwork I forgot about, so I'll need to leave early as well. After I do my part, of course."

As I watch the pair stuff, I'm grateful for their help, but I can't help but notice that Virginia Kate does look worn out. I wouldn't poke fun about it like I would with Sloane because Ginny Kay's always been more sensitive. Hopefully it's nothing a good night's sleep can't fix.

"Anyone need anything? Food? Drink?" I ask.

Eliza signals to her loaded plate, then flashes a thumbs-up, and the rest of them decline. So I grab the remote and click around for a movie that will please the crowd. All the new stuff seems too young for us—we've long outgrown tight dresses and expensive cocktails.

"Everyone okay with an oldie but a goodie?"

I receive only a few grunts of agreement, so I forge on and click play on *Now and Then.*

I settle myself on the rug in front of my ottoman and start stuffing as I wait. Any moment now one of them will realize what movie I put on and shriek in delight. Like couples have songs, The Five has a movie, and it's *Now and Then*. It came out when we were kids and follows a group of friends who stuck together into adulthood. We didn't know if we would turn out the same—certainly in some facets it would be impossible—but we all wanted it enough to christen it our movie.

As the quiet minutes tick by, my eyes dart between the others more frequently. By now they should've noticed. I clear my throat, and Eliza calls over, "Bless you."

Sloane laughs, and Eliza slaps her arm playfully. "Sorry. Brain fog, you know."

I smile at her. Eliza has long bemoaned the real follies of "pregnancy brain" and I have no reason not to believe her.

I get back to my egg stuffing and wait. Surely it's only a matter of time until someone pipes up. The Five is reliable that way. I stuff each small plastic egg with candy, stickers, or one of several small toys we ordered. As I look at the selection set out across my living room, I'm proud of what my mother and I have chosen for this year's hunt. I came into this expecting the worst—knowing I'd be outside of my comfort zone—but at this juncture, I'm glad I did it.

Things aren't magically turned around between Mama and me, but I think it's done us good to team up on this. And for once I'm actually sort of looking forward to Easter brunch. It'll be nice to see our hard work play out as folks enjoy the event.

Virginia Kate hops to her feet and slaps her thighs.

I perk up, excited that she's the one to decode what's playing in the background.

"Alright, ladies, I should go," Virginia Kate says. She crosses the room in a couple of determined strides, plucks her purse from the hooks on the wall, and pulls open the door. "See y'all soon!"

As the door slams behind her, I look around at the others. Each of them is so zoned out that they don't notice the love letter I've set to play on the large screen before them.

Betsy pops up. "I should do the same. Busy, busy, you know."

Before I can blink, she's clear out the door.

Over on the large sofa, both Sloane and Eliza are fast asleep, a plastic egg still tucked in Eliza's dangling left hand.

The tears are hot as they fill my eyes, and I feel instantly foolish for hoping this evening would go the same as it's always gone, even though things are changing. I get to my feet and dry my eyes with a paper towel at the kitchen sink. What was I thinking? Usually putting on the right movie is a quick fix for the tiffs that crop up among us. Usually a forced Five fun night of community service guarantees us eventually devolving into laughter. But something about this, about where The Five sits now, feels different. Whether we call it life getting in the way or a peachy rift, there's no question that it feels heavier.

I drop onto a barstool and swallow the rest of the tears that want nothing but to spill over. Through the large opening into the living room, I can still watch the movie from where I sit. Alone. I let Sloane and Eliza sleep.

I guess there won't be a good moment to ask them to meet Jasper.

CHAPTER 26

Delilah

WHEN I SWING OPEN my front door the next evening, Jasper stands with arms stacked with craft store bags, head turned toward Mrs. Chopra's house, chatting animatedly.

"You know, if I wasn't weighed down, I'd come over and greet you appropriately," he calls toward the house next door, a wide smile on his face. "I've heard nothing but the best."

"Oh, no worries, young thing. The two of you enjoy your evening. Don't mind me!" Mrs. Chopra's voice calls in reply.

I lean out and wave as she shuffles inside her house.

Jasper turns to me and a lazy smile settles on his face. "Finally, the main event. All day I couldn't wait to see you. Not that meeting Mrs. C isn't a lovely opening act."

I feel the pinch in my cheeks as the corners of my mouth lift into a smile, my face warming at his words. "Come on." I wave him inside, and he heads straight for the soap-making table, where he drops the bags.

"Wish I had a better place for them," I say.

Jasper looks over the table, and when something outside the window catches his eye, he pushes up onto his tiptoes to look. "You've got a shed out there?"

I nod. "It basically sits empty. Not even a mower in there since I pay one of the high schoolers from down the street to mow."

"Hmm. Mind if I use it?"

I pull my brows together, confused. "Uh. I mean, no, but—"

"Beer making. I know I don't have a ton of time left, but I could do a quick brew. It's one thing I miss out on with my lifestyle. Promise I'll leave your shed in even better shape than I found it."

I partially deflate at the mention of his inevitable departure but brush it off. "Sure. Why not. Now"—I prop my hands on my hips—"how about these craft supplies?"

Jasper's gaze goes back to the bags and his cheeks redden. "I may have entirely missed the mark on this, but"—he unloads a few bound books, fancy patterned paper, scissors, some fun pens—"I had an idea."

"Scrapbooking?"

He reaches back and pulls a shoebox from one of the bags. Not a fancy one designed for storage, but an actual box that once housed a pair of tennis shoes. It's beaten up and aged. He holds it in front of him and pops the top.

"Take a look."

I step closer, the shoebox holding the only space between us.

I look down, and his box is packed with stacks of postcards and envelopes with the tops ripped open, all bound into bundles by rubber bands. Some look newer; some are yellowed with age. Some look on the verge of falling apart, and some look practically brand-new. All of them have been written, stamped, and sent.

By me.

"You kept them all," I say.

"Didn't matter where I was, I always tucked your postcards away. I kept them until I got back to wherever home base was and slipped them into the shoebox. Lately, they lived in a storage unit close to the Atlanta airport."

My chest squeezes in joy. I hold up a finger before him. "One second."

I half skip, half run up the stairs and into my bedroom. On the top shelf in my closet, I have my own box—a fancy craft store one with a bright, funky print. Back downstairs, I open the box in front of Jasper.

"You did the same?" he whispers, surprise in his voice.

"Of course I did."

"Thank goodness. Otherwise we'd be scrapbooking only my postcards, and, I don't know, that feels a little weird."

A laugh bursts from me.

"Come on, let's start."

As Jasper pulls out various sheets of paper, he explains why he picked each one, what he envisioned for them, and continues to say everything is "just an option." My insides are practically glowing at his thoughtfulness in every step of putting together this activity for us. The only thing I don't understand is how he ever could've considered the possibility of me not keeping all of his postcards. In fact, I figured he had no choice but to trash the ones I sent him as he hopped from location to location.

Minutes later, we are spread across my living room floor between stacks of paper, cellophane wrap, and specialty scissors.

"I'm going to be honest," he says. "Mine looks like absolute garbage, so you better be nice when I show the final product."

"I'm sure it's better than you think."

"I bet your bunnies have done better."

"You know you didn't have to do this . . . *activity* . . . for me, right?"

Jasper looks directly into my eyes through his thick glasses' frames. "Anything for you. Not to mention, that's how things work—give and take."

The corners of my mouth twitch, and I go back to trimming a border for my title page. "You should come teach a life lessons seminar to my class. Bring the crafts, and they might never let you leave."

"I might just let them keep me." Jasper yelps as the scissors nick him.

A red droplet of blood forms on the side of his finger, and I hop to my feet, head to the kitchen, and dig in the cabinet for my rudimentary first aid kit. I pluck a Band-Aid from the pack, carry it back to our crafting station, and kneel beside him as I unwrap the thin paper packaging.

"Surely you don't mean it. About giving up your jet-setting. You're practically Mr. Carmen Sandiego." I unpeel the paper tabs, wrap the Band-Aid over his wound, then glance up, grinning.

He's not smiling, and he delivers no comeback. I keep hold of his hand, keenly aware of the warmth radiating from his palm into mine, and I can't help but wonder if I accidentally hit a nerve.

"The way you left the last assignment . . . It must've been difficult. Is it still bothering you?"

Jasper pulls in a deep breath. "I've never rushed off an assignment like that before. My boss made the call, but I didn't argue. It's sort of put some things in perspective, made me think about the job as a whole."

I squeeze his hand. "I'm always here if you want to talk about it."

"Part of me wonders if I'm just getting too old for it, but I also can't see a way to leave it behind."

I have to admit that part of me hurts, hearing confirmation that it's simply not in his nature to stay put. I have dreamed of Jasper deciding he's ready to be done and settle somewhere—preferably Pearl—but I'm also not naive. The travel bug is intrinsically part of him.

"Maybe this break could be a reset?"

Scooby jumps onto Jasper's lap, our hands break apart, and the papers he'd arranged on a page of his book slide around. Jasper runs his hand down her back.

"Maybe. That and this sweet kitty of yours. Plus, I have to win over Doo before I go or I'll be leaving without bragging rights."

"He's a tough nut to crack."

Jasper grins at me. "I'm up for the challenge. I landed a couple of the freelance jobs I went out for, so I'm tethered here for a bit."

"Amazing. You're practically a local already."

He laughs. "A symptom of my work, knowing how to make fast friends. How're the *actual* locals—The Five?"

I wrinkle my nose, settle back into my scrapbooking, and deliver the update. I tell him about yesterday's egg stuffing, how strange it was, everyone out of sorts, Peach Pit and Eliza's reaction lingering in the air like a bad smell they were all determined to ignore.

"Have you thought about sharing this? I meant it when I said local publications would be interested, and honestly the public deserves to know if there are issues. You—*we*—could write the article." His eyes linger on me with curiosity.

"Not really. I'm not sure it's my style, but Mrs. Chopra agreed to sign up to be a Darling."

Jasper begins cutting a strip of paper. "If you change your mind, an article would go over like hotcakes with the local editor. Peach Pit is massive around here, and an insider look would definitely get clicks."

"Thanks." I have been thinking about it, but I can't get past how it might impact the already struggling Five. "It'd be a last resort."

Even if some in Pearl weren't yet familiar with Jasper's name when they read it in the byline, the people in my circle would know I was involved—The Five, other friends, my family. I would be taking a public stand.

"I was thinking I could help with the farmers market on Saturday. Be your roadie," Jasper says.

It pulls me out of my thoughts. "Yes! Please!"

I couldn't imagine a more fun moment than having him see Bubbles & Suds in action, considering that he's been hearing about it since its inception. Even if Peach Pit has taken its toll, my little soap business is still alive and kicking. As are my dreams for it to one day blossom even further.

"Bright and early?"

"It's my Saturday routine."

Jasper looks pleased when he turns back to his crafting. Eventually my stomach rumbles and we order food to be delivered—barbecue from a local spot. When it arrives we break to eat, then head back to the floor to our projects. By the end of the evening, we both have a decent start on our respective pen-pal scrapbooks, and we get to our feet and dust off the small scraps of paper stuck to our clothing.

When Jasper holds up his work to show it off, I can't help but giggle a little at the lopsidedness and the hacked off edges.

"It's a great effort! Especially for your first time."

"Sounds exactly like something you'd say to your students."

Before I can speak a rebuttal, he pulls me into his arms and my thoughts turn to soup. The softness of his shirt presses against me, and I breathe him in. He smells the same as last time, and I mentally catalog it as his signature scent. I don't want the embrace to end, but he pulls back.

"I should go."

I grab his scrapbook from the back of the sofa where it rests. "Don't forget your masterpiece."

He smiles to himself as he heads for the door, and I follow. He opens it, then stops on the threshold and turns back to me.

"It's the postcards that make it. Your words, your stories, your company even when I was continents away. That was the real masterpiece."

He waves, then pulls the door shut gently behind him.

I might be standing still in the wake of him, but every fiber of me thrums like I'm being supercharged. I'm not sure I'll sleep tonight. Unless perhaps I convince myself I might see him again in my dreams.

Heavens above, Jasper Rowley is sending me for quite the loop.

CHAPTER 27

Delilah

THE MORNING SUN WARMS my back where I stand at the edge of the playground, my usual post guarding the only gate in and out so no bunny escapes the fold. Amber stands over by the small climbing wall on the side of the jungle gym, reminding our students to look where they're putting their feet and soothing the occasional tears. Jack and Huddie are pushing around a pair of jumbo dump trucks, adding sound effects as mulch kicks up behind them. Earlier the children enjoyed making a spring lamb craft with cotton balls, a new project I can call a great success—well, aside from the moment Cici tried to take a bite of hers.

Three days have passed since Mrs. Chopra agreed to pledge allegiance to Peach Pit over pasta and blueberry cobbler, and yesterday she was officially signed up on the team of her friend over at the fifty-plus community. To be frank, I couldn't imagine many Darlings letting a single hour elapse between stated interest and a signature on the dotted line, but it seems the senior factions of Darlings may very well operate at a more relaxed pace. Though perhaps not entirely so, because my phone tucked in my back pocket has been buzzing incessantly as Mrs. Chopra updates me in real time as her inbox is flooded with onboarding emails.

Did you know I'm a Boss Babe Business owner?

They sent me 8 emails in the last 3 hours! It's a full-time job reading them.

I have to pick a starter kit. Cheapest is $699. Most expensive $1,299!!

Shoot, they just sent another email to send in my next month's order, and I don't even have a kit yet.

Behind me the door from the school to the playground clicks and swings open, and I tuck the phone back into my pocket. I glance over my shoulder, and Donna from the office is marching in my direction as she smiles at the children happily playing, waving as she teeters on wedge sandals below her cropped teal pants and cardigan set.

"You're so good at this, Delilah," she says, still taking in the playful crew. "I don't know what we'd do without you."

"Thank you. I love my days with them." It strikes me how true this statement is. With everything going on with my friends, school is a reprieve. A place I'm skilled and appreciated.

Donna stops and leans on the waist-high iron fence instead of moving down the path. "I wanted to check in with you."

My mind goes straight to worrying that I messed something up. "Sure thing."

"I know you and Virginia Kate are friends, and I'm sure it's nothing, it's just—" Donna cups her chin. "The boys haven't been in this whole week, and it's not like them."

"Really?"

Donna pulls herself back upright and steps closer. "And there hasn't been illness in the threes class. Mrs. Roberts called, texted, and emailed, and there's been no response from Virginia Kate."

"*Really*?" A tightness floods my chest, pushing my breath out. "That's unusual."

"Exactly. It's not like them to take off or disappear. They have great attendance, and she always notifies the school when they're out sick. She's one of the few who brings a doctor's note. I guess I'm a bit worried. Has she said anything to you about it?"

My body stills and a coldness blooms in my middle. I just saw her two days ago, and she didn't mention anything. Virginia Kate, just like the others, bemoans childhood illnesses, the wrenches that are forever thrown into the schedule, so keeping the boys out of school for a full week is something she would typically mention. My conscience gets in the way of the words I try to say.

"I— Well— Um, not really."

I wouldn't know how to start to explain how and why things have changed between us, not monumentally but slightly then increasingly over time. Like Peach Pit is a tiny wedge in a small gap that seems to be swelling in real time, forcing the space wider. What if I'm no longer one of the people Virginia Kate would come to? What if she's closer to Darling friends than me? The night when her parents told her they were getting divorced replays in my mind, the way I loaded up my bag with anything I thought might help, the lot of us spilling out of Eliza's mother's van and running to her.

I'm not sure a Leo DiCaprio *Tiger Beat* would do the trick this time.

I swallow the lump that throbs at the top of my throat.

"I'll talk to her. I'm sure it's nothing, but thanks for the heads-up."

Donna nods and reaches for a walkie-talkie in her cardigan pocket that crackles with garbled voices. "Let me know if there's anything we can help with."

As she walks on down the path, my mind churns. This has to be about the money. Surely this is about them being behind on tuition. I wish it wasn't, but I know Virginia Kate, and as Donna said, she's not the type to pull her kids from school for a spontaneous trip. And even if she were, she would let the school know, respond to the teacher's messages in the rare case she forgot to mention it.

Virginia Kate is the most organized of us, with her rotating meal plans, color-coded calendar, and well-balanced weekend schedules. She's the furthest thing from this.

I shoot a quick text to Virginia Kate but don't expect a response. If I'm about to show up on her doorstep unplanned, as I very well intend to, I have to try to contact her first. I'll call during my break, leave a voicemail. If she ignores me, I'll stop by her place later.

After we line up the bunnies and I lead them back inside the classroom, I mentally prepare to see Betsy for early pickup. To my surprise it's Jared who comes for Huddie. After lunch and nap time, I clean the classroom and set up supplies for the next day. All throughout, my phone buzzes, and every time my heart leaps in anticipation that Virginia Kate has replied. Mostly it's Mrs. Chopra, her texts stoking questions and intrigue, but she and I already have plans to meet later to go over the Darling emails.

> They've sent me an infographic about the "science" and I can tell you it's horse manure.
>
> Oooh you'll love this one about how to find sales opportunities. LOL.
>
> Gird your loins for this evening.

When the last student has been picked up and ferried home, I grab my bag and head for the door. Virginia Kate has not replied, despite my many attempts to reach her, so to her home I shall go.

* * *

Less than a half hour later, I stroll down the brick path that leads to Virginia Kate's ranch-style house. The TV plays through the large picture window, a children's cartoon series I know is a favorite of the boys. It's practically proof of life for the two littles. I make it to the solid mid-century door and knock, internally cursing the architect for not going with large glass panes that might allow me some snooping. When no answer comes at the door, I knock again.

Someone is home with a television left on.

I'd be lying if I said there wasn't part of me wondering if the whole family had been swiped by some kidnapper, mid-TV watching, but those are the outlandish places our minds go when our loved ones are out of touch.

I dial Virginia Kate's phone and listen for that familiar grating buzz of a phone vibrating on a hard surface inside. If I hear it, I'll grant myself permission to call out some version of *"I know you're in there! Open up!"* I step down from the door and cross in front of the picture window. With the lighting I can't see far inside, and what I can see looks like any normal day at their house. Probably I should be comforted by this, but I'm not in the slightest.

If it were a normal day, Virginia Kate would text back.

I return to the car, crank it, and sit in the driver's seat trying to work out what comes next. Usually I'd text The Five group chat, but this feels like a conversation I need to have directly with the others—Sloane, Eliza . . . and to my chagrin, Betsy. Starting a side chat feels catty, even if it's done out of concern for Virginia Kate. I put the car in gear and dial Sloane's number, and when she picks up, traffic noise and voices surround her.

"Where are you?" I say by way of greeting.

"Twenty-four-hour trip to Chicago. A deposition gone wrong. Don't make me go on."

"Something's going on with Virginia Kate."

"What?" She must duck into somewhere, because the noise behind her quiets.

"I don't have all the info." I fill Sloane in on the school situation, the concern.

"Maybe she just decided to say 'screw it' and go live a little."

"The only issue with that is that it's far easier to live it up without kids in tow. Why wouldn't she drop the boys off at school?"

Sloane sighs, the noise resuming around her. "Don't ask *me*. I don't have kids."

"I just left her house. The TV is on, but it's like no one's home."

"My dad used to leave the TV on for the dog. Cooking shows."

I stop at a red light, then make the turn toward SweetGum Lane. "It just felt . . . *off*. Wrong in some way."

"Have you called the others?"

"Eliza's basically on baby watch, and I don't want to put her into early labor, especially with everything that just happened with the tea. Which leaves Betsy."

"Suck it up and call her. I know y'all are weird right now, but this is about Ginny Kay, so you need to get over yourselves."

I squeeze my nose into a furrowed mess but only because I'm too afraid to roll my eyes at her even when she's hundreds of miles away.

"I'm about to walk into a meeting," Sloane says. "Call Betsy. Between the two of you, there's very little y'all can't figure out. Smooches!"

Sloane hangs up before I have the chance to argue, and it's probably for the best.

She's right that I need to call Betsy.

I pull in a deep breath, pull up Betsy on my phone, and dial. The line rings but only a few times before it goes to voicemail. A text comes through while the voicemail message is still playing.

Betsy: In the parent meeting for Rex's big game tomorrow. Little League World Series. Call you back?

Delilah: Sounds good, and good luck to Rex!

I make a point to keep my phone at my side so I don't miss her call as I head to Mrs. Chopra's house. I take her recommendation and gird my loins.

Whatever that means.

CHAPTER 28

Betsy

BETSY HAD JUST ENOUGH time after the baseball parents' meeting for a quick shower before shifting into Peach Pit mode. In her formal living room, she sets out cut-glass tumblers, a pitcher of Peach Pit Palmers—a blend of lemonade and Peach Pit Tea—and a platter of fruit and cookies. She hopes her regular Friday afternoon Darling roundup with her team of incredible women will finally help shake the slimy feeling that stuck after visiting the Queen Peach a few days ago. Ever since, she's struggled to pull in a full breath.

The women arrive mostly on time in sundresses or jeans with blousy tops, hair and makeup done. Everyone squeezes in on the formal velvet sofa, a few armchairs, plus a handful of high-back dining room chairs she asked Jared to drag in earlier.

"Hey, ladies! Welcome. I hope everyone got themselves a little snack. I'd love to welcome our latest addition, Miss Eliza, but she wasn't able to make it today because she's about to pop!"

The ladies giggle politely. No doubt most of them have referred to themselves as such so late into a pregnancy. So it's cute, not mean.

Before Betsy digs into the routine meeting bullet points, her clammy palms remind her to first address the thing that's been following her around like a persistent gnat all week.

"I'm so grateful for y'all." Her breath hitches when she pulls it in.

"And there's something I wanted to mention before we get too far in. It's come to my attention that there have been folks having bad reactions to some of the products. Now"—her tone tightens—"we hope this is just certain folks not being a good fit for the product, people whose biology doesn't love the peach pit like we do! But I want to keep a log of any and all complaints y'all get. Please come to me with any issues. No one is going to be in trouble."

Around the circle, several sets of shoulders release, and a sigh or two escape.

Rosie McKean raises her hand. "I'm glad you mentioned it, because Cara from Pilates blew up like a blowfish after using the lip gloss. I refunded her—of course—and I hoped Peach Pit would reimburse me too."

Chantel, in the seat beside her, speaks. "The same happened to my friend Leah. I let her use some lotion before Mommy and Me class at the library, but she had to rush home when her forearms broke out in hives. They were burning so badly she had to call her husband for a ride."

Betsy gulps hard, mentally willing herself to look composed. She never expected this response. Maybe she's been imagining that the reactions were nothing more than isolated events, but the revelations only add to the swirling uneasiness inside her.

"The body spray makes one of my best friends sneeze like crazy, eyes running tears like it's just a spray of pollen or something," Lorna says.

Samantha nods. "Same for my mama, except she gets a rash of red bumps where it hits the skin too."

Virginia Kate looks rigid as she raises her hand, and Betsy notices how gray and sagging she looks, like she's carrying the weight of the world. "All good on my end."

"You feeling okay, honey?" Betsy asks her friend. "You look . . . tired."

Mikka, the Darling sitting beside Ginny Kay, pats her back tenderly, and Virginia Kate almost jumps through the roof.

"Sorry!" Mikka says, drawing a bashful hand to her mouth. She turns back to the group. "But if I can add, I had the Peach Pit Tea two days ago and got so sick I had to call out of work. I thought I had a stomach bug until my girlfriend who came over to watch a movie the night before had the same thing."

At the mention of the tea, Betsy's mind goes to Eliza, and her gaze meets Virginia Kate's. Betsy hasn't had a chance to fill her in on her jaunt to the hospital. In fact, she sort of decided that she wouldn't mention it unless pressed, after the way Delilah took it. But now concerns are mounting over the Peach Pit Tea—the very same ones Ted made clear after Eliza's incident.

The air feels thin as Betsy breathes in, and she leans on a nearby chair. She realizes the impossibility of her position, trapped between her allegiance to The Five, that to her Darling sisters, and her dependence on Peach Pit as the thing she's built herself upon.

"Hmm." Betsy knows what she needs to say, but the words sit like lead pebbles in her middle. It feels like betraying herself to admit it, but she forces the words out. "Our friend Eliza, our new Darling, also had a bad reaction to the tea. So"—she didn't plan this part—"let's table the tea for now. Y'all don't drink those Arnold Palmers. Set it aside, and I'm going to try to get it sent back to corporate and the funds recouped."

Mikka nods. "I appreciate it, Bets, because I bought a whole case. I was going to dress it up like a wedding favor and sell it to the brides that come into my mama's dress shop."

"Of course."

Betsy rolls through the rest of the meeting agenda in a daze similar to the one Virginia Kate appears to be in. She performs robotically, congratulating the women on sales, cheering in excitement over potential new recruits, and signing off with an encouraging sales story about how Peach Pit saved a woman's life. Today for the first time Betsy wonders how much fiction is blended into fact. If any fact at all exists.

Behind her cheery eyes her mind rumbles, turning over how she can possibly hold on to what she has gained here in Peach Pit but also make things right. Betsy's almost certain she'll be on her own to cover the cost of the tea she's promised to take from her team. The no-return policy is strict and in place to "prevent bailing out poor saleswomen"—the exact wording in the *Top Darling Training Manual.*

Betsy's heart picks up just like it hammered that day as she carried the manual to her car. She hasn't checked on it recently where it lives in her Lilly Pulitzer storage box on the top shelf of the closet. But it'll be there. Weeks after the training, when it was business as usual, she'd wished she could put it back, feeling disloyal, but now she's grateful to her former self.

Not knowing if she'd ever need it, she gave herself a trapdoor.

When the meeting ends, Betsy says goodbye to all the Darlings, and her energy levels are so low they're blinking. But something in the way Virginia Kate looks makes Betsy stop her before she leaves.

Betsy sets her hand on her friend's smooth, tanned arm. "Honey, you okay? You look like you saw a ghost. And not a friendly Casper."

Virginia Kate's mouth quivers as she meets Betsy's gaze, but she drops her head almost instantly, shaking it. "I'm fine. Really. Just tired."

Betsy furrows her brow, leaning in. "I'm not convinced. What is it?"

Virginia Kate takes a fast, deep breath as she pulls herself upright. "I'm just having a hard time with it all."

Betsy presses a hand to her chest, closing her eyes with each deep nod of her head. "Oh girl, I *get* it. I've got the kids, my own small business, and a household to run and keep clean. Jared does some, but let's be honest, it's more work to make him the checklist than just do it my dang self."

Virginia Kate's mouth pulls up at the corners, and even though it doesn't reach her eyes, Betsy knows Ginny Kay is harnessing a can-do attitude. It's part of what makes her such a good Darling: She keeps her head down and makes the sales.

"Alright. Well, considering how much we both have to do, I'm going to head home." Virginia Kate pushes open the storm door and walks down the porch steps to her car.

Betsy waves before closing the door. Her shoulders drop as she turns and strides purposefully toward her bedroom. She wants out of this dress that's still a little tight since Hattie's birth, but first, she needs to check on that *Top Darling Training Manual* to make sure it's right where she left it.

CHAPTER 29

Delilah

I'M SQUEEZED IN BESIDE Mrs. Chopra at her glass-top dining table, watching as she scrolls through her email inbox on her laptop. In the kitchen she has dinner simmering on the stove, an earthy blend of tomatoes and turmeric wafting over to where we sit. My stomach rumbles, and at the sound, she looks up and winks.

"The emails can wait," she says.

I shake my head. "I've been wondering about these all day."

"There are already ten, and I was only officially on board last night." Mrs. Chopra points to the screen. "Here are a few intro and welcome emails, some with company stories that are . . . eye-opening."

"How?"

"What they're saying about the scientific process of creating these products, it doesn't make much sense. It's one thing to create a line of cute, fruity lotions and call them fun lotion, but it's a whole other thing to make the claims they do—about anti-aging and revitalizing human flesh, about creating energy out of thin air. I'll need to check some reliable sources, but I'm actually under the impression that some pretty nasty chemicals can come from the pits of these fruits."

"The allergic reactions!"

She shrugs. "Maybe yes, maybe no, but I'm betting the claims they're making are bogus at best, dangerous at worst."

"How do you find out? What's the plan?"

Mrs. Chopra takes off her reading glasses in a slow, deliberate manner, then casts a loving look my way. "Child, you must slow down. We need to take this one step at a time, gather information methodically. Not to mention, there's dinner to be had." Mrs. Chopra gets to her feet and heads for the kitchen.

"A few more minutes?" I crow like a small child.

In all honesty I don't remember the last time I felt so genuinely curious about something. Peach Pit is an interloper in The Five at this point, and I'm in a frenzy to find out its true intentions. My suspicion is that it's up to no good, but I'm trying to be nice and give it the benefit of the doubt. Even if that sentiment is shrinking by the moment.

Mrs. Chopra turns back. "Under two conditions: You pause in about fifteen minutes and set the table, and second, you don't look at any of my online shopping. That's my battle to fight privately."

"Yes, ma'am."

I start with the first email, skimming the welcome and all the sections about boss babeing. I stop when I reach the "Tips on Getting Started" section.

> Sometimes the hardest part is just getting started—it's true of so much of life! But you, boss babe, are up for the challenge. Below we've sourced some tips from our TOP earners as to how to get your gorgeous business off the ground.
>
> 1. Start with your best girl pals! Who would you invite to your engagement party? Baby shower? Those are your people.
>
> 2. Start simple. A picnic in the park, a BBQ on your deck, a coffee and donuts morning for the moms after school drop-off. It doesn't have to be a gala-level production, but

remember: Details matter! Treat your guests to something good to eat or drink, a little catering order from a local restaurant, one small business to another!

3. Look the part. What better way to make a sale than by someone asking, "How on earth do you keep your skin so glowing?" Similarly, get dressed up and do your hair. Darlings who care go further.

4. Don't be afraid to invest. We know—the start-up phase can be tough. The starter kit includes all of our basics and products you can absolutely sell, but do you want to be the go-to IT girl for beauty and glam on the block? Consider upgrading with a simple purchase of our luxe package. Remember: If you're not invested, how can you expect someone else to be?

I navigate to the next email and lean in, speed-reading. The hair on my arms stands on end.

Grow your own team!

Do you love Peach Pit products? Do you love a good Peach Party? Imagine doubling the fun by inviting your friends to join in sharing these life-changing products with the world. Women are weary. Their glow is stolen by pregnancy and the withering effects of aging, but Peach Pit is here to help. Our products not only pluck women from the perils of sagging skin and irritable moods, but we also offer a new financial opportunity. Joining Peach Pit as a Darling business owner will change the trajectory of their lives! Providing a flexible work schedule, unlimited opportunity for earning, as well as the lifetime friendship of fellow Darlings, Peach Pit is the answer to so many of the modern-day issues plaguing women.

TIPS:

- Approach friends who could use some extra cash. Do you know a stay-at-home mom who would love to earn money for an upgrade to her car? Or some cash for a fresh new wardrobe? She might just be your girl.

- Peach Pit is as much about life-changing products as it is about creating sisterhood among Darlings. Consider extending the invite to someone who is lonely or isolated. What better way to gain a boost of confidence than by striking out on a business adventure with new friends?

- Sell it, girls. Tell them how much fun we have, how well the products work, the dream we're living. Leave the boring numbers talk about financial commitment and ordering requirements for later. As we always say: A good attitude and a can-do spirit is all you need to sell a mountain of Peach Pit. The product does the rest.

"This is absolutely unhinged," I say into the computer screen, realizing only when my breath almost gathers on the screen that my nose is close to touching.

Mrs. Chopra sets her hand on my shoulder and pulls me back. "Rapt as I was, little bird, but let's take a breath."

I drop back into the seat. "It's unreal."

"Mm-hmm," she sings from deep in her chest. "I particularly loved the section of tips on how to prey on the weak."

I grip my temples. "It's terrible, but"—I pop upright—"we can use this. This is exactly the sort of thing we could put in an article."

I sit, and it's as if the information percolates inside me, as I imagine what moving forward with an article would mean. My insides lurch, a nausea creeping in as I consider the blowback. I am not the type of person who does this. I am the furthest thing from bold or brave enough to expose something. I stew in all of the worst-case scenarios, and I'm almost convinced that the article is a terrible plan when I consider the alternative.

Peach Pit continues to weather The Five. Other women get sick. Betsy or Virginia Kate get sick. Our friendships fizzle under the strain of not only Peach Pit but the other forces of life we are already pushing back on: work schedules, children, illness, relatives, the mundane work of fulfilling basic needs. Even here and now it's not easy to keep The Five together. We make sacrifices in order to see one another as much as we do. We take time to text and reply. It's work, but it's also love in action. It's showing up for someone because you care too much to let them fade into the background.

Maybe love—the sort I have for The Five—is also being willing to get uncomfortable with myself for once. To realize that I have a voice for a reason, and that maybe this time it's my turn to step up.

I've almost lost my appetite when Mrs. Chopra sets a gentle palm on my shoulder. "You okay? You look like you're suffocating in a room full of free air."

I open my mouth, and breath fills my chest like a brand-new sensation. "This could get ugly before it gets better."

Mrs. Chopra pauses and tilts her head to the side. "You're probably right."

I glance up. Her honesty is the heartbeat of our relationship, the way she mirrors the truth of my life back to me, a rare gift. More than once I have wondered if I'd be a different person had I not moved into the lavender bungalow next door to her.

"Do you think I can do it? Show some truth about Peach Pit without destroying my friendships?"

"If you can't respectfully tell the truth to a friend without things being ruined, I'm not sure you had a friendship to start with."

I drop my gaze and nod. She's right. I have to trust the strength of The Five. If we were to look back over its history, there are plenty of examples of disagreements and arguments that didn't unseat the group. It's just that this will be my first time being in the center of it.

She pats me gently on the upper back. "You have time for one more email—take it or leave it. Then we eat."

"Take it," I say and turn back to the computer. The next is titled "The Magic Behind the Products."

> Dearest Darlings,
>
> Welcome to the Pit! Now that you're on board, we're delighted to share with you the science behind our dazzling products. Shhh! Don't tell a soul lest we risk our trade secrets being stolen. (Please see NDA attached and required of all Darlings PRIOR to starter kits being shipped.)

"Mrs. C, did you sign the NDA?"

She pokes her head through the doorway to the kitchen. "What's this about the NRA?"

"No. NDA. Nondisclosure agreement."

"What now?" She crosses the room, an apron attached to her front and a wooden serving spoon in hand.

"It says your kit won't ship unless you sign an agreement to not disclose stuff . . . I don't know what it says." I click the PDF open and am met by a fifty-page document in small, single-space type. "Shoot."

Mrs. Chopra points her spoon at the screen. "I'm not signing anything."

"I could ask Sloane to look at it."

"For how much?"

"Pshh. She'd do it for free." I pinch the bridge of my nose. "I think you're right. I need to eat before I try to dig through any more of this, but thus far I guess we know why you don't have your stuff yet."

"They must know I'm a spy!" She chuckles to herself as she makes her way back to the kitchen.

I stand, sighing at the madness of this organization, and begin clearing the table of the computer and other stray items. I pass into the kitchen where Mrs. Chopra hands off the silverware and napkins wordlessly. She joins me at the table with water glasses and a pitcher, and I follow her back into the kitchen where she releases the spout on a beeping rice cooker. Before long, we're digging into hearty bowls of rice with chicken and vegetable curry.

"So tell me, how are things with Betsy, the rest of The Five? . . . Jasper?" She scoops a fresh bite of food into her mouth.

I skip over the mention of Jasper. Everything between us is so precious yet delicate that speaking about it aloud feels like running the risk of it evaporating right before me.

"Betsy is . . . *Betsy*. And I'm me."

That sums it up: We're two separate things connected by an aging string of memories, of friendship—of what I hope is love. It started back when we were kids when she ended up becoming exactly the young woman my parents wished I was. With her own parents relatively absent, Betsy was more than happy to bask in the compliments of Mr. and Mrs. Thomas.

She never meant to hurt my feelings, but she did. It was—still is—such sensitive territory for me.

From there we grew into two very different women. Betsy is put together, beautiful by all exacting Pearl standards, and ambitious. I'm happy blending in, taking care of others, and finding meaning in my work. Probably Peach Pit is meaningful to Betsy too, but I can't rationalize her looking past the red flags that continue to mount.

"Have you spoken to her?"

"She owes me a call back."

It reminds me to check my phone, and when I glance at the screen, no notifications wait.

"You're both headstrong women. You won't always agree."

"It's not that simple when it comes to the Peach Pit stuff. This company is predatory. I mean, the NDA only backs up my claim. How could Betsy not see this? I love her, but I just want to shake her until she wakes up. The Betsy I know would have a problem with these things too."

"What if she sees something else?"

"You'd have to be closing your eyes as you walk through the motions of it not to see this."

Mrs. Chopra shrugs, and I take it—finally—as some admission that I have a point.

"I'll call her again in the morning. She's probably caught up with baseball parent stuff."

"Friends as old as you I'm sure can find a way through."

We finish eating quickly, the conversation running out as we both silently enjoy our dinner. Mrs. Chopra serves coconut cookies for dessert, and I'm yawning before the sun is even completely down.

"How about I forward you the emails and send you on your way with the leftovers?"

I gladly accept, and when she appears from the kitchen with Tupperware, she pulls me into a hug that soaks all the way through. I savor it, the warmth of her arms around me.

When we part and I head home, it's as if she's left part of her hope with me.

Between everyone, maybe we can figure this out.

CHAPTER 30

Delilah

I PAD DOWNSTAIRS EARLY the next morning when I hear a knocking on my front door. Jasper waits on my porch, his hair still damp from the shower, to-go coffee and a paper bag in hand. He smiles through the glass panes in the door.

I rub the sleep from my eyes, my chest warming.

As I unclick the locks, the morning light filters into the front of my little house. It's my favorite way to see it, houseplants illuminated, the cracks and scratches on the floor highlighted, the dust that hangs in the air a sign that I'm busy living.

"I almost texted, but I didn't want to wake you." Jasper hands off a cup like it's payment for entry, and I step aside.

"I'm never one to turn down breakfast on my doorstep. Or you on my doorstep for that matter."

My cheeks flush briefly at the surprising boldness in my words.

I guide us through the living room to the kitchen, and I slide onto a barstool as Jasper unloads the tinfoil-wrapped palm-sized packages. The savory aroma of bacon hits me.

He slides in beside me, and I dig in. The tortilla of the breakfast taco is soft and fluffy, and I don't even try to hold back the groan that escapes me as I take a big bite.

I cover my mouth. "So good."

Jasper nods. "A guy at the paper told me they were voted best breakfast in Pearl. I got to chatting with the guy at the counter this morning and apparently it caused quite the stir."

I squint, my eyes still blurry from sleep. "Why the stir? Also, how are you basically already a local? I've lived here my entire life, and you fit in better than I do."

"Per Elijah—the guy at the counter—the diner used to hold the honor year over year, but once Big Mike retired and sold it off, it wasn't ever the same. What can I say? I'm a good journalist. I know how to make friends and find the story."

"You'll be even better than I imagined at the farmers market booth."

Scooby rubs up against the sides of my barstool purring, lured by the promise of feeding time. Jasper reaches down and pulls her into his lap.

"You might just get a bite of bacon if your cat mom is okay with it," Jasper says to Scooby.

"A tiny one, but—"

I stop mid-sentence at the sight of Doo standing in the middle of my kitchen, the morning sun casting his rotundness into shadow behind him.

Jasper gasps. "Does he know the word *bacon*?"

My mouth hangs slightly agape. "He won't even come out for The Five. Barely for me."

Jasper shrugs, plucks a small bit of bacon from inside his tortilla, and breaks it in half. He feeds one to Scooby, then stands and slips her onto his barstool. Slowly, in measured tiptoe steps, he approaches Doo, bacon out. Jasper lowers himself and drops the offering.

Doo scoots up, keeping his wary eyes trained on Jasper, snags the bite, then turns and hauls rear up the stairs.

Jasper bows. "Some of my finest handiwork."

I shake my head. "I cannot make it make sense. Story of my life, I guess."

Jasper reaches out and grazes my forearm with his fingers, running them slowly along the length. "So tell me all about last night. Did Mrs. C get anything good? Are we writing an article?"

By now and with all the text updates I've been giving him, Jasper seems quite invested in exploring Peach Pit's behind-the-scenes conduct.

I lean in close. "Oh, buckle up. I only got three emails in and had to stop." I recount the information I uncovered, the dubious "tips," the NDA as the grand finale.

His eyes grow wider and wider behind his dark rectangular glasses' frames, and my heart races when I catch the sparkle in them. *He gets it.* Like sitting alongside Jasper is what it feels like to be understood for who I truly am.

He lets out a playful mocking scream when I note that the beauty supplies won't be released until the NDA is complete. "You were right. This is unethical. And downright weird, to be frank."

I nod forcefully. "I mean, how am I only now hearing about an NDA? I have three friends in it, selling products, so they must've signed it."

Jasper swallows a gulp of coffee. "Maybe they're embarrassed. I mean, I wouldn't expect an NDA from this sort of company. But then again, maybe it's what makes consultants feel like they're part of something bigger than themselves. Like a selective club where only the people who promise not to spill the secrets get to join."

I've known all along this was a component of it; it's just not until right now that I'm seeing how well they create the sensation.

"I have to call Betsy again today." It comes out like an admission.

"Okaay?" Jasper stretches the second syllable so it sounds like a question.

"I'm worried about Ginny Kay. She's not sending the kids to school and wouldn't answer the door when I went over."

Jasper's brows shoot sky-high.

"I know. Anyway, we need to team up and figure out what's going on."

"I hope it's nothing major." Jasper squeezes my hand.

My heart hitches. "Me too."

I eat the rest of my breakfast quietly, and Jasper does the same. I wonder momentarily if he's letting me have room for my thoughts. It's a new frontier of the in-person side of our relationship, but the ease between us makes it feel like it's been this way all along.

Eventually Jasper nods to the metal prep table of soap supplies where I've stacked the boxes and bags for the farmers market. "Is that all we need to bring?"

I nod. "They provide the rest."

As he starts loading smaller items into bigger boxes in preparation for hauling them out, his face cracks into a grin.

"What?" I ask, feeling immediately self-conscious.

"Remember when you drew me an illustration of your dream soap shop on a postcard? It was sweet."

"Oh, I remember. I went through so many versions before I found the right design." I laugh through a wave of embarrassment.

"You weren't afraid to play big back then."

That younger, unweathered version of me seems light-years away now that lagging sales are center stage and the peachy monster is on the horizon.

"I'm not sure it's ever been further out of reach."

"We'll see about that. First things first, you need a shower before the market. In the meantime, I'll get to loading."

I pad upstairs and start the shower to warm the water. It takes forever in this old house. And in the meantime, I dial Betsy. When she picks up, she's surrounded by outside noises, voices, shouts, possibly the crack of a bat.

"Hey." Her voice is lacking its usual pep. "What's up?"

I launch carefully into an explanation of the Virginia Kate

school situation plus my visit. "I'm pretty sure she was there when I stopped by last night."

"Oh, that? No, we had a Darling meeting at my place. She's alive and . . . well?" Betsy pulls in a quick breath. "Well, I don't know. Maybe we should just check in. I agree that the boys not coming to school is super strange."

My shoulders drop, the pressure that's been wrapping my head for the last few days finally releasing. "Oh thank goodness. Sloane flew back in last night, and I'm sure she'd come, too, this afternoon."

"We're up in Blue Ridge for baseball World Series. The final." She pauses. "And tomorrow's Easter . . ."

Every year Pearl assembles at the country club outfitted in offensively bright pastels, screaming prints, hats so wide they're a collision hazard, and not a one of us is spared. Not even me. Photographs are taken, babies scream, and eventually the little boys yank off the long socks their mamas pry them into. Deviled eggs, bunny cake, and alcohol are consumed like the very best of football tailgates, and one might even hear the occasional mention of Jesus rising from the dead.

"I don't think we can bank on her showing up for brunch, with how things've been looking, Bets."

Betsy sighs. "Well, I guess if I'm honest, she didn't look great last night. I asked her, but she explained it away—at least to satisfy me in that moment—saying she was stressed with responsibilities piling up. Hunter is constantly working, so I think she's solo *a lot*."

I want to tell Betsy about the missed tuition payments, but I know I can't. I shouldn't even know myself, and it would be more of a betrayal to Virginia Kate than a help in getting her right side up.

"I'm going to keep calling her," I say, but even as I hear the words come out of my mouth, I know she's not going to tell me anything over the phone.

"It's a nice gesture, Lilah, but she ain't going to crack unless the lot of us show up as one. The Five is a force unlike any one of us alone."

It's a truth I already knew in my heart. "I'll get everyone on board for tomorrow?"

"I don't think we have any other choice, and we owe it to our girl. Plus, we can't let this mark our first Easter apart, can we?"

The smile that folds into my face pulls so hard it promises to be permanent. The feeling is the same thrill that shot through my chest when The Five cheered me on as elementary-school me swung on the rope slung up on a tree by the lake. Pride that felt like helium balloons tied onto me, lifting me up and up, as the vision of their pumping fists blurred when I hit the water.

We may not always see eye to eye, but there is nothing quite like the feeling of having Betsy McCleary on your side—even if it's just for a moment in time.

The brightness sticks with me for the rest of the day. By the time I get showered and dressed, Jasper already has his truck loaded, and we drive to the farmers market together. Since it's the Saturday before Easter, the crowds are lighter, but I don't complain. It allows for more moments for Jasper and me to bow our heads together, chat, and laugh. He points out all the delightful features of the market—the collection of senior men who bring their dogs, stopping to create an unofficial "dog club"; the Girl Scouts who rush up to any young girl who passes them to deliver an invitation to join their group; the handmade treasures on display from local artists. Considering that he's seen many of the most interesting corners of the world, I'm surprised by how taken he seems with Pearl.

When Roxie arrives, she and Jasper hit it off, chatting about soap making, travel, and Pearl in general.

When a customer approaches the tent, it's as if a switch flips inside Jasper, and he becomes the consummate salesman, rushing to assist with selection and payment. Charming the customers' socks off. When the crowd grows noticeably thin in the hour leading up to market close, he slips away and buys burgers for us from the food truck at the end of the road.

In all senses, it's the perfect day. In every way, it is a practice run of precisely the life I wish for most. I savor it, and I savor him. Because the bliss of today won't last.

It can't be a forever thing.

CHAPTER 31

Delilah

THE FOUR OF US women must look like a pastel mafia as we case Virginia Kate's house on Easter morning. It wasn't ideal to come dressed in our Sunday best, but we all agreed it would be too tight of a turnaround to go all the way home, change, get made up, and make it over to the club on time for the egg hunt before brunch.

Thanks to her double-wide white straw hat, Betsy can barely make it within a foot of the window she's peering into.

I slide in behind her, eyeing the clutch tucked under her arm. "That could've stayed in the car."

"Didn't your mama tell you to never leave your bag in the car?"

"And when was the last time you heard about a smash-and-grab in Pearl?"

Sloane is dressed in a white pantsuit with a silk necktie scarf. Her jewelry is gold and thick, glinting in the early light as she marches up to the door in a terrifyingly high pair of heels.

Eliza borrowed a floral print maxi dress in pastels for the occasion, but the fabric stretches so tight over her belly that the flowers warp, resembling something psychedelic. Her makeup is done as usual, but even at a distance she looks uncomfortable beneath it, like everything is an effort slightly too much.

Eliza stands the farthest back from the house, her hands planted on her lower back. "Stop!" she whisper-yells to Sloane.

Sloane whirls around.

"It's Easter morning, let's not go in like a SWAT team," Eliza says.

"And how would you recommend we proceed?" Sloane crosses her arms, a playfully challenging look on her face.

Eliza pulls her phone out of a pocket somewhere in the folds of her stretchy dress. "I'm just going to text her and tell her we're here so she can come out without making a scene in front of Hunter."

Out of all of us, she, the one with oodles of hormones coursing through her veins as her body works overtime to put the finishing touches on tiny toes, tiny major organs, an *actual* brain, is the one to keep a level head.

Betsy gasps from in front of the window, ducks, and backpedals away. "She's coming!"

I suppress a giggle. "Betsy, she knows we're here. That's why she's coming out."

She halts in her tracks, then slowly tugs at the hem of her fuchsia shift dress. "Fair."

Virginia Kate comes to the door and cracks it open, appearing in the sliver of space, wearing her robe. "What the heck are y'all doing here?"

Betsy clears her throat. "We're here to check on you. I know you told me you were just 'stressed' on Friday night, but even then you didn't look right. Then Delilah said the boys haven't been to school all week, and you're avoiding her. We know something's up."

"It's Easter," Virginia Kate says through the crack. "You shouldn't be here."

"Take it as a sign of how worried we are," I say.

Sloane, closest to the door, meets her gaze. "It wouldn't be Easter if you're not part of it."

I close the last few steps and slide in beside Sloane. "Will you come out? Or let us in?"

Virginia Kate's eyes fill with tears as she tightly shakes her head.

Eliza is at my side, leaning in. "Honey, there ain't a thing that could be happening that would scare us off. Remember when Betsy had the raccoon in the house years ago?"

The Raccoon Affair of 2019 was a major event on the timeline of The Five. Jared was out of town, and a raccoon found its way into Betsy's house. When she came down for breakfast with the kids, the thing had raided the pantry and torn up the whole place, scattering some unbearable smells about. The rest of us suited up in whatever we could scrounge—hazmat suits, scuba gear, a forgotten baseball helmet. Sloane even brought her daddy's shotgun, which I made her leave in the car.

"Or when Sloane got that awful spray tan and we had to execute full body makeup for senior prom?" Betsy adds, crossing the grass to join us.

"It was one of the first spray tan machines. In hindsight I'm not sure why I'd want to be the guinea pig, but at least it makes for a good story."

Virginia Kate drops her head and lets go of the door. It swings open, and inside the kids are tearing through their Easter baskets, paper grass flying left and right all over the carpet. Each of them has smudges of chocolate on their faces as a cartoon blares on TV in the background.

We file into the house, the boys greeting us with squeals about the Easter bunny, and Virginia Kate trying to hide her tears. She stops in the middle of the living room, surrounded by strewn Easter grass, candy wrappers, and the odd pair of striped kids' pajamas.

"Hunter is gone," she says.

Eliza springs into action behind me, calling the boys to follow her as she guides them to the playroom in the back of the house with promises of a movie and a five-dollar bill for anyone who sits quietly and watches.

The four of us hover beside the couches arranged in a right angle, and after a pause I step forward. "What happened?"

Virginia Kate drops onto the sofa, a sob flooding out. "It was my fault. I lied, and we're in trouble."

Betsy comes to Virginia Kate's side, pats a hand on her back, then Sloane follows and perches on the arm of the sofa. I crouch in front of her.

"Tell us everything. We're here for you."

"Y'all know Hunter's pay can be sporadic, but things were starting to dry up about six months ago. We decided it was time for me to go back to work. I mean, I used to be a corporate hotshot—I should've been able to scoop up something without issue, but . . . the licensing issues were a headache and so time-consuming. I was so connected in Charlotte, and then when I came back here, I lost all my business contacts. Here, I'm dragging around my family's scandalous history, so when Betsy told me about Peach Pit, it felt like exactly the thing we needed: some extra income while I could still be there for the kids. No need to hire a nanny or anything."

Betsy shuffles in her seat, her face growing pinched, and Eliza rejoins us, taking a seat on the catty-corner couch.

Virginia Kate sucks in a shaky breath. "So I signed up for Peach Pit and got started. I sold some stuff, but"—she glances over at the door to the basement—"I just couldn't keep up. I had to order a minimum each month, and it didn't sell. Even friends who liked the lotions or the lip gloss simply weren't going through it that fast. I tried to find new customers, but most of them already had a seller—or were already sick and tired of being pitched to buy products off their friends. I—" She pinches her brow, bowing her head. "I couldn't bring myself to tell Hunter that not only was I not making money but I was *losing* money. So I lied. I told him things were going well, all the while running up a balance on our credit card—both for the cost of the Peach Pit products and also the expenses my supposed income would've covered."

Betsy's face has drained of all color and life, and she appears frozen.

Virginia Kate turns to her. "I don't blame you, Bets, only myself."

Betsy opens her mouth, but not a word comes out.

Virginia Kate looks back to the front and continues. "Hunter found my stash of unsold product in the basement and from there it all unraveled. Our finances are wrecked. We can't afford to pay for the kids' school, and I don't have the audacity to keep bringing them when I know we're already behind." She looks right at me. "I'm sorry we sent them as long as we did without paying."

Hurt explodes inside my chest. "That was never it, Ginny Kay. We were worried about the boys, all of you, not chasing you down for payment."

It's not the moment to say it, but there is a long history of families at Pearl Prep falling on hard times, missing payments, and every time it's figured out. Pearl may be well-groomed flower beds, freshly painted fences, and high-tech street crossing flags, but not everyone can keep up. To this day, I'm convinced a great number of residents are over-leveraged and driving around in most of their wealth.

"Hunter is livid. He left almost a week ago now to stay with a friend." Fresh tears well as Virginia Kate admits this. "Our marriage might be over, and it's all my fault."

"You made some mistakes, but you were set up to fail," I say.

"The Pearl market for Peach Pit is saturated," Sloane adds. "It's an economic truth you cannot bootstrap your way out of."

Virginia Kate shakes her head. "It's only excuses that keep a Darling from being successful; with enough effort and enough creativity I should've been able to sell all of this. I let myself down—and my family in the process. All I needed was a better attitude."

I shoot Betsy a desperate look, one that begs her to *say something*. Again, she opens her mouth, and I implore the universe to give her words, but despite my hopes, she closes it, then opens it again, beginning to resemble the animatronic fish that were once popular to mount on a wall.

"It's a lie," I tell Virginia Kate. "All of those things are lies. But you're too deep into it to see it right now. Believe me, this is an impossible task. It's like setting up a lemonade stand at the North Pole and being told that if you just believe and try hard enough, you can will customers into existence."

Virginia Kate nods tentatively. "But Hunter . . . I don't know what will happen, don't know if he'll be able to forgive me."

Eliza moves to stand behind me. "Honey, this is fixable between y'all, I just know it. Is he coming home today—for Easter?"

Virginia Kate must be stressed about Easter brunch at the club. It's $150 for adults and $50 per child for the all-you-can-eat buffet, including one lobster per person and bottomless mimosas. Even for me, on a preschool teacher's salary, it's quite the stretch. Every year I debate accepting the offer to put it on the Thomas tab—their annual generosity extended—but every time I inevitably decline.

"I've got y'all's brunch on my tab," Sloane mentions. "No arguments."

Virginia Kate meets her gaze sheepishly, pulling a grateful smile.

"Can I call him?" Eliza asks. "Ask him to at least come to Easter?"

Virginia Kate squints. "I'm not sure I even have outfits for the boys—"

"I can help with that!" Betsy says—*finally*. "I have a whole closet of Rex's dressy outfits I'm saving for when the stuff will fit Huddie. I won't have a matching set for the two, but I definitely have something good. A smocked Jon Jon or some sort of spring theme jumper."

"I don't—" Virginia Kate starts.

"We're the same size, and I have a closet full of the chic stuff none of y'all mamas can afford with the way you have to constantly replace kids' clothes." Sloane smiles. "It'd be fun for me to share."

"I know no one wants my fashion, but I'm here to tag team getting the boys dressed," I say. "Wrangling them back into pants after a diaper change is Blissful Bunnies 101."

Virginia Kate gulps before she lets out a tight breath. "Okay. Might as well try. But Eliza, I want to hop on the call after you get him hooked. I have to be part of putting me and him back together."

The rest of us spring into action as Betsy jogs out the door, car tires squealing. Eliza and Virginia Kate head to the deck to make the call, and Sloane takes off—more leisurely—toward her place.

I stay with the boys, but before we're even through a few rounds of hide-and-seek, Betsy bursts back in, best Easter options in hand. She helps wipe the boys' faces with plush washcloths, hands them off to me to dress, then together we manage to hold them still enough to dampen their hair and run a comb through it.

"Oh, shoot. I forgot about shoes," Betsy says.

"It's no biggie. They've got to have something."

I dig through their coat closet and find some slip-on shoes that will do. They aren't the fanciest that Pearl tots will wear for the occasion, but they're clean enough to pass. As they slide on the chubby feet of both boys, it's a complete Cinderella moment.

Eliza and Virginia Kate pass through the slider from the deck, looking hopeful enough, just as Sloane pops through the front door.

"He agreed to come," Virginia Kate says.

"I'm right on time then," Sloane says, carrying a few dresses on hangers. "Let's go to your room and you can pick."

Within the hour, the lot of us roll up to the Pearl Country Club looking well-dressed with our shoulders back and heads held high. We might not have solved every part of the big problem at Virginia Kate's feet, but we've come to her rescue for today. We won't miss an Easter together yet.

It's the perfect reminder of what happens when The Five come together: We save the day.

CHAPTER 32

Betsy

AT EASTER BRUNCH, BETSY sits at the large circular table, squeezed between Huddie in a booster seat on one side and Hattie in a high chair on the other, marooned from the other adults now deep in conversation. Rex sits beside Hattie and occasionally slips chunks of food before her. Jared chats with Betsy's father, and her mother is deep in conversation with Jared's mother.

The ballroom is a bright pastel rainbow of Pearlites rumbling in conversation. The buffet is refreshed near constantly, and the children wiggle in their seats. The egg hunt went off without a hitch—thanks to Delilah and Mrs. Thomas—and the little ones delighted over a new array of trinkets and candies hidden inside. But now they're ready to move again. Betsy spots dessert being carried in and knows it'll be mere moments until at least one chocolate-covered tot streaks through the banquet hall.

Delilah and her mother must've been pleased with the way the egg hunt went. Betsy's eyes find Delilah sitting across the room, talking closely with her niece, Roxie. The rest of the Thomas crew are most concerned with themselves, unable to see the gem of a daughter they have in Delilah. Even Delilah's mama has the foot of Pearl's expectations so squarely on her throat that she can't fully appreciate the baby of her family. Betsy just hates the way Delilah still tries with them and—probably forevermore—still seeks their approval.

Betsy's gaze lands next on Darcy, and a switch flips inside, a flame that heats her.

Darcy sits there throwing back mimosas *again* as if Darlings—like Virginia Kate—aren't struggling.

Betsy feels sicker the longer she thinks about it, shoving away her gold-edged plate that still holds a half lobster as she sips from her champagne flute. How can Peach Pit feel so good to her when it causes harm to others? It feels like being caught in competing tides that leave Betsy confused and exhausted. She blinks back tears, remembering Virginia Kate looking so broken. How could she not have noticed? Even if she did sense something off about Ginny Kay, she didn't push hard enough to get to the bottom of it. Why didn't she push for the truth?

The answer hits her like a cartoonish weight thrown onto her from a cliff: She didn't want the truth. Not when it comes to Peach Pit.

Of course she didn't.

Because if Peach Pit, the very place she's found her new lease on life, is all smoke and mirrors, what does that say about her? Without Peach Pit, Betsy is nothing. She'd disappear on the breeze like morning fog.

"Bets, you okay?" her mother asks.

Betsy looks up from where she stares into the tablecloth, startled from her thoughts. At that moment Huddie shovels mashed potatoes onto his fork and accidentally launches them into the air as his utensil becomes a food seesaw. The potatoes hit the side of Betsy's face, warmth covering her as they slide off and pile in her lap.

"Jared's mama was just saying she's thinking about buying her own Peach Pit starter kit, and I said you were the one to talk to about that." Her mother turns back to her mother-in-law, apparently unaware of the mashed potato explosion.

Betsy shoves her chair back as she hurries to her feet, mashed potatoes stuck in her blowout. She doesn't utter a word and only turns and makes a beeline for the women's bathroom. The tears start before she makes it inside, her tall heels teetering precariously below her just like the life she's built herself upon. If she falls, so be it. Probably she should take her turn to hurt.

Inside the bathroom, sweet Mrs. Rothburn from the church stands washing her hands. She looks up from the sink as Betsy lets out a pained sob.

The woman pulls her cardigan tight over her wide middle as she meets her with a worried frown. "Oh, child, let me help you." She snatches a paper towel from the dispenser and dabs gently at the mashed potatoes in Betsy's hair. "I know how you girls love getting dolled up for the day. I'll fix you right up."

Mrs. Rothburn wears the same outfit today as she usually does when she runs children's choir on Wednesday nights. She has always reminded Betsy of Delilah.

Betsy's eyes burn and a fresh deluge runs down her face.

"Oh, honey, I've got you. I just got gum out of my granddaughter's hair last week and we didn't even need the scissors. This is a cakewalk."

Mrs. Rothburn finishes dabbing the food from Betsy's hair, wipes a few stray potato smears from her dress, and finishes by fluffing her hair ever so slightly.

"I don't deserve this. I don't deserve your kindness."

Mrs. Rothburn turns Betsy to the mirror. "Sure you do, honey. You're not shower fresh, but not a one of them out there would know the difference." She pats Betsy on the back and heads out.

As she pushes out the door, Mrs. Rothburn says, "Excuse me" to someone on her way out and holds the door for the next person. When Betsy looks up, in the mirror she sees Delilah standing behind her.

Betsy's face is lined with streaks of mascara, and Delilah, basic makeup still intact, sets a hand on Betsy's shoulder and squeezes.

"I saw you get up. Are you alright?"

Betsy pulls in a quick breath and speaks without thinking. "I didn't have any idea Virginia Kate was struggling like this, that she had boxes of overstock. I don't hear about what people actually sell—not unless they tell me."

Delilah's face turns serious, her words heartfelt. "So why didn't you say something in her living room? At least that it wasn't her fault."

"Well. It's— I do believe—" Betsy pauses as her brain rushes to grasp at justifications. It's like her wiring makes it impossible to break out of the Peach Pit mantras.

"What? What do you believe?" Delilah's words are gentle, her eyes wide and sincere. Painfully hopeful.

Betsy pulls back and stands upright, a couple inches taller than Delilah today in her heels. "I believe it didn't have to be a mess this big if Virginia Kate had just been honest. I'm sorry that this is the situation, but this isn't Peach Pit's fault."

Betsy knows as soon as she's said it that it was a mistake, but nevertheless, she also doesn't have the wherewithal to backtrack, to apologize, to take blame.

If she admits Peach Pit is a sham, then it means she's one too.

Delilah deflates, and when she lifts her chin, her eyes burn with fury. "That's the best you've got? We're friends for decades and you can't pick Virginia Kate over Peach Pit? Not even in private? It's a crying shame, Betsy."

"I mean— What I'm— I tried talking to Darcy, I tried to report the issues with—"

"Wait—*Darcy*?"

Betsy's insides jolt to alertness as she realizes her misstep. "It's nothing. Really, nothing. I meant—"

"No." Delilah steps closer. "Darcy is part of Peach Pit?"

Betsy closes her eyes and gulps. She has no choice but to admit it, and perhaps, if nothing else, it'll bring some relief. "She recruited me. At first I figured you knew, that surely she'd mentioned it to you somewhere between the conversations she and I had. But it wasn't until after I signed up that she said we'd need to keep it a secret."

Delilah's face turns beet red, and Betsy can't tell if she's angry or ashamed or possibly a blend of both. She shakes her head as if she's trying to find a place where this information can live.

Betsy reaches out for her friend. "Once my team grew, I barely thought of her. Until recently with the issues. It was as if she didn't exist."

Delilah's eyes grow misty. "Virginia Kate is in financial trouble—marital trouble too. Eliza ended up in the hospital. And you've been keeping this from me this entire time."

Betsy throws out both hands to grip Delilah. "I know. I'm sorry. *Please*, it's Easter. Let's keep our wits about us."

Delilah meets her gaze, and there's a heated flicker in her eyes that Betsy hasn't seen before. Not from easygoing Delilah.

Betsy's chest patters, and she pulls her friend closer. "Seriously. *Please*, Delilah. I'm sorry, okay? I don't want to ruin today."

"I barely recognize you anymore." Delilah stares back unblinking.

With that she slips around Betsy and out the door. It feels like the blood drains out of Betsy as she watches her go, like losing her friend in real time, watching her recede as she inevitably will from her life entirely.

Betsy pushes out of the bathroom door and tails Delilah, knowing she has only herself to blame for this.

"Delilah!" she calls. "I'm sorry."

But she's already gone, bound for the ballroom.

CHAPTER 33

Delilah

IT'S AS IF MOTHER Nature has turned her winds behind me and carried me all the way through the Easter celebrations and back to the table where my terrible sister sits. I could've picked her out blindfolded, knowing the exact fake laugh she lets out of her mouth filled with blindingly white teeth and lined in a Barbie-pink lip gloss. I count my lucky stars when I see Roxie over by the soda fountain chatting with some girls her age, deep in conversation and looking away.

No one notices me coming, the purpose in my strides, or maybe I'm too focused to clock it.

I drop into the seat beside Darcy. "Hey."

Her eyes narrow as she drags her head to face me. "Ugh. What?" An arm crosses over her middle as her head cocks to the side.

"You're part of Peach Pit. You didn't tell me. You recruited Betsy." I hate the way my voice wavers when I want it to sound assured. I hate how tender my heart feels behind words that sound so weak. I hate how much of a rookie I am at confronting her.

She shrugs. "It's not a big deal. Who cares?"

The familiar feeling of being an outsider, a member of this family who is simply incapable of belonging in the place I was born into covers me, and my insides sink. *I* care. It's a big deal *to me.* Because Darcy—and most likely my parents—intentionally kept this from me. It hasn't been mentioned once at a family dinner or gathering, and I haven't been absent from any event I've been invited to. The only conclusion I can reasonably draw is that they agreed to hide this from me, to keep me out of it.

"Why would you tell Betsy to keep this a secret if it's 'not a big deal'?"

Darcy sighs. "Because of this annoying moment happening right now. Not to mention, all your friends would've eventually joined anyway. I just got to Betsy first—girls like her are built for it."

"You're avoiding the question. This 'moment' wouldn't be happening if there weren't all these secrets being kept against me."

A loud, mocking laugh spills out of her. "*Against* you? Come on. Literally none of this—nothing about my life—is about you."

"You told Betsy to keep it from me. You intentionally hid this." My voice is strained but low, and the rising tension inside me pushes against my good manners. Like my body is determined to explode from the hurt of it but my mind knows I have no right to tell any of these women what to do.

Darcy looks up at me, her face slack in boredom. "Can we not? The same old 'Delilah's jealous of Betsy' because she and I are more alike than you and any other Thomas. It's boring. And you're going to make us *that family at Easter* everyone talks about for the next week."

"Oh yeah?" I raise my voice, and my insides buzz at pretending to be far more courageous than I am. "I don't really mind being the talk of the town."

Darcy's groan sounds like a roar. "You are so self-righteous, Delilah! No one cares about you and your weird life."

At that my mother is on her feet, her cheeks flushed as she tugs us from our seats toward the closest exit. "Delilah, what on earth's gotten into you?"

I'm so weary, aching to my bones, with the pretending and the glossy surfaces of this town. I'm tired of the generational denial of the fact that being human also includes ugly parts. That disagreements are part of relationships. That life, any life, includes real suffering as well. Maybe if I'd been allowed to disagree all along, we wouldn't be here now, dipping a toe into making a scene at Easter brunch.

Mama pulls us out into the hallway and then ushers us through a set of French doors onto a small patio.

"I've never noticed this space before," I say.

"Most people probably haven't, Delilah, because most people aren't psychopaths who start arguments with their family at Easter brunch," Darcy spits back.

Mama stands off to the side like a referee, her eyes darting between us as she chews her lip worriedly.

"So what's your deal in this whole thing? How close to the top are you?"

Darcy rolls her eyes, crossing her arms over her chest as she pops out a hip. "I'm, like, the top girl."

I look to Mama. "You knew about this too?"

Mama pulls her arms around herself, hugging herself as she appears to shrink, despite the bright pinks and blues of the seashell design on her dress. I can only bear to glance at her quickly because it's a reminder of how and when she lets me down, predictably, like clockwork. It doesn't matter how many times we do something together, like the Easter egg hunt—which went off swimmingly, mind you, only an hour ago—because when the going gets tough, Trudie Thomas won't be on my side. Time and time again, she assumes the comfortable position: cowering to the wills of the loudest Thomases.

"I'm not going to apologize," Darcy says.

"I never expected you would," I say. "But why are you lying? Never once before have you cared to protect my feelings or even put an ounce of effort toward keeping the peace."

Mama stares intently at the ground.

"I guess there's nothing to lose at this point, not now that you've ruined the day and we're guaranteed to be the gossip of the week." Darcy pulls in a breath, and her eyes briefly flutter nervously. "I was there from the start."

"What do you mean? *How?*"

"I'm 'the creative.'" She looks upward like she's barely resisting an eye roll. "I come up with the ideas and pitch them. The investors loved the concept, so we ran with it. Then when it was time to hire salespeople, I decided to head up the group and sprinkle my own take on it. You know, using all the tricks I learned along the pageant-to-sorority circuit. We all know I'm not the type to sit at a desk and crunch numbers all day."

"There is no way you came up with Peach Pit."

It's then the memory returns to me, of how Darcy joined in on the soap making when The Five and I were in middle school. She threw in glitter and even sold it at a local craft fair. Not that it bothered me at the time—it felt good that my way older sister thought what I was doing was cool enough to copy. My sister who usually paid little attention to me. It was a fun thing to share.

Or so I thought.

When I look at Darcy again, it's as if she's watching me come to the realization in real time. "You stole my ideas."

Darcy sighs. "I mean sort of, but also not at all. Just look at Peach Pit—it's nothing like your rinky-dink soap operation. It's modern, chic, and glam. I saw how your 'natural, organic' shtick worked, so I copied it. So what? There's barely any other resemblance."

The air leaves my guts in a swift swoop, but I stand firm and silent.

Darcy knew what my soaps meant to me. Well, if she was ever paying attention, she would've known. And *that* of all things, she's taken from me. She had the pageants, the adoration, the popularity, the all-access pass to belong with the Thomases, and she couldn't let me have a little homemade soap deal. Even that was too much.

"You are so cruel," I say.

Darcy's icy veneer finally shifts, and she looks upon me with withering pity. "You just make it so easy."

CHAPTER 34

Delilah

I'M RUSHING OUT OF the country club in a daze when I bump into someone on my way through the bar.

"Hey!"

I look up, and there stands Jasper looking dapper in a seersucker suit with a pastel-pink tie.

"What are you doing here?" The words sound like I'm not convinced he isn't an apparition.

"You've told me all the tales of Easters at the lauded club, so I had to see it for myself. Plus, with the Virginia Kate rescue mission and everything else going on, I figured you might need me for moral support. Or to tag in. Or for a 'Please, oh please, let's get the heck out of here'?" Jasper loosens the tie at his neck.

Usually I would melt into giggles and rosy cheeks at the prospect of unexpected time with Jasper, but there is nothing usual about today. I take him by the wrist and tug him behind me, and together we press on through the crowd. Once we're out of the main entrance, past the valet parking stand, and into the parking lot, I finally pull in a breath that makes it all the way into my lungs.

"I'm sorry. I should've invited you myself. Then again, I wouldn't wish the Thomases on anyone." I let go of his wrist and click the remote to unlock my car, then slide in.

Jasper climbs into the passenger seat. "The egg hunt went south?"

"That part was great. It was everything after. *Darcy*." I gulp hard, my eyes stinging at the threat of tears.

Jasper's eyes pop wide enough to fill the glass in his frames.

"I shouldn't be surprised. It all tracks. But *still*, every time with them I hope for the best."

I hit play on my favorite early 2000s music mix, roll down the windows, and hit the gas.

"Want to talk about it?" Jasper asks over the noise.

I squeeze my face into a grimace.

"First stop, Milkshake Barn then," he says.

"It's Easter. It'll be closed."

Jasper shakes his head and grins mischievously. "Rick at the gym said he always opens on Easter so he has an excuse to get out of brunch." He taps his temple. "I made note."

All I can manage is an incredulous look. Jasper is friends with Rick? He has a *gym membership*? Really and truly he's making himself quite comfortable for someone who barely has two weeks left on the clock.

I click on my turn signal, knowing exactly where I'm going. The Milkshake Barn was a weekly stop for The Five years ago. Sometimes more than once a week back when we didn't need three to five business days to recover from the dairy overload of a milkshake. I can't think too long about it, not after Betsy today.

Never before have I wanted to throttle her like I do right now. What she's done—what she refuses to fix—is too much.

I cannot lose The Five, but I also will not make nice with Betsy in this moment, not when she refuses to admit she messed up even a little. Not when she falls back into Peach Pit sales language instead of rushing to the aid of her friends. Her *true* friends.

"You're thinking, Lilah. I can as good as see your brain whirling from over here," Jasper says.

I sigh, then launch into the briefest overview of everything that's transpired. I speak as factually as I can so I won't be reduced to a puddle of tears, but still my voice wavers with hurt.

"And it's all worse because Peach Pit is essentially what I wanted for Bubbles & Suds."

"Darcy took something that wasn't hers."

"I keep replaying how excited I was when she asked me to show her soap making all those years ago. Of course, she wouldn't have been planning it at the time. But my memories of it: I thought she liked the projects. I thought she finally liked *me*. And now, years later, when I'm clearly still pursuing it myself, she steals it." A rushing breath escapes me as I pause. "Mama knew. She kept it from me too—while we've been running around organizing the egg hunt like we're a happy family."

"I hate how they treat you."

"Darcy didn't even steal it right."

"Peach Pit is not the same as your dreams. It's rotten on the inside."

I pull into the Milkshake Barn parking lot and whip into a spot. As soon as I shift the gear to Park, I drop my hands in my lap and sigh.

"The worst part is that every time there's a Thomas family issue, there's part of me that hopes it'll go differently. That *this time*, one of them will care enough to consider what I'm saying. My feelings. I don't even expect a full turnaround, not even an apology, but a basic 'I get it.' *Any* acknowledgment."

"*I* get it." Jasper takes my free hand and squeezes gently.

"I know you do. But *Betsy*." The adrenaline that's carried me thus far deflates as a deep heaviness covers me. "Darcy recruited her, and long story short, she's kept the secret the whole time—over a year. She basically lied to me."

Jasper rears back.

"I— It's—" The tears I've held at bay up until this point fill my eyes and run down my face. "Truly that hurts the most. *She*, I thought I could trust. The Five have always been the family I didn't have. Now Betsy's gone and crossed enemy lines, and where does that leave me?"

"Did she help Darcy steal the idea?"

I shake my head. "She came in later, but she should've known. She should've told me."

It would be awful to say it out loud, and I'm not convinced I completely believe it, but in this moment what I want to say is what I feel screaming inside me: I would've traded the lot of the Thomases for Betsy if pushed. I would do anything to keep The Five. And Betsy's choice to be loyal to Peach Pit throws it all into question. Does she actually care about me like she once did? Or have she and her priorities changed? Because all of this is so out of character for my friend of a lifetime.

Alas, perhaps lying to the people we love is easier than admitting certain truths.

"Did she seem sorry? Betsy, that is."

I nod. "Yes. Very. In fact, back there is the first time I've seen her truly upset about this whole thing. She usually has that glossy front perfected."

"Maybe that counts for something."

"Maybe." I sigh. "I can't help but wonder if this is somehow my fault too. Maybe if I'd just kept quiet and not said anything, everything would still be okay. The Five wouldn't have problems. I'd still be in good standing in my family."

Jasper takes my hand. "Delilah, you didn't cause this. If you hadn't said anything, Virginia Kate would still be in hot water, and she'd be there without help. If you hadn't said anything to Darcy, she'd continue to feel free to go around and take advantage of people."

"There's already so much fallout."

"Don't let it scare you out of being brave."

In the depths of his brown eyes, I catch a warmth that makes me believe that perhaps things won't always be this rocky. One side of my mouth ticks up.

"I can't promise to take away all the hurts of the world, but one thing I can: The world always looks better on a full stomach." Jasper takes out his phone. "Rick said I can just text him with the order. Let's get you fed."

"You have his number? Besties already."

"Gym buddy for sure."

Jasper texts our order, and ten minutes later, Rick arrives at the car window with chocolate shakes and fries.

"Thanks for hooking us up," I tell him.

"Sure thing," he says. "This place is my safe haven from that fancy brunch."

He waves and heads back to the restaurant.

I open the lid of my shake to dip my fries before slipping them into my mouth. The salty-meets-chocolate sweetness is irresistible and hands down three times better than the lobster station at the stuck-up club. Jasper and I eat in quiet for what feels like only moments as we make quick work of the fries, and soon we're left sipping the remnants of our shakes.

I drop my head back onto the headrest behind me and roll it to face him. "Thanks again for coming."

I have wished so many times that my mother, anyone from my family, would do the same in moments of distress.

He really is remarkable, this man.

Jasper smiles, leans closer, and reaches out a hand. He cups my cheek. The sensation of his rough palm pressed against the tenderness of my face silences everything happening around us. Goose bumps run down my arms.

"Being here for you is one of my new favorite things," he says.

He moves closer, and I feel an overwhelming urge to meet him in the middle. Or melt into him. To drop my head on his chest, to wrap my arms around him. Perhaps even to set a kiss on the side of his neck. I stare into his eyes, and when he smiles, the skin around his eyes wrinkles. I want to tell him that I want him to stay, that I want to be more than friends. That maybe after all these years and being with him now in person, I am finally sure that I might love him.

I edge closer, and his mouth parts ever so slightly, and I wonder if he's thinking the same thing. Craving the same thing. My heart rate picks up, my breath shallow, and my gaze is trained on the mouth I wish only to kiss.

But without fail, my trusty brain kicks in and reminds me that this is all impossible, and it feels like losing my sparkle in real time. The pulsing electricity inside me falters as I remember: He leaves in two weeks. The last thing I need to add onto today is messing up the friendship I have with Jasper, backing him into an uncomfortable corner by confessing romantic feelings after he's come to my aid. He could never stay here, not happily.

I pull back, and we retreat into our seats like nothing ever happened, like the tail ends of sparks aren't still lingering in the air between us.

"Ready?" I ask.

It takes him a second, but his face relaxes into a lazy smile. "If you are."

He looks back at me with his lopsided dimple, his dark hair that's probably overdue for a cut. I'm so lucky to have my Jasper, especially if everyone else is dropping like flies around me.

"Good," I say. "Because I have Peach Pit emails that need reading."

He laughs as I crank the car and pull out.

CHAPTER 35

Delilah

THE NEXT MORNING, THE alarm on my phone blares its shrill demand for me to wake, and I paw around on my nightstand for it. I've barely managed to silence it when the memory of Easter runs right over me like a dump truck, sending a tightness all the way down to my toes. On my phone wait a few individual texts from Sloane, Eliza, and Virginia Kate, commiserating over Easter. It seems Betsy must've filled them in on the contents of our fight. I "heart" the messages, drop the phone, and pull the bedcovers over my face for a moment of extra rest.

Thank goodness it's a school day. Thank goodness I get to spend the day with the world's sweetest beings, my bunnies. Never once has a one of them conspired against me. Well, aside from the occasional smuggling of a bug inside from the playground.

Yesterday afternoon Jasper and I read through the Peach Pit emails together, both leaning in, inhaling the written word of this curious company, dissecting their language. Though Jasper admitted that the emails were only perfunctory information, he did say an op-ed was well within reason.

Later at school it's like magic the way I let the classroom absorb my entirety, and the rest of the world falls away. Inside the walls, I manage paint, glitter glue, and any messes made. The giggles of glee that come from the squish of a glue stick on construction paper lets me breathe easy. The hugs at story time, circled up on the purple rug, are a balm to my heart. Both Jack and Huddie ply me with special hugs.

On my way out that afternoon, I swing by the office and poke my head into Donna's office where she sits typing on her computer.

"I checked in with Virginia Kate, and she and the kiddos are fine. Did they show for school by chance?"

School fees didn't quite rise to the top of the priority list for our Easter intervention, but I'd hoped it was implied that she should bring the boys back to school today—especially so she and Hunter could work on patching things back together.

"Let me check." Donna grabs her mouse and clicks around. "Hmm. Looks like they were not present today." She glances up at me in a way that suggests she might like some details on the situation, but she doesn't push.

I hold up a finger. "Let me see what I can do. I'll stop by in the morning?"

"Sure thing, Delilah. You have a way of working wonders around here."

On my drive home I call Virginia Kate. This time she picks up without pause.

"Hey!" My tone is far too peppy, a total giveaway that I'm calling with a motive.

"Hey, what's up?"

"Oh, I just wanted to call after yesterday and everything."

"From the sounds of it, I should be the one calling *you*. Betsy was a wreck after you left."

"Yes, *that*. From what I hear my family members went right back to the festivities as if not a dang thing had happened."

Virginia Kate is quiet for a beat; she must've observed it firsthand.

"I'm sorry, Delilah. It's— I don't know. I had no clue Darcy was involved since Betsy's above me. Peach Pit isn't exactly an open book."

I clear my throat. "Well, you've got enough of your own to deal with, thanks to Peach Pit, without worrying about me. I wondered why you didn't send the boys to school this morning."

"I appreciate the thought, but we can't afford the tuition, and I'm not sure it makes sense when I can't see us being able to make the payments in the near future."

"Donna can meet with you, see what she can do—"

"Thank you, Delilah." Her words are kind but lined with steely resolve. "But I'm up to my nose in credit card debt and probably heading for a divorce, and the last thing I need is another bill—even if it's smaller than it was. I've got a homeschool plan for the boys, art projects, and library trips until they . . . go to public school eventually, I guess."

"Okay." I know better than to press her. "That makes sense. Well, let's talk again soon, but I should go."

We say goodbye, and I swallow the lump that forms. I can't help but compare the kids being forced to leave school to Virginia Kate being forced out of so many social circles after her parents' ugly split. Fortunately the boys are too young to get it. There is no social hierarchy for them—not yet.

My mind is tired by the time I get home, my thoughts occasionally returning to Darcy, Mama, and Betsy but quickly retreating as if they've touched a hot iron. I head next door to Mrs. Chopra's house as soon as I park, and she welcomes me inside. The smell of something simmering on the stove greets me, and she directs me to wait in her living area where two mugs of tea sit waiting on the trunk that serves as a coffee table. She takes off to the kitchen and shuffles back moments later with a plate of cookies.

The layout of Mrs. Chopra's house is the same as mine, but the afternoon sun hits her living room more directly, making it a comfortable place to sit in the cooler seasons but a beast during the summer. Two vining plants hang from macramé slings attached to the ceiling, and smaller potted plants line the windowsill, a few bursting with colorful blooms. She sets down the plate beside our cups of tea.

I blow on the steaming mug. "So what did she say exactly?"

"She said I needed to sign the NDA soon or I'd be kicked out. Can you believe it? I've only been a Darling for the weekend, and they're ready to kick me to the curb." She laughs to herself at her rebelliousness.

"Well, I knew they wouldn't send you the stuff, those shady fools." My gut clenches at the reminder that my own sister is among the top brass of fools.

"Right, but they've sent me all these emails saying that my 'subscription' will be canceled if I don't sign."

"They're scared about you getting their info and not having the NDA to cover them."

Mrs. Chopra takes a bite of a cookie and holds the plate out to me. "True. Most of the emails have been spammy, but I've been getting ten to fifteen a day—even on Easter! I figured they'd let someone have the day off."

"They're all automatic."

Mrs. Chopra clicks around the screen. "I did get a particularly interesting one today." She spins the computer so I can read it for myself.

Subject Line: A Peachy Hiccup

Hello, dearest Darlings,

It's been brought to our attention that some community members have reported difficulties with certain products. Please remind your shoppers that topical cosmetics are one of the most common causes of skin irritation and localized allergic reactions. However, an allergic reaction does not serve as evidence of an issue with the product; rather it demonstrates an intolerance on the part of the individual consumer. Peach Pit will not be held responsible for individual intolerances, and shoppers should use products with consideration for their own biological limits.

Some batches of Peach Sheen lip gloss have been so packed full of the deep pit nutrients that some of our more fragile customers have been unable to tolerate the plumping burn. These products are still safe and may continue to be sold at Peach parties.

We have chosen to discontinue the Peach Tea recently distributed, but this product may also be sold until stock runs out. Returns will not be accepted.

At Peach Pit we're dedicated to continuous improvement while standing by the quality and effectiveness of our products. We are proud of our peachy life-changing items and all of you, our Darlings.

"So this is like an admission and a denial swirl, like vanilla and chocolate soft-serve ice cream."

Mrs. Chopra nods. "I had the same thought. Only, I'd also like to get to the bottom of these products—the scientist in me—see what's *actually* in them."

I look down into my tea, wrapping both hands around the mug. "I'm not sure it matters to them."

"What's going on with you? You really don't seem yourself," Mrs. Chopra says.

I launch into an explanation of everything that happened on Easter. The news from Virginia Kate. Betsy's accidental admission that led to the heated conversation between Darcy and me. Mama an accomplice to it all.

"So as you might imagine, I'm sort of low on energy. School was an absolute godsend to keep my mind off it, with all those sweet bunnies. Just what I needed."

"You're a master in the classroom, Delilah. I'm not sure there's anyone more skilled with those children."

I shrug. It's a nice sentiment, but I've never felt like it was that important of a skill even if I enjoy it. It wasn't the dream I set out to reach, after all.

"I can't help but feel like settling into that job for good is a cop-out."

Mrs. Chopra pulls her face into a shocked frown. "What on earth?"

"Everyone who's been raised here knows bigger, better accomplishments are the way to get along. Just ask my family." Building a business was supposed to be my one checked item on the Pearl must-do list.

"With all due respect, I can't see a thing better in your sister—who did a crude job attempting to complete this so-called dream—than you. In fact, quite the opposite."

I smile weakly. "Thanks. It just seems like I can't win with them."

It's obvious now how continuing down this road, poking around in Peach Pit, is going to do nothing but estrange me further from my family. I just wish for a moment that Mama could see my side, stand up for me too. Surely Daddy couldn't be bothered less about cosmetics, but if put to it, he'd take Darcy's side in a blink.

"We'll have to send this information to your man friend," Mrs. Chopra says.

"'Man friend'?"

"Somewhere between a friend and a boyfriend because I'm too old not to call a spade a spade."

A true smile opens across my face. "The article idea's got me nervous."

"Like I have said all along, if Darcy and her cronies have nothing to hide, an article about their business will be nothing but free marketing."

I nod. I do agree with Mrs. Chopra, but digging in to Peach Pit—saying *anything* about it publicly—also feels like staring up at a cliff face I've been tasked to climb. Not only is it going up against

Darcy, but it's also pressing on a fresh wound in The Five. The potential for problems is enough to send a shiver down my spine. Nevertheless, I'm old enough to realize that none of the paths forward will be easy. None will be pain- or drama-free.

Perhaps it's simply about picking the path that has the best chance of getting me through to a place worth belonging.

A place where I hope beyond hope that The Five is still intact.

CHAPTER 36

Betsy

BETSY ACTUALLY LAY DOWN and slept for a few extra hours this morning after she dropped off the kids at school; Easter was such an *event.* She later texted Virginia Kate to let her know she was thinking about her and the family, but Betsy knows that fixing the situation will require much more than a single text. She holds herself responsible. Undoubtedly this will impact their friendship, but Betsy can't make sense of why Virginia Kate didn't *say something.* Betsy of all people would've been there for her, just like she was when Ginny Kay's mother's credit card was declined at the movie theater. It was a quick fix to use the credit card Betsy's father had given her—the card one of the few reliable things he did provide—to cover her ticket and popcorn.

As far as things between Betsy and Delilah, she can't quite bear to think about it right now.

All along Betsy thought she was doing the right thing, but every part of yesterday was like a reveal of every way she can't help but get it wrong. She has not a clue how, but she's going to have to find a way to make it right with Delilah. And Virginia Kate.

By now, Betsy has the kids home from school, dinner in the Crock-Pot, and little Hattie bopping happily in her jumper while the boys bounce around the playroom. Betsy fills her tall plastic tumbler with nugget ice from the specialty ice maker on the countertop, a splurge from a recent online sale thanks to her

Peach Pit check. She cracks a diet soda and pours it over the top, then fastens the lid with the attached straw.

She plops down into her new rattan-back dining chair, a set she simply had to get when she saw a favorite influencer share them online, and opens her laptop. To be entirely honest, it's been a while since she's really looked at the budget she and Jared supposedly follow. As soon as she started getting sizable monthly checks from Peach Pit, counting every dollar seemed like a waste of precious time, and impulse buys weren't such a big deal when there was money sitting there. Betsy could schedule a facial at her favorite spa without worrying that Jared would call, angry about the ensuing banking alert for low funds in the checking account.

It goes without saying that her relationship with The Five is paramount. It's the reason she's looking at the budget—to prepare for the worst case, where she has to walk away from Peach Pit—even if she's still holding on to hope that far off, somewhere, there's a solution. To have both.

Betsy doesn't even have to look at the spreadsheet to know that their yearly beach vacation would either have to shift into a maybe category or evolve into a different sort of trip if the paychecks from Peach Pit were to stop. Those Instagrammable houses at Rosemary Beach don't come cheap.

Just as Betsy has the spreadsheet open, Huddie barrels in, tears running, with blubbered complaints about a Nerf gun and his older brother. She scoops him up and cuddles him in her lap, dotting kisses over his fine baby hair.

"Oh, you poor thing."

Huddie lets out a shuddering breath and settles into Betsy's chest like a heavy weight. Could it be a possibility they wouldn't be able to pay for the increasing school tuition without Peach Pit? With Hattie coming up, there will be a good chunk of years when they have three children in the school. Betsy would need a different job, and the thought of starting over—from *nothing*—is daunting. Especially for someone like Betsy who's never been particularly talented. In contrast there's someone like Virginia Kate who is smart and bright and certain to land on her feet. Sure, she sort of lay down and let the tide of motherhood and Hunter take her where they pleased a couple years ago, but Virginia Kate at her core is unsinkable.

Huddie pulls back and places his hands on Betsy's cheeks, and in response she puckers her lips into a kiss she touches to his nose. Huddie writhes around as he giggles, sliding himself onto the ground and off in the direction of what sounds like a popping Nerf gun.

Before she can get back to the spreadsheet and figuring out a path forward, the door to the garage rattles open and in walks Jared, his work bag slung over his shoulder.

He passes behind Betsy and drops a kiss on her head. "What're you up to? A Peach Pit manifesto?"

Betsy tries her best to smile in response to the joke. "The budget, actually."

Jared sets down his work bag on the table. "Really? Since when are we looking at that?"

Betsy's insides tighten. She hasn't yet told Jared about the extent of the issues orbiting Peach Pit. Her own mounting concerns. He didn't even get the full rundown on Easter with how chaotic it was trying to chase down the sugar-charged boys.

"It's sort of a long story." Betsy pulls in a breath and gives Jared a barebones overview. "And if it's true that the company is shady, which it's looking like it could be, I can't keep working there."

Jared sighs, running a hand through his hair. "What if it's nothing? Let's not risk so much by jumping on the bandwagon after a few rashes."

"Virginia Kate and Hunter are to the point of getting divorced over it—it's important."

Jared's eyes go wide. "Dang. Okay, well that puts it in perspective." He drums his fingertips on the table. "I just want you to do what's best for you—for *us*. I mean, it can't be the whole entire company that's rotten to the core, right? Things are never that black and white. Plus, they have you! How bad could they be?"

As much as she wants her husband's words to be true—how often she has reassured herself with the same thoughts—Betsy can't deny her mounting suspicions. Because even if Jared is right and things aren't clear-cut, if the core of a company is rotten, it's difficult to reconcile any good that comes from it as untainted.

Does that mean Betsy's tainted too? She's already staring down the possibility of being cast out of the place she actually makes a difference, and now she's being forced to consider if all the good she did was somehow canceled out by a few bad apples.

It's almost unbearable.

"You didn't see Virginia Kate."

"You didn't force her into any of it. What if she'd spoken up when she had a hard time selling? Surely she could've paused monthly purchases. Or even left if it was no longer workable."

Betsy shrugs very slowly as the memory of Virginia Kate's own words on Easter return to her: *"It's only excuses that keep a Darling from being successful; with enough effort and enough creativity, I should've been able to sell all of this . . . All I needed was a better attitude."*

It's what Peach Pit teaches, what *Betsy* teaches.

It's that plus the pressure of this town, the things, the services required to function here. Like the spa she's sure to have to cut ties with once she loses her income. Who's to say what looks she'll start getting once her roots grow in and her Botox fades. Perhaps she needs to take Delilah's advice and start embracing her aging body as evidence of a life well-lived.

Betsy sighs. "That's not what it's about. That's like being a drug dealer and arguing that it's acceptable because you're not forcing people to buy the drugs."

"You're a good person, Bets, and I know you want to do the right thing, but we've talked about this before. I'm not getting another promotion without an MBA, and those are expensive. So if you don't do Peach Pit, it's my earnings, and . . . that's it unless you spin your magic on something else."

Betsy drops back into her seat, her stomach turning sour.

Jared heads for the fridge. "Beer?"

He's already popping the top when Betsy replies, "No thanks, I've got my soda."

Jared rounds behind her and massages her shoulders. "I don't want to fight about it. I know you're stressed—it's tough combining business and friendship, I get it. Maybe we can table it for now?"

Betsy nods, and it's almost a relief when her phone rattles to life on the table, the name of one of her Darlings on the screen with a peach logo. She grabs it.

"Let me take this real quick, five minutes tops."

Jared nods as he heads for the playroom, calling out to the kids.

Betsy pushes open the French doors leading to their deck that overlooks the golf course and accepts the call.

CHAPTER 37

Delilah

IT'S BEEN FOUR DAYS since Easter, and I haven't spoken to Betsy. Or Darcy or Mama, but with them it's less out of the ordinary. Surely within a day or so I'll get a casual text from Mama, business as usual, as if not a drop of drama unraveled at Easter brunch. That's her way. Still, I'm surprised Betsy has been absent every day from school pickup, sending her babysitter or Jared—who, despite his work flexibility, is usually only tagged in for pickup in a bind—instead.

I'm filing out of the conference room after a teacher staff meeting this afternoon when The Five group chat that's sat dormant for four days springs to life.

Eliza: I have typed and retyped, reworded and deleted all of these words so many times because I'm not really sure what to say. I don't remember the last time we went four days without talking, and that even includes when Sloane did study abroad in France.

Sloane hearts the comment immediately.

Sloane: Same same same.

Sloane: I have cycled through a ton of jokes but never sent one in case it didn't land.

Eliza: Also selfishly I don't want to go into labor with everyone weirdly not talking.

Virginia Kate: I love y'all. I'm just working through a lot right now.

Delilah: Same.

It feels like The Five is stuck, like we've wandered into a tar pit, and despite all of our good intentions there's no simple way out. I wait for Betsy to say something. Her admitting some of the bad sides of Peach Pit could truly help us get back in the right direction.

She knows things are strained between Darcy and me, so she would've known—Pit Peach or not—that keeping the information from me would hurt. Instead, she chose to try her luck at keeping it under wraps, and it's thrown my confidence in The Five out of whack.

Nevertheless, the small voice that lives inside me, the one that urges me to keep the peace and smooth things over, the one that reminds me how impossible it would be to lose this group, gets my fingers typing again.

Delilah: I love y'all. I know we'll be fine.

It's not what I actually want to say. I want to say that Betsy broke my heart. That what Peach Pit has done to Virginia Kate and Eliza should be enough for Betsy to turn in her keys to the castle. No amount of money is worth selling out your friends. I look again at my phone to see if Betsy has said anything, but of course she hasn't. Betsy doesn't like to admit the bad parts. She hates acknowledging any hurt or sadness she's experienced, as if it's a weakness, and just the same, she won't admit when she's done something wrong.

Because if we keep up the act that everything's fine and everything's perfect, we can really and truly fool ourselves. At least to a certain point.

When I get home, Jasper is at my house working in the shed, and a few of my boxes have been pulled out and sit in the sun. We'll see if there's actually time for him to finish the brew before he goes, but since I have more than enough problems on my own plate, I'm leaving it up to him. Not to mention, I know less than zero about beer making, so I wouldn't be much help even if I tried.

He's sweaty and dusty when he knocks on my side door later, smiling through the windowpanes. It's become a routine I look forward to, and today I welcome him inside, take a pitcher of sweet tea from the fridge, and pour us both a glass.

"I started drafting the Peach Pit article," Jasper says after downing a healthy amount of tea. "The local paper is interested in seeing it once it's ready."

My stomach doesn't drop at the mention of it this time, and I'd call that a reliable sign that it's a reasonable idea. Despite the fact that I have a front-row seat to the messes Peach Pit is creating, so many members of the Pearl community don't. If Peach Pit is going to be held accountable, the information should be public.

"Do it."

Jasper's brow jumps. "You're sure? It won't 'mess everything up'?" He quotes my own words, and again, my chest squeezes at his attention to detail.

"Honestly? I'm not sure. But I am sure that things can't stay the way they are."

There are so many possible issues that might come from the article, but it's ones that impact The Five that flood my mind. I worry that I'll break us somehow. Or are we already there? I'm not sure I know how to live in a world without The Five. For as long as I can remember, I was Delilah and also a member of The Five.

"If we're publishing this, we should dig into the ownership of the company." Jasper takes the pitcher to refill his glass.

"It's definitely not listed on the website. I doubt it's anywhere else online."

"We can submit a public information request from the attorney general's office, I think." He pulls out his phone and clicks around. "I did it for another story once before. It could take a while for them to get back to us, but we should try."

My phone lights up with his text, and I click the link he sends over for the information request. "I'll send it in."

I start the process of filing the request online as we chat.

"And while we're on the subject, do you want to read what I've got so far?" Jasper's eyes open a pinch wider, then he slides his phone toward me on the counter.

My typing fingers slow as I momentarily forget the form at hand. I nod tentatively, despite uncertainty creeping in, that familiar voice that tells me to keep quiet.

"What's up? Change of heart?" He slides it halfway back.

I slump onto the counter. "No. I mean, *maybe*?" I sigh. "I don't know. Why am I like this?"

"Is this about Darcy?"

I drop my chin into my palm. "I have no qualms about Darcy getting caught up in the storm she created. The way she sneered and blew me off, it's clear she's not open to having a civil conversation."

"So what are you worried about? Betsy?"

I glance off to the side. "I'm always worried about Betsy. And it kills me that we're not really talking, at least not like normal. But I also don't know how to fix it. Maybe speaking the truth to the town could be a way. Maybe if Peach Pit starts to shrink, the hurts that've been caused by it will do the same."

Jasper shrugs. "I can't make any promises either way."

I press my lips into a line as I consider the rest of it. "Mama is going to be unhappy about this. She doesn't want the family caught up in public riffraff, and everyone will know that even if your name is on the byline, I'm involved. I have to imagine all her friends know about Darcy being a Darling, so at the club there will be whispers of daughter versus daughter."

"Sure. But the alternative?"

My heart pounds painfully as I consider it.

The alternative is allowing Peach Pit to sit pretty, conducting all of its ugliness undercover, letting The Five remain planted in the middle of its mess. The alternative is allowing more and more Pearl women—many of whom might be vulnerable—to be pulled into the mess. The alternative is that Peach Pit remains and the newer generations are pulled in, our girls who are on the precipice of becoming women: Roxie and her classmates.

"I guess if Mama's never cared to stand up for me thus far, it's not unreasonable that I take my own stand—whether it ruffles her feathers or not."

Jasper reaches out and places a heavy palm on my back. "Sometimes doing the right thing also feels like doing the hard thing."

It's a basic life lesson that was hammered home throughout years of elementary schooling, but it's a whole other endeavor to actually live it out. To step out knowing I'm going to upset the very family I'm desperate to belong to. Because if I don't, I risk losing the found family I've come to love and rely on instead.

"Betsy won't be happy."

"She's also not in a position to call the shots right now."

"True."

A quiet passes between us, Jasper hanging back with optimistic eyes as he waits for me to say something.

I pull myself upright off the counter and take a sip of my sweet tea.

"Alright, let's take a look at this draft. If we're stepping into the public arena against this peachy beast, we best not have any spelling errors."

CHAPTER 38

Delilah

THE ITALIAN RESTAURANT SLOANE picked out for her birthday celebration the next evening is cast in dim lighting, and chatter from the surrounding tables is already at a hum. My face is pressed deeply into the tall, leather-bound menu propped in front of me like a shield.

Eliza sits to my right at the round table. "I know Sloane's busy, but she's late to her *own* birthday. I don't know about y'all, but I think they need to go ahead and bring the bread basket."

"Agreed," Betsy announces from across the table.

She scans the interior with bright eyes, and when she catches the waiter's attention, she gives him a winning smile. He's at her side in a few strides, nodding at the beautiful woman as he promises to deliver a bread basket right away.

She turns back to us. "Easy peasy."

Virginia Kate sits on my other side and pulls out her phone. "I'm going to call Sloane and just make sure everything's okay."

It's the first thing she's said since she walked in and greeted everyone, and I understand why she's quiet. I patted her on the arm earlier when no one was looking—just to let her know I'm thinking of her and Hunter.

"Good idea," Eliza says.

I risk a glance at Betsy across the table. She's been wearing a permanent smile since she walked in here and is yet to make eye contact with me. It's possible that she genuinely feels this upbeat tonight, but I suspect it's an act. An all-is-well front put on in the name of keeping things nice for Sloane. In fact, Betsy can be the queen of putting on a good face—and not even in a bad way. At times, it's the fake-it-till-you-make-it attitude we all wish we could muster when things get tough, a force to propel her through life's hardships.

Finally, Sloane marches across the restaurant and lets out a dramatic huff.

"Sorry! My boss is awful. Just awful. She even knew it was my birthday. Let's hope she's not harassing me this weekend." She and Anton have a quick but luxurious getaway planned for tomorrow night only.

"We're glad you're here. And we started on the bread without you, so no hard feelings on the tardiness," Eliza says.

Sloane drops into her seat. "I'm glad. Have y'all ordered?" She reaches out and takes the bottle of red wine in the center of the table and pours herself a glass.

"Not yet," I say. "And happy birthday! How do the late thirties feel?"

"Late? Thirty-seven is definitely still mid-thirties."

"It doesn't matter what the number is, honey, you're fabulous." Betsy throws her arm around Sloane.

When she looks up, I catch her eye, and for a moment I see the facade slip. Behind her cheery eyes, pain flickers. It was the exact way she looked that one Christmas night she came to my house after her parents ditched her like the self-seekers they were. I could see in her eyes that she wanted so badly for it to not be a big deal, so of course I played along. I fluffed up the daybed and acted like it was any other Friday night, *no big deal.*

A sharp pain radiates through me as the realization hits me again: *I can't play along this time, Bets.*

Sloane pulls herself upright just as the waiter returns to the table. The rest of us order first, allowing Sloane a few minutes to choose, and after gathering our heavy menus into a stack, the waiter disappears. They prepare the dishes quickly, and after we engage in some surface-level chitchat about our days, the waiter returns with the food. Spaghetti and meatballs. Chicken Parmesan. Sloane gets a steak with mashed potatoes. We all lose ourselves in the comfort food that tastes like a hug come to life.

Once the plates are cleared, a quiet hums at the table. Betsy has pulled out her phone. Eliza is playing with the seam on her napkin, and Virginia Kate is staring off into space.

I meet Sloane's tired eyes, and she shoots me a look.

I shrug.

"Alrighty," Sloane announces confidently. "Well, I'm not going to sit here in silence, so we might as well name the elephant in the room."

A mix of relief and terror covers me. I probably shouldn't be surprised, but I figured we'd leave things swept under the rug for tonight for the sake of it being Sloane's special day.

"I don't want everyone to be upset because of my situation," Virginia Kate says. "I appreciate what y'all did on Easter more than you'll ever know, but I'm not going to be myself again for a while."

Only now do I appreciate the depth of what Ginny Kay is going through, the fact that even if the financial mess is on its way to being cleaned up, the emotional scarring between her and Hunter is real. Possibly lasting. All of us are rooting for them to make it through, but that doesn't mean it won't hurt along the way.

"Same," Eliza says. "I shouldn't have used any new products—especially heavily scented ones—during pregnancy. My OB is happy with my health and the baby, so I think we can call what happened to me water under the bridge."

Eliza is sometimes too nice for her own good, and I wonder if she could use a share of the gumption I've been working up myself. *"Water under the bridge"?* The fear of her rushing to the hospital is still fresh in my mind. I look around the table at the others who are sitting still, listening. Am I the only one who feels this way?

Betsy nods. "I agree. All of these issues are water under the bridge."

She doesn't look at me, and it plants a lump in my throat. It's as if the harm I've come to at the hands of Peach Pit doesn't even count.

"Hey, now," Sloane says. "What Eliza said is fine, and we can accept that. Ginny Kay, we're all here for you—whatever you need—and whichever version of you is standing is the one we'll love. But they don't speak for everyone."

All eyes turn slowly to me, and I gulp. Inside the privacy of my thoughts, it's so much easier to be righteously angry over my hurt, but when I'm invited to speak it out loud, it always feels like my confidence scurries away into the shadows. The fear of breaking The Five rises to the top. My voice shakes as I speak.

"I'm glad Eliza and Ginny Kay aren't holding hard feelings, if that's honestly how they feel. I know it's always nice to move past things, to find peace. But I'd be lying if I said any of this was 'water under the bridge' for me. I've been lied to and left out, and I've sat back too long and watched this company hurt good people." I pull in a shuddering breath as my heart hammers. "It's so hard to even admit it. I *hate* creating problems. Especially with the people I love. But also, The Five is too good for faking things between us."

"You didn't create the problems. That was Peach Pit," Sloane says.

"I'm not going to sit here and listen to a Peach Pit bashing session," Betsy says.

My heart picks up.

Betsy crosses and uncrosses her arms, she shifts in her seat, she flips her hair in exaggerated swoops. It's as if she's caged and desperate for a way out.

"We're not going to. It's my birthday celebration," Sloane sings as a gentle reminder. "But Delilah has a right to an opinion. To disagree."

Betsy sighs. "Since when did Delilah become so outspoken?"

"I'm sitting right here," I say.

She only glances at me, then back down at her lap. "Sorry." The word is so quiet that her regret is obvious.

"I appreciate you standing up for me too," Eliza says. "It's hard to say something about Peach Pit when everyone else in town thinks it's the bee's knees. And with the pregnancy hormones, I'm constantly second-guessing myself. Like, am I overreacting? Am I making a mountain out of a molehill?"

Virginia Kate reaches over the table and squeezes her hand. "You're not crazy, Liza. Peach Pit did you dirty on the tea."

Betsy drops still in her seat, and a frown creeps across her face.

"There's going to be an article. About Peach Pit. I wanted y'all to hear it straight from me before it lands next week. It's an op-ed Jasper put together," I say.

Usually, at the mere mention of Jasper this group would erupt into catcalls and cooing about our budding romance. Demands for updates. Plans hatched to finally put us together. But today it's crickets.

"You're serious?" Betsy says, her mouth hanging slightly ajar after she finishes.

"I think it's important that people know the truth," Virginia Kate says. "I don't wish my situation on any other woman."

Eliza nods. "Definitely for the preggos too."

"Sharing the truth is never a bad thing," Sloane says. "Plus, it's the local paper, not national news. How far can it even go?"

Realistically we all know that Sloane is simply trying to soothe Betsy's nerves. The local paper is far more widely read here in Pearl than any national publication. People want information on local happenings, not the latest messes unraveling in Washington.

Betsy's face heats to a deep red, and the table shakes as she jostles her knee up and down vigorously. She shakes her head, and the words erupt from her.

"So it's just like that, huh? Y'all are going to leave me behind? Just because I like Peach Pit—because I can see the good parts—I'm excluded?"

"Whoa, whoa, whoa." Sloane holds out her arms. "The comments are about Peach Pit. Not *you*. No one ever said anything about leaving you out."

"They *are* about me."

"Really"—Virginia Kate's voice is laced in warmth—"the bad feelings aren't about you."

Though I think there are absolutely still unfortunate feelings between Betsy and me over the way she lied to me about Darcy's involvement, never once have I questioned her place in The Five. It's not a gossipy social club where people are cast in or out as the direction of the wind shifts. It's a family. I know and love Betsy, and even if I'm upset with her now, I know we can get past it.

"It is about me, and y'all are ganging up on me. I am Peach Pit." Betsy jams a finger hard into her chest. "It is part of me. And when you say all of these things, it's about me."

"We don't mean it that way," I say.

Betsy stumbles to her feet. "You're going to leave me just like everyone else. I thought I'd always be able to count on you four to be there"—she grabs the purse looped on the back of her chair and slings it onto her shoulder—"but obviously I was wrong." She turns to go. "Happy birthday, Sloane."

As she heads for the exit, I get to my feet without a second thought.

"Betsy!" I call after her, garnering a look from a nearby table of senior women sipping white wine.

She pushes out into the night air, and I call out again.

"Betsy!"

She turns just as Sloane arrives at my side, Virginia Kate behind her.

"I'm sorry, but I really need to go."

"Okay," I say. "But we want you to stay. You're part of this, no matter what." I look at her intently. "Always."

Betsy pulls a tight smile. "Thanks. It's just—" She pulls in a breath, sets her shoulders, and lifts her chin. "I need to—I don't know. I just can't be here right now."

I nod despite the ache that rolls through my chest. As she turns and walks toward her car, I feel the heat of tears threatening in my own eyes. She might've hurt me on Easter, but it feels far worse to see her walk away from us right now. To hear the suggestion that being with The Five somehow doesn't work for her even if it's only in this moment.

The three of us turn back to the restaurant in silence, Virginia Kate holding the heavy door open at the entrance. Eliza waddles up to the hostess stand as we reenter.

"What happened? Y'all know I move slower these days."

Sloane shrugs. "I need to pay the tab."

Virginia Kate follows her in the direction of the table.

I take Eliza's hand and squeeze it. "She wanted some space. For now."

I add the last words as if they're for Eliza, but they're also completely, entirely, *desperately*, for me. There is no world I can imagine in which Betsy doesn't belong in The Five. It doesn't work that way and never will.

That is one thing I am simply unwilling to find peace with.

CHAPTER 39

Delilah

ON MONDAY I REARRANGE the morning to make sure I get the local paper in hand first thing, hoping with every bit of me that it'll be worth it, that publishing this article will actually be for the greater good. That folks in town will be grateful to hear the truth.

I flip through the thin layers of newsprint to the op-ed section and read.

APRIL 17, 2023

OPINION: PEACH PIT PRODUCTS CHANGE PEARL LIVES FOR THE WORSE

By Jasper Rowley

An invite to a Peach Pit Party, a multilevel marketing (MLM) company peddling purported health and beauty products, has become as common as an invite to an SEC football tailgate in Pearl. At the events, local women become consultants, sell product, and recruit one another. But are things as sweet and fun as the fruity-scented products might claim?

A source who has gone through recruitment with Peach Pit has given the *Pearl Herald* exclusive access to how this company trains and manages its sellers—dubbed "Darlings"—and what it truly takes to make money in this endeavor.

In only two days of membership as a Darling, a consultant might receive upward of fifteen emails. These messages urge the consultant to purchase more product—before any has been shipped or received—to start planning parties, honing high-pressure sales strategies, and mapping out recruits to build their own team. And all without products to sell. The company continues to blast consultants with emails, urging them to purchase more product, assuring them of the benefits with vague claims and references to "science" without providing facts or evidence. The Peach Pit website also does not offer scientific evidence to support its claims. Although one might reasonably expect a company to guard its proprietary trade secrets, this company has thus far not publicly demonstrated how it is able to harness any health benefits from the pit of a Georgia peach.

Could it all be smoke and mirrors?

Darling consultants are regularly urged to develop their business by "growing their team," which requires the recruitment of other sellers to work underneath them in an upward stream of product sales. Pyramid schemes, which are illegal in the United States, are defined as companies in which recruitment is the sole way to make profits. A legal MLM operation is one that focuses on sales of products. Peach Pit does equip consultants with product—and even requires a monthly minimum purchase of $499 per consultant—but in the span of three days, our source received only a single email with flimsy tips about selling product but five about how to recruit new sellers. The line between MLM and pyramid schemes has historically been contested, leading to lengthy legal proceedings.

In addition to its questionable business practices, a recent wave of consumer reports of allergic reactions and issues with products has flooded Peach Pit. In an email to consultants, Peach Pit assumes no responsibility, describing customers who experience reactions as "fragile" people with biological deficits all their own as the company encourages consultants to continue selling these products. Peach Pit Peach Tea is the sole product recently discontinued without explanation, but consultants have been instructed to continue selling the tea in question until their supplies run out because the company will not issue refunds. Emails to consultants did not disclose any specific actions on the part of the corporation to test or implement new safety protocols for the product range.

Pearl has long been a tight-knit community full of people who look out for one another. Is it possible that Peach Pit is taking advantage of our goodwill?

A small group of anonymous Pearlites has come together to investigate Peach Pit, how it operates, what benefits it actually offers, and whether there is science to back their promises.

Join the efforts: Do you know someone personally affected by Peach Pit? Please contact the *Pearl Herald* Opinions section at opinions@pearlherald.com with information.

CHAPTER 40

Delilah

AROUND NOON MY PHONE starts ringing off the hook in the front pocket of my overalls, my mama calling again and again as I monitor the lunch tables. I already know it's about Jasper's article, and I can only imagine she's calling with her concerns about Darcy being dethroned as the queen of Peach Pit. A billowing tension expands inside me at the thought of facing my mother over this.

Cici cries out as her container of Goldfish slips from her grip and clatters to the floor, and it pulls me back to the here and now. I rescue the crackers that didn't fall to the floor and pull her tenderly into my arms.

"It's okay," I whisper into her ear.

She settles quickly, the fat tears that came on instantly vanishing in much the same fashion.

Throughout the rest of the day, Mama continues to call, and I do my best to focus on the Blissful Bunnies. Eventually the clock ticks to 3:00 p.m., all of the children have gone home, and I reluctantly pick up my mother's next call.

"Mama, hey, you okay?"

Her voice is tight, words pressed through a clamped jaw. "You were part of this, weren't you? And how is Jasper involved when he's halfway around the world?"

"He came to visit."

She sighs, probably rolling her neck out, gold jewelry glistening in the sun so that she looks like an Egyptian princess. "You have no idea the trouble you're starting."

"Nothing Jasper said in his article is untrue, but they wanted it in the Opinion section because there are still too many holes in the story. The emails, the selling questionable product, the recruiting to make money is all real. How is discussing that a bad thing?"

My words sound confident, but inside my stomach is churning.

"Your sister is basically the top girl over there, what do you mean, 'how is it a bad thing?' You're not thinking about all the other people making money from this."

"The people making money from it—like Darcy—aren't thinking about the people they're taking it from."

"*Delilah*." She spits my name out like a foul bite of food. "Darcy is your flesh and blood. And—"

"She didn't even give a second thought to stealing my ideas."

"We all know it was only a tiny piece of it, and she didn't mean it like that. She didn't rip off your brand—all the differences are so obvious."

"She didn't care that I was hurt, that she lied to me, made Betsy go along with it."

"That was difficult—"

"You just cannot help but take her side." I pause, and I'm met by silence. "What about me?"

Mama sighs. "Well."

I don't fill the silence. I want her to answer.

"This is a lot for us all to think about. I just don't want more mess. We should just cool our jets and let it pass. Let me let you go, honey."

I'm sure most of the town is gossiping about the article, asking their friends and friends of friends what they think, wondering which Darlings are pulling in the big bucks and which are floundering. It's clear to me that Mama is most concerned about the fact that her daughter—and by extension the Thomas family name—is connected. At least to those who are privy to her part in it.

About an hour later, I've put the finishing touches on getting the classroom ready for the morning, said goodbye to the office staff, and made my way home to SweetGum Lane with a quick stop at the grocery store. When I pull into the slim driveway between my lavender house and Mrs. Chopra's tangerine one, I notice a figure on my porch. She paces up and down, crossing in front of my door, apparently muttering something to herself.

I grab my paper grocery bag from the passenger seat, provisions for this evening, and at the sound of my car door slamming shut, my guest's head whips in my direction. Darcy's big, extensively highlighted mane looms closer like a warning flare as she crosses the porch toward me.

She skips down the steps to meet me, her face scrunched into a scowl. "How *dare* you!"

My heart beats so fast it's practically in my throat, and I have to concertedly stop myself from cowering. "Darcy, *stop*."

"One of my down-line sent me this freakin' article. What are you thinking?"

I climb the steps and stop on the porch, Darcy hot on my heels.

"If you're messing with the company, you're messing with me."

"All of it's true." I keep my eyes down on the key I slot into the lock.

I don't mention the fact that she's on some rocky moral ground coming at me for sharing the truth, when she sold my concept to investors in exchange for her spot as Top Darling. Like she has a leg to stand on. I push inside, and being on my own territory calms the flurry of nerves.

"It's exaggerated, that's for sure. Twisting the truth."

I raise my brows and shrug. I'm not giving in, but I'm also not engaging in the verbal brawl she desires.

"Even if it's true, why do you have to air *this* dirty laundry? Lord knows the junkyard over the bridge has basically been selling drugs for decades, Mr. Clark at the gas station takes illegal bets on Georgia football, and the minimart sells beer to Pearl Prep football players every year."

"It's doing real harm."

"Why can't you let me have anything without trying to mess it up, Delilah?"

I can't help but laugh out loud at my domineering sister's comment as I make my way into the kitchen. "Really? *I* never let *you* have anything? Because the way I remember our lives together, it worked exactly the opposite way. And what about Bubbles & Suds? That's my baby, and you know it."

She groans like the air is under extreme pressure, balling her fists as she follows me. "Why can't you just be like everyone else?"

"So is it that you don't want me digging into your shady business or that I still embarrass you because I couldn't care less about looking Pearly perfect?"

Darcy crosses her arms, her hair puffing on her breath as she releases a huff. "Everyone knows we're nothing alike, but yeah, I don't care that you're all offbeat or whatever it is you are. Both of us have done what we needed to get by. What I care about is that you're trying to take money out of my pocket."

"Yeah, life's always been quite the struggle for you."

Darcy rolls her eyes. "For being Mama and Daddy's show pony all those years, the least I deserve is having this business. And again—get your nose out of it."

"No one is saying you can't sell product that's safe. As in, *isn't sending people to the hospital*." I drop my grocery bag on the butcher block counter. I refuse to acknowledge Darcy's so-called childhood hardships—even the mention of it feels like a slap in the face to me, the person who was constantly told to stay quiet, keep out of the way, to watch my big sister and follow. Complaints about the show ponying? *Please*. She loved it.

"Oh come on." Darcy lets the silence hang, but even if we have less than nothing in common, I can read between the lines. I can as good as hear the words she refuses to say out loud. We both know she doesn't make money off selling Peach Pit product.

I raise my brows as I examine the wood grain in front of me.

"What?" my sister demands. "What was that look?"

I shrug, feigning innocence. "You tell me."

"You can be such a miserable party pooper sometimes, Delilah, just ruining it all for the rest of us."

"Again, you can still sell product."

Darcy closes the gap between us in strides like an antelope. She whispers the words pressed and tight. "You and I both know that isn't how I'm making money, and I'd appreciate it if you'd shut the hell up about it."

I turn to look at her, eye to eye. She needs to know I'm not afraid of her—not anymore—that she can't intimidate me like she does everyone else, that she can't bend me like she can everyone else. I'm done with that.

"And for what it's worth, your sweet little Betsy knows it too. She loves to act all prim and proper and like she really thought the other gals were making money by selling, but let me be honest: She's not as dumb as she plays herself out to be."

The comment lands just how my big sister wanted it to, searing through my guts, a reminder that if I'm lumping my sister in with the wrongdoers, I can't forget about my dear friend either.

The vision of Betsy in tears just a few nights earlier, claiming The Five was in some way abandoning her, returns to me, and it feels like my heart cracking apart in real time.

"Don't ever talk that way about Betsy. Not to me or anyone else."

Darcy starts—barely, almost unnoticeably—then smiles. "You're not going to win this game. Even if I do sort of prefer this new side of you."

Darcy spins on her heels and marches toward the door, letting out a scream that sounds exactly like the ones my students release when things don't go their way. Before she pulls open the door, she stops, turns, and sneers.

"This runs a whole lot deeper than you'd imagine. Think hard before you push any further." She slams the door shut behind her, the photo frames on the walls rattling in her wake.

I pull in a deep breath, stopping to notice the way it fills the little crannies of my chest, and as I release it I let go of Darcy and her tantrum to the universe. I'm done trying to make sense of her behavior, and I won't wear myself out over it. Darcy is known for her empty threats, for her blustering, and I don't have room for her intimidation to take up space inside my mind.

I start by lighting the candles around my small abode, the ones set alongside miniature ceramics and trinkets I've collected throughout my life. I pull the gauzy curtains over the picture window where the sun floods in and turn up the overhead fan in preparation for my guest. I fluff the worn pillows that have grown tired with time. Back in the kitchen, I unpack the grocery bag, a small selection of cured meats, unusual cheeses, and fresh fruit, then mix up a pitcher of virgin margaritas.

When Roxie arrives on my doorstep a half hour later, it's hard to reconcile that she is the offspring of the furious woman who departed not long before.

She skips right over the threshold and wraps me in her arms. "I've been looking forward to this all day. I brought oils I found online."

"Awesome! I've got some cornflower to try putting in this time." More than ever, I appreciate Bubbles & Suds, these soaps and the repetitive motion of making them that always settles me in moments of restlessness.

Roxie heads for the kitchen and drops her supplies on the metal table before whirling around. "Ooh! Yum!"

She heads for the island where the food and drinks sit, then reaches into the freezer to scoop ice into the waiting glasses.

I join her. "Can I make you a plate?"

"Yes, please." She sniffs the pitcher of yellow juice, her eyes flying wide. "Are these *margaritas*?"

"Minus the tequila."

Roxie pulls her nose into a wrinkle. "Fair enough."

We stand at the butcher block island eating charcuterie and sipping our drinks as Roxie catches me up on school and her plans for the summer. Eventually we have no choice but to land on the topic we've been circling.

"I want you to know that whatever issues come up between me and your mama, it doesn't affect us," I say.

Roxie's eyes drop to her plate. "I know she means well. I promise she's better at home. With me, she's—"

I reach out and set a hand on her arm, and it stops her. "You don't have to explain. I know you love your mama, and of course you do. I love her too—even when we don't get along."

Roxie bites her lip. "She is a good person, I just know it. I think she—"

"It's for us adults to figure out." I flash her a smile I mean with all of me. I only wish loving Darcy was as easy as loving her daughter.

"No, I know that. I just feel horrible because I . . . I think . . ." Roxie fidgets with her hands, eyes darting left and right. "I think I helped her. Accidentally."

"I'm sure you didn't."

"She came to me a couple years ago. I'd forgotten about it until the Easter thing." Roxie blushes deeply and drops her gaze. "She asked me to show her how we make things naturally. I showed her the soap-making process and the oils. I thought she was just interested in spending time with me, but . . . but I think she was rooting around for ideas for Peach Pit."

I round the island and tuck her under my arm. "That's on her. Not you."

I set aside my rising anger that isn't for Roxie but for Darcy at putting her daughter in the middle. Her lack of appreciation for Roxie's devotion.

Roxie drops her head on my shoulder. "So you're not mad at me?"

I smile wide. "Not even a little."

Roxie looks up. "Good, because I've been waiting all day for soap making, and it takes both of us."

We abandon our plates where they are and start setting up the soap-making table. We know our roles, and we work together like a pair of figure skaters, twisting and sliding around each other as we gather and set out the beakers and measuring equipment. Soon we experiment with scents, deciding quickly that the rose essential oil is far too stuffy and grandmotherly for our brand, and eventually we concoct a delightful blend of lavender and white tea. It's floral enough to hit the mark but modern and interesting.

"We'll have to see how it turns out," I say as Roxie drops the agreed-upon scent into the test batch of soap.

She fills a second mold with the liquid soap, and then together we sprinkle and poke our flower heads and petals into the blocks before finally putting them aside to set. Once we clean up, Roxie pulls out her phone to show me some of the design ideas she put together for an updated Bubbles & Suds logo.

"This looks like someone with years of professional experience put it together," I say, meaning every word.

"I just think this company could be something big. Something way bigger than it is."

My heart pitter-patters with excitement, longing for exactly what she describes. Nevertheless, for today at least, I'm feeling grateful for what I already have. Mentally I list everything out: my sweet niece, soaps, the Blissful Bunnies class, Jasper in town. When I get to The Five, my heart hitches; we haven't talked today, not in general, but also not about the article.

I reach for my phone to check it. The group chat is still silent.

CHAPTER 41

Betsy

WHEN BETSY FIRST READS the article on Monday, she is fighting mad, imagining all the rebuttals she might insert between Jasper's points. She goes for a power walk—probably looking like she was on her way to start a fight—but to her surprise, the exercise helps a little. She fields texts and calls from her team, reassuring them that there's no need to worry. Darcy calls an emergency video chat, spends the entire time barking her complaints, and doesn't even ask for questions before she logs off abruptly.

By the following day, Betsy can admit that Delilah was right that nothing in the article was factually incorrect. And it's true that some of the women—specifically Darcy—don't care enough about their Darlings; it's hard but she's come to accept it.

But Betsy does. Deeply and genuinely she cares, and she can't give up on that.

Maybe Betsy has bought in more to the Peach Pit promises than many of them. Believing so fervently that she bought in not only with the dollar amount on the starter pack but with her entire identity.

With all of her.

This afternoon, Betsy's heart hammers as she walks down the school hallway decorated with sweet art projects, monogrammed totes from the older classes hung on their hooks, quiet punctuated by laughing children. It might've been over twenty-four hours since the article came out, but her body is still on high alert, especially knowing that today she'll have to face Delilah.

Betsy knows she shouldn't have kept the Darcy thing a secret from her friend. Really and truly, she was wrong. It sounds like an excuse—and perhaps it is—but it was simply another thing Peach Pit forced her to rationalize when they flooded her with so much acceptance and positivity. It's a phenomenon that would be impossible to explain to someone who hasn't experienced it firsthand.

Until the Easter blowup it never occurred to Betsy that Darcy would've taken any ideas about the soap making from Delilah. She now sees—with very fresh eyes—that the similarities between Peach Pit's soap and Delilah's are obvious. With all of the allergic reactions Betsy's been tallying, not a one has come from the soap.

Delilah stands at the classroom door like she's been waiting for her. She smiles widely, polite and professional as she hands off Huddie's bag.

"He had a great day."

Betsy pulls a small smile back, then releases it. There are so many things she wants to say to her friend. *I'm so sorry. I didn't know what I was doing. I should've done better. Please don't leave me.*

"It's good to see you, Bets," Delilah says.

It sends a dagger through her heart, hearing those words. "You too." She opens her mouth and pulls in a breath, then stops. Where does she even start? How much can she admit? What happens to her when Peach Pit falls apart? Huddie digs his fingers into her thigh like claws and lets out a dinosaur growl.

Delilah glances at Huddie, then up to Betsy. "It's okay. We don't have to. Here and now probably isn't the right time."

Betsy nods once and turns to leave. Why can't she just get this right? She's been friends with Delilah for her entire life, and every time she opens her mouth, tries to make it any sort of alright, she misses the mark. Betsy loves Delilah, adores her, but still something inside her seizes up when it's time to fix things.

Probably it's because Betsy's just not good enough. She wasn't good enough for a real job. She wasn't good enough for her parents to stick around. So why would she be good enough to do this right? Even with The Five, the ones who have loved her despite her faults, nothing she does is right.

Betsy packs the kids into the car and is overwhelmed by a sudden loneliness, as if she's deserted on a peachy island, everyone else on rafts drifting off into the distance.

It hits her: She has to do something. Even if it's not enough, she cannot let The Five drift away without trying everything to prevent it.

* * *

An hour later, Betsy pulls up to Virginia Kate's house with a large edible arrangement riding shotgun. It's her first step forward on the path of making amends, and Betsy feels pretty tickled about it. She stops in the driveway under the shade of trees, rolls down the windows, and leaves the kids buckled in the car. She hops out and gathers the gift basket from the passenger seat, then shuttles toward the door.

Betsy pushes her sunglasses to the top of her head and knocks, looking back over her shoulder repeatedly to check on the kids.

The door clicks open and there stands Virginia Kate, her eyes landing on the arrangement of fruit in Betsy's hands.

"Hey?"

"Sorry I came unannounced. I was just going to leave it if you didn't come to the door."

"That's for me?"

Betsy's eyes drop to the fruit in her hands, and for the first time she wonders if perhaps this wasn't the gift to bring. Perhaps for a woman whose family is in financial straits, a bouquet of fruit misses the mark.

"It is," she says, flushing with embarrassment. "Actually, I'm not sure why I brought this."

Virginia Kate's eyes open wide, and Betsy continues.

"Well, I do. It's because I'm sorry. I wanted to say sorry—for once—but now I'm realizing how terrible I really am at this. Admitting that I'm wrong, taking responsibility."

Betsy's shoulders drop, and she wishes she could rewind this tape and do it all over. It's as if shame might just roll over her like a mammoth wave and smother her when she feels Virginia Kate's hand on her forearm.

"Thank you," Virginia Kate says. "The boys love cantaloupe, so we'll be set for a while."

Betsy nods. "I'm sorry, Ginny Kay. I don't— It's hard for me to put it into words."

"You don't have to." Virginia Kate takes the basket Betsy slips into her arms. "I'm still trying to figure it all out myself."

"I am so very sorry." It's as if she's practicing, knowing deep down that it's a phrase she'll need to get used to saying.

"We'll figure it out," Virginia Kate says. "At least, I hope we do."

"Delilah." The name falls from Betsy's mouth like a heavy weight. Tears well in her eyes.

Virginia Kate pulls her mouth into a concerned line, her eyes softening. "I know."

When a chirp from Huddie emanates from the car windows, it grabs Betsy's full attention. She sighs. "I guess I should go before I can add 'leaving children alone in a hot car' to my list of mistakes."

Virginia Kate waves, heading back inside. "Thank you for the fruit."

Betsy blushes slightly as she heads for the car. Edible arrangement? What was she thinking? Ginny Kay is her lifelong friend who she accidentally led into financial ruin, not an office colleague celebrating a retirement. She's going to have to get an awful lot better at this if she's ever going to make up with Delilah.

If she's going to keep The Five alive.

CHAPTER 42

Delilah

IT'S THE DAY AFTER the article was published, and Jasper and I sit on the tailgate of his rented truck, chowing down on our Milkshake Barn burgers and looking out over Ford's Pond.

"So how'd the article land with everyone in your circle?" he asks.

He was working in the shed when I got home from school this afternoon and rushed to close up.

"You don't need to listen to me hammer away after school," he'd said. I caught a whiff of something he was using, something that smelled too chemical for beer, but he reassured me he wasn't cooking anything illegal.

"I think my mama is about ready to disown me if she wasn't there already after Easter." I can tell people around town are talking about Peach Pit, asking questions, speaking about it honestly for the first time. I've heard rumbles of questions, overheard mutters that sound like *"What do you know?"*

I intentionally leave out mention of The Five. There's too much to unpack, and for tonight I want to escape with Jasper, savor the time I have with him.

Jasper's face breaks into a wide smile. "And to think, it's just a local paper."

"Oh, you're a city boy and it shows. Around here the *Pearl Herald* holds far more authority than a major broadcast network."

A few ducks pop out of the water and approach the truck. Jasper reaches into the oversized bag of fries and starts tossing them.

"You're going to give them high cholesterol."

He shrugs. "Let them live a little, enjoy their ducky lives."

"I can't argue with that."

The sun is dipping below the tree line that surrounds us tightly at the pond's edge, and I can't help but notice the magic of this moment. We're alone in my hometown, eating from a favorite local spot. It's a moment I have dreamed about for years, and now it's happening. Jasper makes me happy—fully and deeply in a way I'm not sure I've felt before. It's not the good feeling that comes with the delivery of a gift, the receipt of an award, or even a raise at work. It's the feeling of real peace that comes only from being fully oneself and welcomed for it. Because he accepts me, I don't have to hold back. I am enough as is.

I turn and look at him. His profile is lit in a warm orange from the setting sun, and I savor it. I want to reach out and run a finger down the shape of it, let my body memorize the landscape of him. Never before have I been more certain that I love every bit of Jasper Rowley.

When he catches me looking, he wraps me under his arm, cradling me.

"I'm so glad I came. When I got on the plane after the last assignment, I felt like I'd never come out of the chaos. Little did I know, all I needed was you."

I smile as the warmth of his words covers me. I rest into the strength of his arms and relish the sturdiness of him as he holds me up. I reach up and snake a hand around his neck.

"You're welcome here. Anytime. Always."

Jasper edges closer. "This time I get the official royal invite in advance."

"You've earned it. All of Pearl seems to be charmed by you." I let my hand hang heavy behind his neck, and I won't deny the fact that I hope it pulls him closer.

Jasper gives in to the pressure of my arm and leans into me. His face hovers before mine, and the quiet between us feels like it lasts a lifetime. Even in the escaping light, every dip of his face, every patch of his dark beard is clear. Every part of him looks like everything I want. His lips are full and hover open, and I wonder if he's thinking the same as me. *Kiss me.*

"There's only one Pearlite I've set out to charm," he says. His voice is deep, and I feel it in his chest pressed against me.

"Rick at the Milkshake Barn?"

Jasper cups my cheek and looks intently into my eyes. "Oh, Delilah. If you can't tell by now, I might just have to show you."

The corners of my mouth lift in delight, and it's as if someone else entirely has taken over my body.

Jasper closes the gap between us, my heart hammers, and when his lips meet mine, flutters of a kind I've never felt before rush through me. His arms hold me firm, and I press deeper into the kiss. Somehow it feels like falling in love with Jasper all over again from the start.

He pulls back, and his face cracks into a mischievous grin. "Dang, I've wanted to do that for a long time."

It's all I need to pull him back into me, back into a new kiss. I wasn't wrong about him. All along this is where those postcards were leading, and best of all: He feels the same way.

Jasper's phone starts to buzz in his pocket, and we laugh, eyes darting about sheepishly as we untangle ourselves. My fingers linger on my bottom lip as he answers the call, as if I'm trying to hold on to the moment.

Sitting right beside him on the truck bed, I hear the back and forth on the phone clearly.

"Hey, man," Jasper says.

"Hey. How's your break been?"

"Good, good, man. *Really* good." His eyes flick to me and my cheeks heat.

"Cool, man. Well, I got word on our next assignment, and it's a favorite of yours: Marrakech."

Jasper laughs. "The same guys in the market?"

"You called it. You up for it? I can send you the details in an email?"

"Yeah, send me the details."

It's as if the bottom of me falls out in one swift motion. Slashed are the butterflies and the warmth and left in their place is a hollow cold. Right after *that*, that kiss, Jasper is mapping out his exit?

"Alright, will do," the other man says.

After they hang up, Jasper sits staring into the phone screen, and I can only imagine he's mentally juggling flight schedules, mentally packing his bags for Morocco, Pearl a rinky-dink town fully in the rearview.

Me in the rearview.

My eyes burn with the threat of tears, my throat thick behind it, so I rush to my feet. I can't let him see me like this, the needy girl who is crying over him after two kisses when she knew all along he wasn't here for long. Even if I knew, it still feels like my heart is tearing in two. I knew it would hurt more if I let myself fall for him, but I did it anyway.

Why *would* Jasper stay? Everything he loves is out there in the world, always a plane ride away.

I am so grateful we brought two cars, and I start in the direction of mine down the path.

"Where are you going?" he calls after me.

I stop and turn to look at him.

I want to say, *"Me? Where am I going?"* But he and I both know I don't have the right to say that. His leaving was a prerequisite to everything that's happened since he stepped foot in Pearl. Even if I was too hopeful to admit it to myself entirely, even if I always held that open spot for the possibility he could change his mind, he hasn't broken any promises. Jasper is Jasper, and adventure is in his heart. It's built into the very fabric of who he is. If he stayed, wouldn't I just be caging him? Holding him back from his true desires?

Despite the logic I parse out in my head, the ache that started in my heart radiates throughout me.

"I'm going to head home. I'm getting a bit of a headache."

Jasper gets to his feet, eyes wide. "Everything okay? I'm sorry if—"

"Yup. Really just suddenly not feeling well."

"The kiss—"

"It's not that. Nothing about that. Seriously." I turn and walk quickly toward my car.

"Let me drive you if you're not feeling well."

"I'm fine. It's fine."

"You're sure?" He sounds defeated.

"Totally sure. One hundred percent. See you around, Jasper."

My eyes heat again like they're brewing tears, but I will not be that girl. The one who had all of the information but decided she knew better. The girl who, when the guy promised he would leave, didn't believe him.

The girl who, despite knowing it would end in heartache, fell in love anyway.

CHAPTER 43

Delilah

I'M SO DISTRACTED TRYING *not* to think about my overwhelming heartbreak when I pull back onto SweetGum Lane that I almost miss Arthur's mail van parked in front of my house. He leans back against it, chatting with Mrs. Chopra, who sits on her front porch.

I climb out of my car.

"My wife had a hip done last fall, and she bounced back fast. Don't know what they're doing these days, but it's easier than ever," he says to my neighbor.

Mrs. Chopra sips from a mug. "Well, that's good news. My sister is a warhorse, so I'm sure she'll do well."

"Brittle bones are the problem as y'all ladies age. Trust me, my daughter keeps trying to put a weighted vest on the both of us."

I stop in front of Arthur. "You? Brittle bones? You're basically a spring chicken."

Arthur laughs. "See, this is why I like you, Miss Delilah. Which is exactly why I'm back over here at the end of my shift all because of you and your fancy mail." He slides open the side door of the van and reaches into a box. He turns around with an envelope in one hand and a pen in the other. "Certified mail means something important. I'll need you to sign for it."

"Oh, Arthur, thank you. I didn't know I was getting anything, but I sure appreciate you looking out for me. Tell Darlene her next two soaps are on the house."

"She'll sure love to hear that."

I take the thick envelope and press it against my chest as I sign the delivery slip. My mind goes to Jasper as it always does when happy mail arrives, but I push away all thoughts of him.

I hand the pen back to Arthur. "Thank you, sir. You're the best mailman SweetGum Lane has ever seen."

He heads around the van and starts climbing in. "The only one in your tenure."

"May you never retire," I call.

"Two years, three months, and seventeen days. Not that I'm counting." With the sound of the engine roaring to life, our conversation ends.

I wave to Mrs. Chopra on her step as I climb mine. "I would invite you over, but I'm dead tired."

They say heartbreak can be physically manifested, and only today do I believe it.

"Well, I only have one piece of news for you anyway, and it's that I'm sad to announce I have been officially off-boarded as a Darling. I may never see my full potential." She giggles to herself.

"Because you didn't sign the NDA?"

"You guessed it. Between us, I sort of like the idea of them thinking I'm up to no good. Now go on and get some sleep, little bird."

My sadness trails behind me as I close the door, and I feel like I should kick myself. Could I have been more predictable? I knew I already had some feelings for Jasper before he even showed up, and despite knowing better, I let myself fall into him, get lost in him, and now here I am in love as he's about to board a plane for the other side of the world.

I carry the mysterious mailer to the kitchen and drop it onto the butcher block island. I rip open the top seal and pull out a stack of papers. A cover letter sits in front and behind it are two different packets of information.

My eyes practically peel back when I see the Peach Pit logo on the letterhead, and I read as quickly as my eyes can drink in the information.

Dear Delilah Thomas,

We are writing on behalf of the board of directors for Peach Pit, LLC. Your work with all-natural, organic soap products has been brought to our attention. We are looking to expand our corporate reach and are interested in acquiring your full line of soaps that comprise Bubbles & Suds, LLC.

Enclosed you will find a packet with the pitch for the proposed incorporation of Bubbles & Suds into the greater Peach Pit, LLC, by creating the "Peachy Clean" division. Though we welcome ideas from you as the Bubbles & Suds originator, all final decision-making regarding branding, product design, and all future retail endeavors will fall to Peach Pit, LLC.

The enclosed packet also includes our initial offer of acquisition. Our legal counsel will be available to respond to further inquiries.

Respectfully,
Peach Pit, LLC

The packet behind is printed on glossy magazine paper and professionally produced with stock images layered with fancy fonts and graphics. The Peach Pit logo has been altered to include a green leaf as the dot on the letter *i*, which evokes environmentalism, and "Peachy Clean" is written in a shade of light peach with a highlight effect around it. Packaging designs are shown as well as marketing and branding slogans.

Peach Pit wants to buy my company? A shiver breaks out and creeps across my entire body like a gentle wave. My hair stands on end, just as my chest clenches. I double-check the delivery information to make sure this was actually meant for me.

The breath almost leaves me at the figure they're offering me to buy my company. Surely they put an extra zero or two on the end. I stand staring at the information, stunned, for goodness knows how long. I'm as good as in a trance, and who wouldn't be upon being put in this position?

I hold in my hands my dream for Bubbles & Suds.

This is growing it on a corporate scale, making it big, checking off a Pearly accomplishment for once. This could be the very thing to finally make my mark. Admittedly, the money would also make a real difference to my lifestyle, seeing as a preschool teacher's salary stretches only so far. The bungalow roof leaked more than once in the wet months last fall, and I know it probably needs to be replaced. It won't be long before my trusty Toyota kicks the bucket. Life would certainly have more wiggle room after a payday like that.

The Thomases would also undoubtedly be proud of the accomplishment, and maybe for once something I do might turn their heads. I hate to let myself daydream about it, but what if the deal was a real opening for Darcy and me? Even the barest connection over something shared is better than where we are now.

Still, there's the undeniable other side: Accepting the offer also means selling out to the very company that has torn a slash down the middle of The Five. Turning a blind eye to everything I said must be stopped. The idea of it makes my skin crawl.

Then again, if I were just to accept the deal, I could put everything back in place. I could make the Thomases happy again—and in a new and even better way. I could patch things up with Betsy, apologize. Even Virginia Kate and Eliza have already said that Peach Pit is water under the bridge for them.

In some ways, perhaps taking the deal is the path of least resistance.

I glance at the financials again, and my heart skips a beat. This would be life-changing money for me—new roof, mortgage paid way down, spending money for travel—and for simply handing over the keys to Bubbles & Suds.

Handing over the keys. It's the first time I consider the breadth of that. My heart aches at the thought, of passing off Bubbles & Suds like it's not a child of mine I'd planned on living at home for their entire life. In fact, despite all of my dreaming about hypothetically growing Bubbles & Suds, only now am I considering the practicalities of that. *Other people* making the soaps, other people selling it, other people's decisions weighing in. Maybe I'm a fool, but in my dreams it's always still been me and Roxie at the helm as it hypothetically burgeons in size.

But again, good could come from accepting this offer.

A truce.

It's as if the indecision has me tethered to the paperwork, the only part of the situation that feels like something to hold on to, and I carry it upstairs with me. I look at it again as I curl up in bed.

I fall asleep with the packet on my chest, and I dream vividly that night.

The world is at peace again, and everyone is happy.

Everything has a peachy tint to it.

CHAPTER 44

Delilah

JASPER IS IN THE shed on Thursday afternoon when I get home from a day spent with my bunnies. I don't go over and chat his ear off like I usually would and instead head straight inside and start fixing myself an afternoon snack. Lunch is always odds and ends thrown together, so I'm ravenous and not in the best mood. I'd also rather avoid having to dissect what happened the other night between us.

It's starting to feel like I just can't get it right, or more so that perhaps when I get on the right path, something new is thrown in my way. I thought trying to show this town what Peach Pit really is would be the solution, and it does seem like more people are scrutinizing the company. That more people are taking a hard look. But it hasn't fixed The Five. Betsy's mind wasn't changed by the article.

And now I have this offer from Peach Pit to supercharge my business to Pearl-approved heights. Bubbles & Suds might have to change its name to Peachy Clean, but isn't a bit of flexibility required of any growth? Still, there are too many holes in that plan to rush forward.

I grab the chocolate chip banana bread I baked the other day and slice a healthy hunk from it and drop it on a plate. I grab some washed fruit from the fridge and stand at my island and eat. The snack won't solve anything either, but it might stave off the hangriness I'm feeling.

A light knocking comes at the glass window on my side door. Jasper's unsure eyes stare back, and he waves. My whole chest clenches at the sight of him. Not an ounce of my feelings for him are gone, but now with them sits a permanent disappointment that feels like a boulder hitched onto me.

I'd rather not, but I wave him in anyway.

"You look awful sweaty for someone making beer. Isn't it a small batch?" I say between bites, keeping my eyes on my plate.

"I may have underestimated the job I signed on for."

He lingers just inside the door, then steps closer, his eyes narrowing in concern when I glance up. "Is everything okay? The other night . . . I thought it was going so well, and then you rushed off. The kiss—"

"I know." I toss a hunk of banana bread in my mouth and chew.

"You know . . . what?"

I stare at my crumb-laden plate. The kiss leveled me in the best of ways, ways I thought I'd never feel, ways I'm now certain he couldn't have felt as well. Not if he's leaving.

"It was nice. Zero issue with it."

Jasper rocks on his heels. "*Zero issue?* I guess that's not a bad thing, but it also definitely doesn't strike me as a good thing."

I shrug. I know it's lame, but I don't know what else to do.

"Well, I'm here for you if you need anything," he says.

"Not for long, though." I turn and set my gaze on him, and I hope he sees the sadness that wells in my eyes. My body screams against having this conversation so much that it feels like a physical pull, but I owe it to him to be honest. "I heard the conversation you had on the phone. About Marrakech. I was sitting right there."

Jasper's brow pinches in confusion. "It's my job."

"And you're leaving. Look, it's been awesome having you here, but I guess I'm just preparing for you to go."

He moves a few steps closer, but still the island sits between us. “I haven’t officially taken the job yet.”

“*Yet* is what matters here. If it’s not Morocco next week, when is it? Another location in two weeks? Or three? It’s not fair to either of us to act like a couple when it’s simply a matter of time before you leave.”

Jasper’s gaze falls, and he lets out a tight breath. When he looks back up at me, his face is red and set. “I’m sorry if I came here—to Pearl and into your life—and messed things up. I care about you too much to—” He raises his hands and lets them drop. “I’m sorry.”

“I feel the same—about messing things up. Our friendship is too important to me.” The words taste so awful in my mouth I could choke on them.

“Okay, well, I guess I should get going.” Jasper raises a hand in farewell.

I smile lamely. “See you around. And look out for Arlo on your way out. He’s graduated to a bigger bike, and the thing moves fast.”

Despite the way my heart aches as I watch him leave, I know I need to put more space between us. He and I are destined to be apart. Like we always have been. The longer we play like we’re hometown lovebirds, the harder saying goodbye will be.

When I hear the engine of his rental truck start, I reach for my phone in search of a distraction. I flip through social media but navigate away at the first mention of “bathing suit season” approaching. I refresh my email, then delete a few from retailers who have already notified me of their sales. Among them, one message grabs my attention, one with the subject line “Records Request.”

It’s from the attorney general’s office, the ownership records for Peach Pit. A pinch of guilt courses through me. Jasper and I planned this together; in a perfect world we would be opening it together. Alas, this world isn’t perfect, not by a stretch.

I click to open the message and scan the contents.

Jasper warned me that often the information is useless, an LLC listing that sheds no light on the individuals involved, so I proceed with caution, telling myself this will likely be a dead end. The letterhead ripe with details of the attorney general's office at the top of the electronic notice eclipses the small chart enclosed at the end.

It shows that Peach Pit is the company I entered under the request, and beside it are the relevant details:

Location:	**Pearl, GA**
Established:	**August 2021**
Ownership:	**The Thomas Group Holdings, LLC**

I stop, my eyes freezing on these words. It feels like it must be a practical joke. No. It can't be. *The Thomas Group*—as in *my father*?

It takes only a moment for my shock to vanish, and a searing pain rushes in to take its place, my racing heart pumping it through every inch of me.

My father's investment group owns Peach Pit. He has been part of it all along. Darcy mentioned an investor, but even when it was her moment to confess, she chose to leave out the part where the "investor" was our very own father. Does Mama know too? No amount of wishing, hoping, praying would change the fact that she certainly does.

Tears fill my eyes, and my chest shudders. I turn to the counter behind me and grab the tissue box.

Together, all of them stole my idea and poured my father's money into it to make it boom. Only when it was Darcy's idea did they buy in; when it was mine, they paid no attention. They kept me on the outside for as long as they could, and only now that their need for me to stay quiet outweighs their desire to have me only peripherally belong, do they offer me a place on the inside.

And by way of certified mail.

Truly, Arthur the mailman who made an extra stop probably cares more about me than my own family.

My body shakes as the realization sinks in that things are irreparable with my family. There is no coming back from this. I have tried and tried, and I can't figure out what I did to make them so unwilling to love me. I went along with Mama's ideas for us like the Easter egg hunt, but to no effect. Maybe if I'd only tried one more time at the pageants, maybe if I'd done more to be polished, produced a version of myself they'd be proud to show off.

Perhaps the only reason is that I'm simply that unlovable to them. Maybe it's time to admit that I'll forever be the daughter they never wanted, the surprise baby years too late.

A small part of my mind, a nook inside a corner, goes back to the offer.

Their offer.

I close my eyes and really and truly imagine my farmers market soap table gone, the friendly chatter around it turned off for silence. The lingering fragrances no longer greeting me when I pad downstairs, sleepy the morning after a soap-making session. I imagine not seeing my friends at the market as routine, too long passing between visits. Lonely evenings where I sit twiddling my thumbs as I dream of my soaps way off on the factory line. When I imagine ambivalent factory workers making my soaps, it's a hollowness that's carved out in me, not a buzzy joy or jittery thrill.

It hits me like a slap in the face: I never wanted this dream. Not for myself.

I *like* making my own soap. I *like* going to the farmers market and chatting with customers. I *like* being able to share my email in case of issues with the product. The last thing I want is to carve out these rituals that bring me to life.

Things that make me Delilah.

It's now I realize a new truth in all of this: All I have ever truly wanted was to belong.

I thought growing a company would make me Pearlier, and that would make the Thomases finally want me, finally make space for me to belong among them. All of this striving for my family and for Pearl, but I wonder, was it ever for me too? Have I ever sat down and asked myself that? Or am I so trained to pay attention to the needs of others that I've forgotten my own? What I wanted was to be me and belong as is.

I head for my room in the rafters of this house and dive into bed.

It may take more than a good night's sleep to figure this out, but it's the only place I know to start.

CHAPTER 45

Betsy

BETSY DEBATED FOR SO long whether to attend Darcy's Friday Darling roundup meeting today. On one hand, squeezing into close quarters with Darcy and the other Darlings on her team is the last thing Betsy wants to do, considering how the self-proclaimed Queen Peach has been entirely focused on herself since the article came out. But Betsy's still a Darling—at least for now—and what if this is good news?

Maybe after Jasper's op-ed, Peach Pit is doing some self-reflection.

Maybe a bad batch of product was detected and ferreted out.

Maybe, after Darling feedback, they've decided to alter the monthly ordering requirements.

Maybe it could be day one of putting things right.

An effort that might extend to The Five.

Betsy sits between two other Darlings, each of them in summery dresses much like her own, hair well-groomed and falling past their shoulders. Glancing around the room, Betsy sees that they all look so alike, something she hasn't noticed before. Naturally, she thinks next of Delilah. Even though the Thomases have been in Pearl for decades, Delilah stands out. Betsy's heart pinches as she imagines all the ways that might be difficult for her friend.

The dinging of a pen on a champagne flute casts quiet across the group of women, and Darcy takes her place at the front as another woman carries around a tray of champagne. Betsy isn't sure whether to take one, feeling decidedly less than celebratory herself, but as she notices not a one of the others decline, she takes it but lowers the glass to her lap.

"Welcome, all my Darling girlies!" Darcy squeals the greeting, oozing sweetness and fun just like she did back when she was recruiting Betsy. She teeters around on thin heels, her skin unnaturally tan for the new spring season, her bright dress tight across her curves. "We're popping champs tonight in a celebration of *you*! Each of you have been absolutely killing it on sales and recruitment, and Peach Pit is exploding with new growth. We've hit an all-time high on profits, and I cannot wait to unveil the way we're thanking *you*, our top-performing Darlings!"

A gentle golf clap fills the room. Many of the faces surrounding Betsy break into squinty smiles, and excited whispers are exchanged.

"Now, before I get to our exciting gifts, I want to address the *opinion* article published in the *Pearl Herald*. All of us who are directly involved know that the picture painted is completely inaccurate. We care about all business owners, and there is a real opportunity to make a good living with Peach Pit—but it requires hard work, perseverance, and creativity. It's not going to be handed to anyone, and that includes us in this room too. All of us have worked hard to get to our level, and we rightfully get to reap the rewards." She runs her long, manicured nails over the glass. "We cannot help a Darling who doesn't have the can-do attitude required to sell."

Betsy has heard these words before, again and again from Darcy, parroted by other Darlings. Even herself. But this time her insides prickle as the words land around her, and Betsy's skin grows warm. She wriggles in her seat, suddenly compelled to move, some biological part of her unwilling to sit in quiet acceptance of what she's being told.

She pulls the champagne to her mouth and takes a deep gulp.

"We are ready to move forward from this article, sticking by our products and our methods—by our *Darlings*. Peach Pit is a strong company, and we won't be blown over by some complainers over at the local paper."

A couple cheers erupt, shoulders dropping and sighs of relief abounding as the Darlings who've been wondering if their days are numbered are assured their paycheck is still coming. Waves of nausea roll over Betsy as the champagne bubbles hit her empty stomach, her head pulsing like it's promising to throb later.

"We won't bow down to ugly newspaper articles. We won't waste our time refuting these claims when the bounties of this beautiful enterprise are so obvious to the people paying attention. Are there any questions?"

Darcy's stare is intense in a way that suggests there better not be. The group sits still, a few heads shaking, then Darcy claps her hands, her face leaping into animation.

"Wonderful! It's the fun stuff that comes next. Each Darling in this room will be receiving a $1,500 bonus on your next check! You will also receive a complimentary basket of products to raffle off to your own Darlings as a sign of Peach Pit's continued commitment to our people."

Betsy looks around at the women with whom she's assembled, and she seems to be the only person not wearing a happy expression. Do they not see? This is clearly an attempt to double down without actually investigating company practices. Darcy didn't mention a single way the company looked into the safety of the products, or the pressure put on consultants to continue spending money on new products before they've sold through their existing inventory. These ways that Peach Pit takes advantage of the women who sign on to their ranks.

It's a flat-out denial.

Granted, all of them have signed the NDA documents required, but Betsy searches the crowd for at least one other woman who appears rattled, unsure. Peach Pit was supposed to be small business, good friends, and quality cosmetics—no dark underbelly. When Betsy cannot find anyone else looking even remotely rattled, an electric shock sparks inside her. When Betsy first started, Peach Pit felt like home, a good place to belong and do well, finally being among people who understood her, but sitting here today, that feeling is nothing but a memory. Did the others change or was it her? When did it change? Certainly incrementally, like being boiled alive in a pot set atop a burner.

Maybe Betsy has changed or maybe she's changed her mind, but in this moment she is certain: She cannot be part of this any longer.

It will come at a price. Jared will be upset, and they will have to really buckle down and change their spending habits—particularly if all three children are to attend Pearl Prep. But she can't gain from other people's misfortune, so if it's a less lavish lifestyle that awaits them, so be it. At least she'll have a clear conscience.

And yes, it's also possible that the rest of her worries will come true, that she'll be left adrift, without meaning or purpose, but the alternative is no longer a price she's willing to pay. Betsy thinks of The Five—of Delilah especially, who finally drummed up the guts to take a stand—about how tenderly they presented their worries, how they separated her from this company. About how they came after her when she walked out, how they stuck around, how they never wrote her off—even in moments it would've been easy to.

All along Betsy worried they would leave her like her parents did, but only now does she see how frequently they proved themselves to be the ones who would stay. With all of this Peach Pit nonsense, Betsy has given The Five reason upon good reason to leave her. Most people wouldn't have blamed them if they did.

They wanted to keep her.

Betsy's heart feels like it's exploding when she realizes the rest: The Five will never leave her.

They are here to stay.

And maybe within her place in The Five there's as much purpose and meaning as she thought was available only inside Peach Pit.

As soon as Darcy steps away from the front of the room and chatter takes over, Betsy slips out. The warm air outside brushes through her hair, and Betsy swears it feels like Pearl reassuring her that she's doing the right thing. She shoots Delilah a text: Are you home? I'm coming over.

She has something to pick up from her house before she goes to Delilah. The *Top Darling Training Manual.*

CHAPTER 46

Delilah

I AM SNUGGLED INSIDE my most worn-in quilt and wearing my comfiest sweats, with Scooby curled on my lap, trying to steal the Swedish Fish candies of which I'm making quick work. I went to school this morning, planning to go through the motions, but I got clear confirmation of a truth I'd already realized overnight.

Amber, feeling guilty about her excessive absences, coordinated a special show of appreciation for me. With the help of their parents, each of the bunnies had filled out a form about me as their teacher. At the top each drew a picture of me, and below were their favorite things about me.

All but two of the drawings were covered in hearts, and I read the favorites lists written in the parents' handwriting.

> Miss Delilah sings songs.
> Miss Delilah is safe and happy.
> Miss Delilah laughs.
> Miss Delilah lets us paint with lots of colors at the same time.
> Miss Delilah hugs.

These statements might mostly be of the parents' creation, them inferring their children's favorite things, but that hits me even harder. I am impacting families. A strong teacher sends home happy two-year-olds. Happy kids make for stronger families.

I already knew I would turn down the Peach Pit offer, but this recognition is reassurance.

I wanted so badly to be accepted—as is—into my family that I clung to this idea that a boom for Bubbles & Suds would be that ticket. Now I know better. I also know I won't ever be accepted into the Thomas family fully, not the way I've longed for. My heart races at the knowledge, my throat tightening suddenly when it hits. I am practically an orphan—or I most certainly will be when I actually decline the offer. It's terrifying to think about it, knowing I'll be setting myself up to become even more of an outcast.

But there's still a glimmer of hope, and I cling to it: The Five.

I toss three red gummy fish into my mouth at once, enjoying the nearly painful assault on my jaw required to mash them between my teeth.

I'll call it fish for dinner.

When a knock comes on my front door I ignore it, figuring it's one of the packages containing a few kitchen necessities I ordered. The knock comes again, and I consider getting up and answering but easily talk myself out of it, recalling door-to-door roofing company sales.

A voice calls behind the third knock.

"Delilah, it's Betsy. Please open up."

I pull myself to my feet, wrapping the quilt around me as I make for the door. I flick the lock open, and hinges creak as I pull the door in. Betsy stands there looking penitent, a thin booklet tucked below her arm.

"I'm so sorry. I screwed up so many times. Again and again, I chose them. I don't deserve your forgiveness."

I blink rapidly. Betsy on my doorstep apologizing was the last thing I expected for this afternoon.

"I should've said sorry a long time ago."

I think about all the ways Virginia Kate came to believe the Peach Pit messaging, and I'm certain Betsy, too, was taken under their spell—particularly so as she spent more time in the organization and at higher levels.

"Oh Bets."

"I'm here with a peace offering."

I step back and wave her in. "As long as it's not peach flavored."

Betsy cringes, eyes dropping. "Well, it sort of is, but in a good way."

I shut the door behind us, and she falls into my arms. It brings back every time as kids Betsy would come to us in trouble, throwing herself upon us, knowing that even if we had no solutions, we might have snacks or movies or commiseration. A will to help her get through it.

"You were right about them. I was wrong, and I'm sorry. I hate how long it's taken for me to say these simple words."

My chest opens, and for the first time since my family's involvement was uncovered, a lightness fills me. I *knew* The Five was the hope. I untuck the blanket I have wrapped around me and pull Betsy underneath it with me. My eyes burn and tears run, and in mere moments I'm a blubbering mess.

"I missed you."

A sob escapes Betsy. "I missed you too. I've been awful. So terrible. I can't believe Darcy stole your soap idea."

"*Our* soap idea. You encouraged me."

Betsy pulls back and dabs at her eyes before taking my hands in hers. "What on earth is going on with you? You look like the pigeon woman from *Home Alone*."

I laugh and realize her comparison is not entirely off base.

"What happened?"

I drop back into my spot on the couch, and Betsy sits right beside me, the booklet tucked under her arm.

"I'm not sure you even want to know," I say. "I'll tell you I didn't. Not really."

Betsy levels her warm green eyes on me, concern pressing her brows closer. "Of course I want to know. Tell me."

"Peach Pit is my parents' company."

Betsy hops back as if she has touched a live wire, and her eyes shoot wide as her hands fly to cover her mouth. *"What?"* She removes her hands momentarily for the passage of the word.

I throw a candy fish in my mouth and chew, enjoying the reprieve it offers, and when I hold out the bag, Betsy scoops an uncharacteristically large handful out for herself and begins nibbling.

Once the fish in my mouth is chewed up and gone, I pull in a breath. "They offered to buy out Bubbles & Suds."

"Oh?" Betsy perks up. "What did they say?"

I drop my gaze. I might prefer having a tooth pulled without medication than admitting this part out loud, but I remind myself it's Betsy.

"They didn't even come to me themselves. They sent a formal offer from a lawyer as if it came from anyone else in the world. They have no idea I even know it's them, so I guess they think they're pulling one over."

"Oh my freakin'—"

"Yeah. I guess they must've been planning to just pay me off so Darcy can keep going, and my father and Mama stay out of it."

Betsy's eyes are as wide as they go. "I could be sick. Right here and now."

I nod gently.

"So what are you going to do?"

I can only assume Betsy sees the two sides I saw in the offer as well. The easy way and the hard way. Most likely my family is expecting me to accept the offer because that's what I always would've done: kept the peace.

But now I've come to realize that *their* peace isn't the same as real peace.

"I can't go along with their nonsense anymore. True peace, one that lasts, doesn't come from shrinking yourself and staying silent. It's taken me far too long to realize it, but there's only one real choice here."

"I've got your back, Delilah. The others do too."

Tears well in my eyes. "I'm going to need it, because if I'm not unwelcome in my family now, I'm sure as heck about to be."

Betsy pulls me into a deep hug and holds me there. She might not have gotten everything right recently, but she is still light-years beyond the family I was born into. She won't quit on me or The Five.

I pull back, and another admission spills out of me.

"Jasper and I kissed, and then he immediately scheduled his next assignment. I needed y'all, but I couldn't—"

"What!" Betsy screams, getting to her feet. "*When?*"

"Couple days ago—Tuesday." I shake a hand at her. "No. No. It's not a good thing."

She drops back down beside me. "So we don't get to meet him."

"Sure, you can. I've been trying to find a time. It's just— I was going to ask when—"

"You didn't like him as much in person?"

I shake my head. "He's even better in person, but he's *leaving*. Marrakech, it sounds like." I shrug. "I knew it was coming—even if I ignored the fact for a while."

Betsy pulls me back into her arms. "Whatever ends up happening, you'll always have us."

I pull a tight smile.

"But you need to text what you just told me to the group chat, and I'll act surprised. The others would have your head if they knew you told me without them. You're already going to get heat for holding out on us for *three whole days*."

I smile to myself, knowing the depth of the truth in what she says, then dig between the sofa cushions for my phone. "It's going to take a minute to get the message right—all of the conflicting feelings contained in the situation." I sigh as I get to typing.

After I finally hit Send, I look up and see Betsy biting her lip worriedly.

"What's up?" I ask.

She reaches slowly for the book she brought with her, the one that's since taken up residence on the seat beside her. She stares at the cover, then turns to me, looking nervous.

"And in the meantime, I have something that will help us with what comes next."

I lean in and read the title: *Top Darling Training Manual.*

"What is this?"

Betsy bites back down on her lip. "Top-secret Peach Pit training information. I'm not supposed to have it, but when I caught some bad energy, I slipped it into my bag at my first meeting. Insurance policy, I guess. Darcy was already several mimosas in and not counting the books stacked up, but this . . . this exposes all the worst bits. Now, I might get the living daylights sued out of me if it gets out—NDA and all—but this information reveals Peach Pit for the fraudsters they are."

A shiver runs over my skin, my muscles leaping to life as the adrenaline courses through my veins. Weeks ago this book would have been like a golden bullet, like the buzzer half-court shot that isn't supposed to happen. But it's no longer that simple, knowing my family's involvement.

I mentally set aside the Thomas crew and take the booklet from Betsy.

I sit transfixed, fish candy forgotten at my side, and flip it open.

CHAPTER 47

Delilah

THE BOOK IS THIN, a hundred pages if that, printed on simple shiny paper with a spiral binding holding it all together. The watercolor painted peaches are lined up in a border, the title, *Top Darling Training Manual*, written in a curlicue font. It looks sugary sweet, like a recipe book compiled after interviewing the local grandmothers, but as I turn the page, the table of contents reads far more sour.

Table of Contents

1. Welcome and Why
2. Winners vs. Losers
3. The Look
4. The Sell
5. The Inside Scoop
6. Wealth and Loyalty
7. The Pact

I must gasp or groan, because Betsy squeezes even closer beside me.

"I know. It's shameful." Regret oozes from her.

"You were always too good for them," I say.

"Just like you are for the Thomases."

I start at chapter 1, scanning it all, even though I'm far more interested in the latter chapters, the ones whose subjects haven't been broached in the emails to Mrs. Chopra during her brief Darling stint.

Chapter 1, "Welcome and Why," is the same marketing basics they've emailed repackaged, selling the company as a once-in-a-lifetime, life-changing experience, bemoaning the effects of aging, and urging newly registered consultants to dig deep and identify their "why."

Chapter 2 is juicier.

Chapter 2

WINNERS VS. LOSERS

> Have you ever wondered what it takes to win as a Darling? What it truly requires to be the girl at the top of the list? You're in the right place. This training has been designed specifically for our elite Darlings, our most promising saleswomen, the girlies upon whom we'd bet our peaches. Congratulations, you're on the right track!
>
> Winners like you are shrewd, business savvy, and built to see a sales opportunity like second nature. You've already built something with your own hands, and we're here to help you go the extra mile, then the next, and the next until you're off on the horizon swimming in success.
>
> The defining trait of a winning Darling is a woman who isn't afraid to get a little uncomfortable. Growth doesn't happen in the comfort zone. How uncomfortable are you willing to get in the name of success? If a sale feels comfortable, if your customer can easily

> resist your pitch, you're not selling effectively. Are you recruiting only women you feel confident would sign on for the Darling experience? If so, you're leaving opportunity on the table. Approach someone who wouldn't be an obvious choice. See the potential.
>
> As much as it breaks our peachy hearts, we have to admit the truth: Where there are winners, there are also losers. When a Darling loses, she can blame only herself; all of the tools required to sell and scale a personal Peach Pit business are provided by the company and found deep within the individual's character. If a Darling is lazy, lacks creativity or a strong work ethic, Peach Pit cannot create those traits for them. Peach Pit creates a stage, and the Darling must perform.
>
> Do you have a Darling on your own team who is struggling? Loser Darlings should be swiftly removed from the organization to avoid reflecting poorly on the Peach Pit brand. Peach Pit is a top-tier organization for high-performing women to live out their business dreams, and this competitive environment may not be suitable for all.

The pages crinkle under the grip of my fingertips, and Betsy pats my back with a firm palm.

"*Breathe,* Delilah. Don't forget to breathe." She hands me a glass of water I had sitting on the ottoman, and I sip as she instructs me to.

Chapter 3, "The Look," is exactly what I expected and not entirely dissimilar to the email content sent out to new recruits: Look hot, sell more. The article goes into specific hair and skin routines—unsurprisingly all using Peach Pit products—and explains how the ghastly effects of aging can be sidestepped with these simple, fruity steps. The language used in relation to aging is laughable—"suffering," "pain," "torment," "affliction"—as if the process of growing older is akin to a deadly disease, not the utter gift of time on this earth that it is.

"Ugh, *these people*."

When I'm met only by Betsy's silence, I look over wearing a sheepish grimace.

"I'm sorry. Not you, of course."

She lets out a puff of a sigh. "I was one of them for far too long."

"That wasn't what I meant. I mean look here"—I hold out the page, pointing—"they compare fine lines outside the eyes as an 'affliction of worn-out women.' Seriously? The small dents in our skin made by smile upon smile is a sign of happiness lived out over and over again, a well-lived life. To them, it's a great suffering to bear."

Betsy swallows. "All beauty products are the same."

"To an extent, but this is worse."

"Why?" Betsy sounds genuinely curious, the defensiveness of the previous weeks only a memory.

"Because not only are they telling women they can't age—while men can—but they're also trying to shake them down too. 'Oh, you poor thing, you're looking so old. Why don't you give us $500 every month and sell this stuff to your friends—or not, or whatever—and just go broke.'"

Betsy tilts her head like she's considering it. "I guess you're right."

I dive into the next chapter on selling, a puffed-up list of sales tactics.

> Offer Limited-Time Deals: Customers drag their feet, and there's nothing quite like a limited-time sale to

take a customer on the fence and transition them into an active buyer. Peach Pit recommends adding a small percentage to the listed sales price so that when a buyer resists the life-changing opportunity in front of them, the Darling in charge can offer a limited-time discount to sweeten the pot. But if the buyer walks away, the special offer is lost! Buy now: the only way.

Tell them why Peach Pit products are different: We save our customers from suffering from the ailments of aging as they approach midlife and beyond. Feeling droopy? Glow up with our plumping Peach Gloss and you'll be nothing but smiles. Skin lackluster? We've got you covered with our sun-kissed tinted moisturizer. Low on energy? Try our zesty body wash to wake you up first thing!

There isn't a life gap where Peach Pit doesn't make a difference, and it's up to you to make this clear to your customers.

I pause at the end of chapter 4 and pull myself upright from where I'm peering over the book. Betsy's there waiting for me.

"Did you eat dinner?" she asks.

"The Swedish Fish were going to be it for me."

"We need some food. How about I go pick up some Thai? But you have to promise me you're not going to go rogue while I'm gone. We're in this together now, okay?"

I nod. "Yes, ma'am."

Betsy crosses the room, pulls the door open, and stops on the threshold. "Be back soon," she calls before skipping outside and letting the door bang shut.

She already knows I want pad Thai with chicken and spicy

peanut sauce on the side, and the knowledge of it floods me with warmth.

I return to the *Top Darling Training Manual* that looms open in front of me, and when I remind myself that Betsy is at my side in this now, finding a way out of this mess actually seems possible.

But first, I need to get through this manifesto.

CHAPTER 48

Delilah

Chapter 5

THE INSIDE SCOOP

Peach Pit is a fun company, and when we started this beauty empire, we knew we didn't need to overcomplicate it. If you're reading this training manual, you've been granted access to this exclusive behind-the-scenes tour where we bear our trade secrets. "Why?" you may ask. It's because you've earned it! You've grown a team strong enough to push you to the top, and we want you to stay.* You are the Darlings people will approach asking for the how and why of the products, so we need to make sure you've done your homework—or at least look like you've done it.

*Darlings are required to sign an additional non-disclosure agreement prior to this training that requires them by law to keep this information under lock and key or risk the possibility of legal action.

If you've made it this far, you're probably a cool girl, and cool girls know there's no time or money for all the boring stuff. The "science." Yes, we make sure the products are safe—we want our customers

> alive and well—but the real promise of Peach Pit is the aspirational life we sell. Have our products been proven to reverse aging? No, silly. Are there chemical components that energize? Not that we know of. Is there a shred of real evidence that the post-baby vitamins have bounce-back qualities? Not definitively. Yet again and again, when asked, our customers give rave reviews. The women using these products feel younger, better, more attractive, more active. They believe they are bouncing back because of how we've made them feel. Because of what we've sold them. Even if the chemicals inside the bottles aren't doing the lifting, the dream we sell is. Peach Pit is as much, if not more, about the Darling culture, the hopes and dreams we inject into our eager customers, women who need a boost, a pep put in their step. We show up for them, we make these changes for them because of how we inspire them.
>
> You, Top Darlings, are our true secret ingredient—not the crusty insides of a peach pit. Nothing that basic could hold a candle to you. Peach Pit glitters and you are among the shiniest stars in our peachy sky. We love you. We trust you. And we know you'll forever be on our side in crusading for youth and beauty, the pillars of a good life.

I'M NOT SO SURE I'll be able to stomach any dinner by the time I finish reading this chapter. The gossipy inside scoop is nothing but a veiled confession that their products are worthless, that they're selling a free dream for real money, that every promise they offer is contingent on the receiver doing all of the hoping and believing on their own behalf.

How could they? How could these Darlings agree to simply

go along with it? First, the questions fly through my head like accusations, but as I remember Betsy showing up here, now on her way to get my favorite comfort food, I genuinely begin to wonder: How could good people be turned to this? Before Peach Pit, Betsy had a great life. She was well-liked, social, an excellent mother, and active throughout Pearl. But after Peach Pit, she walked in a new way, her shoulders pulled back, her smile easy. She also gained financially—we all saw the new jumbo SUV that cost more than some folks make in a year, the budget hotel stays swapped for luxurious tropical resorts, the constantly rotating boutique clothing on the kids. I'd bet it was the confidence, the belonging Betsy found that trumped the money any day.

I, of all people, understand how it feels to question one's belonging, growing up keenly aware of my black sheep status in my own family and how I often stuck out in the homogenous Pearl crowd. It hurts to be pushed to the outskirts, the feeling of inclusion a delicious relief—something Peach Pit offers by way of peachy parties and girly fun.

Peach Pit worked out how to offer this up to women whose identities are in flux: new moms, worn-out moms, moms who miss their old selves. Moms who haven't yet accepted that maybe the new version of them is better in countless ways. In their membership lurks a shiny promise: You can be it all, have it all—just *join us*. Not until it's too late, until the Darlings believe it all so deeply, does Peach Pit lay the evidence out before them, throw back the veil, and show itself for the empty promise it's always been.

Oh, Betsy.

She was a victim in her own way.

I push myself to the next chapter like it's a course in a large meal I'd rather not finish.

Chapter 6

WEALTH AND LOYALTY

If you're sitting in this room, you've probably already figured it out: True wealth building happens by recruitment. We can't legally admit this, of course, and it's why these training manuals are counted and kept under lock and key. But in the spirit of inducting you into the Peach Pit inner circle, we can only acknowledge this reality among the top tiers. Peach Pit is a family, and that means keeping the fold tight.

We have nothing but faith in your ability to succeed as a Top Darling, and your continued loyalty to the Peach Pit organization only opens you up to future wealth and success.

Knowing Betsy will be home soon, I plow ahead to the final chapter. Even at a glance the title sends a shudder through me.

Chapter 7

THE PACT

Are y'all even still with us? This has been a lot of words, and we hope you're still up and running. As Top Darlings, we'd expect nothing less.

By joining our group and agreeing to move up the ranks, you've entered into our Pact. Our Pact is our agreement to protect the Peach Pit proprietary information included in this packet, as well as other training strategies. Top Darlings must carefully sidestep probing questions about products, customer complaints, and in general protect the company's reputation at all costs.

Peach Pit is your family.

Peach Pit will watch over you.

Peach Pit will come for you if you cross us.

Just kidding! Sort of. Let's just agree to stick to the rules, and we won't have to do court stuff—okay, sis?

Peachy love and peachy kisses to you, our sweet Darlings. We are delighted to have you enter the inner circle.

Peach Pit forever!

I collapse back into the cushiony sofa, close my eyes, and do my best to reconcile what essentially read as a blood oath transcribed to paper.

Lord have mercy.

CHAPTER 49

Betsy

WHEN BETSY PUSHES BACK through Delilah's front door with food in hand, her friend lies splayed out across the sofa like a ghost just ran through her, limp and askew, mouth hanging open.

"You alright?" Betsy stops in the middle of the room, halfway to her.

Delilah replies from her starfish position. "Depends. I'm not sure I'll ever get clean again after reading that no matter how many showers I take."

Just as Betsy expected. She reread it earlier, and only then did she realize how her own mind had erased the most appalling sections in the months that have passed since she first read it. Self-preservation, most likely.

She passes Delilah and walks into the kitchen, where she sets the brown paper bag on the counter and begins pulling bowls from the cabinet. Delilah is often best revived by food, a lesson Betsy's known since eighth grade when they watched *The Sixth Sense* at a sleepover, and Delilah was so scared she wouldn't come out of her sleeping bag until Betsy lured her out with a bag of Cheetos.

Betsy carries the food into the living room and sets it on the ottoman. "A drink?"

"I've got sparkling waters in the fridge."

"No wine?"

"Help yourself. I don't trust myself to drink anything right now that might make me more volatile than I already feel."

Betsy cocks her head to the side, considering it. "Fair. Two waters, coming right up."

When she returns, Delilah has already dug into the food, and after a pause during which she inhaled the meal, Delilah is back to talking full speed.

"I can't believe that thing." Her eyes bounce off the training manual. "Although yes, I actually really can. But holy cow, the information."

Betsy nods, waiting for her friend to say more.

"With the NDA you signed, we can't share any of this," Delilah says.

"I thought we might try to find a way to do it and shield my identity. No one knows I have the manual."

Delilah shoots her a look. "Come on, Bets. Everyone knows we're friends, and you're one of a few people I know on that level."

"Yeah, but I took it forever ago—months and months—back when I was new. I made it to the top so fast." The last sentence comes out sounding like a confession.

"We need to talk to a lawyer. Sloane."

"We need all of us together. It should be The Five from here, not you going it alone," Betsy says. "How it should've been all along, all of us on each other's side, no slimy company inserting itself. I can't believe I almost let them break us."

Delilah reaches out and squeezes her friend's hand. "They could never break us. Not truly. I might not have believed it myself until now, but just look at what happens when we decide to be on each other's side."

Betsy reaches out and pulls Delilah into her arms, sliding herself closer. In this moment, it's difficult to understand how she ever thought Peach Pit was the only place she mattered. All along she mattered so much to The Five, the ones who stuck around at her side. Turns out, the years growing up with flighty parents really did a number on her confidence.

"Let's call the others," Delilah says. "Hopefully we don't send Eliza into labor."

Betsy pulls back, tears in her eyes again. "I love you, Lilah. I'm sorry."

"Oh stop, Betsy. No more apologies," Delilah announces. "It's done, and there's no gain to be had by your self-flagellation from here on out. You're with us, and we're going to get stuff done."

Betsy smiles so deeply she feels her cheeks turn pink with heat. Goodness, does it feel good to be Delilah Thomas's friend, to be on her side, to be on her team.

To be one of The Five.

CHAPTER 50

Delilah

THE NEXT EVENING THE Five squeezes into a sticky booth at the Pearl Diner, the last available on a busy Saturday night. Yesterday Betsy put out the 911 call, husbands were advised, plans rearranged, and babysitters scheduled. Not a one asked questions before leaping into action.

"Tonight may be mostly business, but I've got a surprise for y'all!" Betsy cries.

When she beams over at me, it takes effort to smile back. It's overdue, of course, for them to meet my friend-and-nothing-more Jasper, so I pushed past my impulses to keep him at arm's length and reluctantly agreed to invite him. For a *brief* stop in.

"I seriously cannot believe y'all kissed and you didn't mention it immediately," Sloane says.

"Holding out on us married-for-a-decade types who live for this stuff," Eliza adds.

"Well, it was awful, that's why," I say.

Virginia Kate rolls her eyes. "Let's not have this argument again: The *leaving* is awful. The kiss was . . ."

I sigh. "Magnificent."

As if the heartfelt word conjures him, the bell over the retro door jangles, and in walks Jasper. He raises a hand and smiles.

My insides flutter and spin, and I beg my brain to take over and talk some sense into me. I don't know if it's scientifically possible, but I've been telling myself that I can talk myself out of being in love with him. Mostly through mantras, like positive affirmations: *He's leaving, he's your friend, he won't ever—not ever—stay.*

Betsy leaps to her feet and stands beside Jasper as if he's a science fair poster board she's presenting at the fair.

"Isn't he just as cute as a button?"

A deep crimson starts in Jasper's cheeks and spreads across the rest of his face until it reaches his ears. "Hey, ladies."

"Come on, take a seat," Eliza says, attempting to shuffle down the booth seat, only to find that her bump lodges her in place.

"Thank you, Eliza, but I'm not staying," Jasper says. His eyes flicker to me as if to point out the reason.

"You already know me?" Eliza pulls a thrilled hand to her chest.

Jasper holds out his pointer finger and goes around the table. "Sloane, Virginia Kate"—he turns to Betsy beside him—"and Betsy."

"Aren't you forgetting someone?" Betsy says back, her words dripping like syrup from her lips.

His deep brown gaze falls on mine, and it sends a shock wave through me that feels like pain and comfort wound up together. When did things get so complicated between us? I long for the postcard days.

"I could never forget my Delilah," Jasper says, eliciting a gasp from Betsy. "And on that note—I will leave you ladies to your business. I'm rooting for you."

The group erupts in a chorus of goodbyes, and he waves as he dips back out of the diner.

Betsy slides back into the booth beside me. "'*My Delilah.*' We all heard that, right?" She lets her eyes roll back like the wording has taken her out.

Sloane laughs. "You two could not be more obvious."

"*Stop.*" I knew this would come, the cooing and the teasing, and even though I'd usually take it in stride, right now I can't. Not when I'm trying my hardest to rectify my feelings back into the friend zone.

"You heard the woman. Y'all cut her a break." Virginia Kate dabs her mouth with a napkin. "Hunter hearing me talk about exposing Peach Pit might've been the happiest I've seen him in weeks, so in the name of saving my marriage, let's get down to business." She laughs, and it hits me. This might be the first time I've seen her smile since Easter.

"I never should have talked you into it. I feel awful, and I should've seen the truth sooner." The Betsy sitting here in this diner is absolutely not the same woman who was running her Darling squad merely weeks ago.

This one is the true one.

"I appreciate it, Bets," Virginia Kate says, "but I'm a grown woman responsible for myself. I should've just called it off instead of trying to force it."

"I get it. I thought it was going to be the answer to all of my problems too, and all I got from it was a nasty rash and a hospital stay." Eliza laughs.

I set down my fork, my all-star breakfast platter now demolished. "Which brings me to our first order of business: Sloane. If I have found a piece of Peach Pit propaganda that happened into my hands, what legal recourse does Peach Pit have?"

Sloane cocks her head, her soda straw between her lips. "Well, if they can figure out and/or prove who gave it to you, they would go after that individual in court, and depending on what you did with it, they could legally go after you too."

"I mean, *obviously* it's me," Betsy says. "I stole an incriminating training manual forever ago, and I've decided it's time to blow the lid off."

A gasp escapes from Virginia Kate, and her face glows with a new energy. Her cheeks fold into dimples as a smile cracks her face. "Heck yeah, Betsy!"

Betsy flushes with pride, but there's no mistaking the way her eyes squeeze briefly in apology when they land on her friend. And here I was thinking this was Betsy's big act of love for me. Perhaps it's even more for Virginia Kate. For The Five.

"I've got you legally, pro bono, if they try anything. Hopefully their lawyers know better, but I'm more than ready to go toe-to-toe if need be," Sloane says to Betsy.

"I think I could get Jasper on board, excited, in fact, about putting this in an article—even if he's doing it remote."

A shiver runs over me, the hairs standing up on my forearms. Could this really be it? The end? Peach Pit gone, removed, erased once and for all.

"Just prepare for them to push back," Sloane says. "A company like that will have lawyers on retainer, the funds, and the know-how to do it with ease."

It's only Betsy at this table who knows the truth about my family owning the majority stake in Peach Pit. Would my family take Betsy to court? Would my own father take *me* to court? I can't immediately rule it out; there's a real chance he would.

My mama, though, she might make a case to Daddy on my behalf—well, at least partially on my behalf, if overwhelmingly her own, arguing that the kerfuffle it would cause in the rumor mill would be unbearable. There is nothing quite like a juicy family lawsuit landing at the courthouse to invigorate the Pearl rumor mill.

My thoughts have carried me away, but I return to the diner booth where my girlfriends' faces are pulled into curious expressions, eyes trained on me as if they're waiting on something.

"Delilah?" Eliza asks. "You okay, darlin'?"

"Yup. Yes. What now?"

"I was just saying, Sloane needs the whole explanation if she's going to understand," Betsy says.

"Oh. Yes, of course. Y'all wanna hear the craziest part?"

"Do they do tequila here?" Virginia Kate asks. "I'm not sure how equipped I am for *more* crazy."

Sloane shakes her head. "Beer and wine only."

I throw out my hands and wave them off. "Y'all just hush and listen for a second."

I don't give them even a moment to sneak in a sideways comment before I launch into the saga of my family involvement in Peach Pit. I describe their formal offer sent via certified mail, my intent to decline, none of them privy to the fact that I know it's them. Eventually it'll come up, but with The Five needing my attention, it hasn't been the priority.

Sloane's mouth hangs open. "So they just all lied to your face this whole time?"

I nod. "Precisely."

"How did a person like you come from that group?" Virginia Kate's words are thick with anger.

I'd be lying if I said it wasn't a question I'd asked myself time and time again. I think somewhere early on in life I saw the pain behind all the polished surfaces of their lives. Mama was always despairing over my father and his awful moods. Daddy himself was miserable, always going on about *"more this, more that"* while no amount of anything seemed to fill his personal void. Darcy surely had holes in her satisfaction with the way she chased attention and accolades all the way through life. I guess because I was so close to it, I was even more determined to make something different for myself.

Betsy throws an arm around my shoulders, and it feels like being covered by a thick weighted blanket, my thoughts momentarily quieted.

"She's the flower that grew up in the pavement cracks is what she is."

I glance up at her and smile.

"Undoubtedly write the article"—Sloane wiggles her brow—"with your lover boy. We'll figure out the rest. Peach Pit has no idea what it's got coming."

We're settling up our check, Eliza yawning excessively at the end of the booth, when a woman walks past us with her two boys dressed in baseball uniforms covered in dirt smears and sweat. Betsy catches sight of her and her brows leap in recognition.

"Hey, Betsy, fancy seeing you here." The woman stops and so do her baseball boys.

"Oh yeah, I'm feeling a little better than earlier."

The woman crosses her arms and drags her eyes slowly across the lot of us assembled. "I couldn't help but overhear a mention of Peach Pit. I sure hope you ladies aren't causing any problems."

My blood simmers, and I imagine all the responses I would like to lob her way.

"Oh, I was just telling my friends how much I love being a Darling! Still working on recruiting." Betsy winks.

The woman floats off, waving for her boys to follow her, but her set expression suggests she might not have been convinced by Betsy's answer.

"Nothing to worry about," Betsy says. "She has a reputation for starting rumors, so no one takes her stories as truth."

Everyone nods along, but I can't deny the energy that hums among us. It might serve us well to keep looking over our shoulders until the article is officially approved and printed, because as long as Peach Pit is kicking, it's also on the prowl.

CHAPTER 51

Betsy

BETSY IS CLEANING OUT the playroom on Monday afternoon when the doorbell rings. The kids are scattered throughout the house, most likely creating new messes for her to pick up, and Jared is in the backyard pruning the dead winter branches off the shrubs. Betsy heads for the door and opens it.

On her doorstep stands a young guy in his twenties wearing a baseball cap, sweatpants, and a light jacket. He reaches out his hand, and Betsy slowly takes a large envelope from him, her face pinching in confusion.

"Ma'am, this is an official document from Peach Pit, LLC, requesting that you cease all activities related to defaming Peach Pit either verbally or in the press. You have copies of the nondisclosure agreements you signed."

Betsy stands stunned, rooted to the spot, as the delivery man takes off jogging toward his black sedan. The hair stands up on the back of her neck as she flips open the slim panel and pulls an official letter from the manila envelope that reads "Notice to Cease and Desist" at the top.

She spins in place, pulls the door closed—and locked—behind her, and grabs her phone from where it's lodged between the kids' stuffed animals in the sofa. She dials Sloane.

Sloane picks up, and Betsy skips the pleasantries. "I just got a cease and desist order hand delivered. From Peach Pit."

"Ah. It seems they're ahead of the game. I'll stop for coffee on the way and come take a look."

"Please."

After Betsy hangs up, she's too distracted to go back to playroom organization as she considers all the things this could mean. She's already having a hard time coming to terms with the reality of losing her income, but now it looks like legal trouble heaped on top. Sloane said she'd help, but could she really do it in a way that they won't have legal bills?

A heaviness gathers in Betsy's chest as she thinks about the *Top Darling Training Manual*, as she imagines all the various ways the fallout might happen. What if—even if she's represented by Sloane pro bono—she loses in court? She could be on the hook for hundreds of thousands owed to Peach Pit. Just because she'd have a good lawyer doesn't guarantee a win. Betsy begins to pick at her cuticles, and when she looks down, her new nail polish is flaked.

She lets out an exasperated huff.

Two hours later, Betsy has caught Jared up to speed, sent him and the kids to the park, and Sloane sits at her kitchen table reading through the letter.

"It's all fairly standard," Sloane says. "They're doing this to show you that they're serious about you keeping your mouth zipped."

Betsy illuminates her phone and begins to text. "I'm going to see who else got one—starting with Ginny Kay."

"It must've been that woman at the diner," Sloane says.

Betsy gulps. Not only were they overheard, but Betsy also considers how she's started to slowly pull back from Peach Pit. In the past week she left a party uncharacteristically early, placed no extra product orders, and even pushed a team roundup meeting two weeks out. Could some of the Darlings have caught on to her change of heart?

Sloane sets the letter down. "Do you want to reconsider doing the article? It's okay if you do. Delilah would understand."

Betsy's stomach churns like she just drank spoiled milk. She could back out, but could she *really*? The *Top Darling Training Manual* was an olive branch that pulled Delilah out of the mires of heartache, that put a sparkle back in Ginny Kay's eyes, that recemented The Five. Betsy can't go back on that, not when things are so freshly patched up.

"Betsy." Sloane stands and rounds the table to Betsy so they're face-to-face. "I see you thinking in there."

"This is really scary. We're already taking a hit with me no longer having my income, and now they're threatening to take me to court?"

Sloane squeezes Betsy's arms. "I get it."

"They're not idiots either, so when the article hits, Darcy will smell it from a mile away that I took the manual and gave the information for the article."

"Delilah will understand."

Betsy is sure Delilah would understand, but she also sees so clearly how this article is also Delilah standing up to her family for once. *Finally.* She can't let Delilah down when she's certainly scraping up every ounce of bravery to do this.

Her phone dings with a text from Virginia Kate.

"Ginny Kay didn't get one." This should make Betsy feel better, hearing that her friend isn't on the receiving end of Peach Pit's bullying, but there's another part of her that feels even more alone. Even more singled out.

Betsy's eyes grow hot, and after a moment she can't hold back the tears any longer. Sloane pulls her into her arms.

"It's okay, honey," Sloane says. "I'm going to talk to Delilah."

"We can't," Betsy says. "We can't let her down like her family does. *We're* her family. Now more than ever."

She knows the feeling all too well herself.

CHAPTER 52

Delilah

I HAVE GROCERIES IN the trunk and am mulling over which of them I'll make myself for dinner this evening when I pull up to my lavender bungalow and spot Sloane's car parked in front. After I park I grab my reusable grocery bags from the trunk and head up the porch steps. Sloane sits curled up on my rattan egg chair enjoying the patch of early evening sun hitting her.

"I know they say UV is terrible for the skin, but I'll never get over how good it feels to turn your face up and let the sun cover it."

I smile at her, admiring the joy radiating from her, despite the fact that I know she must be here for a reason.

I set down my bags momentarily and slip my key into the door lock. "Come on in before you turn from porcelain to lobster red. I didn't see a text or call from you, so I'm assuming you're waiting on my porch for a reason."

She grabs one of the bags and follows me into the house. Once she's dropped the bag on my island beside the ones I carried in, she stops to pet Scooby.

I leave the groceries for now and turn back to her. "Lay it on me."

She sits on the edge of my sectional. "I'm here about Betsy. She got a letter from Peach Pit this afternoon, a cease and desist order essentially threatening that if she speaks out, they will sue. She's saying—with her words, at least—that she still wants to go ahead with the article, but I'm seriously concerned about her."

I steady myself on the back of the armchair in front of me. "You think they have grounds?"

Sloane turns up her palms. "Honestly? Yes. There's a reason companies like these have people sign NDAs."

I drop my head forward, willing away the fire that burns inside. We could let it go. Arguably, The Five is on good footing, but would it remain so if Peach Pit feels no blowback? What if Peach Pit starts bringing harm to other people we know and love?

"Look, I think since Betsy's come around, she wants to do the right thing. She wants to make amends. But I'm just not sure if this is *the* way. Betsy herself won't say it because she feels she's done enough damage, but the legal recourse could be real."

"Jasper has the article set to run in a couple days—Wednesday, I think. If we're backing out, we need to do it soon."

I bat away the shadows that seem to fall inside me. Last night Jasper and I got started and put this story together through email. *Email,* for goodness' sake, as if we aren't lifelong pen pals finally in the same place. I haven't been able to bring myself to think about it for too long or it would surely bring me to tears. In my last email minutes ago, I finally broke down and asked when he's leaving. I think I have it in me to see him once more, some friendly time and an in-person goodbye.

I'm starting to wonder if it'll be the last time I see him when Sloane stirs me from my thoughts.

"We should all take the night and talk tomorrow. Everyone needs to be aligned."

"Good idea," I say.

She pulls me into a big hug before leaving into the golden hour sun outside. "If you find me out here later, it's because of the magical powers of this sun."

I smile at her joke as she climbs into her car, but I can't deny the small ache inside.

I close my front door and turn to slump against it.

I don't want Betsy in legal trouble, but I do want all of Pearl to know the truth about Peach Pit. I want my family to be held accountable. I couldn't bear the feeling of anyone else signing up while we're holding on to this information, keeping it secret, as someone else becomes wound up in the scheme.

But Betsy.

I have no doubt Darcy is involved in this, lashing out at Betsy the moment she steps out of line. My father probably couldn't care less. Of the lot of them Mama is the only one I could reason with. Though she reliably gets it wrong with me, she's also the only one of them who seems to genuinely try.

It's like a small light turns on in my head. Mama will at least hear me out, and she's loved Betsy ever since she stole her heart on the pageant circuit. Between her obligations as my mother and true affection for Betsy, there may be room to work with.

I don't let myself overthink it.

I grab my keys off the counter, head out the door, and drive for my parents' house.

CHAPTER 53

Delilah

I HAVE TO KNOCK at the door of my parents' home several times before Mama appears in the sidelight by the front door, her hair wrapped up in a towel. She swings the door open, revealing herself in pink silk pajama pants and a matching button-up.

"Delilah! What a surprise."

I walk in, and she shuts the door behind us.

"Your father is off golfing with his friends, so it's just me, I'm afraid." Mama says it like a formality because we both know I never stop by to chat with my ornery father.

"It's alright. I'm here to talk to you."

She leads us to the kitchen. "I was thinking about making tea. Would you like some?"

"No, thanks. I won't stay long."

Mama's eyes flash in disappointment, and it confuses me. What is she expecting? A heart-to-heart? A coffee chat like it's routine for me to drop in like this? Not that it would be a first for us in brushing things under the rug.

"I need to ask you for something."

She reaches as if to take my hand, but then she stops. "Yes, honey. Go on."

"Betsy got a cease and desist letter from Peach Pit."

Mama's eyes leap. "Alright. And?"

I hold her gaze for a few beats before continuing. "I know y'all are the owners. Well, it was listed as Daddy's financial firm in the information request form."

Mama's face crumples, her eyes watery as she flushes. "I've been doing my best to figure out a way behind the scenes to make it right. You know, after I heard about Ginny Kay and Eliza."

I stare at her, and it's difficult not to believe her. She looks so convincing the way she says it. In the past I would've hitched my hope to her promises and gone along with it, told myself Mama was "working on it" behind the scenes. But I've learned by now that when things inevitably get dicey, Mama will not stand up on my behalf. If she really wanted to take issue with the company—the one her family owns—she wouldn't need to do so behind the scenes.

"That's nice to hear, but I'm here about Betsy."

Mama pulls back. "I thought Betsy was still a Darling?"

Betsy has intentionally stayed on so as not to rouse suspicion. Her involvement in the article would be obvious if she suddenly leaves the organization moments before it hits.

"Daddy's going after her with this legal stuff. They all had to sign NDAs, and now, I guess, he thinks she's breaking it." I don't want to give my mother the full story. I no longer trust her enough to make Betsy that vulnerable. "Maybe it's all a clerical error?"

"If she doesn't have anything to do with what you and Jasper are up to, I can't see it going anywhere. Your father only sends those notices out if he's got good reason to believe someone is sharing proprietary information."

My brow creases. "How do *you* know what I or Jasper may or may not be up to?"

She drops her gaze, as if the terrazzo tile below her feet is the most interesting surface in the world.

"One of Darcy's friends heard y'all at the diner. She's got Peach Pit minions in all sorts of places."

"Of course." I swallow the lump in my throat. "All I'm asking is for one thing. One favor. Please drop it and leave Betsy be."

"I just don't understand why it matters if she's not doing anything wrong."

Mama's words cut right through me. She shouldn't need to understand. She shouldn't need more information from her daughter than this. It's Betsy. Betsy, whom she loves and admires. Betsy, the daughter of her friend Mary. Betsy, whom she trained up in pageants just like the second daughter she always wanted.

"Go to Daddy and tell him to let off on Betsy." I point a finger at the ground.

She releases a tight breath, her mouth set in a rigid line. "He's always been ornery, but your father's mood has turned dark recently. I'm not sure he's in a place to be reasoned with."

"You tried to buy me out." I try to swallow the tears that threaten, but despite my best efforts, my eyes burn with their arrival. "And secretly, not even face-to-face. You helped Darcy steal my idea. This is the least you can do."

Mama has the decency to drop her head. "I was just trying to avoid issues. You know your father and your sister both have such mood swings. At the slightest bump in the road, they're through the roof. After Easter, I don't know, I guess it seemed like a good idea to give you something to make up for missing out on Peach Pit. Part of me dreamed it might be a common ground for you and Darcy to finally make nice."

I shake my head. To my ears, her reasoning sounds so lame, like such a weak attempt at patching years' worth of damage with a little swipe of glue. But deep inside, I understand. I've hoped and wished for the same harmony among us, and in the moments I let my mind wander to those places, I, too, dreamed up easy fixes, imagined a world made right.

I, however, am no longer naive enough to daydream about outlandish scenarios wherein we're made whole by the waving of a magic wand—or the writing of a check. It's not real. And the wishing and hoping about it are a waste.

"Go to him and ask," I say. "*Please.*"

"I can't be sure he'll listen to me."

I throw out my arms and pace. "Maybe so, but you have to *try*. How can you just let all this go? Don't you *care*? Even a bit?"

Mama's eyes fly wide as her head whips up. She spits the words at me. "Of course I care! And you should know better than to question it. I gave up everything to be a wife and mother. This family is my life's work, and I've done my damnedest to hold it together."

Her comment slams into me, and I reel back from what feels like a physical blow. "I am a part of that family too, you know? That is what's always lost."

"But I can't blow it up for you, Delilah. There's a bigger picture here."

"I never asked you to blow anything up. I'm asking you to appeal to your husband. On Betsy's behalf. It's not difficult to understand, and frankly it's not an unreasonable request."

"You don't know the whole story."

That comment sails through me like an icy wind, and my animated hands drop to my sides. My jaw hangs slack. There it is. Again. Of course I wouldn't be included in the inner workings of this family, because to them I'm not a full-fledged member.

I should've known better than to hope Mama would see. Hope she'd understand. Hope for a better outcome. Hope things would be different.

Hope is my problem, my mistake I continue to make over and over again with her.

I turn and go. I walk out, no goodbyes.

I already knew who she was: a woman who is happily pushed

around by the bullies she calls family, unwilling to stand up for herself in the name of keeping some sort of ugly peace. A peace that can't be genuine, not if it requires so much hurt.

As I start my car, tears flow. Tears for myself and again for the relationship I know I'll never have with Mama. But my tears are also for Betsy, my dearest Betsy, whom I wish I had the power to protect from the meanness of my family.

Perhaps being on the outside of them isn't such a bad place to be after all.

CHAPTER 54

Betsy

"THE ARTICLE IS SET for tomorrow, so today—right here and now—is the last opportunity to pull it." Jasper hands out copies of the article to The Five arranged in Delilah's living room.

Sloane leans back, skimming quickly. "Factual, tight, and to the point. Nice work."

"It presents them exactly as they are," Eliza says. "And I can't imagine anyone wanting to sign up after hearing or reading this."

Their voices float over Betsy as she looks down and reads. She's halfway in when Ginny Kay speaks up.

"I love it. Love, love, love it," she says.

The group reads for a few more minutes and finishes the succinct article.

Betsy looks up. "Honestly, it's so good, it makes me even sadder."

Everyone stops their paper shuffling, their eyes going to her. The final decision will be left up to Betsy about whether to publish it, but she walked into Delilah's house today feeling confident. Peach Pit might go after her—probably will—but it's long overdue for her to be on the right side of this. To make up for ignoring the warning signs for too long. Even if it means consequences, she's done letting down her friends and letting down her hometown.

Fortunately she'll have Sloane to help her with the legal stuff, and she can trust her.

Betsy spent her entire stint in Peach Pit trying to control the narrative, and admitting that she's tired of it takes a weight off her soul. Perhaps legal issues will come, but she's prepared. She'd rather be right with herself, with her conscience, than be protected.

"I'm ready to go on it," she says.

"You're *sure*?" Delilah asks. "We won't be mad, not even a little, if you say no."

"It's the right thing to do," Betsy says.

"You're still a good person even if we stop on the article," Virginia Kate says.

"Agreed. It's up to you, Bets," Eliza adds.

Jasper sits quietly, only occasionally casting adoring looks at a clueless Delilah, her eyes razor focused on Betsy. He must know he's second string to this group, but why won't he just *do something* to fix things with Delilah? Betsy went to the bother of finding his email address and inviting him to Pearl—not that he needed much convincing—but she can't do it all. As much as she'd love to direct their love story like a movie, it's not her place.

"Thank you," she says. "I'm ready to go on it."

Sloane smiles first, and soon the rest follow. Delilah lets out an excited cry. "We're doing this thing!"

Betsy throws her hands up in the air in celebration, and the others melt into laughter. The Five get to their feet and exchange hugs.

When the burst of excitement fades, Eliza clears her throat.

"This may not be the ideal moment to announce it, but I might need a ride. I think my water just broke," Eliza says, eyes wide.

Betsy's heart quickens, happiness running through her like it hasn't in a very long time. "Oh my goodness, *seriously*?"

"It's time?" Virginia Kate cries.

"For real? Like, *yes*, actually?" Sloane asks.

Betsy walks around behind Eliza to examine the back of her leggings. "Oh yeah, girl." Then she leans in and wraps her in a hug. "It's time for your baby girl to come." Happy tears well and cascade down her face.

"We're all becoming aunties again!" Sloane cheers.

"What do I do?" Jasper asks, a mildly panicked look on his face.

"Nothing," Delilah says. "You're not on deck for this."

With that, Eliza pulls out her phone and calls Ted. Her voice shakes with her fear about the delivery, that it'll be bad like the last one.

Betsy goes to her and pulls her into her arms again. "You can do this, Eliza. You are strong enough to bring her here into this world," she whispers.

When she pulls back, Eliza's face is resolute. "You're right. But I should go now before contractions really start. There's enough time to go to the house and ride with Ted."

"I'll drive you," Delilah says. "My overnight bag for Jack duty is stashed in the car," she calls over her shoulder, heading for the door.

Eliza beams as she loads into Delilah's little car.

"You get to meet her today, Liza. How about that?" Betsy mutters to herself as they go.

She was already certain, but it's the only confirmation she needs. There's about to be another of them—a girl this time. Another Pearl woman who will grow up here among them, following in their traditions, learning the ways of this town. Well, as much learning as she pleases beyond a certain age.

For now, she has a chance to influence what those traditions are. The rituals the women of Pearl subscribe to, the standards they set, the lessons they teach, and the things they believe about themselves. This is so obviously the right thing to do. For The Five *and* for the little ones who will come after them, watching, learning, and following their mothers' examples.

Pearl will no longer be the place for Peach Pit's "looks trump all" approach, if Betsy gets a say in it.

CHAPTER 55

Delilah

ELIZA BRINGS A BABY girl, Harper Rose, into the world later that evening in a remarkably smooth delivery, and the next day the article goes out. I'm at school for the day, and I leave my phone intentionally set aside, tucked into my purse out of sight. If there's a true emergency, my people will call the school office. Anything that happens during school hours will still be there for me to find out about after car pool, and I'm savoring every hour with my bunnies.

Eventually, once all the messes are cleared, all the children packed up, and the classroom closed down, I head home. I turn my phone on only once I'm stowed away back at the lavender bungalow, Scooby curled in my lap, and a snack already fixed to eat. When I power on the phone, the notifications I anticipated rush in.

Several acquaintances across town—everyone from old knitting club friends to former class parents—send texts congratulating me on the article. I guess word of the Jasper-Delilah connection has gotten around town sooner than I expected, a fact I can likely attribute to Jasper's quickness to make local friends.

He has also sent me an email. I read it when I check my inbox for anything important before powering my phone off for the day. He has a new offer for an assignment in two weeks—Marrakech.

This time the news doesn't sting quite as badly.

The Five group chat is full of messages that've gone back and forth over the day, mostly Betsy celebrating how well things have gone with the women she's heard from. Darlings, former or soon-to-be former, who finally feel validated after feeling misled for months. Virginia Kate explains how Hunter came to her, finally able to fully understand the grips the company had on her and how lucky she was to get out when she did. Sloane drops heart emojis all around, celebrating, but I know from her quietness she's likely also biding her time until she has to go to war legally. Eliza sends replies, oddly misspelled messages, as she juggles brand-new Harper Rose.

I told them my plan, so they knew my phone was off.

I type out a reply, but then stop and backspace, knowing I'll need to see to the messages from my family members first. I click back and look.

Surprisingly, there's no missed call or voicemail from my father. Probably he's so cocky he doesn't think the article will have an impact. That or he's simply disinterested in engaging with me now that my knowledge of their involvement is known to them. Darcy has sent a whole slew of ugly messages, wishing me and mine nothing but the very worst in this very unfair world that's out to get her.

Mama has sent a single message, and it knocks me off-kilter: I'm proud of you.

My insides feel like they're soaring at the words. Does she truly mean it? Then again, she's stating it quietly over text, not shouting it from the rooftops, and most likely neither my father nor Darcy has a clue she sent it.

I head back to The Five group chat and type.

Delilah: Not much more than expected over here. Business as usual with my family. A few winks at car pool and a few excited whispers in the halls.

I hit Send and set the phone down, then lift my snack plate from the ottoman. I pop a grape in my mouth and chew, and a wave of relief comes over me. The unraveling of Peach Pit, as much of it as happens, will come out over weeks and months, and it's a relief to be done with my part in it. Of course my mind goes to my family—Mama mostly—wondering how my father is choosing to explode about this.

I keep thinking about that text, knowing that even if things between Mama and me aren't destined for improvement, I'll keep that message.

I'm proud of me too.

CHAPTER 56

Betsy

WEDNESDAY'S ARTICLE IS BARELY in the hands of readers before the rumor mill kicks into gear, texts sent with a link to the online version, phones dinging with *"Did you know this?"* and *"Can you imagine?"* texts, Darling emails hitting Betsy's inbox with their termination requests. For all the time Betsy worried over what a world without Peach Pit would mean—imagining crippling anxiety, chest palpitations, thick tears as blame fell at her feet—today is remarkably peaceful.

Betsy feels lighter than she has in months as she strolls into the hair salon, knowing full well she can be proud for her part in the article. Knowing full well that she belongs wherever she plants herself, and for starters that's among The Five. Knowing that she's doing good and *that* matters.

The receptionist does a double take when her eyes land on Betsy. "*Oh*. Hey, I didn't know if we'd see you today."

Betsy smiles, true peace ballooning inside. "And whyever not?"

The receptionist falters, then eventually shrugs. "Of course. You have an appointment."

"And if this is about the article," Betsy says in her sweetest voice, "I couldn't be more tickled that the truth is finally out."

She gets a few looks on the salon floor as she follows the receptionist to her stylist's station. She ignores them, shoulders back and head held high. She's practiced this stance ever since she was a little girl, each time her parents left, but for the first time she actually experiences the confidence inside to match her outside presentation. Betsy doesn't wait long for Monica, her usual stylist, to arrive, and she greets her warmly.

"I'm so glad to see you. I was hoping the article wouldn't come back on you."

"Oh, girl, I'm *relieved*," Betsy says. "It's time for the scheme to fall. I was under the spell for far too long—took one of my friends getting swindled by the program to see the truth."

Of course there's more to the story, but the less she says, the clearer Peach Pit shines as chief villain.

The women in the chairs around her are listening in, and she doesn't care. Every time she speaks the truth out loud, she feels lighter, like she can like herself more, like she doesn't have to pretend. Betsy wants everyone to hear. She wants them to know she's wholly off board from Peach Pit.

The hair salon is the best place to start, and it was no coincidence that she scheduled this appointment for today. While Monica puts color on her roots, Betsy types an email that includes every Darling on her team.

> To my Darlings—scratch that—to my friends,
>
> By now you've likely seen the latest article about Peach Pit in the *Pearl Herald*. Although we are all restricted by the NDA documents we signed in what we can say about the company and its practices, I want to extend my personal apologies to anyone who might've been harmed by this company. Whether it's mental—being made to think you weren't enough if you struggled—social, or financial, it's not your fault.
>
> I, too, was under the Peach Pit spell for too long, and it took a friend's terrible experience for me to finally see the truth. I will be completing my own Darling termination

form today, and I am attaching the form for anyone else who would like to terminate their membership. Note: If the form is completed and submitted by 5/15, you will not be charged for another month's worth of product.

All of you are incredible, fabulous women, and you have valuable skills that I have no doubt will carry you into new opportunities in the future. If I can be of help with references or referrals, please do not hesitate to ask.

All my best,

Betsy

An hour later, Betsy is done with her hair service and has sprinkled a couple dozen comments around the salon to stoke the rumor mill. It's those women's lucky day to have gossip gold to take with them.

"I heard it right from Betsy McCleary at the hair salon. Well—overheard it."

Back in her large SUV, Betsy sits for a moment with the engine humming. It feels like a relief to be honest about Peach Pit, to wave farewell, but she'd be lying if she said there wasn't a gap left in its wake too. She staked so much of herself on it, so much of her family's lifestyle on it, but much like she said to her team in that email, Betsy is certain that she, too, has skills that will serve her.

She's certain there is a path forward for her and—who knows—it might even be bigger and brighter than anything she did at Peach Pit. Certainly, it'll be built upon values she can be proud of.

CHAPTER 57

Delilah

AT SCHOOL FRIDAY MORNING, I'm kicking myself for not making the same plan to turn off my phone, because it keeps buzzing and ringing, and as soon as I think it's done it does it again. There are only two weeks left of school, and I want to be mentally present for every day that remains. After that Fox, Neil, Madeline, Collin, Cici, Asha, Morris, Braylen, Tia, Jack, and Huddie will move on to the Buzzy Bees class for three-year-olds. Every year I cry on "graduation" day. Sure, it's a bit over the top, but celebrating so many of them learning to use the potty, remembering to say "please" and "thank you," learning to sit in the circle, and pouring their creative spirits into craft after craft is never too much.

I am so proud of each and every one.

When I step aside to check my phone, I'm surprised that it's Mama trying to get in touch with me.

I sigh.

I can only imagine she's just trying to talk me out of something. Or into taking a shady deal from Peach Pit to save them face and a few bucks. Sure, most of the town doesn't yet know that the Thomases own the majority of the company, but it will be only a matter of time before it's common knowledge. Probably Daddy will have a PR firm in the wings ready to spin the story of them being some silent investor, the malpractice all unknown to them.

I read her texts in order.

Hi Delilah, I need to talk to you.
I have news. Please call.
I need to tell you, honey. Pick up.
Where are you?
This is an emergency. 911!

The last message stops me in my tracks. Immediately my mind goes to the worst: She's deathly ill or injured, in the hospital actively dying. I whisper to Amber that I need to step out. I walk all the way outside, the sun warm on my shoulders, and dial. She picks up on the first ring.

"Oh thank goodness. Delilah."

"Mama, are you okay? What's going on?"

"I need you to meet me."

"Are you safe?"

"Yes. I think." Her voice is quiet. Alarmingly so.

"I can come to the hou—"

"No!"

A coldness runs over me, and the image of my steely, cold father crashes through my mind.

"Where? Mama, I think we need to call the police."

"No. Honey—"

"Mama, I'm worried."

"The Waffle House on Montgomery Boulevard by your father's office."

I nod even though she can't see it. My heart is racing so fiercely I can feel the pulse in my throat, and I swallow to flush it away.

"Are you okay? Are you sure you're safe? I can call the police."

"I'll be fine. And Delilah?"

"Mm-hmm."

The pause that follows feels like ice running in my veins.

"I already did call the police."

She hangs up, and I scramble to gather my things, to get to her.

* * *

I don't even make it inside the Waffle House because Mama stands outside in the cracked parking lot, a long cardigan pulled tight around her, despite the warm spring sun. I'm immediately comforted by the sight of her bodily unharmed. Her face is makeup free, her hair pulled back under a ball cap, and it strikes me that I can't remember the last time I saw her out in public not put together and dressed. I park beside her and jump out of the car, then instinctively pull her into me.

"Oh, Mama, what's happening? Are you okay?"

When she leans back, her eyes are watery and red from whatever distress she's been enduring. She looks tired, her natural ease erased. Across the parking lot, a group of teenagers spill out of a car, chatting animatedly.

She laughs half sincerely. "Just look at me. Guess this is what Peach Pit does to you!"

I reach out and run a hand over her shoulder. "Whatever it is, I'm here."

Knowing how much I mean this—knowing that it'll never go both ways—causes my skin to prickle slightly.

A whirring police car siren passes behind us with flashing blue lights, and it causes me to step back. Another two police cars ramble by, and then it clicks.

"Mama, are these the police you called?"

Tears fill her eyes and spill down her lined face. She manages a tight nod.

"Where are they going?"

Mama turns her body to face the small business complex beside us. It's built out of redbrick with bright white trim, gold lampposts throughout the parking lot. A place where all the successful independent finance and business guys around here set up shop.

I gasp.

"*Daddy*." I say it as much as a fact as I do a question for my mama, and the way she meets my gaze, bereft, I know I'm right.

"Our family was my life's work."

We move to the grassy divider between the restaurant parking lot and that of the office complex, floating closer to the scene like an invisible force is pulling us.

A line of black SUVs tears down the main road and turns into the lot one after the other. Soon uniformed people spill out of the large vehicles, their dark blue coats reading "GBI" on the back: Georgia Bureau of Investigation.

I reach out and take my mama's shaking hand, adrenaline coursing through my own muscles, as my feet move faster to keep up with her as she rushes toward the gathering officers.

Tears run down Mama's face, and I squeeze her hand.

The GBI agents disappear into a business front door, one in the very direction of my father's office, and soon they reappear with boxes loaded with electronics, paperwork, and files. Police radios chirp, muted voices passing over before fading into white noise. Eventually, the vehicles begin to leave, their back ends loaded with evidence.

Daddy storms out onto the sidewalk behind them, marching like he's going to do something about the imposition.

"*Absurd*. Completely absurd! Surely whatever information was sent to you was doctored up by somebody looking to start trouble for me."

I weave through the police vehicles, Mama on my heels, and when I get to him his eyes squint in confusion.

"Delilah? What're you doing here?"

Mama rounds from behind me to face him, and he does a double take when his eyes land on her.

"What's this all about?" I look at Daddy, making it clear the question is for him. "Why are the cops unloading your office?"

Red in the face, he huffs. "They won't tell me anything aside from that they've got a warrant. I need my lawyers here *now*."

My mind runs. How could Daddy have gotten into something warranting a police sweep of this size? Sure, he looks for tax loopholes like all the other finance guys, but there's a reason he keeps lawyers on retainer. I guess I wouldn't put it past him to push the rules a bridge too far if there was money to be made. If even on the outskirts of the law. Surely he'd tell himself that as long as most of his business is law-abiding, being a little outside the lines won't harm anyone.

I turn to Mama, and finally the other puzzle piece clicks: She called me here, so she must know something about this.

Daddy was caught off guard.

Mama drags her eyes up from the asphalt and meets my father's gaze. A moment passes between them, and whatever silent messages they exchange, something dawns on my father.

"You knew?" he demands. Then he turns to me, leaning in. "Or you? That's why you're here."

My heart thumps loudly, but I step up to him. "It looks like you're the one who needs the talking-to if the police are ransacking your workplace. Don't come at me and Mama like we're to blame."

Mama's hand is on my forearm. She steps forward and addresses her husband directly.

"I looked into the records after you threatened to go after the girls legally. I know what you've been up to."

Daddy throws out an incredulous hand. "Really? *Please*, enlighten me."

"Stealing money from the Peach Pit coffers to pad all your bad investments. Reporting record highs to your clients to drive more business when you're taking the gains from the poor women slinging peach products all over town."

He blinks. His mouth falls open, but no words come out.

"I guess you thought I'd be either too dumb or too afraid to report you, but I'm done. I'm done with this company creating problems in the family. I'm done with you pushing me around."

Mama's arms are planted confidently at her sides, her head held high.

He scoffs. "There's only one person who has an issue with it." He turns to me. "Sorry, Delilah, but we can't all quit making money because you got your feelings hurt."

Mama shakes her head. "At least two people. Delilah and me."

"So you reported me?" Daddy asks.

Mama cocks her head as if she's suddenly confused. "Well, here I was thinking there was no crime—since you so directly stated any accusations are false."

"Answer the question."

She whips her head back upright. "Yes. I called the police. You wouldn't be convinced by me alone to cut the crap and put family over profits, so you left me no choice."

Daddy steps closer, nearing Mama like a circling predator. "After all these years, all this time, you betray me? I've done nothing but be a good husband."

I know firsthand he hasn't been anything close to a good spouse. He's unkind to Mama as a practice, isolates himself to "work," and spends all his free time on the golf course. He doesn't make her a priority, and it's only when there's something amiss with the household that he wants to chat.

"Well, that's where our opinions diverge, Jim. I loved you—probably still do in there somewhere—but you've been selfish and mean and this stealing money bit was just the grand finale."

"I can't believe you."

"Well, I guess you can say I've finally had enough."

A pair of officers strolls up, their hands propped on their belts. One clears his throat, and we turn to look.

"Excuse me, sir. We'd like to bring you down to the station to answer some questions."

Jim nods. "Fine, but I'll need my lawyer. Trudie, I need you to call him."

When Daddy looks over at her as he's done for years to clean up his messes, she clears her throat.

"Actually, Jim, Delilah and I are about to go grab coffee at the Waffle House, so you'll need to call your own lawyer."

Mama turns and strides away, shoulders back and assured, and I follow. She's like the Pied Piper of finally getting it right, and I join her parade heartily.

CHAPTER 58

Delilah

SITTING OPPOSITE EACH OTHER in the sticky booth like mirror images, Mama and I wrap our hands around warm white mugs. The teenagers from earlier are eating, and their chatter creates a hum in the background.

Mama looks down, shaking her head. "Ever since you came over and told me about the legal notices, I've been digging, but I was listening even before that."

"What do you mean?"

"First I searched in your daddy's home office looking for something, anything, to stop him. Later I snuck into his business place and got into his laptop."

"But how did you know to do it?"

Mama meets my gaze and presses her lips into a flat line. "I've been married to the man for decades, and yes, he's always been irritable, but recently it's become something else. For a while I wondered if it was a medical issue, so I decided to listen in when I could on his calls, trying to gather information. He went to his physical and got a clean bill of health, but from the snippets of conversations I grabbed, it became obvious there were issues with money. His investments weren't going as planned or something, and the business was struggling."

"*His* business, *not* Peach Pit?"

Mama nods. "Of course I didn't really know what exactly I was looking at, all that financial information I snuck out, the spreadsheets and balances, but I had a feeling it might not be right. The money Peach Pit was making was significant, but then the balance of the accounts didn't match. I had your uncle Mike take a look at it, and within hours of having it, he told me someone had been stealing from Peach Pit accounts, siphoning off funds."

"Daddy."

Mama nods. "He was the only person who had access to them—refused to let Darcy touch them. Now, perhaps my hunch will be proven wrong in a court of law, but I'll eat my hat if I'm wrong. He's always been squirrely about letting any other professionals in on the accounts, strange about hiring help he needs keeping the books. I thought he was just particular, but now I suspect he might've had things to hide."

In the silence that passes, I wonder if his own money too—his and Mama's—is somehow mixed up in this impropriety, but I bat it away. Surely whatever is going on, the GBI will get to the bottom of it with everything they took.

"But why? Why are you doing something now after going along with him for all these years?"

"After you came over about the letter Betsy got, I went to him like you asked. I asked him to withdraw it—or whatever would need to be done to take it back—but the cruel man just laughed like I was joking."

My mind feels like a shuffling deck of cards as I scramble to make sense of her words. "So you reported Daddy to the police . . . for *Betsy*?"

Mama's eyes brighten as if it's all she can manage instead of a smile. "No, honey. I love Betsy, but no. After I pushed him, trying to assure myself he'd never actually take legal action, he went off on a tangent about how he'd take all of y'all on in court for going after his cash cow. Told me he would sue you. *You,* his very own child!"

I drop my eyes and stare into the deep well of black coffee inside my mug. It hurts to hear the confirmation, but I can't say I'm surprised.

She reaches out and takes my hand as she stares into my eyes intently. "I'm doing it for *you*, Delilah. Maybe it's all too little too late, but I say better late than never. You inspired me, honey, and I'm so sorry it took me this long to wake up."

"It's okay—"

"It's not." She sits back, still holding my hand, and turns to look out the window as a police vehicle drives calmly away from the scene. She dabs at her eyes, and her voice comes out in a thin whisper.

"I feel terrible. Just awful. About how you've been treated. About having to report your father. About how spoiled your sister is. But it had to be done." She drags her eyes back to me. "I couldn't let him hurt you again. Or your beloved Five this time. I know they're like sisters to you."

My chest feels like it's breaking open as the words meet my ears, the words I've yearned to hear for years, but even more than the words, the action. Mama finally standing up to my father's bullying is a small miracle, and it opens the door wide for this family—whatever remains of it after the dust has settled—to grow fresh upon honest ground.

"You did the right thing. He was stealing from our friends and neighbors, our town. Even Darcy."

She nods like she's trying to convince herself. "I married your father so young, gave up everything else. It was the way back then. He had a job lined up with his own father, so we married and started a family. Only years later—quite recently, in fact—did I wonder what else I gave up in those choices, as he became colder to me. As he grew greedier."

"You're worthy of so much more."

She shrugs. "Who knows. I made my own fair share of mistakes with you kids and with the family. I gripped it too tight, the only thing I had."

"You're the hero in this story, Mama. The one where Peach Pit gets the axe. Sure, the article would've cast speculation, people would leave the company. But as long as Daddy was at the helm, it would've been like a bad smell we couldn't quite kick."

She shrugs. "I'm not sure I'm a hero, Delilah. In fact, that'd probably be you and the girls. Jasper gets a nod too. I just hope there's something to be remade here. A family of some sort. A worthwhile life."

"Mama, I am here, your family. And I have a sneaking feeling that life's about to look even prettier, even better than what we'd counted our best yet."

Mama's eyes brim with tears, and she manages a smile. "I couldn't be luckier to call you mine."

Before long we pay for our coffees and head for the parking lot. I follow Mama in my car as she drives home. At her house I make sure she's settled and has something to warm up for dinner. I feed the dog so she doesn't have to worry about anything. Being inside my childhood home with the knowledge that my father will be brought to justice for his wrongdoings makes the place feel different. Perhaps it's me that's changed—certainly I am—but the air feels fresher, and I take my time like I can never remember doing before. For so long inside these walls, it was every person for themselves, it was bickering and brute force, but now Mama has reset the expectations.

I did ask her about her plans when my father gets released from the police station, and apparently she's already discussed it with the lawyer: Jim can stay at the beach house or the mountain cabin, but he's no longer welcome at the Pearl estate.

Part of me feels sad, but only about how hard this is on Mama, how hard it'll hit others. It's difficult to feel entirely torn up when my father has been a bully for as long as I've known him, that he's wielded Peach Pit, knowing full well the unethical ways they pulled in their profits.

I drop a kiss on Mama's head before I turn to go. "Maybe silence your phone. Or even turn it off for a while. I'm sure the news will get around before long."

She nods. "Thank you, honey, but I'll keep it on. I'm expecting I'll hear from your sister eventually, but I wouldn't mind one more night's sleep beforehand. Call me in the morning, alright?"

"Yes, ma'am," I say, then dip out the front door.

CHAPTER 59

Delilah

THE MORNING AFTER MY father is taken in by the GBI, I head for the farmers market like I do so many Saturdays. It's strange to go about something so routine when the world feels completely off-kilter, but me sitting at home isn't going to change anything. Nevertheless, I'm tired, my muscles worn from the adrenaline of the last few days, and as I sit, every detail of the market comes into sharper focus.

The first scent of coffee on the breeze as the coffee shack comes to life; a burst of laughter into the quiet air as two friends reunite; the rainbow of all my soap creations, the abundance of them; the feel of the tablecloth I painted below my fingers. Probably my previous ambition was all wrapped up in my desire to get closer to my family, but this morning it seems silly that I ever wanted to make my beloved small business into a corporate beast. It's simply perfect as is, small but sturdy, chugging along despite the competition. All I could use is a better organization system at the house to keep the soap table neat and perhaps Bubbles & Suds would be a thing dreams are made of.

The mini soaps are almost set up in their tower when Roxie's voice meets my ear.

"Morning, Auntie Lilah."

I turn and she rushes into my middle, and I wrap her in my arms.

"I'm so sorry." She pulls back. "Peach Pit. My mama. I think the earth might swallow me whole."

I cradle her face to stop her. "It's already been dealt with by the adults. And when it comes to Bubbles & Suds, it'll always be you and me in my kitchen."

"You're sure? I swear Mama is so different with me, I—"

"She's a good mom?"

Roxie pulls her nose into a wrinkle when she nods. "Even though it doesn't make sense."

"I believe you."

I mean it when I say it. Darcy and I don't see eye to eye, we are not friends, and probably won't ever be. But we also grew up in the same household, and now more than ever after Mama's confessions, I realize that the toxic family culture impacted all of us. Even if it seemed like everything came easy for Darcy, it's possible there's more to the story. Maybe Darcy, just like me, became who she needed to be to survive among the Thomases. Perhaps her performing and demanding was her version of my fixing and smoothing. With today's fresh eyes, I'd say the lot of us Thomases could use a little extra compassion.

Roxie lets out a sigh. "Thank goodness. Bubbles & Suds is way better than Peach Pit anyway. Maybe one day we can get an outdoor sink set up, but even if not, there's no complaints from me."

"Agreed, honey. Agreed."

Roxie pulls the tablet from its bag and begins setting up the payment station.

"Where's lover boy this morning?" Roxie's messaged me more than once about Jasper since the two met a couple weeks ago.

When I stop and think about Jasper, my heart squeezes. He leaves next week for Marrakech, and part of me is grateful he decided to forgo the market this morning, promising instead to go by my house to clean out his beer brewing operation from the shed.

It's probably best that having him here is already starting to feel like a fever dream. Hopefully, with time, the marks he left on my heart will start to fade too. Nevertheless, without his journalistic input none of our lives—mine, The Five's, Mama's—would be in the fighting shape they are in today. Maybe he had some impact on me finding my voice as well. It's as if he was sent to us for a reason.

Even if my heart will break to say goodbye to him, I'm determined not to let it ruin the memories we made during these weeks. Even if he won't be my forever person, he will remain one of my most cherished friends. And I'll keep writing to him. As always.

For better or worse, I love Jasper Rowley.

"He's off this morning."

Roxie looks over. "He seems like a pretty good guy."

"You're right," I say. "In fact, he's better than 'pretty good.' The world is lucky to have him, wherever it is he lands."

* * *

When I arrive home to my lavender bungalow, sweaty from a morning outside in the heat, I have no plans but to take a shower and watch movies for the rest of the afternoon. There wasn't much to pack up at market close, due to our record sales that left Roxie and me scrambling to schedule a soap-making date. Perhaps it's the outcome of Peach Pit falling out of favor or perhaps it's the universe giving me a nod. Confirmation that I'm on the right path.

My car door slams behind me, and when I approach the house, Jasper stands in the middle of my porch.

"Hey." My stomach drops at the unexpected sight of him. He said he'd be done cleaning the shed before I returned. "Everything okay?"

He looks up, unsure.

Is he leaving early? This must be it. Goodbye.

"I have something I need to show you. Out back," he says.

Relief floods me. "I thought we agreed on no Walter White."

His face remains serious as I unlock the door, and he leads me through the house to the back door. He opens it and steps down onto the concrete pad, and as I follow him I almost lose my footing on the bottom step at the sight before me.

My shed is lavender. To match my house. My hands rush up to cover my mouth as a gasp escapes. I look at him, his deep brown eyes keenly watching my response.

"It's . . . *purple*," I say.

"Do you like it?"

"*Of course!* It matches my house."

Jasper's face stretches into a grin. "Let me show you the rest."

I follow him to the front where he's sanded down the door and replaced the rusty hardware with sparkling gold fixtures. He's even potted some flowers and set them out on either side.

"You didn't have to do this. You know I let you borrow the shed with no strings attached."

Jasper stops with his hand on the doorknob and looks at me. "That's the thing: It wasn't beer I was making inside." He turns the knob, and as the door swings open, I see the rest.

I'm speechless.

He has cleaned out the interior and painted the wooden slat walls a bright white. Two smaller metal prep tables line the walls, and a laser-cut wooden sign hangs on the back wall with "Bubbles & Suds" in the new font I recently chose with Roxie for the branding.

"You asked her?" I say, pointing to the sign.

He nods. "I wanted to get it right, make sure the place actually worked for soap making, and who better to pull in as my accomplice in the design?"

I step inside and see fairy lights strung up where the ceiling meets the walls, a lamp in the corner. The wire shelving along one wall is already stocked with our oils, scents, the mix-in ingredients.

Below sit our beakers and mixing bowls. Even the electric burner has a permanent place.

I whirl around, and even inside my brand-new soap-making shed, I only have eyes for Jasper. I go to him and wrap my arms around him, searching my brain for the right thing to say.

"Thank you." I say it with my entire heart, but it still feels like too little.

"You're welcome."

I look up at him from where I'm pressed against his chest. "But why?"

"Why did I make over this shed?"

I nod only once. He takes my hands and steps back just enough to lock our gazes.

"I built you this shed, Delilah, because I didn't know a better way to show you, to tell you—*finally*—that I love you. And probably for longer than I knew. First because of the loopy handwriting that always lifted my spirits, next in the thoughtful replies I waited for, genuinely desiring your input in my life. When times were rough, everything changed at the sight of a postcard or letter in the mail. And then in person." His eyes glint. "Beautiful you, right here before me. Being with you is all of the best things that ever kept me going every minute of the day."

I push up to my toes, my heart racing like the wings of a hummingbird, and I brush my lips against his. Jasper pulls me into him and returns the kiss with fervor. Warmth floods me, and I hold on. His fingers creep up to the nape of my neck, and the touch sends a shiver through me.

I pull back. "But Marrakech. Next week."

His mouth curves into a smile. "I didn't sign the contract. I didn't take the job. I don't know what's next, but I can't leave you, Delilah. I didn't come here planning to stay, but after being with you *here*"—he gives me a little squeeze—"in my day-to-day life? I can't let you go."

"You're staying?"

"If I get the royal decree."

"For how long?"

He shrugs. "Indefinitely."

I throw my arms around his neck, and he lifts me off the ground and spins me in slow circles.

I was prepared to settle for the parts of Jasper I could get through the mail even when I wanted the rest. I could never bear to imagine a life without him. But with just a few words, it's all changed. I know how much it means for him to *stay*. He's willing to try something new—for me. I don't know when it started, the exact moment when I fell in love with Jasper Rowley, but I know I want to hold up my end of this deal too.

"I need to get a passport. If you're staying, you still need your travel bug itched."

He sets me down, beaming. "Yeah? We'll plan around school breaks to go together?"

I nod, nerves fluttering. "Slow and steady."

He leans down and kisses me again, tenderly as if he's taking his time. "A balancing act."

"Not that we can go too far for too long now that you've built me a soap shed."

I grin at the shed, the perfect space for my work, but also a real-life symbol of Jasper's dedication. Together we look around at his handiwork. Undoubtedly it took hours—far more than I was aware he was spending here—and I'm not sure I could imagine a greater act of love.

"*This* is my dream for Bubbles & Suds, and I didn't even know it. Maybe you're just a really good guesser or maybe you've come to know me better than I even know myself."

"Your postcard illustration from 2003 gave me a head start. I have a dry sink I'm going to put in next week on the exterior—for mixing the noxious stuff—but I had to paint first and I knew it'd be a dead giveaway once you saw it. Hence the farmers market paint job."

The sound of his words, ones that speak so casually about his extended stay here, cover me in a warmth only he can create.

"I love the sound of you staying."

He nods. "Thank goodness for Betsy."

"Huh?"

"She didn't tell you?"

"Lay it on me."

"She tracked me down and sent me an email. She said I needed to finally come to Pearl so we could meet in person. Hang on, let me think of the exact words . . . 'I can plan y'all some supercute dates, or you can figure it out yourself, but the lot of us Five are sick and tired of you lovebirds being kept apart.' Now, of course I knew Betsy even if I hadn't met her, and I sort of figured maybe she had a point."

A giggle bubbles out of me. "I did wonder why now of all times. Thank goodness for Betsy."

I am so lucky to have her—and the others. The fact that The Five almost broke apart now feels like such a distant memory, even if only days have passed. And we can add the new role to Betsy's résumé: matchmaker.

"I think we owe Betsy something. A nice bottle of wine?" he says.

"Just as long as it's nothing peach."

Jasper pulls me into his arms, and I hold on.

And I might just never let go.

CHAPTER 60

Delilah

DARCY WEARS A SURLY pout on her made-up face as she stands reluctantly beside a Peach Pit lawyer before a crowd gathered at the Pearl Community Center Gardens. It's been exactly a week since Jasper turned my world upside down by revealing the soap shed and his plans to stay, and Darcy is reluctantly hosting a community impact meeting as unrest among Pearlites mounts around Peach Pit. Probably it's an attempt at outmaneuvering legal action from locals.

The setting is far too beautiful for the postmortem conversation, flower beds freshly mulched as blooms spring up in a picture-book rainbow spread. The paths are freshly power-washed and the fountain bubbles like a melodious backdrop.

I came not to rub salt in the wound but as an invested observer, so I pick a seat in the back, hoping to remain out of sight with Jasper at my side in support. Secretly, I hope for a small moment, a blip, of redemption for Darcy.

She's still my sister, after all.

Our father's lawyer, one who has since brought on a whole slew of colleagues to manage Peach Pit's many legal issues, hands Darcy a microphone.

Without introducing herself, Darcy jumps right in.

"Hey, everyone. If you're here, you want to know the deal with Peach Pit, and I'm here to explain. Honestly, this is, like, zero fun, so let's just do it so we can all get out of here."

The crowd remains silent, and Darcy appears to deflate slightly at not having her usual crew of Darlings-in-waiting applauding her every move.

"Anywaay," Darcy stretches the word. "Here's the deal: Very sadly we've been forced to close Peach Pit effective immediately due to some unforeseen financial issues." She pulls a paper from her pocket and reads directly from the script. "'Consultants, also known as Darlings, will be eligible for a buyback of product up to $2,000 per seller for remaining stock. It should not be sold as is. Darlings should no longer host Peach Parties and may not offer new memberships. All Peach Pit business must cease as of this notice.'"

The crowd is quiet for a moment, and when sound erupts, it's animated chatter. A couple of hands fly into the air.

"No questions," Darcy says. The lawyer nudges her with an elbow, leans in, and whispers something. She groans. "Ugh. Fine. *A few*."

A woman I recognize from school who has elementary-age children stands and asks, "What about Darlings who have more than $2,000 worth of product?"

"Yeah, it's a no. Sorry. Next?"

The lawyer beside Darcy grits his teeth, appearing to be saying something to her from between them.

Another woman stands. "This is not a question but a PSA for folks gathered. We are creating a class action suit against Peach Pit, so if you would like to be included, you can find us at . . . " She gives a website address, then repeats it as people jot it down.

"Did you know this was all a scam, Darcy?" a disgruntled-looking man calls out.

The lawyer beside Darcy yanks the microphone from her hand before she can answer, but for the first time she looks shell-shocked.

"Peach Pit was created to provide gainful sales opportunities for local women," the lawyer says.

"What about the women who lost friendships or relationships because of this? Where's their restitution?"

The lawyer clears his throat. "Again, they will be eligible for the buyback program."

The grilling continues for a while longer, with Darcy looking increasingly alarmed, eyes growing wider while the lawyer, sweating rivulets, answers questions lobbed his way with unsatisfying, canned answers.

Eventually the lawyer calls an end to the meeting, and the crowd begins to disperse. The lawyer guides Darcy by the elbow in the opposite direction. I push and jostle through the crowd to get to her, apologizing as I accidentally bump others around me until I reach the clear path she takes to the back lot.

"Darcy." I break into a jog to catch up.

She glances over her shoulder, and when she sees it's me, she stops. "Come to gloat? Revel in my humiliation?" At a closer glance, dark bags sit below her eyes.

"Not at all. I just want this to be over."

Darcy turns to the lawyer. "Go ahead. I'll meet you at the car."

She comes closer. Her eyes are watery, and it strikes me that I don't remember the last time I saw her cry. "You destroyed everything I built."

I stop and let the silence do the talking. I might've turned a light to the truth of what Peach Pit was, but I didn't make the company what it was.

"I wish it hadn't had to come to this."

Darcy's head drops back, and it looks like surrender. "I didn't realize how many people were actually mad about it. It seemed like such a small thing. *Cosmetics*."

"Looks have always been a big thing around here."

She looks off to the side. "Guess I can't argue with that."

As Darcy softens momentarily, I take the opportunity to ask, "What was causing the reactions? Do you know?"

She folds her arms. "We did look into it. We're not quite the big, bad wolf you'd have us painted as." She sighs. "We were grinding up peach pits as a small component of the products—an attempt to be honest about the ingredients. Turns out there are some dangerous chemicals—cyanide, I think—in them."

I think about the claims Peach Pit made publicly about allergic reactions being the fault of the consumer, how they doubled down on their products.

"And just so you know, we didn't figure it out until after the second article, but by then it was sort of a moot point. You know, after everything with Daddy." Darcy looks off in the distance.

"I just wanted to make the company stop hurting people. My friends."

Darcy starts walking backward and throws up her hands like it's outside of her control. "It's the way the world works, Delilah. Every person for themselves." Her voice hitches like she has no choice but to question her long-held belief.

I don't say anything else as she turns and walks away. I won't kick her when she's down. It's hard to see a place and time when things improve between Darcy and me, but I'm nothing if not hopeful.

After Darcy disappears Jasper comes up behind me and pulls me into a hug, then kisses me tenderly on the side of my neck.

"Well, that was a doozy."

I smile and reach up to hold on to his wrists. "Come on. We're going to be late for Betsy's."

Jasper takes my hand and we walk toward the car. "You want to show me off like a prize pig, huh? Can't say I had that on my bingo card."

I pop a gentle whack on his belly. "Oh, stop."

"I get it. I'm a catch."

I drop a peck on his cheek. "Now *that* I can agree on."

CHAPTER 61

Delilah

JASPER PARKS IN BETSY'S driveway, and we walk around to the deck, following the sound of familiar voices layered on top of one another. Excitement flutters in my stomach. We pass the older children, who are running around, grass stains already abundant, and I spot a couple of the husbands leaning on the ledge of the deck, beers in hand. As we climb the steps, I reach back and take Jasper's hand in mine, pride radiating through me.

Sloane and Virginia Kate are in deep conversation at the top of the steps, and when Sloane's eyes land on us—*us, hand in hand*—she stops mid-sentence. Virginia Kate turns in search of what has her friend tongue-tied.

When I reach the top, we stop before them, and matching slow grins creep across my friends' faces.

"*Stop*," Sloane says, like she's begging for it to continue.

"Oh my gosh, look at y'all, a real-life couple!" Virginia Kate's hands fly up to cover her face after the words come out.

"Thanks," I say, letting my expression and the radiant Jasper beside me do the talking.

Although The Five—minus a freshly postpartum Eliza—came over to admire the soap shed and get the play-by-play of Jasper's proclamation of love a week ago, this is our debut as an item to a Five gathering.

"Betsy and Eliza are in the kitchen. You must go show yourselves to them. Like, immediately!" Sloane demands, then jumps up and proceeds to steer and prod me in that direction.

I play along and drag a happy Jasper behind me into the kitchen. Eliza sits in a dining chair, the baby wrapped up and cradled in her arms. The sight of the precious child grabs my entire attention, and I pull Jasper alongside me.

"Oh my goodness!" I gush, and Jasper leans in close behind me. "Just look at her."

Eliza and Betsy freeze, their eyebrows slowly creeping up as they take stock of Jasper and me and a giddy Sloane and Virginia Kate behind us.

I lean down and hug Eliza as best I can with the baby in her arms. "Can I hold her?"

Eliza is smiling with her mouth dropped half open as she eyes me meaningfully. "I'm not sure I'll ever get used to this"—she flicks her eyes between Jasper and me—"being for real. Just the best!"

A giggle escapes me. "Me neither, but it sure is sweet."

Jasper laughs along with me, and before I can get my mitts on the new baby, Betsy nearly tackles me with a massive hug, as she whispers in my ear, "I'm so happy for you, Delilah—you two together! *Finally!*"

"Thank you for pulling some helpful strings," I whisper back, and she steps away smiling ear to ear.

I give Jasper a peck on the cheek to prove my love for him but also to thank him for going along with this performance. He blushes and stuffs his hands into his pockets before approaching the other men as I get back to baby snuggle requests.

Eliza sets a sleepy Harper Rose in my arms, and happy tears run down my face. There is nothing in the world like a brand-new baby, an innocent soul to serve as hope for the rest of us. That maybe she and her friends will grow up to get all the things right that The Five have gotten wrong. Or perhaps they'll make the same mistakes, despite warnings, and still—*again*—they'll make it right with apologies and repair.

Maybe that's what it's about in the end anyway: making the best out of the unavoidable bad parts and finding our way back to the light. Knowing that despite the recurrent ugliness in life, we still get the pretty parts too.

Like forgiving your friend who got caught up in something that was promised to be a good deal. Like sneaking into a hospital to lay eyes on a friend you worry you might've hurt. Like putting yourself in the crossfire, in the name of making things right. Like forgiving your family for letting you down—then and now. Like forgiving yourself for being slow to stand up for the right thing, to find your own footing.

I look up with teary eyes. "Thank you, girls, for being the hope in this world."

Eliza fans her face. "Dang, girl, you're making the hormonal one cry too. We want the deets on your crush here. How's it going? We've only been waiting since the fifth grade!"

I give in, and I tell them a few more details about the soap shed moment, the plans we've made since, the unflattering passport photo I had taken yesterday. About letting the tide of my love for Jasper take me. About how he's looking for long-term work at the paper, that we're planning a big trip for the upcoming summer break. Eventually I hand Harper Rose back to Eliza. My insides hum.

When I look at this group, it's astounding to think that only weeks ago I wondered if we were coming to an end. I started out trying to will this scene before me into existence, but now I'm certain it's come not only at my hands but at the magic that solely happens when it's the five of us in something together. It requires us all.

Now that we've survived the ghastly Peach Pit and lived—together, as friends—to tell the tale, there isn't anything that could break us apart.

Not considering the deep love that always has, and always will, run among The Five.

EPILOGUE

Six months later

AUTUMN LEAVES ARE FALLING from the trees on SweetGum Lane as Mama arrives at my house. Today is the SweetGum fall festival, a glorified potluck where the lot of us spill out onto a roped-off street with a dish, a chair, and a festive spirit. It's not fussy or particularly official, and that fits us just right.

"Good morning," Mama sings, breezy like she's living the good life as she pops my door open with the key I gave her.

"In here," I call from the kitchen, now far roomier since my soap-making materials have been moved to the shed.

"How's it taste?" Mama asks, nodding at the bubbling pot of chili we started yesterday. She pulls off her fleece jacket.

I dip a spoon in and hold it out for her to try. "Divine by my estimation."

Mama squeezes her eyes shut and takes the bite. "Couldn't agree more."

With my father gone, Mama's actually started to bloom, as I long suspected she might. Instead of running the massive household my father always wanted, she goes to yoga three times a week and volunteers at the Boys & Girls Club. She comes over to my house for dinner at least once a week, and we walk in the park when weather permits. She even tags in beside Roxie and me in the soap shed on occasion.

Initially I wondered if the increasing time we spent together was due to her guilt—an apology of sorts—but the longer it's continued and the closer we've gotten, the clearer I've been able to see it for what it is: mother-daughter bonding. It's what I've always wanted from her. From my family, even if it can't be all of them.

Finally, it's about both of us. Not me fitting into her girly-girl routine.

"It's this little house," Mama says, pointing at the pot. "I could never get it this good back at home."

Now that Mama's been forced to put the house on the market, she's become far more frank about her feelings regarding the sprawling estate she shared with my father. Practically all of my parents' assets have been seized by the government, and my father bides his time in a new, low-budget apartment as the authorities gather their evidence for a yet-to-be-scheduled trial—or possibly a plea bargain. The change seems to have been good for Mama.

"Well, the kitchen is always open for chili making. You've got a key."

She pulls me into a hug, and a moment later there's a knock at the door.

Mama releases me from her arms. "I left it unlocked for him."

Jasper cracks the door and calls in, "Hello?"

I skip to the door that's drifted open, leap into his arms, and drop a kiss on his cheek. We pass through into the kitchen, where he hugs Mama, who has since tied on an apron. I stop at the butcher block island, and over at the stove she dips the spoon into the pot and stirs. Jasper comes up behind me and wraps his arms around my waist. I smile to myself as I think about the past six months we've spent together.

During summer break, we went to Peru, and having Jasper at my side quelled the most intense of my nerves. I soaked in the bright colors of the clothing, the vibrant greens of the mountains, and the ephemeral mist and clouds that hug them. Memories of the delicious food will stay with me forever, and I left knowing that the way I see the world is forever changed.

Maybe I am more suited to adventuring alongside Jasper than I thought.

He has continued to immerse himself in Pearl, snagging a permanent job at the Atlanta paper, making friends of his own, and doubling down on the gym membership by joining an early morning workout group. That is one activity I'm certain I'll leave to him.

I turn and look over my shoulder, where his head rests, and smile. "I love you, Jasper."

He presses his lips to mine and lingers, and when he finally pulls back he says, "I love you too."

Telling him those words and hearing his response has become a favorite ritual. I turn my head back front just as my mama spins in place at the stove.

"I'm so happy with how it turned out." She casts her eyes proudly to the simmering pot.

"Me too," I say. "Me too."

An hour later, the rest of the crew shows up, bringing camping chairs, coolers, and dishes to put out on the long plastic tables in the middle of the street. Kids ride scooters and bikes, music emanates from speakers in neighbors' yards, and the odd sparkler firework is set off, much to the concern of the parents in attendance.

I sit in my camping chair, lifting my face to enjoy the cool breeze.

Virginia Kate sits beside me, dabbing at her eyes. "I'm going to miss you guys so much."

Sloane hands her a beer from her cooler. "It's for the best."

Virginia Kate announced a month ago that her firm in Charlotte had offered her a position there. After discussing it with Hunter, together they decided to make the move, his job being flexible enough for him to work remotely. The financial firm was even paying for Ginny Kay's licensing paperwork, plus helping with moving expenses.

"We're going to miss you, but Charlotte is close. And y'all will be back." Betsy stands in a wide stance, wearing brown riding boots, leggings, and an oversized sweater. "Plus, I might have some events there soon!"

Shortly after Peach Pit collapsed, Betsy started her own event planning business, and in only a few months it is already well off the ground with multiple high-end affairs under its belt and several lined up on the calendar.

Eliza arrives at the end of the street, which we've closed off with traffic cones. She waves, Harper Rose propped upright on her hip, Jack running in front.

Sloane stands and takes the baby in her arms and drops a kiss on her head. "I've missed you, little peanut."

Now that Eliza works at Sloane's firm as an admin, Sloane gets glimpses of the newest addition at the company day care downstairs whenever she's in town. Eliza loves it, too, because she's also been able to nurse Harper Rose on her breaks.

"How was your trip?" Eliza asks.

"Eh. I told them it's my last for the next several months," Sloane says. "I'm finally ready to admit that I need to slow down. Take breaks."

I spot Roxie heading our way, and not far behind her follows Darcy. Roxie waves as she skips past me to the soap shed and calls out about checking on a setting batch. Darcy approaches slowly and quietly, sets a box of baked goods on the table, then opens up chairs for her and Roxie. She sits with us but joins without fuss. When I wave, she waves back, and we exchange tentative smiles.

It's not perfect, but it's definitely a start.

Mrs. Chopra's front door bangs open, and I get up to help her as she carries out two large platters of food covered in foil. Just last month I received confirmation that what I'd once believed to be her tall tales were in fact complete truth. All it took was her offering to show me her photo albums, and unless she is an accomplished forger, it's all true. ABBA. Royals. I fish for more stories every time we get together.

"Thank you, little bird. Can you grab the rest from the kitchen?"

"Sure thing," I say, then head inside for the rest.

Now that Peach Pit is a memory, something we all endured like a collective blip on the Pearl timeline, it's sometimes as if it never happened. Sure, my father is almost certainly headed to prison and Darcy has been dethroned as the Queen Peach, but my life has pulled together into exactly what I want.

Even if it's not the picture I'd planned for myself.

I can't help but feel proud of us—of The Five, of Mama, Jasper and me, of Pearl. Even Darcy.

Life might not always be pretty, but it sure is sweet.

ACKNOWLEDGMENTS

Pretty as a Peach was a book I adored writing so much so that once it was finished I told my editor, "I don't want to let this one go! I want to keep her for a while longer." Nevertheless, sharing it with you, my readers, is always the greatest honor, and I hope you enjoyed it. Without readers there would be no reason for books, and I remain steadfast in my belief that book people are the best in this world.

There are so many hands that have touched this book throughout the process of its creation, refinement, and delivery out into the world. So many people who have supported me.

To my editor, Laura Wheeler, the third time really was a charm. Thank you for being an incredible partner in bringing these stories to life, to tending them with such care, and for your keen vision and insights. I am so fortunate to work alongside you, and especially so when we can occasionally read each other's minds. Can't wait for the next one!

To Margaret Danko and Kim Perel for your support in making this whole show happen. Not only for your work on *Pretty as a Peach* but also for your commitment to the long run, fielding my emails, and helping me steer the ship. Thank you for always being game to hear my next crazy idea.

To Jodi Hughes for another wonderful line edit. Thank you for your eagle eyes that catch all of the small details I miss. I always learn something new from your edits.

To Sarah Berke for reading the earliest version and giving feedback. For being an incredible friend, a sounding board, and a tireless reminder that good people still exist. I aspire to be like you in so many ways.

To the team at Thomas Nelson who worked diligently on all of the behind-the-scenes tasks required to make a manuscript into a book and to bring it into the world with fanfare. Savannah Breedlove, Taylor Ward, and Colleen Lacey for handling this book with such great care. Amanda Bostic and Becky Monds for your leadership. The support of the rest of the team: Margaret Kercher, Nekasha Pratt, Kerri Potts, Natalie Underwood, Ellie Long, Cayla Rusielewicz, and Fred Sakai.

To the many book bloggers, Instagrammers, and reviewers who I have had the pleasure of getting to know online. Every post, share, or mention makes my day, and I am always grateful for your willingness to pick my book out of the sea of incredible options.

A special thank you to the BTP book club: Since my debut, y'all have stood beside me in shouting from the rooftops about my books, and I'm still not sure how I managed such luck. You women are the real deal, voracious readers with golden hearts, and I'm honored to call you friends. A special shout out to Annissa Armstrong and Dawne McCurry for your friendship.

To the independent book sellers who have recommended my book to customers or hosted events spotlighting my books. You are the lifeblood of the book business, and we cherish you!

To my friends who have stuck with me as I launched three books in less than 18 months, checking in, attending my events, and excitedly purchasing copies. My original mom crew, Megan Drummond and Sarah Schneider. Amazing VMS moms and staff. My beloved WOW/St. David's girlfriends. Author friends who have become such incredible companions in navigating this crazy business. There are too many names to name, but y'all know who you are!

To my family. To my mom and dad for *everything* but also for always jumping in on childcare for events and travel. For taking such good care of the kids when they came down with the flu at the end of the *Good Hair Days* tour. For asking about my work and saying, "So where is everything you're working on standing these days?" I, too, lose track sometimes.

To my children for being the best supporters and for making sure there aren't too many leftover snacks from the book launches. I am so proud to be your mom. You are the two very best things I've ever made.

To my husband, Kyle, my biggest supporter. Simply put, none of these books would exist without your love and support, your belief in me, and your willingness to jump in on the wild world of publishing (even when I sideline you on "brainstorming" ideas). Thank you for being my chauffer and videographer on the road, for being an equal partner willing to share the responsibilities of our family. The life we have is better than anything I imagined.

DISCUSSION QUESTIONS

1. Peach Pit is a multilevel marketing (MLM) company that uses network sales. Have you ever worked with an MLM or been pitched to join an MLM? How is Peach Pit different or similar?
2. Pearl, Georgia, is a "glossy" town that prioritizes achievements and outward signs of success. How does this impact The Five and the decisions they make? If the location of the story were different, how do you think the story would be different?
3. Within both Pearl and Peach Pit there is pressure to focus on success only, and it lands some Peach Pit Darlings in financial trouble. What do you think about the "keeping up with the Joneses" phenomenon and its relevance in modern society?
4. The events in the story force Delilah to find her voice, and she transforms from meek to courageous and outspoken. Do you relate more to her "keep the peace" starting point or the outspoken woman who is willing to speak out that she becomes by the end?
5. Outwardly Betsy seems to have it all—a happy family, a lucrative job, and an abundance of friends—but on closer glance she still doesn't feel like she's enough, worrying that if her Peach Pit wins are erased, she'll be reduced to nothing.

What do you think about the pressures modern women and mothers face to "have it all" and put on a good face?

6. The Five have been friends since childhood, and although their lives have changed significantly since, they still show up for one another and prioritize their friendships. What are your experiences with "friend groups"? Is it similar or different to The Five?
7. If you were to cast The Five in a movie, who would you pick for each character?
8. It wasn't long after they were paired as pen pals in fifth grade that sparks started between Jasper and Delilah. Can you imagine yourself feeling sparks from only letters?
9. By the end of the book, Delilah realizes that she prefers her homemade soap operation small and abandons the vision to expand it. Do you have any hobbies? Have you ever transformed a hobby into a small business?
10. Delilah's relationships with her family undergo quite a reckoning. In her shoes, would you have made similar or different decisions?

ABOUT THE AUTHOR

Photo by Lisa Liberati Photography

GRACE HELENA WALZ received a master's degree in social work from the University of Houston and has worked with children in foster care, as a medical social worker, and in a mental health capacity. She currently resides outside of Atlanta, Georgia, with her husband and two young children. She writes women's fiction in the moments between sticking Band-Aids on scraped knees and coordinating pint-size social engagements.

* * *

Connect with her online at gracehelenawalz.com
Facebook: @gracewalzauthor
Instagram: @gracehelenabooks
Pinterest: @gracewalzauthor